For my Friends – the Best

A compilation of thoughtfully selected previously published short tales

by

Richard J. Small

Front cover: intrinsically safe miner's lamp, as used by the author in the fire brigade during the mid-seventies.

Published by
Goodness Me Publishing Limited
www.goodnessmepublishing.co.uk

Other books by the same author

I want to tell you a story
Edward Gaskell Publishers

Ghosts and Things
Edward Gaskell Publishers

Tales from Merlin's Pal
Edward Gaskell Publishers

Simple Poems
Edward Gaskell Publishers

Tai Chi and Aikido – exploring pathways beyond choreography
Goodnessmepublishing.co.uk

My Devon tales
Goodnessmepublishing.co.uk

The Writer's Bin
Goodnessmepublishing.co.uk

Bones of Contention
Goodnessmepublishing.co.uk

Dedication

If you were my greatest friend, then these are the stories I would dearly wish to share with you.

I write for you, in order that you too will know.

Tragedy that seeks your empathy, humour that brings you laughter, philosophy and the supernatural to engage your soul and finally a somewhat sceptical foray into the world of politics and those who serve the cause, often their own!

All of this is in here, in these easily readable stories, they are the best that I could write, and they carry my own beliefs and spirit forward in the written word.

For what that is worth, only you will be the judge.

My eternal blessings to Jocelyn and Samuel for an adventurous but safe and happy life.

**

Contents

Life the way it is . . . or certainly was

Philosophical or Spiritual

Adventure, Camaraderie, Sacrifice

Humour

Supernatural

Bureaucracy and Politics

The purpose of storytelling is to invite you to quietly visit with your soul, and to think differently about your own perceived version of normality. It is a beautiful alchemy that can turn ideas into dreams and mind into spirit.

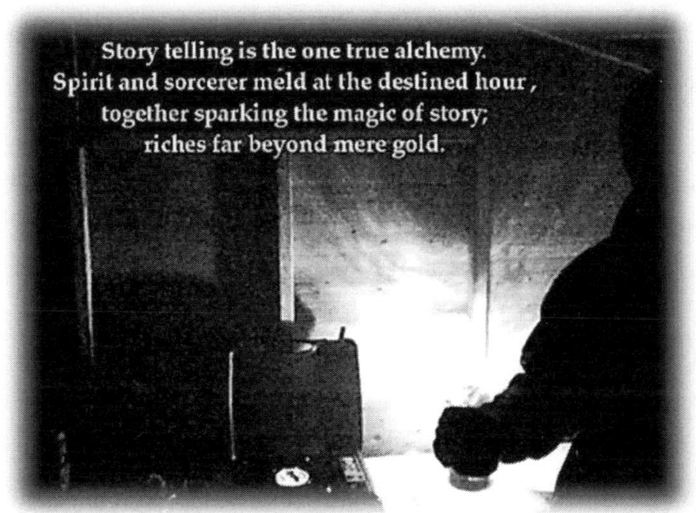

Life the way it is . . .

or certainly it was

The Cornish Archer.

Trevellyan was a yeoman free,
whose son was born, to archer be.
To stand the ground, and bend the bow,
his father taught, his boy to know.

The years passed by, till he was grown,
great archer he, the seed was sown.
And in the crowd, did such a feat,
that Cornwall's finest archers beat.

No stronger man, when in his prime,
did hunt King's deer, though 'twas a crime.
To warnings dire, he would not hark,
and every arrow, hit its mark.

As story goes, ten strong it took,
when sheriff's men, the village shook.
They dragged away our hero sung
to gibbet dire, and there was hung.

Some say they see, brave archer still,
as twilight mists, do hush the hill.
When noble stag, he lifts his head,
our archer's home, back from the dead.

**

'Greengates' – a fire and a life – so what?

About an ordinary man in extraordinary circumstances, his feelings and his actions at a dangerous fire

He was a far younger man than now as he stood on the night-time gravel road by the big red engine. It was an isolated place far from the lights of the City, but it had its own light as a fierce fire swept through the workshops and cars of Greengates scrap yard.

The gates themselves were indeed green, big solid gates, higher than most men could ever see over. They were locked fast against intruders, of any description, good or bad. The younger man was fully conscious of his thoughts that reflected on life and death. At this time in his life, neither of them had any importance, neither life nor death mattered.

Up and over the gates, strong arms first pulling and then pushing his body over to the other side. Heavy boots dropped into the fire lit compound, it was only then he thought, 'guard dogs,' but thankfully none appeared. Soon hose and branch were passed over from the men on the outside, and one other joined him, Paul, a good colleague. With a shout for 'water on,' they advanced the heavy hose across the compound, hitting the fire where experience had taught them had the best effect.

The all-devouring fire roared and crackled; bright flames lit up the poisoning black smoke pouring into the winter night sky. Closer still they went, closer still to slay their enemy dead. In amongst the glowing workshop fire, pressure was building in gas cylinders; he was aware of the dangers of such, knowing on occasion bursting like bombs, throwing flame and hot metal in all directions.

Still alone, and closer still they went; then a heavy loud 'crump' and the ground burst instantly into light all around.

The younger man crouched lower still, not daring to look up to see what might be coming down. Life or death mattered not, but pain was a different beast; he could still feel that. Burns were a horror they respected and avoided at all cost. Would this demon fire fall, like the angel of death, from the heavens and engulf this crouching figure in the yard?

He waited; it was to be life, and life with no pain; after the fright, now it was their turn and onwards they pressed, now supported by more colleagues, and after many labours and many hours the demon was finally slain, though it had taken much with it while it lived.

Still, to him, this younger man than now, life nor death mattered naught, but survival with honour would do him for a while.

Photo: author 1984 about the time of Greengates Fire. Story was written then.

When danger came . . .

Not for them to say, 'We're brave',
though risk their lives they would,
when danger came, with threat of death,
through hope and hell, they stood.
To a man, the foe they'd fight,
regardless of its form,
and danger comes, with threat of death,
in darkness, fire, and storm.

I know their thoughts; I feel their pain,
for with them, once I stood,
and danger came with threat of death,
but not once cry, they would.
When fearful shouts for help came in,
loud bells would raise alarm,
then danger and its threat of death
was met with strength and calm.

The siren wailed, the road had cleared
and urgently they'd drive.
While danger stalks with threat of death.
'Hang on, 'till they arrive.'
That dreadful fire, it seemed to breathe,
and life to terror give,
as danger grew with threat of death,
they must not let it live.

Fire is dead and people saved,
the crew returned to base,
all danger quelled from threat of death,
relief on every face.
No coin they ask, but honour due;
reporters, ask their name,
though danger lurks, with threat of death,
none, who's there, seek fame.

Photo by author, National Fire Training Centre, oil fire.

It's what we did

While most lay safe and sound abed,
we're out, in engines red.
While they, in land of dreams, no care,
we fought the fires, in choking air.

While they could eat their pie and mash,
no time for that, had we,
the dead need pulling from some crash.
Cos that's our job, you see.

As years of life approach December,
long past, we risked our all,
but dreams still come, as we remember,
every bloody call.

A fairy story, with magic, tragedy, and adventure.

It was late, with the rain-swept road lit by his lone car headlights he took the old road through hills and trees towards the sea and home. Beautiful, soul touching music filled the air from the car's speakers, and though not easy to discern the words, it mattered not, for the rise and fall of tones in her voice sent the story of the song direct to the soul. It was the sort of road and the sort of song that spirits your heart and soul to younger years, to a world of hopes and dreams entangled in the memories of life and love's realities. Music that wakes the very life force that fires the spirit to all that is brave and noble, invoking feelings that inspire the ordinary to greatness; feelings that were you to try and describe would melt away, for they themselves know they cannot be shared, for they belong to you, alone.

As he listened, his mind drifted to thoughts of a story he had half wanted to tell.

One part of him said, 'Tell it, tell it, it is a story of magic, love and tragedy, it's worth the telling, tell it!' Another in him spoke also, 'but if you do, it will not be easy, for you will find demons to fight along the way. If you tell it, then everyone may know you and judge you and all the things you would want not from the telling.'

As his journey travelled with the clock, hour by hour, so his inner conversation continued; brilliant ideas and flowing moving words would appear, then a darkness of fear and doubt cover them over. Then, one winter evening shortly after his return home he picked up his pencil and he wrote,.... ....

'The Princess and the China Bell'

'Where on Earth do you start old boy?' he asked himself.

Himself replied, 'Just anywhere will do, don't worry if you miss something out, if you wait for perfection, you'll never do anything. Why not start with your early trips to Russia?'
Some ten years earlier his long-held dream of going to Russia came true, when his Martial arts teacher, and indeed good friend, was invited to teach there. He had no wife at the time and lived alone, dedicated to his work in the Fire Brigade and absorbed by the Aikido he practiced with likeminded people. This was seemingly all life had to offer at the time.
Russia was good to him, welcoming, and flowing with food and vodka – at least, where they were, it was. He was to go there several times, normally during autumn or spring when the five-month snows still covered the land. One of the highlights of the visits was the family gathering mealtimes; he would sit at the table surrounded by fellow students, teachers, and family of the hosts. The feeling of welcome, of family, was like coming home, and so different from his empty house back in England.
Much vodka was drunk, and many toasts were made. Once you had a full glass, which was almost constantly, you could raise it and say, 'Toast,' and all present would stop and listen. It was your chance to speak of great things or little things, to inspire with poetic grace the gathered company to lift their glasses and drink with the joy of fellowship.
Two years into these regular visits to Russia, he noticed among the many students a young woman who stood out from the crowd, short, pretty, and exceedingly smart and cleanly dressed, long blond hair in a plait under a skewed brown beret. She was a dedicated student of the art and was often used by the teacher to demonstrate throws.
Another year or two go by and the same little woman stood quietly, now with shorter and darker hair, in a corridor at a sports camp in the snowy forests of north west Russia. She

smiled her lovely smile and looked up quietly at him while the men spoke, for there it was the domain of men to rule and speak. Although by now, she was the force behind organising the events for the visiting teacher, it was not her place to enjoy any of the benefits. While the men drank and sang heroic Russian songs in the sauna and tucked into fresh kebabs cooked in the snowy forest over a living fire, she was somewhere else.

Often small gifts would be exchanged between visitors and their hosts, but one such gift was to have a special place in his life. She offered the wrapped gift and as he opened it, he saw it was a pretty little china doll, but more than this, it was a bell. He rang the little china bell and asked, 'When I ring this bell, will you appear?'

Next to his old armchair, bought cheaply in a farmyard sale, in his home in England stood an old bookcase that his late father had acquired for him for a tenner; on the shelves were various mementos of people, places and family, and among them sat the pretty china bell, and sometimes, as he sat in his aloneness, he would pick up that bell and ring it gently, and make a wish.

More visits and more years passed their way and each time he would see her smiling face again, always helpful always friendly. 'Such a nice girl,' he thought.

Then, one year, she came to England, to stay for three months as a live-in student at the Aikido training centre, (dojo). He was to see her often now, as he trained there as much as he could with his teacher. It had always been his habit to befriend all the visiting students, taking along good food for them and where possible taking them out on sight-seeing visits, and it was no different for her. Boating, shops, museums, and botanical gardens; and their friendship grew. She confided in him of her life in Russia, of an alcoholic mother, sister on drugs and the murder of her only cousin in his own flat, of long hours of work with poor pay and no prospects, and little chance of true freedom and happiness. Although she was young and strong, she suffered from stresses and health problems and he did his best to help her overcome them. Their friendship grew more and more strong and turned to love, a love that they could not show to the world, and even then, complaints were made to the teacher by some that thought this relationship was harmful to the peace of other students.

They hatched a plan whereby each time they might be lucky enough to spend time alone they would say ,'hallo,' and each time before they re-entered the training place they would simply say 'goodbye' to each other. They gave no outward signs of their love but had secret signals in the training hall, (dojo) whereby they could reassure each other of continued affection. Though there was much to gain by this relationship, there too was much to lose.

The huge gap in their ages was a great source of embarrassment and despair to him, more, he sensed, than to her; the sort of feelings that few on the outside of them would ever understand. On those rare occasions when they were free of the martial arts centre their talk was always open and honest; there was an implicit trust in each other. Fears grew that it would soon be goodbye, as her visa came closer to expiry; they imagined a fantasy world in the future, when being reborn to a new life they could meet again and be the same age; he was to live in China in the foothills of some great mountain and would be, of course, an accomplished martial artist, she was to be a pretty Chinese princess and they would meet again and feel the same way, unburdened by the weight of age.

Phone calls from Russia mounted pressure as they insisted, cajoled, and begged, for her return, such foreboding calls

were never welcome. They comforted each other as the emotional torture worsened.
In all his years in the Fire Brigade he had never carried out that 'heroic, dream rescue,' which so many hope will be theirs. Yes, he had always been willing to place his body between the danger and the helpless, but to know for certainty that he had directly saved a life had eluded him despite those long years of dedication. In his mind it was as though he was at the head of a ladder looking into a brightly burning house, into which he could not enter, and in the room she simply stood. In his mind he reached out a strong hand to save her, but he could not reach her, she must reach out too, to be saved. Many a time this dream would come to him and each time the girl would turn her back and quietly and silently disappear into the burning room. Then, one day, she did reach out and he knew at last, he had saved a life. Against much opposition and all advice, they realised only marriage would keep her from a return to a dangerous world of little hope and unhappy future.
One autumn day they set off together to the mountains of north Wales; her own, native land was vast but flat, snow covered for five months, then swamp and forest during the thaw, followed by a noticeably short hot summer, so mountains had excitement and magic in them. As they sat on Snowdon's summit, he took a ring from his pocket and asked, with hope and with fear if she would marry him. She thought quietly for a few minutes, while he sat and waited, then turned and said that she would. They stayed a short while on the summit then set off on the long trek down. They had not gone so far when they looked down into a cloud filled valley below to their right. Behind them the Sun shone brightly casting the shadow of the ridge path on the clouds below, and there amidst a circular rainbow stood their shadows, one tall, one short; they waved down, and their

shadows waved back, then the clouds drifted away, and the wonder was gone, like all that fades in life, leaving only memories.

She secretly journeyed back to Russia where she met up with her mother and father to say goodbye properly; it was already too late to see her grandmother who had sadly passed away in her absence. She returned to England where they were married quietly with only another retired fire officer and his wife for witnesses. It was a private affair of necessity. They made their home in his old bungalow and were rarely separated. He had the habit of calling her, 'a little sweetie,' which she promptly adulterated to, 'swootie.' To their friends they became known as the 'Swooties' much to everyone's amusement. One day, while sitting at the old pine kitchen table as she prepared a huge saucepan of brilliant tasting soup, he asked her what her wishes for life were. She replied, 'a house by the sea, chickens and a dog.' This had been his dream too for many, many years and he knew it was within his reach. Sometimes when it comes to making a dream real it is not so easy, so, no dog, no chickens, but the house near the sea was on. Not long after this they moved to the land of his ancestors in the South West, he practiced his martial arts and to him she was his Princess.

She studied and worked hard. For a couple of years there was much happiness, and they did the silly things you do when uninhibited, childlike happy things like dancing round the living room and singing aloud some silly made up songs.

Then she found a dream of her own, a dream that would take her away to fulfil her ambition hundreds of miles away. A melancholy fell over the house and the writing was on the wall, though none of it bitter, only sad. He had saved her life for freedom, now freedom beckoned her away.

As she gathered her belongings into cardboard boxes, she eventually came to the little china bell. She held it in her hands and looked up, saying, 'You won't be able to keep this, will you?' She knew it would be a constant reminder of the fairy story that once was, a story of gain and loss. He kept back the tears and said, 'No, you take it.'

So, the little bell has gone, no longer there to ring again in his aloneness to call her back. And though life moves on, the memory remains.

The story could end there, but while we live, we can live to change the ending, and some months later he went to China with a martial arts group of travellers and in a Temple in the foothills of Wudang Mountain he knelt and silently, in front of some great statue, told his story of the Princess and the china bell; adding that he had no plans yet to die, in order to meet his princess in a new life.

The young Chinese girl, who was their guide on the mountain, gave him quite a surprise when she said her Chinese name, but that most people called her, 'Sweetie.'

For some unknown reason, as he waited with the group leader, last to board their train, she gave him an impromptu hug. Perhaps this meeting with 'Sweetie' fulfilled the lover's bargain, only time will tell.

As he put down the pencil, he was grateful to the other in him that had written his story for he could not have done so, and he hoped that in the life he had saved lay the power to save many more.

He was tired now and as he closed his eyes to sleep, he smiled with gratitude for all those special happy times he had spent with his little princess and her china bell.

**

'Sometimes we need to be quiet,
or we will never hear the echo.'

**

The walk is over.

All it needed was the Dales,
to finish off my walking tales.
Having crossed them, I could boast,
that I had walked from coast to coast.

In the past I'd had some fears,
that's why it took me sixteen years.
To make it right and bring me smiles,
t'would only take me eighty miles.

To win such prize, four days I planned,
and off I went, with map in hand.
I did get lost – as others hinted,
path had changed since route first printed.

Committed now, to progress chained,
three flipping days it rained and rained.
When the storm ceased, from the skies,
out came in force, the biting flies.

When weak on hills in hungry mood,
I dropped to village low, for food,
Soon stomach thought the throat was cut,
the only, village shop, was shut.

When to Richmond town came me,
no room there was in B&B.
Though, in the house, *'no room,'* they said,
'You can use our garden shed'.

Grateful for their kindly thought,
and sleepless in a bed too short,
blistered feet were racked with pain,
while on tin roof it beat with rain.

Worst rain for nigh a hundred years,
felt glad sometimes, it hid my tears.
The mud, the pain, the sweat, the path,
God, I craved a nice warm bath.

At long last, to car returned,
my muscles ached, my feet they burned,
but after rest and after dinner,
this old man drove home, a winner.

Life, on the moors.

As in life, a story could provide various endings, each of them created by choices made in the mind of the reader.

In this story you will inevitably come across choices with which you may or may not agree. Such is the way of life.

This is the thought-provoking tale of a late 18th Century peasant family, as they struggle across desolate moorland seeking a better life on the other side, a place free from betrayal and starvation. Will they find it? Will they make the right choices? Would you?

The date is 1786, and like many peasants of the day, George Dinnicombe was another hard-working victim of the social system, often surviving on subsistence wages in return for giving his all, his life, his family, and his soul. He was hungry, not just for decent food but for the opportunity to provide well for his children. George himself was born to pauper parents in the winter of 1752 and when old enough to work was given away and bound to a Thomas Reid, owner of a blacksmiths and farriery business not far from the pretty Devon village of Loxhore.

George did well as apprentice to Thomas Reid, a kindly and likeable gentleman with an excellent reputation for horses and ironwork. George proved himself over again as a willing worker and a keen learner and soon became indispensable to the Reid's family business. Life was as good as could be expected for a working-class man.

Earlier, in 1774, at age twenty-two, George had married Phoebe. Phoebe Goulde was a God fearing and kind-hearted young lass from Stoke Rivers, she also came from an impoverished family, her father having succumbed to smallpox the year before she became twenty and married. The couple were blessed with three children, all healthy and strong – William eleven, Thomas nine, and their little sister Sarah, six.

Old Mr Reid, the owner of the business, had two grown sons, Mark and his younger rival sibling Luke, of whom it must be said was a downright wastrel and a most disappointing son for the fair minded and kindly Thomas Reid. It was a bad day for all when Thomas Reid was finally laid to rest. Thomas' funeral was a fine affair and well attended by the local community, particularly by the many that were in his debt for past favours. None were surprised by the absence of the spendthrift Luke, who had ridden into Barnstaple town to celebrate his inheritance in the only way he knew. Subsequently his drinking and gambling incurred debts upon the business and despite his brother Mark's best efforts they soon had to let workers go and evict loyal and trusty servants of many years.

On the third of March 1786 it was George's turn, and he was the last to go. The business had failed completely by then, due to Luke's so called 'friends' calling in their markers.

Mark Reid retained a small cottage from the estate in which he continued to live with his grieving mother. None of their employees could be afforded such luxuries. None of these events were going to be easy for anyone. By the dying heat of the forge, the two men stood in solemnity already aware of the other's mind, 'I'm deeply sorry George. We've grown up together here and I had great hopes we would all grow old in dignity and peace together too. It's not to be. The cottage you live in is no longer mine. You will have to move out, I'm truly sorry. I can tell you how bad it is, the horses we have, those few that are left, I cannot even afford to feed.

I'm not sure how I will survive but am hopeful one of my father's friends may have pity on me and find me a position.'
'I'm sorry too sir for your loss, don't you worry about us sir, I shall think of something. . . don't you worry sir. I shall go and speak with Phoebe and we'll make our plans,' said George with a confidence in his voice that belied his sense of total loss. Mark had been like a brother to him all these years and old Mr Reid had been like a kindly uncle all through his service. It wasn't the first time George had struggled alone and he didn't suppose it would be the last either. As he walked away from the smithy, across the once weed free, inner cobbled yard and under the barn to the lane outside, he met Luke coming the other way. As usual he was the worse for drink but treated George with the respect that bullies often have of those who are in nature and in stature their betters, 'Sorry to see you go George old chap, you're a fine fellow, fine wife too I'll say.'
Something in the back of his mind stirred George to ask a favour, 'Luke, sir, if you cannot feed the horses, could you see your way to let me have one in payment for all the times I saved you from troubles in the past?'
'George old chap, help yourself, no, tell you what, I'll pick one out myself and tether her outside the barn for you. That big bay with the black mane is a fine horse. You leave it with me. You can trust me not to let you down.' With that he staggered off to confront his poor brother over some trifling amount he still needed.
George walked thoughtfully to the comparative hovel they called a cottage but nevertheless a home of happy times, an emerging plan taking shape in his mind. At the back of the cottage was a rundown open farm cart in need of some attention, what with that fine horse Luke had promised and a few running repairs to the cart, they could use it to start a new life where there was more work. Many a traveller

seeking the farrier at the smithy had shared their tales of riches and fine living in towns such as Bristol. Riches fostered by the ships that sailed to and from the new world. This was a bold but fine plan.

Phoebe listened quietly as he broke the news. She thought a while then said quietly, 'Why, George dear, could they not tell you last week when you would have had a chance of work at the hiring fair. You are a good man with fine skills, you would have found work to be sure. . . and now it is three months to the next one. . . and us homeless with winter not yet past. That Luke will surely go to hell, for certain he should, I pity his poor mother, God bless her.'

The children, though not fully understanding the implications, had heard the news. They had such faith in their father, they were not afraid, it seemed like an adventure.

'We will leave tomorrow morning. While I prepare the cart, you must gather what little we have, to take with us. There may be a few root vegetables still good enough to lift. . . William, you can do that. Otherwise just help your mother in whatever she asks. While there is some daylight left, I will begin on the old cart,' and with that he was gone to the rear of the cottage, tools in hand.

That night they all had a good supper and kept the fire banked well, no point in leaving firewood for the next tenant. Nobody slept well that night, all minds in turmoil over the unknown.

As a pale grey March dawn approached slowly from the east bringing with it a cold wind off the moors, George was already preparing to leave. He had on his working clothes and thick coat, as his old boots clumped up the stony lane for one last time to the stables. He was in for a dreadful shock, no fine bay horse awaited him, just an old nag of

twenty years or more. The poor animal was more suited to feeding the hounds at his Lordship's hunt than pull a cart.
George was staring at the old grey mare in a mixture of disbelief, sorrow, and surprise, when Mark's voice startled him from the barn doorway. 'George, George, my dear friend, I am so sorry this has happened. Luke was angry I had no more money for him yesterday, so he took all the horses, leaving only old Molly here. He said she probably wouldn't reach town alive anyway. It's all there is my friend, all there is and nothing anymore to be done about it.'
'Never you mind sir, not your doing, we'll care for her, make the best of it as we always have,' George assured, as he released the tether to walk Molly down to the cottage.
Mark held out his hand, George took it and the warmth of fellowship flowed in their veins. As Mark released his grip, George looked in his hand. . . a golden Guinea looked back.
'No need to say anything George, take it for any emergency you might face. It's all I have, I wish it were more, for you were ever a better brother to me than that wastrel drunkard. I wish you all well and tell you, I will never forget you and your loyal service to my father. Goodbye George.'

Outside their humble cottage, Phoebe looked in astonishment at the old horse, but young Sarah instantly loved the quiet gentleness of the old grey. They'd never had a horse before.
'I know, I know,' agreed George, 'I know she's old but if we are careful and do our share of walking too, we'll survive. If we stay here, we will starve for sure. We must always make the best of what we have. Come on boys, you can help me harness her in the shafts.'

Their adventure to a new freedom had begun. Most roads in those days were extremely poor, almost impassable in places. It became fashionable for the rich to improve some important roads and charge people for using them. George chose instead to take isolated and remote moorland tracks, for several reasons, it would be very many miles shorter, it avoided the levies of toll roads and there would be free grazing for the family's new horse.

It all began well, with the children and Sarah walking alongside, George leading the horse, encouraging with kind words gleaned from so many years of his trade. After a few miles they left the small tree filled valleys behind and started the steady climb on to the wilds of Exmoor. They stopped only briefly near mid-day, for daylight was still valuable in the month of March. The pace was slow and dependant on Molly the horse, each hour would only see them another weary two miles along the ancient tracks.

Then, George smiled and looked back at his despondently trudging family, 'Look there, lady luck is smiling upon us.' He pointed to a small but well-situated farmstead ahead and down to the right. It was only a gentle slope to the farm, it looked a touch run down but had all the essentials, running water, sheltered valley, small orchard, a wood for fuel and even a low-lying pasture field that could be cultivated. Little Sarah wandered alongside and chatted to her newfound childhood friend Molly the grey horse, who ambled slowly on at the perfect pace for the charming six-year-old. George waved an open hand to the farmer who was struggling with a broken fence. As they approached, they greeted each other warmly, one for the comfort of shelter and the other the comfort of company.

The farmer introduced himself as William Beer and as he did so, a pleasantly smiling plump lady wiping her hands on a cloth appeared at the open farmhouse door, 'and this is my good wife, Sarah.' And then, after hearing the traveller's story, William Beer insisted, 'You shall dine with us tonight and the barn is sound enough for shelter... it looks like your old horse could do with a rest. . . a long rest!' They all laughed, forgetting all their troubles in that passing moment of joy.

The coincidence of two Williams and two Sarahs was not lost on them, it created an impression of kinship, as in those days, children were often named after their grandparents. Old Sarah made a fine fuss of young Sarah and the boys sat by the fire with their mother.

George, having seen the needy state of the farm, offered a day's work from him and the boys in return for the hospitality.

'Gladly accepted George my friend, gladly indeed. Sadly, we were never blessed with children strong enough to survive their first years. We're getting older now and yesterday I strained my shoulder trying to keep a wayward ewe from jumping that broken fence you saw me struggling with. Sarah's not up to lifting heavy things either!' Old William smiled a knowing smile.

In the two days the Dinnicombe family chose to stay at the farm, situated not so many miles north of Challacombe, they transformed the place, fences mended, wood collected, chopped and stacked, barn hinges straightened and replaced, weeds cut, water fetched, roof patched. It was a hive of activity, a gloriously happy time, but then it was time to leave. George was destined for a somewhat different future.

The morning of their departure, old William the farmer, with his wife close by, spoke quietly and sincerely to George, 'George, you can see the future this farm holds for someone younger, we have no living relatives, no children to take over when we are gone. We would like to offer your boy William a home with us, treat him kindly like one of our own and one day he will be the farmer here.' Old Sarah held her

hands together in hope and Phoebe's hidden hand pinched her husband's arm.
George understood the offer well enough. George had already decided what he must do, he could not give up his child as he had once been. 'In my heart I cannot do such a thing, though I feel the kindness of your words and sense your loss as if it were my own. We must move on and leave you with happy memories and a knowing you will not be forgotten. But our destiny lies elsewhere.'

As they gathered at the farm gate, prepared to leave, and say goodbye, Old William warned George of bad weather to come, 'Winter's not over yet George, the wind from the East and the colour of the morning's sunrise tell me that it's possible we may have snow. . . the moor is no place for anyone when that happens. You are always welcome back here if it proves to be too hard going.' Their handshake was deep in the meaning of lasting kinship.
'Don't worry, William, we shall be fine, two days at most and we'll be off the moor and be on the sheltered wooded lowlands,' assured a confident George, a most able man in his mid-thirties and with great strength and energy.

They walked with the horse to the top of the slope, only young Sarah hitching a ride on the back, waving her many goodbyes to the dear old lady, who'd been like the grandmother she never knew.
William and Sarah Beer stood together as they always had and waved until the cart and all were gone from sight. They walked slowly back to their house; their minds filled with the dreams of what could have been.

The ancient track was still passably visible and usually followed contour lines or ridges. They were making good time until a trial of nature blocked their path. In a small but unavoidable valley, evident from the reed growth and sphagnum moss that spread some twenty yards or so across the valley bottom, was the sort of marshy challenge they could well have done without. 'Everybody off the cart, even you Sarah, lift off some of the heavy things and we'll come back for them,' George was still confident it could be done, but oh for a stronger, younger horse. It was almost as much as Molly could do to lift her feet out of the bog, never mind pull the cart, which only made her hooves sink deeper. 'Come on boys, hands to the wheel spokes, and you too Phoebe,' called George enthusiastically as he heaved at the harness and encouraged Molly to do her best. She was a willing horse and deserved no flogging. The wheels wobbled side to side with their worn bearings and rocked back and forth as the cart teetered on leaving a deep rut. With rests, it must have taken the family a good half an hour to place the cart on firm ground again. It was obvious that Molly was now lame. Experience told George it was probably a tendon in the lower leg, the swelling had already started, she might be able to hobble on for a while but pulling the cart would probably kill her. It wouldn't be the first horse he'd seen broken winded with age and excessive labour. There was little shelter in this valley of mostly grass and dead bracken, though it was less windy than on the tops where the east wind was beginning to carry sleet. The sky was that peculiar grey that had the smell of snow.

'Right Phoebe, we must be a good seven or maybe even eight miles on from the Beer's farm, perhaps over the next ridge there may be another. Shelter as best you can in the cart, I'll be as quick as I can to fetch help.'

Phoebe noticed the change in George's voice, she knew he was worried, she knew that they should have heeded old William's warning and now their very lives were in God's hands. Sleet began to fall more heavily as George, collar up and leaning into both hill and wind that now conspired so cruelly against him, slowly clambered from sight. Phoebe prepared the contents of the cart as best she could to make a shelter, she leaned against the woodworm riddled side and gathered her children close, Sarah on her lap and the boys each side, pieces of sack cloth and a sheet of old darned canvas their only protection from the east wind's determined onslaught. The cold, hunting wind howled through gaps in the cart's sides and the torn canvas flapped noisily about them.

Phoebe knew only too well the truth of the matter, not all of them would live through this storm, but she reassured the children that all would be well, that their father would not let them down and would never leave them alone on the moor. She knew he would always come back - nothing would stop him.

Molly, now free from her traces and lightly tethered, stood resolute with her back to the biting wind and sleet that slowly changed her grey to white, there was only one thing she was waiting for and it didn't disappoint. It wasn't long before she sank quietly to the ground, unnoticed, her work forever over.

George reached the summit with failing visibility but sufficient for him to view the surrounding empty moor. In front was another small valley, it shouldn't take him long to cross it and see if here was a farm the other side, or perhaps a shelter wood. He pushed himself harder than ever, his feet numbingly cold through the worn-thin soles of his boots. The touch of cold sleet pained his hands like a burning from the forge and his hands had lost so much control he could no longer close a button nor adjust his collar. He knew as well as Phoebe, that they would not all survive this storm, but he was not dead yet and he must find help for his family.

'Just one more hill,' he promised himself, and with fading hope, 'just one more hill.'
Meanwhile the sleet had turned to snow, big snowflakes riding the wind towards him faster than galloping horses, almost pretty to watch, practically hypnotising. . . George shook his head from his strange but passing fascination and pressed on.
Meanwhile, back at the cart, Phoebe's mind was in turmoil, what if George did not come back in time, even if he did will they still be strong enough to move? She thought about Mr. Beer's generous offer to care for her eldest boy, William. Possibly seven miles back to the farm it was, but young William was a strong boy, well-nourished and big for his age, he had the determination of his father and the spirit of his mother. She made her decision. Daylight would not last forever, maybe four or five hours left, if William started out now, while still able, with the wind at his back and before the snow deepened, he could make a determined one-way hike to the farm before nightfall. Phoebe gently lifted Sarah, who appeared to be sleeping quietly now, to one side, she took off her coat and made William put it on, she wrapped him up well and asked him, 'Tell me William, do you think you can follow the way back to the farm?' William was sombre but nodded back in reply. 'Then off you go with my blessing, may God be with you and guide you all the way safe to the Beer's farm,' she kissed his cold forehead, pulled his cap down tight and helped him off the cart. 'Don't you stop,' she said, 'if you are tired you do not stop, you keep going, say hello to them and we send our love. Don't you stop William. . . whatever happens, you keep going!' she shouted after him.
William turned, nodded again, and was gone in an instant, he felt very grown up that his mother entrusted him with such a journey. . . he would not fail her.

Sheltered by two coats, with the cold wind at his back blowing the snow past him, his path was clearer, his body warmer and his intention resolute.
Phoebe settled back in the cart as best she could, already little Sarah the youngest was sleeping the long sleep, Thomas huddled closer, his shivering telling Phoebe he was still alive, she pulled the canvas and sacking tight around their bodies and quietly prayed, first for Sarah, then for William, Thomas and for her brave George, wherever he was, and only then for herself.
George's mind was confused, he was still walking but no longer sure in which direction, for snow had covered the ground and filled his footprints. He'd long since stopped shivering and was so tired he desperately needed to rest. Then astonishingly through the curtain of snow, like an apparition, came another man. The other spoke and beckoned him on. Though George could not hear above the wind, bemused, he followed the stranger to a small cob-built shepherd's shelter, it had a simple but adequate heather thatched roof, and best of all a small fire of Gorse wood burned at one end. His host explained that he was a local shepherd looking for lost sheep before the blizzard took its icy grip upon the moor. George, unable to recognise his rapidly worsening condition, replied in a slurred voice, about his family needing help. The shepherd told him of a small farm two miles further east just off the ridge-way track. Though pleased with the news, George again felt extraordinarily drowsy. He took off his big coat to warm it by the fire and promised himself a few minutes rest before pressing on to the farm. Just a few minutes, that's all, it wouldn't hurt. In a moment he fell fast asleep, it never occurred to him that even if he reached the farm he was still lost, he would never find the cart again in this storm.

It was in that same instant that Phoebe ceased praying for his return. Hope and breath lay themselves peacefully down in the snow with the old grey horse, innocents all to the worsening storm.

George snapped awake keenly, his eyes acclimatised already to the dazzling whiteness about him. Feeling refreshed and comforted, with what he assumed had been only moments of rest, he glanced about him to see the shepherd had gone and the cob walls of the shelter now just snow lined remnants. George set off with renewed determination towards the farm the shepherd had described. His mind not in any state to question the events of his journey. He reached the farm with seemingly little effort. His hands no longer burned with the pain of cold, his footsteps were light and easy. He reached into his pocket for the one gold coin he had, the guinea, Mark had given him. He would use it to buy help for his family. His closed fist knocked heavily on the solid farmhouse door, but it remained closed. Twice more he beat on the door and called out in pity for someone to come. In the great muffled silence of falling snow, the door remained steadfastly closed to his desperate pleas. He could stay no longer, something dear to his soul was calling to him from across the moors. He turned and ran westwards, quickly blending into the deepening and all encircling whiteness. He would never give up, all that mattered to him was out there, lost somewhere in a landscape that more often, than not, buried its secrets. A terrible sense of loss had seized his spirit, at this instant, George knew he could never ever give up.

Postscript. *Date: 2016, the 6th March.*

Somewhere out on the wild moors of the Exe, several miles North East of Challacombe stood a part modernised farmhouse. It had been on the estate agent's books for several months. Remoteness and old wives' tales about ghosts had deterred potential clients, but today . . . success.

Fingering the keys of his modern Range Rover in his pocket, the estate agent smiled with satisfaction at the proud new buyers of Ashcombe Oak Farm, 'I just know you'll love this place, especially when you expressed excitement about buying a remote property with a ghost! The previous owners didn't mind either; they told me it's a kindly ghost, possibly that of an old shepherd that is recorded as missing, presumed lost on the moors. Quaintly it knocks on the door of the original part of the farmhouse if the snow falls deep. Lovely isn't it? When they opened the door there was nobody to be seen and no footprints in the snow. People love these silly old wives' tales, makes the moors more romantic, more interesting, don't you think? Still, we rarely have much snow here nowadays. Oh, I meant to say, when the previous owners added the new extension, they had to lift some yard cobbles and guess what? They found a golden guinea dated 1779, most probably dropped by some careless rich chap. Perhaps there's more out there. . . here's hoping for you eh?'

**

Each winter, whenever snow lies thick on the moors and the wind blows fierce from the east, George returns, he is ever lost yet ever searching for his family. Sometimes he chances upon the caring shepherd again, in eternity seeking his lost sheep.

**

Did young William, the oldest child, safely reach the Beer's farm? Did he live happily, marry, have children of his own and inherit the Beer's farm? We will never know, we can only trust, as did his loving mother at the time.

**

Now is the time for you to read the gift sequel called 'Surviving the blizzard' on page 391.

'First, abandon hope, all ye who search for certainty.'

**

**

Nature speaks – but who listens?

The telephone rang interminably, eventually he switched the video game to pause, and answered. 'Yes?'

It was his wife Maggie, who was calling from the moors where he had dropped her off earlier. Maggie was a pleasant kindly lady in her mid-forties and slightly overweight, she'd recently bought a new pair of walking boots and a map of Exmoor. She was on a mission to become fit and enjoy a better life – and a longer healthy one, with luck.

'Oh, it's you,' he said sharply,' giving up already eh? Thought you might.'

Her voice was tense, 'Well to be honest, I'm not feeling so good.'

'To be expected dear, it is your first long walk, you'll be okay. Is that all?' He fidgeted with the game controller in his other hand and stared wistfully at the locked screen.

'Well, my hands are tingling. . . '

He interrupted, 'I'm sure they will, what with swinging them about on a walk like that.'

Maggie continued, 'There's a small farm down to my right, do you think I should call in and you can pick me up from there?'

'No, no, are we men or mice? You keep going, you're doing well. I'll pick you up at the agreed place, the Shepherd's Flock by the crossroads and we'll have a pint or two to celebrate.'

Maggie was insistent, 'but that's not all. . . there's a crow and it keeps following me. It's a bit frightening.'

'Okay, that's enough now, you're just being paranoid. Great big lump like you afraid of a little crow. They're nesting at the moment so it's probably out looking for worms or something. Don't phone me again until you are near the pub, okay?'

Suitably cajoled into continuing her walk against her better judgement, 'Well, alright, if you say so dear, but it doesn't feel right, and the mobile signal is getting weaker all the time . . . ch, ch, derrrrr.'

'Thank god, she's lost the signal and I bet she'll be late to the pub too.' The TV burst into life as he pressed the start button on the controller.

He lazily glanced at the clock after finishing his game. 'Curses, is that the time? I'd better get a move on or I'll be late myself.' There was a good football match on TV that evening, perhaps the pub would be showing it, it was the European cup after all.

He duly arrived at the Shepherd's Flock and ordered a pint of local ale, then sat down to wait.

And wait he did, though he couldn't drink anymore as he'd had three already. The landlord asked him if he was okay?

'Waiting for the wife, she's walking from Parracombe way, but she should be here by now, must be two hours overdue for sure. Probably lost I suppose, good job it's only six o'clock.'

The landlord spoke calmly but with authority, he knew people could die out there, especially the ill-equipped novice. 'Right sir, you sit there while I call for some help. Local boys in the moors rescue they are, they'll go and find her.'

'Oh, we don't want to cause any trouble, she's only trying to get fit, nothing to worry about I'm sure.'

The landlord ignored him and made his phone calls.

An hour later while our friend was watching the big match starting, a young man entered and spoke quietly to the landlord, 'you'll need to call a doctor and the police, we've found her and they're bringing her body in now. Who's the husband?'

The landlord nodded in our friend's direction, 'the bloke there watching the match. Leave it to me, I'll make the calls then have a chat with him... keep him calm and the like.'
Sunset was about an hour away when the moors rescue team arrived at the pub's private rear yard. The landlord had broken the bad news and walked him outside to meet the team and find out what had happened. When he saw the body covered by a light tarpaulin, he stepped forward to have a look. A strong hand on his chest stopped him, it was one of the rescue team. 'I wouldn't do that sir, looks like heart attack but I'm afraid it's worse than you might suspect. I fear it's not a pretty site when the crows have been at the eyes. Just remember her how she was, that's my advice.'

'And there was joy in the home of the Ravens
that their young would eat their fill.'

**

Suspicion.

A rural Edwardian tale of adversity and courage during hard times.

The oil lamp hanging from the beam, swung wildly on its hook and the flame flickered desperately as the old Inn door opened to a wild night, hurriedly ushering in a wind battered visitor.

Old Seth the village mole-catcher pushed his body hard against the door to close it tight and secure the latch. 'By God,' he said, 'that be devilish windy this night it be.'

'No moles to be caught tonight then Seth,' joked the burly innkeeper, pouring him a tankard of ale from the big jug.

'If I know ee moles, they'll take advantage of this bad weather and be all over his Lordship's lawn by teatime come morning's night,' muttered Seth and, like a pack of hunting wolves, the wind around the ill-fitting windows howled in agreement.

Seth shuffled his old boots across the sawdust floor and sat in his favourite chair. Nearby, were four men, strangers they were, and though next to the inglenook wood fire they still wore their greatcoats with collars turned up. Caps, the mark of a working man, covered their heads, and their boots looked the worse for wear. Occasionally a gust of wind forced smoke down the chimney, oblivious, the men talked on, absorbed deeply in their secretive liaison.

Seth's friendly greeting, 'Eeenin to ee gents,' was largely ignored, only one man, the larger of the four, thickset men, grunted back, 'An' yerself squire,' then quickly turned his face away for the work in hand.

'Ah well,' mused Seth, 'obviously strangers, not a local accent, seemed sort of … well, not sure really … anyway, strangers they were, and mean looking ones at that … wouldn't want to meet them on a dark night.'

Seth supped his ale in a peace of his own making.

Now, Old Seth might have been getting long in the tooth, but there was nothing wrong with his hearing. Some said he could hear moles moving underground – some even said he talked to them. Though some would also say, 'old wives' tales mostly – mostly'.

Seth didn't hear all that was being said, he just caught bits of the conversation; 'gotta get money soon', 'counting on us, back home', 'take our chances when we can I say', 'what about the rich geezer's big house down the road', ' shh, not so loud.' …..

William, the big innkeeper, came close and placed a callused and powerful hand on old Seth's shoulder, the hand of part time village blacksmith, 'See 'ere old Seth, I'm putting ee another fine log on the fire to keep ee warm and happy. Now don't ee forget that kindness when ee next sees his Lordship's woodsmen.'

'Ar, to be certain, there's always plenty of useful men about at his Lordship's,' Seth said, loud enough so as the four men could not fail to hear. At the same time, he spoke to William with his eyes, indicating his distrust of the strangers with a sideways look and an enquiring expression.

Seth went back to the bar with William on the excuse of obtaining more ale, but as they huddled over the bar it was other things that occupied their minds. For some half hour they chewed over what they should do about their suspicions, but before they could decide, the Inn door burst open. Standing in the open doorway, with no intention of closing it, was one of his Lordship the Earl's gardeners, 'Big trouble up at the House and we need help quick.'

By now, he has the attention of everyone in the Inn, including the four strangers who are now all looking straight at the gardener with earnest intent.

'What's wrong, old chap?' asked William, peering past the wind flickered lantern.

'Fire, Fire, ... stables on fire … the horses trapped … his Lordship is begging for help to save his horses ….. will you come?'
'We're on our way old chap, we're on our way.' As William threw on his rough old coat, he shouted at the strangers, 'I'm sorry lads, but us have got to go, ye'll have to leave the Inn, I'm sorry.'

The men stood quickly in unison.

'Nah worries guv, we're coming wiv yer,' shouted back the big fellow. With heavy chairs pushed back like they were feathers; they all reached the door together and out into the dark night. William grabbed two lanterns and they set off hurriedly on the gravelled mile to the manor house.
Soon they were close enough to smell the fire and hear the horses' tortured cries of fear.
It was a scene of total chaos at the stables; stone built of two stories, the stalls being on the ground floor and storage above, wooden beams, floors, and partitions everywhere. Straw and winter hay were well alight with ever thickening dark yellow smoke, servants ran and shouted, even the kitchen girls were there ... not that any could do much to help.
William, Seth, and the strangers found his Lordship by the closed main door to the stables. Though quite beside himself with pain for an impending and horrific death of his beloved horses, he managed to explain, 'Fire, started in loft, burnt through floor, far end of stables, the end where we usually get in, horses down this end but we can't open doors from here ... only from inside. The way through is barred by fallen beams and fire .. My God, just listen to those poor creatures. What can we do?'
'If it can be done sir, it will be done, ee have my word on it,' William said, with impassioned promise in his voice. And with that, the six moved as one to the burning end of the

building. There was a small bucket chain from the well in use, but to little avail, they would never extinguish such flames, the only hope was to open the doors from the inside and save the horses, for the barn was already condemned to a fiery hell. William and the big fellow looked through the door together, much of the fire was still on the upper floors, tiles could be heard breaking on the floor above as parts of the roof failed, in front of them, a few feet in, was some smoking, water damped straw and a muddle of fallen timbers, some of them huge beams of oak.

William turned to the big fellow and said, 'Look, I can't do this on my own, but I reckon it's clear past this point and I feel I can open they far doors an let they horses out. Can you, ... will you ... help me by yon beams?'

'Count on us squire, what we've been through in life, we ain't afraid.' Pulling their collars higher and wrapping some old hemp sacking around their hands and arms they entered through the doorway to hell.

'Seth,' shouted William, 'get ee to the main door, tell his Lordship to be ready for they horses.' And with that, he disappeared choking into the yellow grey smoke.

Seth glanced in horror as five men disappeared as if gone forever. He hoped upon hope that the building would stand long enough for William to do his work, he then, quick as old bones would let him, went to find his Lordship.

Strong as William was, the beam that barred his way was beyond his strength, as he crouched low to gain some fresher breath for one last attempt, he heard the big fellow shout, 'go for it mate, we can't hold it up much longer.' William saw through stinging, tear blinded, eyes the four strangers had lifted the beam enough for him to get through. He didn't waste any time, for with every second he was getting weaker and more confused. As he'd hoped, it was cleaner air further down the stables, he followed the stall fronts on the left to the great doorway and, fumbling with shaking but powerful hands, he found the bolts and locking bar that freed the door to open. With an almighty shove, fresh air rushed in to greet him as the heavy door swung open.

As good as his word Seth was prepared, along with the stable boys and his Lordship, to guide the frenzied horses away to safety. It was going well, despite the horses being panicked and some kicking out, they were all released safe to a corner field.

'Let it burn now, let it burn,' called his Lordship, 'don't risk yourselves anymore, my beautiful horses are safe, God bless you all for your help.'

His composure soon regained, his Lordship ordered the kitchen staff to prepare refreshments for his helpers, and for everyone to stand back from the now collapsing building. The roof caved in first and carried the first floor down with it, the falling twisting beams levered the stone walls as they fell, and it was all but over for the old stables.

It was a smoke laden and sweat smelly throng that gathered in the great kitchen, his Lordship mingled with his servants like they were bosom friends, the like of which was never seen before, nor since.

'William, Seth, good friends that you are, heroes both that you are, you will know my gratitude in the days to come, you can be sure of that,' beamed his Lordship, who had been liberal with the port as much as with his thanks.

Seth drew his Lordship aside, 'what of they four strangers, milord, I'm not seeing they since the fire, perhaps they need a watching sir.'

'Nay Seth, good men all, they saved the day for us with their strength and camaraderie, without their bravery our noble William could not have prevailed against the odds as he did. Good men all, simple working folk, iron ore miners walking their way to Northamptonshire for the promise of work to

feed their families. I've had the butler sort them out some fresh clothes ... not burnt ones, eh? ... Here they come now. Here lads, here, come join us for a meal,' he called.
They sat about the great pine table, food and drink a plenty, there they sat, his Lordship the Earl, the mole-catcher, the black-smith and ... no, not four strangers anymore, just four good men that could look any other in the eye and tell their tale of heroism.

But I doubt they ever would, so here,
I have done it for them.

**

A Tale of Two Otters.

Young grass gleamed vibrant green in the warm late spring sunshine and small birds happily sang their little hearts out from the safety of a clump of ancient Yews that had stood sentinel in that special place for centuries. Apart from the bird song and the soft and almost reverent crunch of shoes on gravel, for a town, it was remarkably peaceful here.
So reminiscent of those childhood days long gone when children could ride their bicycles unfettered along miles of country lanes, their only care to make sure they were back in time for tea, when coal was delivered by horse and cart, when summers were hot, and winters were cold; He smiled and felt the feelings of his childhood days.
His closest friend, his old childhood pal, Bob, had lived a few doors away from him in a small, rented cottage on the edge of the village, backing on to a wild wood bank and crystal stream, and only shouting distance from their favourite

'conker' tree on the village green: the place of so many happy hours.

He himself had moved on to better things of course, upgrading his house frequently, manipulating his finances and credit to buy the latest BMW or Mercedes and striving to make even more money by working longer hours further from home; an investment in a way. 'For a happy and eventual retirement,' he used to tell anyone who asked. His eye was caught by a bee, busy on some dog daisies, and he smiled again. His pal, Bob, was an artist; my goodness was he skilled, why, his paintings of wildflowers were always on display at the school, no doubt that less-than-adequate 'Art' teacher bathing in the reflected glory of Bob's genius.

Every few years or so, when on business down that way, he would detour among quiet lanes to the secluded and still much untouched village of his childhood. Many of the other folk had moved on, as had he, but Bob was still there, still in the same old cottage, with its apple trees, vegetable plot and outside toilet. Bob was still the artist – and getting better every year too.

He smiled again and recalled how, on one visit, and over a cup of tea, he had asked Bob why he'd got that gnarled old tree stump on his kitchen table: bits of soil and twigs and all. 'Why' Bob queried surprised, 'Can't you see the pool, the otters and their holt?'

A dismissive glance told him he could see nothing of the sort, just some dirty old lump of wood.

Well, next visit, a couple of years later, the lump of unimportant wood long forgotten, he called on Bob for a chat about old and happy school days and a cup of tea and piece of homemade apple pie, and there, on the table, was a wonder to behold.

Never in all his born days had he seen such a piece of work, never, ever, in all the galleries, museums and books, never, not ever. In differing and subtle shades of brown there were two playful otters, with bushes, rocks and pool, and even a fresh caught fish lay on the bank. The detail was so fine he wanted to gently stroke the otters to see if it was real fur and not wood. My goodness, did he want to buy this incredible symbol of life and beauty to display in his City home.

'How much Bob?' He asked eagerly.

'Sorry, old chum, not finished yet, lots to do, could take years, just can't tell,' replied Bob leisurely.

'But it's wonderful as it is, I will be the envy of all my friends. Name your price Bob, I'm not short of a penny or two,' he implored.

'No, really,' Bob insisted, 'I feel I've much more to do on this work.'

He reluctantly resolved to drop the subject, but not in his memory, for in the future, when it was finished, it would be his. He felt it would be worth waiting a whole lifetime for such a purchase.

It was about ten years before he again visited Bob and his old home village, he'd been very busy on many and very important business matters. Though he might have forgotten to visit, he had not forgotten the two otters sculpture, how could he?

'Come on in,' welcomed Bob, 'sit yourself down and I'll put the kettle on.'

Bob had not changed a bit, well, perhaps a little bit, he was a little thinner, losing some hair and had a slight stoop, but all the same it was still his good friend Bob inside.

He sat at the table wondering where his otter sculpture was, and at the same time admiring yet another, but quite smaller, masterpiece, a pool, a kingfisher and a butterfly all in perfect detail and harmony in wood. 'A fleeting image forever captured,' he thought, 'truly beautiful.' 'Where's my otter

sculpture, Bob?' He called across the kitchen in as positive manner as he could muster.
Bob replied with a childlike chuckle, 'You're looking at it, I found them there hidden inside the rocks and otters, kept the pool, couldn't see anything in it yet, water too muddy at the moment perhaps.' He chuckled again and poured the kettle water into his grandmother's old china tea pot.
What had Bob done? His dream, of owning the otters all for himself, was dashed, such perfection, gone, gone, and gone forever, no coming back, never, no not ever.
'May I buy this one off you please, Bob? He asked in a more humble and now subdued manner, remembering his previous attempt to buy Bob's work.
'Sorry old chap, not done yet, just a bit more, just a little bit more, not far to go now, getting near the end, soon be journey done,' rambled Bob.
It looked like a tear in Bob's eye, he thought, as Bob eased himself into the old wooden carver chair at the end of the pine table. Bob sipped his tea carefully, and then spoke like he'd not heard Bob speak before. 'It's all a journey you know, that's really the only bit that counts, the sculpture; you know, first you find something that appears to be nothing and you embark on a journey of discovery, and you find what you want not by collecting but by discarding, discarding the bits that aren't worth keeping and you end up with something truly beautiful, as your journey takes you further you find other bits that can be discarded to make it even more wonderful – and when finally you can discard it all , well , now then, that's enlightenment and your journey is over – the beauty of spirit is all yours and the original object, is long gone.' Bob sipped his tea again.
'Right,' he said, 'most interesting,' while not really understanding a word of it. 'So, when can I buy it then Bob?'

'When such a journey is finished, my beloved childhood friend, it cannot be bought, for any money, by any person, the price was paid long ago by the traveller himself,' he said with an air of knowingness and wisdom.

Back in the spring sunshine he half imagined he now understood what Bob had tried to say in his last ramblings. The skill Bob had, he had paid for dearly himself, perhaps in the way he'd lived life, who knows. It was a skill money could not buy. As his feet quietly crunched the gravel once more, he overheard others talking .... 'What a waste of such talent' ......could have made a fortune you know ... could have been rich .....they say he left nothing, not a thing he left, ... the cottage was rented, and his furniture was the old stuff his parents had left behind ....'

The voices faded into an obscure distance, and he thought, 'Maybe he took everything with him, or maybe he took nothing, and simply enjoyed to the full his time journeying on Earth. He journeyed his path with love in his soul and if anything was left by him it's going to be in us, and in how we now live our lives.'

His slow-paced footfalls changed from gravel to tarmac and the sound of bird song to passing traffic. The great iron gates of the old town cemetery clanked shut behind him.

**

'Some things are hurrying into existence, and others are hurrying out of it; and of that which is coming into existence part is already extinguished. Motions and changes are continually renewing the world, just as the uninterrupted course of time is always renewing the infinite duration of the ages.
In this flowing stream then, on which there is no abiding, what is there of the things that hurry by on which a man would set a high price?' Marcus Aurelius

The Second Chance.

Based on real events, real people, my people.

It was a Saturday morning before six am, the 28th May 1887 and along with his sons and nearly 200 other miners, James Richmond was preparing to go underground.

James was a widower living at High Blantyre and at age fifty-eight was past his prime for coal pit working but the pay (at today's equivalent of 16 pence an hour) was better than nothing, which was the second of two unenviable choices.

Many a time James reflected on his Irish past and that of his ancestors. He thought on his grandparents, who in better times owned farms in County Antrim and once sailed lime ships across the Irish Sea. The great potato famine of 1845, which he'd barely survived as a young man of fifteen, had diminished any family wealth and those same grandparents were destined for a pauper's grave on Scottish soil. They were too old and weak to take their second chance of building a new life in Scotland. Nearly all the family became coal or iron ore miners; it was the only way to earn a living if you could call it that.

James and one of his sons, John age 25, stood together by the cage of one of three lift shafts. Little did they know that within 3 hours it would stop working. In the semi gloom, weary eyes drained of life's joys looked around at once fit men, now with crippled fingers and dust choked lungs.

But they were comrades all, bonded in the face of a common adversary.

Omen like, James' safety lamp flickered and went out. He hurriedly returned to the pit head storekeeper and showed him the dead lamp.

'Give it here, I'll try it again and if it doesn't work, you'll have to miss this shift.' The lamp gasped at its second chance and spluttered into life.

Not long after, the unlucky lamp was illuminating a coal seam some 130 fathoms below ground. (780 feet)

With picks, shovels, and bare hands they toiled tirelessly to earn a pittance from the rich and distant mine owners to whom they were all but slaves.

At 9 o'clock it was break time underground, they downed tools and ate their breakfast in the gloom and all-pervading smell of coal stale air. At approximately 7 minutes past 9, the ground shook and dust filled the air - a dust that would carry the fire through much of the mine workings. The lucky ones died instantly from an explosion that destroyed everything in its path. 182 men were in the pit at that time. 73 would die, 53 from burns and 20 asphyxiated. The latter were brought to the surface with calm on their faces, entreating the unknowing observer to think their deaths had been peaceful. Trust me, this would have been far from the truth, but it was better the wives and mothers think otherwise.

The fire that issued from the mine, ignited the pit head gearing and jammed all the cages. It was four hours before an exploratory party could access the mine, to save the living and recover the dead. Miners from other pits in the Hamilton district rushed to assist, for the Udston mine workers had been shocked and decimated.

Regrettably, none of this need have happened. The explosion was later deemed caused by unauthorised blasting without properly checking for the miner's insidious old enemy, firedamp. (Methane gas)

But what of James? Did he survive? His lifeless body was brought to the surface along with his son John. Though terribly shaken and bleeding from the mouth, John survived.

He had tried to save his father but had been overcome by fumes, though he had already succeeded in saving a younger brother.

John and his brother lived on to take their second chance at life, working once more in the pit that had claimed the lives of their father and friends.

Four of the men who were pulled from the pit alive and sent home were to die later the same day – their own second chance revoked. Such events we call disasters, but that word is a trifling euphemism for the reality.

Forty-five hours after the explosion, almost all the bodies had been recovered and at the bottom of pit 2, after nearly two days among their gruesomely deceased comrades, unbelievably two men still lived to tell their tale.

The tale of a second chance.

**

**

The Victorian Fireman's Axe.

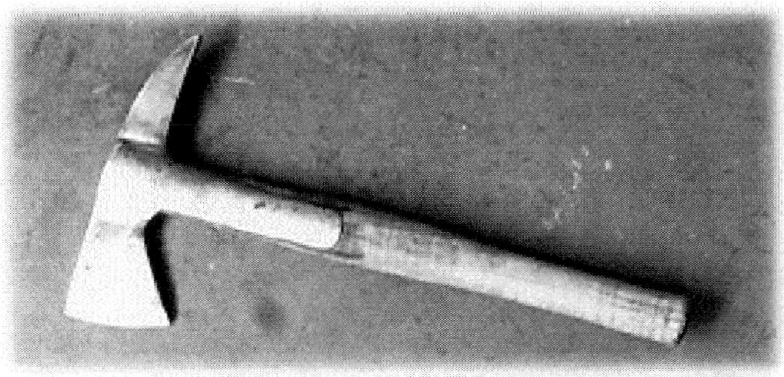

These events are told from the perspective of the axe itself, for who are we to say that the inanimate has no right to share its story?

We were such good comrades, that old fellow and me; constant and dependable companions; we'd been together for over thirty years; faced death and disaster many a time, side by side; the crumbling stairs, the choking acrid fumes; just a way of life for us both.

I suppose, in a way, we were both forged in fire. He was born around 1874 and I in 1892. We worked together in a small but industrious little estuary town. The tidal river ebbed and flowed carrying various cargoes for the warehouses not so far from our station. Often, the firemen would pick up a few 'silver darlings' for dinner from the herring fishers on the quay.

Though it wasn't a big station it saw many changes, even whilst I was there. The horses and 'steamer' were still there when I started, the place was heated by a coal fired boiler and there were various outbuildings storing hay and the like – I never went in there myself, had no need of me I suppose – but others told me how it was.

Though the place was somewhat spartan, it was clean. Twice daily the tile-red painted floor was washed and was clean enough to eat off; the brass work of doorbell, steps, fire door mechanisms and all the equipment was so polished you could see to shave in – not that they did – many of the men had fine sets of whiskers. A row of polished brass helmets rested on hooks above smart, collarless double-breasted tunics – the sort of tunic that inspired every man to stand tall and proud that ever felt its fit. It was with this tunic I would wait, waiting for the bells to go down and my comrade to come and fetch me.

For a few years, until it died of old age, a scruffy stray dog was adopted by the station. They used to laugh a lot at his antics, but greatly admired the dog's courage so close to fires; I think they called it 'Braidwood', though I cannot tell you why, but it did seem to amuse the firemen considerably. Anyway, that dog lived the life of Riley, well fed, slept by the boiler, and then, when the alarm sounded, would run out into the street and follow the men to the fire. What a life, what a lucky old thing, ah, how I envied that dog.

Where was I? Ah, yes, change. The station was to have the new electric light, and later, though the big brass hand bell still hung on its bracket, we were to have a big electric bell fitted. Every few years the station would be sent a new pumping appliance, (those on the outside, who I was informed knew nothing, called them fire engines). The old one would be zealously polished and cleaned with pride as it would be sent to a less busy station, and we had a reputation to honour. The new one would take its place and result in a flurry of activity, starting it up, stopping it, starting it up, pumping water, men running with hoses and ladders with lots of shouting going on from the watching silver helmeted officers. My comrade never wanted to be one of them, it just wasn't for him, for he had a deep sense of

duty which he felt was only truly satisfied at a place the men called, 'the sharp end'. For this I am eternally grateful as it's the only place I can work. He was good at what he did, come to think of it, so was I, we were a formidable team, us two.
Then, one day, he didn't come in to work; I was placed alongside some boots and on top of some folded uniform and fire tunics, then taken by the Brigade wagon to a place I later learned was called 'brigade stores'.
After all my valiant and unstinting service, I was to be incarcerated, in a small dark room, in a box.
Occasionally the door would be opened and, along with the store man's hand, light would come in and bring a glint to polished and waiting steel. The hand would fumble then select from the box, and one of us would be taken. Sometimes the choice was rejected and the 'un-chosen one' was thrown at the back of the tiny wooden room, never to be allowed back with us in the box.

We, who had given so much to change other's destiny,
were now uncertain of our own.

Sometimes, when this door was opened, we could see young men in new uniforms, with buttons bright and thick black polished leather belts. One time, when the door was left open by accident, we saw one of our brothers, a chosen one, being handed to one of these keen smart young men. He grasped the ash handle and made some amateurish chopping action with the blade. It amused us - he would learn. He was only young and now he had one of us to look after him – to stop him sliding down a roof to his death, to open locks that barred his way, to quick release the pressure in a snaking hose dangerously out of control, oh, so many things our brother would show him. He put the axe in his belt pouch and the cupboard door was closed. We were never to see either of them again.

It seemed forever that we stayed in that small wooden prison. When all was quiet outside and the store men home to bed, we would share our stories .... of action, of noble strength and relentless courage; like our comrades, we were prepared to do all that was required and to make sacrifice when duty beckoned. We often wondered why, when we had served so well, and given so much, what we had done to deserve a fate such as this. Strange, but one morning, about lunchtime, we overheard the store men discussing the state of an axe that had been returned much the worse for wear, chipped blade, scorched handle. Finally, we heard, ...'If only they could talk, what stories they could tell us, ... ah, well, ... I'm afraid it's in the bin with you,' and so saying, the store man dropped our valiant brother into the rubbish.... Too bad the cry for mercy fell on deaf ears.

If only they knew of the stories that were being told, just a few feet away.

I well remember telling my brothers, one cold night, about the last shout I went on with my old comrade ...

It was a deadly dark and bitterly cold November night, a winter wind pattered sleet on the dormitory windows, it was the last of our twenty-four-hour duty and tomorrow would be a rest day. Then, in the small hours of the morning, the big six-inch electric bells burst fearsomely into life. Men, driven by duty, habit and a shock of adrenalin leapt up from their beds, blankets cast aside and eyes wide staring open as they rushed for the rest of their firefighting uniform.

They could smell the smoke filling the air as they prepared themselves to turn out, the driver doggedly hand cranking the petrol engine into life. Two more men pulled the thick ropes that unfolded the great red wooden doors of the appliance room and they looked in to the winter street to see, by the light of the engine's lamps, a mixture of driving sleet and billowing thick, yellowed smoke.

They knew, tonight of all nights, this was a working job they had on their hands.

It wasn't far to go, just down the road at one of the old wharf buildings that backed on to the river.

It was a hotch potch of a building, part stone, part brick, that had been added to many times over the years, making a labyrinth of secret places the demon fire could sneak undetected to trap and cut off the unwary. It was a building of three floors and part basement, about one hundred yards deep and about thirty yards wide. It was used mainly for storage of mixed goods, almost anything could be there, wool, timber, grain, jute, anything; the fire seemed to be located on the second floor and was 'showing a light', flames being visible through breaking windows. The Sub Officer had himself and six men; he sent two of them quickly away to locate and set into a hydrant, the pump man stood by the controls. The Sub Officer pointed and shouted his orders, 'take a line of hose around to the windward side and play the jet through any windows on the second floor .... Break them if you need' .... and two more men were gone, struggling with their heavy canvas hose into the dark. Now they were three, 'Right,' he said, trying to sound confident but deep down knowing this to be a daunting task, they would need the Angels with them tonight, 'Come with me; we'll have a quick look inside. Bring a couple of lamps; let's go.'

So close we were to the fire, and so far, we were, from help, it would be twenty minutes at least before another crew might arrive, we were on our own.

The main door was padlocked against us, it was a job for me and I didn't hesitate, with my brave but aging comrade ... a tough steel point through the hasp and a wrench of the ash handle and the lock was in two. Just as we took our first wary footsteps through the doorway, one of the men from the hydrant reported in, out of breath, gasping, 'Line in from hydrant, Sub, but jet's hardly reaching second floor!'

The town only had a two-inch diameter water main and the pressure was never much good at the best of times. There were no ponds and any wells in the vicinity would not last a minute.

The Sub seemed to stare into the air as if looking for an answer, then, realising that something must be done quickly or the fire might spread to other buildings, for sparks and glowing embers were already being carried in the wind, he made his choice, (as we too must make our choice in time), he shouted loud, above the roar of the fire now competing with the roar of the engine running nearby, 'Right! Get the pump moved to a corner in case the building comes down, find anyone in the street that can help and set into open water, get a second jet to work.' As the man turned to leave, the Sub Officer shouted after him, 'and take him with you, get going!' This left just the Sub Officer and us two. I think he kept my comrade with him for a couple of reasons, to save him from all that arduous, heavy work setting in to open water with that awful cumbersome rubber and wire suction hose, and secondly because of all the years of experience and knowledge that could prove invaluable inside this growing inferno.

'Come on,' shouted the Sub, 'let's find the stairs.'

It wasn't long before we found them, they were made of stone, not good this, stone stairs had been known to collapse without warning; give us timber stairs any day, you knew where you were with them. The noise increased as we made our way ever upwards, so great was it that we didn't hear the call from below. 'No water!' The tide was out, too much mud ....

They fell back to setting into the hydrant, exhausted and covered in cold mud from their exertions to reach the water's edge. They had, however, improved their water supply by shipping another standpipe into a water main a street away.

The crackling jet was now beginning to play through an open window, quickly turning to steam and occasionally hitting a glowing cast iron pillar, one of many that supported the floor above.

Sharp and very hot slates were now cracking and sliding off the roof to the ground below, tiny burnt holes sprung leaks in the canvas hose, the crew with the jet sheltered as best they could. They didn't know what else to do; they could only follow the last order. They waited amongst the falling debris for assistance to arrive or their Sub Officer to return.

'What a God forsaken mess,' cursed the Sub officer, as we surveyed the stacked goods of the first floor. Timbers above creaked and the sound of falling slates and spalling stonework filled our ears, 'If only we could salvage some of this ….. but… just the two of us ……..' His voice trailed off, then, 'what the hell was that?' The Sub stared at us disbelievingly. We had heard it too. It was a scream, almost inhuman in nature. 'For God's sake,' the Sub gasped, 'there's someone up there; what the hell are they doing here?'

'Night watchman, that'll be my guess Sub,' said my comrade in a calm but urgent manner, 'it'll be old Fred, he's got a gammy leg …. that's why they gave him this job. …….. I'm pretty sure I can find him Sub.'

'Go for it then, take care, you damn well come back safe; I'll check on what's happening outside and get help in to you as soon as it's possible,' with that said, the Sub Officer's big, dirty hand patted him admiringly on the shoulder and in an instant he had melted away down the dark stairs to the ground floor.

I had a moment to reflect on this … what did my comrade mean, **'I'm** pretty sure **I** can find him', what happened to the '**we**', after all we wouldn't have even got this far without my help. Then I realised I'd fallen into the old ego trap, I'd forgotten that what endeared us most to the Brigade was adherence to our motto, *'Service needs no praise,'* it brought us the greatest of respect and status. We asked for nothing but to be allowed to serve, we were almost invincible.

We found the next stairs, now of timber, and had to brave a small fire on our way upwards.

I tell you, I remember thinking, 'I hope he knows what he's doing!'

Frantically, and beginning to choke in that killing air, we searched for old Fred; we found an open window and looked out and down, there in a crumpled heap on the cobbles below, lay the reason for the scream, it was indeed old Fred. Just out from the window to the right was an old cast iron rainwater down-pipe, when young and fit it is easily possible to climb down such as this, if you know how.

Perhaps Fred had considered this his only way out; it was a young man's game that, even for us it looked decidedly dangerous, and we'd done it before. We turned to leave but that demon fire had sprung its trap and spawned destruction and chaos behind us; now it was we that must find another way out!

Water sprayed in through a broken window on the far side; with plaster off the walls in places, timbers creaking and bits of broken slate peppering the floor we made our way across, at least there some fresh air came in. My dear comrade gulped in some clean air, then called out to the men below. At first, they could not hear him but then they did, almost everything was dropped as they rushed to retrieve the wooden ladder ... we could hear the orders snapping out apace, we knew they would be here soon .... 'Head away ... extend.... well ... lower.... under run .... heel to building ...' A panting, red and whiskered face suddenly appeared at the window. .... 'Bloody bars!' ..... 'Bloody barred windows!' .... 'Give us yer axe 'ere and I'll try and break one free!' I was quickly passed out through the broken glass into the slippery new hands still numb from the soaking cold of holding hose and branch.

I fell; clonk, clonk, clonk as I hit the rounds of the ladder on the way down, accompanied by an anxious cry of 'stand from under!' I heard the heavy fire boots thumping down the ladder ... 'pawls, step out!' screamed the now shocked and solitary fireman footing the ladder, then I was passed from hand to hand and we returned to the head of the ladder, at first he shouted out to my brave comrade that all would be well, that we were back and he wasn't alone anymore. Using my chisel shaped spike our whiskered rescuer hacked at the stonework that held the bar in place. There was no voice from inside, there was no sign from inside .... I wondered if he had gone back to try the drainpipe ..... all we could see from outside was the deep red glow of a big fire in a slow rolling sea of choking dark smoke, then it happened .... Whether it was the roof that gave in or the hot gases had ignited – suddenly all hell broke loose and searing hot gas and flames appeared at every window with a loud but dull 'crump'. The fireman on the ladder was forced to duck down and away from the window to save himself. He climbed quickly down, shouting, 'get some water in through that window – quick – for God's sake ......'

The Sub Officer turned up, extra crews had arrived, water supplies had been improved and progress was being made. My comrade? I don't know, I heard others talking .... 'he must have found another way out' ....and another say, 'yeah, if anyone could, he could. I wouldn't be surprised to see him come out that front door any minute.'

I didn't hear or see any more as the initial crew were relieved and sent back to station, and I with them. They made a pot of tea, opened the door of the boiler and stared silently, with both hands clutched around hot mugs, drying their wet clothes, at a fire that was now not their enemy but their friend. I remember thinking, as we warmed up safe in our station, 'I pray he's alright.'

Dawn was beginning to break, and a new day commence.

Well you know the rest, I can't imagine anything bad happened to my comrade, if it had, I should have been with him, much guilt remains in my heart that I didn't stay with him, if only I hadn't slipped... but I just can't think that, it's too much to bear.

I've been many places since first being forged in fire and I can still do today what I could do one hundred years ago given the chance. I spent many wasted years lost and alone in various cupboards, but for the last ten I've been an ornament on a shelf in a retired fireman's home – I don't think his wife likes me .... hang on ... here she comes with that damned duster and polish .... must stop now got to go ... thanks for listening to me, not many give me the chance you know .... if only they would .... that's all we ever needed .... just a chance ......that's all... not much to ask.

'It is not because things are difficult that
we do not dare.
It is because we do not dare that
they are difficult.'

The Walker's Rest.

(The brief tale of a stranger's life altering discovery while out on the moors)

Dave Baker, ever the friendly, dedicated and conscientious man, was now embarked on a life-changing adventure of great significance. He'd only just emerged from a reluctant and unhappy divorce and at age forty-three had also been made redundant from his long-term employment.

Now, with nothing and no one to hold him back and with just enough money in his pocket for a simple life, he decided to pack a rucksack and see some of the world, well, the world of nature anyway. To this end on one fine and sunny September day he found himself walking the high moors. Not even sure of the day of the week, Dave surmised it might actually be a Saturday, but truth to tell, along with most of his belongings, track of time had gone significantly astray. He'd been walking remote parts of the moors for a few days by now and his down-to-earth clothes were somewhat in need of a good wash, as indeed was he. A respectable cooked dinner wouldn't go amiss either under the circumstances.

As the warmth of the day began to diminish and the omen of dusk foretell its reality, he started to walk more purposefully down a long slope into what appeared to be a lifeless but never the less curiously alluring valley. It wasn't long before rough heather under his boots turned to wilting autumn bracken. As the autumnal sun eased its tired way towards the horizon, Dave felt his boots undesirably squelch into Sphagnum moss, while all about him clumps of grass like reeds decorated the shallow boggy ground. Approximately ten minutes later, Dave carefully scrambled steeply down through a small deciduous wood of lichen speckled trees. At the wood's lower edge, he had the rarest stroke of good luck. . . it was a metalled road; not one worth writing home about you understand, if indeed you still had one. None the less it was a narrow metalled road and it beckoned and enticed him with the promise of civilisation. 'Choices, choices,' he thought, 'Please God let me pick the right one for a change.' Dave flipped a two-pound coin he'd found in his pocket, heads for left, tails for right. Heads it was but Dave glibly rejected the result, for it seemed a far more inviting and easier proposition to go slightly downhill to the right.

'Silly coin,' thought Dave, ignoring its solemn counsel, and popping it back in his pocket, 'what can a mere coin possibly know?'

And was he right!

For, indeed, only just around the next bend, set back off the road among some trees and backed by an old quarry wall, was a Pub, '*The . . .,* ' well Dave couldn't make out the Pub's name as the landlord obviously wasn't over keen on either decorating or gardening. The faded sign was ardently embraced by Old English Ivy. 'Could be *'The Highwayman'* with a bloke on horseback or in a Gibbet,' mused Dave with a big smile, 'or better still, *'The Walker's Rest'* with a picture of a big dinner.' He chuckled happily.

'It must be a popular place', he beamed to himself, as he eyed the display of posh 4x4 vehicles parked outside in the roadway.

The enticing aroma of fresh cooked food filled Dave's hungry nostrils as he approached the Pub door; a low, ledged and braced door so typical of the old cob and stone cottages of the moors, he stamped his boots a couple of times to knock off any unwelcome debris, then squeezed the latch and opened the door. As Dave stepped inside with head lowered, the pub went quiet, it wasn't too well lit inside so he was trying to accustom his eyes when he nearly jumped out of his skin; A loud and burly voice said, 'Mind yer 'ead of they beams laddie, you can get a good whack off they if y'ain't careful.' Dave turned sharply to see a big solid looking man in dark, scruffy but clean clothing standing just behind the door he'd come through. 'Strewth, you gave me a fright,' stuttered Dave, thinking that this bloke was one sort he'd rather not meet on a dark and lonely night; great big bloke he was, had the build of a blacksmith or woodcutter. . . perhaps he was.

'I've been walking the moors a while and I'm hungry, possibly looking to find a room for the night too,' Dave explained. The murmurs of conversation in the pub continued as before, as if he'd not only been accepted but was in fact a most welcomed guest.

'You've come to the right place for food,' said a pretty young maid standing behind the bar, 'as you can see, we're very popular around these parts for our fine specialty food, you'll not find its like again on these moors. Now sir, what would sir like to drink? You'll find the menu is on the

chalk board down by the inglenook. . . mind your head on the beams, you being such the fine tall fellow that you are.'
Dave, being a light and casual drinker, surprised himself by ordering a pint of cider, *'local stuff'* it said in chalk on the pump label; why not, he'd give it a go. As he walked to the chalked menu board and minding his lowered head as he went, he had a chance to see what others were eating.
'Good job I'm not a vegetarian,' Dave thought, as he surveyed the meat pies, stews and steaks all in vast portions. Some of the ruddy faced diners nodded to him and then to each other as though it was a ritual of some secret society. 'God, these moors people are a bloody weird lot,' Dave thought, 'My God they are odd, still the menu looks good.' In fact, the menu didn't have anything written down that he hadn't already seen as he made his way among the smiling patrons at their tables. 'No wonder they are smiling', Dave thought, 'I haven't seen such low prices for ten years. Are they poachers? Rustlers? Who cares eh, let's eat?'
Dave returned to the bar and was gifted another smile from the girl behind the counter, 'I'll have the stew please,' he smiled back, 'and I'll have another cider if I may. . . do you have a room for the night?'
'A good choice, the stew, sir, I'll get Chef to do you a big portion. Sit ee over there by the window sir and I'll send your drink over. I'll check on room availability sir, it won't take long,' she smiled an adorable smile again. It was a long time since Dave had seen a smile like that, in fact any smile at all come to think of it. With his first cider nearly downed, yet another young lady carefully carried over his second brimful pint.
After having walked the moors with only his self to speak with, Dave was craving a little conversation and, fired with the effects of wild unadulterated local cider, he asked, 'Have you worked here long?' Dave thought, 'What a dopey

question,' but the girl was quite amenable to answer, 'No sir, I ain't been 'ere more than a week or p'raps two. I lives with me Ma in the village, if you can call it that, about a mile that way,' she pointed in the direction that the coin had earlier advised him to take. 'You walking with a group sir, you know, like them rambler people sir. . . we don't often see them come round 'ere overmuch?'

Before he could answer, the young lady, of dubious social grace or intellect, was promptly called away.

'Betty, you're wanted in the kitchen. . . at once, please.'

Dave would only see her once again that day, then no more. The pretty one from behind the bar, and now the sole subject of Dave's fickle and slightly inebriated affections, brought over his dinner, a huge portion of meat stew with mashed potato, 'There you are sir, mind the plate, it be hot. Enjoy your meal sir, and if you don't mind, we'll sort you out a room when the pub is a bit quieter. Okay my dear?' Dave nodded enthusiastically while salivating over a piece of succulent and tender meat he'd popped into his mouth. This was wonderful, just what he needed, good company, superb food, a pretty young lady who'd just elevated him from 'sir' to 'dear' and the promise of a bath and a bed for the night. At last he'd found a temporary heaven on earth.

By the time he'd finished his dinner and his fifth cider, *(yokel strength, complete with the obligatory dead rat and a horseshoe no doubt),* most if not all the customers had left. He noticed they all did that eccentric but seemingly knowing nod, to each other, to the girl behind the bar and to the pub exit's rugged sentinel, who replied somewhat undertaker like, unsmiling and with his own sombre nod of the head.

'My God they're a weird lot out here, talk about Wicker men and hill billies, they've got nothing on this lot,' mumbled Dave silently to whoever else was in his own head and still sober enough to listen.'

The growingly adorable, pretty one approached Dave with a smile, ‘Here you are luvvy, here's a coffee and nice chocolate biscuit for you; it’s on the house. Oh, and here's a registration slip for you to fill in for the room. . . It'll be just the one night won’t it?’

Dave smiled back a soppy smile as he was now at odds with his face muscles, having surrendered complete control of them to that firewater cider of the moors.

‘Yes, please you dear young thing you, by the way, I can't seem to get a mobile phone signal here, do you have a telephone I can use?’ Dave had a foolish plan to phone his ex-wife and tell her how well he was doing and how he'd met new friends that cared for him . . .

‘Nay, sir, you'll not get any mobile phone signal here, not in the whole valley you won't, we can't even get a TV signal you know. As for the pub phone sir, you'd be most welcome to use it for free sir. . . but the line is down and we must wait for someone to go into town and report it for us. Sorry about that, but you won't be lacking for anything after a stay here sir, you can be sure of that.’ The pretty one smiled her smile, gave a little curtsey then turned with a swish to return to the bar, from whence she took a keen interest in Dave's presence.

Dave looked at the registration form, lifting it towards the wall light to read each question before placing it on the table to write his answer. ‘Strewth, bureaucracy gone berserk even out here in the Styx,’ Dave mumbled under his breath, ‘soon they'll want next of kin too. . . . 'Blimey', they do too!’ Dave thought of putting his ex-wife down, *(blissfully unaware of the Freudian slip)*, as she was the closest he'd got left in life; he thought again and simply wrote, 'Not Applicable. That'll do them, it's only a room for the night, not as if I'm signing away my life,’ he snorted a little drunken laugh.

A combination of moor weary legs and the local brew contrived to make standing more of a struggle than he'd

thought it would be. Success in standing drew a little smile of achievement to Dave's face and he wandered slowly across to the bar with his registration form in hand.
'There you are my dear, shall I pay up front, and will there be a breakfast for me in the morning?' Dave inquired. Not waiting for an answer, Dave continued, 'Lovely stew that, tasty meat in it, where does the pub get its supplies, local farmer?'
The pretty one was studying the registration form intently and only half heard his questions. . . 'No need to pay until morning sir, breakfast is full English with local sausages, from seven thirty onwards here in the bar. . . oh, the meat supply sir is one of our Chef's greatest secrets along with his preparation methods . . . but between you and me I reckons there's a lot of cider goes along with it.'
'Betty will show you to your room sir, Betty! Show the gentleman to his room please,' have a lovely stay sir, sleep well.' She smiled her lovely smile again.
Betty, roughly prodding his arm, disturbed his day dream, 'This way sir. . .'
Ducking to miss even more beams and low doorways Dave followed Betty along poorly lit corridors adorned by dusty hunting scene paintings and the occasional chest of drawers or dresser. As they reached some rickety old stairs, lit only by a lamp in a small curtainless window at the end of the hallway, Betty stopped, she opened a dark cupboard under the stairs and said, 'You can leave your walking gear in here sir if you like, it's what most other folk do.'
Dave peered into the shadows to see heaps of walking gear, boots, sticks, rucksacks. . . 'There's a lot of stuff in here Betty, whose is it?' Dave asked.
'Oh, it's just things that mostly them walkers must have forgot to take when they're leaving Sir, your gear will be quite safe in there, but if you'm be afeared sir you can take it

to your room, it's just that this is where the others seem to have left their stuff, that's all.'

Dave, any trust he'd had in the past having all but been beaten out of him, chose to keep his gear, his life's possessions in fact, with him. Anyways, he'd secretly contrived a plan to wash some of it when he had his bath.

He had a chance, the chance to set off tomorrow with a clean slate as well as a clean T shirt, a chance for a proper new beginning.

Life encouragingly beckoned him with a smile at last.

The room was simple and comfortable enough, yet seemed furnished with things likely to have been there since the building was first occupied. It was one of three attic rooms at the back of the pub; Dave could barely see the grey quarry rock face through the small grubby rooftop window; he wiped a little grime off the glass with his sleeve; thinking out loud he mumbled he could just make out a Raven's nest, heaped with sticks on a high protected ledge. Dave wondered if the birds might roost there and, in the morning, he could observe them much closer than those he'd seen quartering the open moor, where intelligence and years of experience had made them such a wary and elusive creature.

As Betty began to close the door and bid Dave goodnight she said, 'Great big fat birds they Ravens sir, they're always hanging about around the pub. . . give me the creeps they do. You'll be seeing them again sir, you needn't have no fear of that. . . well, I'll bid 'ee goodnight sir,' and the door closed behind her with the soft click of a time worn Yale lock.

At least the pub had been modernised; although about thirty years before! However, it did have a proper bathroom and enjoying a good long soak with some of his clothes for company did him the world of good. In fact, Dave drifted off quite peacefully in the warm bath, only to be woken by imagined footsteps creaking their way along the landing floorboards outside his room. Though it initially startled him he was too tired to be bothered and was in any event still under the delusional influence of the mind-numbing local brew he'd supped so rashly. He settled into the old sprung bed, pulled the too short blankets up to his chest and wondered what, if anything, the morrow might bring about. Comforted by the good food and drink, the hot bath and the fatigue of worthy effort, Dave soon fell into a deep sleep. Normally he would wake frequently and mull over the many thought provoking and oft times disturbing dreams that broke into his mind like the unwanted robbers of peace they were . . . but not this night, this night was for the sleep of the dead. . . un-waking and unknown.

The sound of a nearby Raven's call, *karronk, karronk,* brought Dave slowly out of a disorienting slumber and an almost amusing struggle to remember where he was. Slowly it all came back to him and then he dressed quickly in a clean T shirt that was now only slightly damp after a night on the bathroom towel rail. 'It'll soon dry on my back,' he thought as he tried to find his way back to the bar for breakfast. As Dave passed by the under-stairs cupboard he briefly shivered as if a chill had suddenly engulfed him, he put it down to his own silliness of wearing damp clothes to dry them off. 'Dopey burke,' he privately admonished himself, 'When will you ever learn?'

The bar was as though he'd never left it, everything in its place, even the pretty one was there with a smile for him. 'Morning to you sir, hope you slept well. Would you like tea or coffee with your breakfast? Juice and cereals are over there by your usual table,' she said with summer in her voice.

'My usual table eh?' Dave thought, 'It's a long time since I felt I was at home and welcome. . . lovely, this is the life for sure, I wonder why I didn't do this earlier.' Dave selected a *'hair of the dog'* apple juice and sat by his window, gazing out on a bright new day, the sun already gently warming a strip of autumn road outside.

'I might go left this time old chap,' he said to another, somewhere deep inside himself.

'Yes, why not, let's see Betty's village that she spoke of,' came an amenable reply.

When the breakfast arrived, Dave had serious doubts about being able to finish it.

'Mind the plate, it be very hot sir,' said the pretty one, 'we're not short on meat here and I asked the Chef to pop some extra of the special sausages on for you. Chef's compliments and he's given you four of the little beauties, now that'll set you up fine for the day sir.'

Dave had other thoughts, well, more than one actually, four substantial sausages along with all the other breakfast items wouldn't set him up, it would probably set him back, and his other thought was how much he would miss that pretty smile. 'You can always come back old chap, you can always come back, there's nothing to stop you now; we are free at last. . . ,' again he was speaking silently to the converted, the inner self that he was only now beginning to rediscover.

Breakfast finally done and all washed, gear packed and bill paid in cash according to the pub's preferred and only method, Dave turned grudgingly towards the pub door and the beckoning outside world; he'd found a place that fulfilled his long search for happiness and he was reluctant to let it go.

'Damn it all to blazes,' Dave cursed to a shocked himself as he suddenly became aware of the big silent fellow standing by the door again, then loudly to the big fellow Dave joked, 'Do you stand there all night? Strewth, you make me jump; if I was older, I'd be dead with a heart attack by now.' Dave

smiled and found himself involuntarily returning one of those weird nods that the pub seemed to like so much.
The big fellow opened the door, 'Mind yer 'ead sir as ee goes, mind yer 'ead, them beams can give ee a good whack sir, you won't ever know what's 'it ee.'
Rucksack in hand, Dave Baker aged forty-three, dreamily walked to the doorway, only hesitating to stoop and lower his head. . . the walker in him was about to begin a breathtaking new journey. . .

'You are the mapmaker of your own life.'

**

A rocky road to nowhere.

Fiona Fiddlesticks was retired. Not that she had contributed much during her fruitless employment but had graciously retired with a suitable civil service pension to a quaint cottage in Devon. As far away from the bustling, ignorant and rude ways of the big city folk as she could manage.

However, things were deteriorating fast, all manner of undesirable riff raff seemed to be moving into the neighbourhood. With crisp and sweet wrappers left by young children and cider cans and big mac wrappers by the older ones, their parents obviously having learned to drive while speeding from drugs gangs or the police . . . both meaning the same to some of them.

Oh, how Fiona longed for the good old days when small children carried shopping home for little old dears and men gave up their seats on buses to ladies ... now they mostly rested their feet on them.

As she was driving leisurely home from her newly renovated beach hut at Comfycombe, she swerved sharply to avoid a surprise rock in the road. Fiona was fuming, it could so easily have damaged her new Jaguar. In the old days someone would have stopped, picked it up and thrown it off the highway. Not any more they didn't. She could not wait to arrive home and phone her only friend and confidante, Lizzy Listner, she clicked the button on her mobile. 'Beep, beep, beep. Hello, you are through to the voicemail of Lizzy the good Samaritan, please leave your name and a message and she'll get back to you.'

'Damn woman, never there when you need her,' cursed Fiona.

It wasn't far to her home, just a couple of minutes, so would phone from the house. Safer that way. Lucky for Lizzy, she was in this time. 'Having a bath Fiona ... that's where I was and by the time I had reached the phone, you'd rung off. Pity really as I had all the candles, herb essence and music going too. What is it you want?'

Fiona threw herself wholeheartedly into a raving mercurial tantrum and ranted mercilessly about the rock in the road and how nobody had the sense to move it.

After listening for about thirty minutes, Lizzy managed to get a word in, 'Well Fiona dear, you are the kind and thoughtful one in this matter, why not set an example and walk back to the rock and throw it off the road? You'll feel better for it, I'm sure.'

Fiona conceded that she was indeed truly the only decent person around willing to do something for others out of the goodness of her heart and stomped off along the road before darkness fell. She soon located the rock, its presence marked by dozens of swerving cars, as soon as possible she retrieved it and threw it on to the grass verge. 'There, a good deed done, pity no one else had the idea and good sense to do it, pah.' and stomped back to her house for a gin and tonic nightcap.

The next day as she drove to her beach hut, Fiona was killed in a freak accident.

The police investigation, later confirmed by the coroner, found that in a multimillion to one chance, Fiona had been driving by as the grass cutting machine hit a hidden rock in the verge, causing the said rock to fly off and strike Fiona fatally on the temple.

Later, WPC Miss Taken told the Gazette.

'Death was instant. She would never have seen the rock coming, and the tragedy is, she could have done nothing to prevent it.'

Going home again – a young miner's tale.

An autumn darkness arrived unexpectedly early that evening at the little farm cottage. Henry lit the oil lamp before thoughtfully putting the last of their coal on the fire.
'That's the last the world will see of that small lump of coal,' muttered Henry under his breath. The significance of loss and coal was particularly poignant to Henry, whose father had been killed in a terrible mining disaster many years previously. 'Dust explosion they said,' mumbled Henry, reliving the day he heard that sad news, as he watched fleeting sparks of coal dust flash across the dwindling fire.
'What was that dear?' asked Martha, his caring wife of some twenty-five years.
'Nothing Martha, just mumbling about the last of the coal. It'll be early to bed I reckon tonight. There's damp in the air for sure,' replied Henry, hiding his real feelings once more, for it's what men did back then.
Though born into a mining family, Henry was encouraged by his late father, James Richmond, to seek different employment; something cleaner and away from the near slavery to which miners were still subjugated in Victorian times. Brave men all, and their families too who often were underground with them, brave men all with scant recognition offered by the wealthy mine owners. It seemed it was their lot in life, indeed their fate, in service to the Empire.

Henry had taken his father's advice and moved south to become a farm labourer and he would not see his father alive again. Henry found a fine young woman from the Henderson family to marry; she was a domestic servant and they met at a hiring fair in a nearby market town.

To be honest it was still a poor life but at least it was free of the choking grime of the pits.

Henry and Martha had only one child, a boy they called James. James was an adventurous soul. One of his regrets was being too young to enlist for the First World War, by the time he was old enough it was over. He remained disappointed at having lost the chance to escape the abject poverty of life as a farm labourer. James had watched his parents work so hard for so little. There they were now, huddled by a tiny fire and with precious little food in their bellies to keep them warm and well.

Wind-blown rain tapped like an impatient visitor on the small cottage window, as if to make an announcement, but it was James, standing by the mantle's edge, who spoke, 'Father. . . Mother. . . I have something important to tell you . . . I have made up my mind and you will not dissuade me.'

In the 'before their time' tiredness of their faces, he could see that they already knew what he was about to say. They had often wondered when the day would come, for as with death, come it does.

'In the morning I leave for Scotland, in Lanarkshire they are employing miners to dig for coal. I want to be a miner, like my grandfather . . . I feel it in my blood to do so,' he said, trying to make it sound like his only reason for leaving. The truth was, he was a drain on his parents; he was an extra mouth they couldn't afford to feed. He knew that in the past his mother had pretended that she had already eaten earlier so that her son could have a meal. He'd seen his father limp and struggle with labouring that was all but beyond his ability to survive. The farmer wasn't a bad man but like most landowners of the time was exceedingly frugal with the wages of servants. The very reason the middle classes could afford them – they were cheap and easily disposable; many would find a pauper's grave on common ground.

Henry and Martha knew they must accept James' decision and the three of them sat by their last fire together and exchanged words of advice, wisdom and comfort.

Later, as Martha and Henry lay shivering in a cold and un-comforting bed, their minds savaged by the impending loss of their only son, Martha spoke, 'In the morning we must smile and be happy for him though it breaks our hearts, we will give him whatever money we can find and make sure he knows he can come home as many times as he likes . . . and he must write us and let us know how he is . . . we don't want him being a stranger.'

Henry hid a deep sigh and said with as much fortitude as he could muster, 'we will dear, never fear, we will.'

Morning came with lighter rain than the previous night but James had already left. He'd left early so that darkness would hide his tears, tears for the loss of his family and home, for he could watch them suffer no more. It was now his turn to meet the world alone and find his own destiny, whatever it might bring. He promised himself that he would return one day, yes, he would find great wealth and return to repay his ageing parents for all their sacrifice.

A heavy sadness fell like a great stone upon the little cottage. Every night they would dream of James' return. As the years wore on with never hearing a word, their dreams became less frequent, more forlorn but not lost forever, no, not lost forever, surely James will return one day.

James had little except coat, boots and his own dreams to carry away with him that cold, portentous morning, as he sadly but resolutely walked the 13 miles to the Railway station. His ticket was paid for as part of an agreement with the work agents employed by the mine owners, but he had to pay it back from his wages. There were a few other men waiting at the station; as the great black smoking steam locomotive pulled in and past the short platform, names were called and those who answered were ushered forward to one of the goods wagons. There was to be no comfort on this journey. The men, now some ten in number, excitedly introduced themselves. As the journey wore on, the warmth of their meeting was replaced by the cold and hungry reality of their journey. The wooden boards were cold, the only light was through a small dirty window at one end and the only fresh air from a gap in the door to the coupling landing of the wagon.

After a few hours James could stand on his feet no more and wearily slumped down against the unrelenting timber walls of the rumbling wagon. For a while the mesmerising, steady clickety clack of iron wheels on iron track amused him, until his thoughts were interrupted by a playful nudge on his shoulder.

'Hi mate, my name's er John, John Smith, from London. What's yours?' The voice came from a wiry young man sitting close by, about his own age and with a cheeky grin.

'James, James Richmond, my first time away from home,' he replied with a shiver.

'No worries mate, you'll be fine . . . you stick with me, I'll see you're al-right,' reassured John.

With just a couple of short breaks to take on more coal and water, the train took some ten energy sapping hours to reach a small and dirty station next to a coal marshalling yard.

They were soon jolted out of their dog tiredness by the screeching, rumbling noise of the sliding door and a brutally uncaring shout, 'Come on, off ye's get and look sharp about it, I'm soon awa for ma supper. Quick, quick, make haste . . . ,' it was one of the mine foremen come to walk them to their lodgings.

All the lodgings and houses were owned by the mining company, if you couldn't work in the mine then you couldn't live there . . . simple as that. Everything was owned by the mining company, which in turn was owned by Sir Hubert Montague De Vasey, one of those families that had owned land ever since the Normans invaded. He wasn't a man inclined to visit his mine, his estates in Surrey kept him amused enough.

James, along with John and five others were put up in what looked like an old inn from the outside but inside it was very spartan, wooden boards, big rough dining table with benches, and stairs that went up to a number of equally spartan tiny and scantily furnished rooms . . . their new home.

A little old lady, Helen McLeod her name, a pleasant enough soul but with a voice that commanded instant respect, brought them to attention, 'There's clean water in the wash basin in your rooms ... keep it like that, I'm not your mother and I'm not here to act like her. The bedding should be clean. . . keep your dirty boots off it and keep it that way, it won't get changed for a month. Breakfast is at five . . . don't worry, you'll hear the bell, even the devil himself could hear it. The well is out the side of the hostel, toilets at the back of the yard, you can have a hot bath for two pence in the laundry room by the kitchen. Don't burn all the candles, when you need more you have to buy them yourself at the mine shop.'

James wondered if she was ever going to stop giving orders and if at all he was ever going to remember them, it was so much easier back home . . . he almost wished he were back there already, but John timely slapped him on the back and

said, 'come on James, race you for the best room in the house.'
Mrs. McLeod was right about that bell, 'It must be being rung by someone already deaf,' thought James as he eased an aching body out of bed and splashed some cold water on his face. By the time he was downstairs several of the resident miners had already finished their porridge. Mrs. McLeod put a bowl in front of him and threw a great ladle of sticky porridge into it, some of it seemed reluctant to leave the safety of the ladle but with a hefty shake it landed solidly in the bowl. James was starving, he'd had nothing to eat for more than a day, and he was so looking forward to the sweet taste of porridge.
'Yuk', James thought as he screwed up his face, and much out of character angrily demanded, 'Who's put the salt in my porridge?' Even Mrs. McLeod laughed, they all laughed; it was one of the few laughs they ever heard again.
It being their first morning they were to visit the company stores where they would be kitted out with suitable clothing and instructions. They had to pay for this too, nothing was free, only the air they breathed and for many a poor soul there was eventually a terrible price to pay for that too. Unsurprisingly James had no money of his own but the agent, for a small undisclosed commission, had arranged for James to pay his debts directly out of his wages. The miners were one short step from slavery; many would be hard pressed to tell the difference. Their camaraderie, sense of purpose and personal achievement was mostly what sustained them, that and the spirits of ancestors who'd walked the same path.
'Ye'll no be wearing they boots down this mine laddie,' said the burly store man, pointing accusingly at James' boots.
'But they're all I have sir,' James replied apologetically.

'Well, they're no use here laddie, do you want to kill us all? The nails on the soles laddie . . . sparks and gas dinnae mix. I have some old boots o'er here, come and take a look, see if any fit ye.' The store man ushered James over to a shelf upon which several pairs of secondhand boots looked back hopefully at him.

There was a pair there that looked just right, they called to him from the shelf, it was without doubt they that chose James, not he them. They fitted fine, in fact they felt fine, better than James imagined someone else's boots could feel.

'Aye, a fine choice laddie, a grand pair of boots, they belonged to the late 'Sad Tam' you'll find his name written inside, you can change it for your own later. That'll be five shillings on your company bill.' 'Next!' he shouted, 'Come along lads I've not all day.'

James was blessed with an easy day, his mentor, an old miner he only ever knew as Danny and who had something of an Irish accent to him, told him to make the most of it as it would be his first and last easy day at the mine. Danny was to show James the ropes so to speak, where he must go and how he must act, to what work he would be put and the key safety rules he must obey. They both ate that day at the lodging house, which James had noticed often seemed to serve meals for many of the miners even though not actually lodging there.

'Tripe and tatties again James, we get a lot of that .... On special days it might be good beef mince, turnips and tatties, that's a lovely dinner, we look forward to that to be sure,' Danny said, wiping his sleeve across his mouth, 'I see you've a fine pair of boots James, are they yours?

James looked down at them proudly, then across to Danny, 'Yes, they are now, five bob they cost, I think I'll not be seeing any wages for months at this rate. They have 'Sad Rab' written inside, did you know him?'

'To be sure I did, everybody knew Sad Rab. His real name was Robert, he had no other name we knew of, neither I suspect, did he. He was an orphan and joined the mining as a boy; he had no bad habits, no drinking, smoking or other wild pursuits, he was careful with his money, as you can tell by those fine boots you wear today. He always wanted a family, the family he missed so much. He was a good man, and his name belied the kind and warm-hearted soul that he was, we all liked him and wished he could fulfil his dreams . . . as we'd like to do with our own too.' Danny continued, 'I can see in your eyes, you want to know if he found his family. Well it wasn't ever to be; Rab was killed in a roof fall about a year ago . . . that's nothing special by the way, for the mine is full of the souls of accidentally killed miners. Look, you can see the scuff marks down the heels of his, I mean your boots, where they dragged him out. He was a good man, and you couldn't walk in a finer man's shoes. He'd be happy for you, to be sure.'

Life was hectic for James for several months, as his body and mind slowly became attuned to the strenuous labours of mining work. Mostly he was just labouring at the beck and call of the experienced men. He was stuck on all the worse shifts that older men avoided wherever possible. 'It's the way of it I'm afraid, Richmond,' explained the foreman one day, 'it will change eventually, vacancies will appear for one reason or another and new miners will arrive . . . then it'll be their turn but until that day you're stuck with the shifts you're given.' The foreman was sympathetic enough but an authoritatively stern man; he appreciated that James was a likeable and conscientious worker and should do well in the future; James would just have to learn patience.

The seasons and months rushed by with nary a thought from James of going home, he was now far too busy.

He'd soon made good friends with John from London who he'd met on the train. John, though always somehow behind with his debts, couldn't be described as a troublemaker though it frequently sought him out. About a year or more into their service, John persuaded James to go with him and a few others drinking in the nearest town. It didn't suit James really as he was just clearing his debts and had begun to save money for his dream trip home. He thought of his parents and how pleased they'd be with what he had achieved, him standing on his own feet . . . making his own way in life, yes, they'd be proud of him. Not being a drinker by habit it went straight to James' head and it wasn't long before John, his so-called friend, had talked him into buying drinks for all and sundry. The next day while feeling very much the worse for wear, James was a very remorseful man when he felt in his now empty pockets. He knew that he'd not get home again for a good while yet. . . he must save again. He had a faint recollection of some sort of brawl at the pub but he himself had no marks to show he was involved. At breakfast James saw the evidence of trouble all over his friend's face and hands. John dismissed any questions out of hand, ''t'was nothing, I've been in worse, they might well be sorry they picked on me, that's all I'm going to say.'

A few days later when John didn't appear for breakfast or lunchtime, James asked if anyone had seen him about. It was Mrs. McLeod who spoke, 'I think we've seen the last of yon young John, the Polis took him away in the night. Not your local Bobbies either . . . all the way from London they were. They said John wasn't his real name and they'd been looking for him for some time. Just his fate eh, he's obviously been a very naughty boy and now he's been called away to pay for it.'

James felt some sympathy for his taken friend, for no matter what he may have done in the past he'd been a good friend to him, James only knew the good in him . . . cheeky as he was; Must have been something serious, mind. They never heard any more, it was as though John never was and, in any case, soon another would take his place. It was simply the way of the world they inhabited.

Months turned into as many years and still James never made it home. Sometimes he felt he'd been away so long that should he return he would find his parents angry with him. The longer he stayed away the more guilt he felt. It almost became easier to mindfully abandon his parents and never think of going home, he felt ashamed that he had abandoned his family so.

James worked hard and saved as much as he could, but fate transpired against him to spend it on a journey home. Once it was spent on maintaining the rent on his lodgings after an accident damaged his hands and he could not work for a few weeks. Nobody could live in a miner's house without being a working miner, widows and their children weren't immune from eviction either, for no profit was ever to be made by such charity. Nobody said life was fair.

Sad Rab's boots eventually wore out and James bought another pair; they were just ordinary boots not like Rab's. He'd thought most often of his parents and home when he wore those boots, the new boots had no such effect but until his feet had broken them in, they gave him many a blister; so much so he began to wonder which was actually being broken in, those boots or his feet.

Sometimes all James knew was the dark. The dark of night and the dark of the pit blended seamlessly into one, especially in the winter. The pit was relatively warm; sometimes he reckoned it was warmer than his lodgings. The pit was not without its moments of fear for James, though in general he was lucky. However, the accident that damaged his hands brought the occasional nightmare to his

sleep. After an unconnected incident in the same mine, the fear became a reality and he was awake to it, oh so wide awake. They were part of a rescue team to reach miners the other side of a roof fall and the gap they had to squeeze through seemed to James like some evil unrelenting beast that sought to trap him and grip him underground until he could breathe no more and he turned to bones. James remembered how he had anxiously hesitated and another miner had taken the lead and gone first, making it through the dark, twisted gap to shine his safety lamp back through. The first miner was a bigger man than James and so he knew he shouldn't get stuck – but still frightening none the less. James would ever carry a tinge of guilt for his self-presumed cowardice. James had great respect for his mining colleagues, they were a tight knit community and they looked after each other like a strong family. In fact, they seemed to have become his family. When asked when he was going home, he always said perhaps this year, but the years rolled on inexorably. Sometimes just before sleep, 'I must go home, I must go home,' he would say to himself, 'I wonder how you are Mother, are you both well?'
In the morning though, it was back to the routine world of work and survival.

Now was the year he intended to go, 'I'm definitely going home this year, perhaps in the autumn, yes it's home for me this year,' he told his pals one winter breakfast time.
'You see that you do boy, you see you do,' Mrs. McLeod admonished him, 'your mother and father must think you're past dead by now, this year you make sure you go and see them … time to go home boy.'
'That's telling ye laddie, ye'd better make sure ye go this time, James,' said one of the old timers, stoutly slapping

James' back and raising a black dust that slowly settled on table and porridge alike.

'Will you help me write to my mother, Mrs. McLeod? I'll go home to see them this year. . . I'll let them know I'm coming,' asked a newly excited James. It would seem, that having made a firm decision, the weight that had played on his mind was lifted, he felt good about his choice, very good.

'That I will, James. Remind me later and we'll put pen to paper for your mother,' replied Mrs. McLeod, who had taken a liking to this worthy young lad over the many years he'd stayed at her lodgings.

One of new recruits to join the mining village, the unfortunate soul, was to bring with him the inevitable seed of disaster, a terrible disease of the times. It wasn't long before the few contacts he had made went down with a debilitating sickness. Typhus, rumour said it was; however, the mine was kept open and the miners kept working, they had targets to meet and their wages depended upon reaching them. After about a week, James also began to feel unwell himself and took to his bed, to be fair he didn't take to it but one morning he just couldn't find the strength to get out of it. He was to weaken rapidly and within a few days was reduced to a very sorry state indeed. Mrs. McLeod had a word with the visiting doctor; a well-liked fair and honest woman, she was on good terms with all. The doctor examined James and concluded that it was probably typhus he had, chances were, him being a strong young man, he would recover.

'He may well pull through on his own Helen,' he spoke quietly at the doorway, 'I'll leave you some Laudanum for him, it will ease any pains, I'll call by tomorrow. I would keep it quiet a while, for I know the mine owners want any sick miners unable to work to be gone. We'll see how he is tomorrow, must be away now, God bless you for your kind heart Helen.'

'You too Doctor, you too,' she said clasping the small bottle in both hands, 'thank you Doctor, thank you.'

It was early evening before the doctor returned the next day; James was deteriorating and drifting in and out of a delirium, whether from the Laudanum or the fever we'll never know. He could no longer see but could hear occasional voices, sometimes he felt there was a woman's presence, he thought of his mother. In his mind he was going home. In his mind he was at the little cottage door calling for his mother.

'Sorry, Helen, nothing more I can do, the company won't pay for his treatment and want him away. I have persuaded them in their own interest to arrange transport to the isolation hospital at Browick Glen, two stops down the track. They will tend to his needs there. Does he have family?' the Doctor's voice was caring and solemn.

'Oh dear, yes,' jolted by a guilty memory, 'we were supposed to write a letter to his mother one time, I clean forgot, only James knew the address mind, so I'll not be able to write for him. Oh, my goodness and he was going home this year too. . . ,' she said mournfully.

'You've done your best Helen, nothing more you can do now, it's almost over, I'll make arrangements for the morrow . . . you get some rest too,' and with that he turned and left for home.

For James, what was left of life, if you could call it such, was quite weird and wonderful, possibly the drugs the doctor had so generously left or perhaps the delirium caused by the fever. Sometimes he thought he heard voices, sometimes he thought he was flying and could see himself from above; sometimes he fleetingly saw people, not always clearly and afterwards could not recall who they were. If indeed he ever did know them. It was time he went home. In fact, he knew he was going home, he felt the cold outside air on his face and smelled the coal smoke and steam of the locomotive; he heard the mesmerising clickety clack of iron wheels on the familiar iron track. In his own mind, the journey home had begun and how so very much he looked forward to seeing his mother and father. James smiled peacefully as he felt again like he was floating on air, so much easier than that awful journey away from home up to Scotland, he thought, 'so much easier.' At this point in time, he was being stretchered from the station at Browick Glen to the isolation hospital's wagon. 'Never seen one in such a state with a smile on their face before,' uttered the orderly to his companion.

'Nor I', came the reply, 'from the doctor's note we'll be as well to forget the hospital and take him straight to the graveyard.' They both smiled the smiles of men with tough jobs to do but who countered their pain with a humour that few on the outside would ever understand.

James felt the floating sensation again as he was lifted to the wagon, then the weight of blankets to keep him warm.

To James, the steady rocking motion of the wagon, the clip clop of horse's hooves and the crunch of iron rimmed wheels on gravel were just a short and happy carriage ride to the old farm and home.

Meanwhile down south, at the farm labourer's little cob and thatch cottage, darkness was to arrive unexpectedly early that evening. Henry lit the oil lamp and thoughtfully put the last of their coal on the fire. Martha Richmond stared at the rain-dropped darkness of the small windowpane and for one wild moment she imagined she had seen a gaunt unshaven face beckoning her. It made her suddenly think of James, the beloved son she had prayed for every night since he'd gone away, and it made her wonder out loud.

'I just know he'll come home Henry; a mother knows these things you know. . . he will come home, something tells me he'll be home,' she spoke softly with a certain air of prophecy in her voice.

'No use you staring out that window any more Martha, I fear we will not see him again, God bless him. For all we know he could be dead. If he weren't, we'd surely have heard some news from him by now,' said a more stoical Henry, doing his considered level best to comfort his grieving wife.

Henry closed the wooden shutters to the other world beyond the glass and lit the oil lamp. They both sat close by to their dwindling fire, 'Not much coal left dear,' said Henry, as wind-blown rain tapped feverishly like an eager but unheard visitor on their little cottage window and a dispossessed wind howled a timely lament under their door.

Footnote:- *The end; for us as much as it was for them.*

While James' spirit had pleaded to his mother through the rain pattered window, the wagon arrived at the isolation Hospital doors and his body succumbed to the inevitable. As much as his body would never return to the little farm cottage his spirit would never return to his body, for now his spirit had no home.

Even to this day when the dark and windblown rain is at hand he still taps on the window of the little cottage, notwithstanding it has now stood empty for some eighty years or more.

**

'Destiny comes not through chance
but by choice.
You are your own destiny.'

**

PHILOSOPHICAL and SPIRITUAL

Expectation – the park at dawn.

A closed mind is like a closed door, you might never see the other side. . . and it may hide from you the unexpected.

I met this nice lady at the Mind Body and Soul Fayre, Pat was a 'knowing' person to whom I sensed it worth listening. She told me, intuitively, 'Go to the park at dawn, keep an open mind, look up.'

For some reason known only to the inner me, it all made sense. I determined to go the very next day. I set the alarm so as not to miss the sunrise. Several times during the night I would wake and think through the meeting of the dawn, realise it was still too early and return to sleep, wondering if I'd still hear the alarm when the real event was occurring and not the pretend one of daydreams.

The alarm sounded as I was already awake again. As I rose and dressed in warm street clothes, I noticed how bright the sky was already. Had I missed the dawn? What was dawn? Is dawn when the first light appears? Our expectation of what dawn will be like is different to the reality. I considered this as the first lesson and that the second lesson was being prepared, to expect the unexpected, as I scraped ice off of my car windscreen, wondering if this delay would rob me of the planned dawn visit. I arrived before sunrise, but the first signs of sunrise did not come from the expected direction, in fact the exact opposite. Sunshine from below the distant horizon shone on high clouds in the west, the reflected light brightening the sky. It was not what I had expected, though I was keeping my mind open and observing all I could. Instinct took me along a path I had many times viewed but never followed. The Park was much bigger than I expected, surprisingly bigger.

I saw some beautiful views, fast and low flying birds, mist in the trees on the horizon, early morning ducks feeding on the water's edge as the incoming tide made the river deeper, all this and more.

I stopped to take a photograph, and very soon was surrounded by a flock of seagulls, they too had expectations. . . and on this occasion, they were disappointed, no free food from this visitor.

As I returned towards the town I wondered if my ancestors had walked this path themselves and seen the church tower and trees lit by the golden light of sunrise.

I saw a small bird in the water; it was a little Grebe, my first sighting, though having seen many a great crested grebe before. The little Grebe dived gracefully for food and having disappeared along with any ripples, it was as though it never was. I considered this too among my many lessons that morning. We may not see it, it may remain hidden, but we know it was there and indeed is there. Should we point this out to another who did not see the Grebe on the surface, they may doubt that anything was ever there. Therefore, keep an open mind, what you might expect may not come, what you didn't may. . . and not from a place you might suppose, it may be bigger than you ever imagined, it may be hidden from your eyes but not from your knowing.

I must make two visits to this park; I have made one and now must plan the next. . . with still open mind.

Next day . . .

This was my second advised visit to the park at dawn. Nothing in particular happened. . . or did it? These are my thoughts on my visit. You can make all the plans you like, but fate will decide if they are to work out. Be ready, always ready, for opportunities are fleeting. I could have taken a wonderful photo of a bird on a signpost by the river. . . but the bird only waited long enough for me to find the camera and take it out of its case. . then it flew away! Instead of staying in bed and making excuses why it would be hard work to go out, raining, headlight bulb gone, not sure where the boots are etc, just get up and go. . . when you arrive, you'll discover its easy, even in the rain. Those that must live entirely on their wits and own efforts were already there. The Cormorant was there fishing and the ducks gathered around an outfall from the town drains. . . not sure they'd be eating there if they knew what we did. Still, they didn't, and they foraged with joy in their hearts.

Sometimes misfortune can lead us on a path to enlightenment. . . rain caused me to return to my car by a different and more sheltered route. I learned of new and interesting pathways here and saw a dog being put back into an expensive blue tinted windowed Mercedes. I don't suppose the dog saw life any different from the other dogs that walked to the park, only we judge such things.

I wondered at the power of trees that expand cell by cell and push up the pavement with apparent ease. So powerful growing all the while. Then I wondered at what kills them. Do they run out of life force at some time, are they given a limited portion of this elixir? Some use it quickly some take their time, witness the huge buttresses of a London Plane tree in the park. He'll be there for another hundred years or more . . . if we leave him alone that is.

Lastly my gratitude for the money in my pocket that allowed me entry to a hotel to buy a breakfast.

Barnstaple. River Taw

A man called Thomas Carlyle once said, *'he who has sixpence is sovereign. He can call cooks to cook for him and soldiers to guard him . . . all to the tune of sixpence'.* A wise man.

Someone, just like you

High up on a west facing cliff top, the child and the grandfather sat on a bank of soft turf and looked out to sea. There they sat and quietly watched the horizon for ships that travelled the world. They took comfort in the subtle onshore breeze and a pleasant warmth that filled the summer air.

The grandfather spoke gently, 'once upon a time there was a child, just like you. . . 'The child's eyes unknowingly and softly closed. . . a new reality was born. . . the reality of the dream world, coloured and moulded by the sounds only the sleeping can hear.

The grandfather continued, as if reading from a book in his mind, 'The child was afloat in a small but sturdy rowing boat upon a bright and great ocean and being rowed steadily towards one of many mountainous islands that rose up high from a clear blue sea. The rower was Japanese, a warrior, and in Japanese he spoke, though strangely everything was understood. He, the child, was told that each man's body was his own boat on the ocean of life and before we set out, we should ensure we build a good boat. The warrior himself was on his way to his spiritual island where he would spend some hours in harmony with the Kami or spirits, which helped guide him build his own 'boat'.

The wooden hull crunched ashore on a shallow sand and shell beach not too far from dense green and unfamiliar trees at the foot of some cliffs. Beyond which stood the mountains he would later ascend. The warrior beckoned him to step out of the boat. As he felt the warm sand under his feet, he breathed in a deep breath, like a first breath, the life-giving air of this Earth. He turned to help the warrior, but both he and the boat had vanished, and all was quiet but for the gentle lapping of the waves.

What had happened did not seem to bother him... it was as though it was part of his destiny and just one of many strange things that would happen, and each he would take in his stride. Soon his feet left the sand for the soft earth beneath the trees. Among the trees, life bloomed abundantly, and leafy branches teemed with joyous creatures, of birds with rainbow feathers and small mammals curious and not afraid in the presence of his innocence. Time itself had been misted over, he had no idea how long it had been... and nor did he care, yet something was driving him onward, he knew that someone must journey in order to make the footprints... even if only in the mind.

Confronted by the wall of rough grey stone he made his way towards a clearing. Luck was indeed his, for many small paths came into this place though only one left. That single narrow path that seemed to beckon him steeply onwards, appeared to cling to the cliff as though itself afraid to fall. It was a path on which he could not linger, a path from which a fall would end his journey before it had begun, he knew a fear that was absent in the trees below and fear made him strive harder, to climb more quickly, to grip more strongly... while he looked forward and upward it seemed easier. To look down was to realise there was more danger in going back and it ceased to be an option he would ever again consider. One of life's valuable lessons was now permanently his. As he reached the top of the cliff, the ground was feeling good and safer and before him a path of sorts meandered in the direction of the mountains. He stopped only briefly to savour the challenge he had overcome and enjoy the strength he felt in his very bones and sinew. He sensed that the path would be littered with subsequent emotive events of life and set out to meet them. As he topped a small ridge, he had a glimpse of the tallest mountain and if he wasn't mistaken, there was a building near the summit. He felt a strong sense of purpose to go there, for there, may be found the why, of his journey.

Thorn trees, brambles and sharp stones contrived to send him back, but he knew somewhere deep in his heart that this was the challenge that would fulfil his life purpose. If he can do this, he can do anything.

The sun was beginning to set, and he was tired from an all-day climb, yet overjoyed to be so close to the building he'd spied from so far below. Invigorated by his success he hurried on to the door of some ancient temple. As he opened the door, his spirit felt a warm invitation to enter. There was a single chair, a small table with lighted candle and a book. He sat down, relaxed, opened the great book of life, and began to read . .'once upon a time there was a child, just like you.'

**

Success is a word, it's not a way of life.

As a cold grey dawn broke outside the warm doorway of Cayman Executive Finances, Big John, a burly homeless man, gathered his cardboard and meagre belongings. He knew a good thing when he found it and didn't want staff turning up and making a complaint that would cause his relocation. The night had passed with one interesting incident, a false alarm call to the fire brigade from the nearby hotel. John had a good relationship with the hotel staff, who would often find him suitable leftovers from the evening meals. He had shared a friendly chat and a cup of tea with the fire-fighters that night. Big John was a likeable, tee-total man and had previously owned a smallholding business, which gave him an air of respectability. He couldn't cope any more with four walls, it was his freedom that kept him sane. Regardless of the weather, he took life in his stride and with a smile on his face. As he wandered with his few but useful possessions in the direction of the local park, he nodded a friendly hello to the early morning postman and received a cheery wave in reply. They had much in common, both out in rain or shine, while most were still tucked up under their duvets.

An hour or so after John had left 'home' at the prestigious Cayman Executive Finances building, the silence was broken by the arrival of chief executive Clive 'wonder boy' Rothenchild. Roaring into his reserved parking space in his red Ferrari, he was ready to start work and kickass in the world of banking, a euphemism for shifting poor people's money into rich people's offshore bank accounts. Even with the windows closed, his new age 'rock a bully', music almost ruptured the eardrums of a passing stray dog. Clive made his way to the grand entrance, where he had to wait briefly

for the caretaker to unlock. 'Good day sir, lovely morning now,' he welcomed with a smile. Clive stared in fury at the annoying dimwit someone had obviously mistaken as suitably employable, and ignored him. Clive took the lift, only one floor up, and hoped his dim-witted secretary would be in early just as he'd texted, late last evening.
Clive entered his office, turned up the heating and took off his coat, briefly stopping to admire himself in one of several office mirrors. He sat at his desk, turned on his computer and drummed his fingers impatiently while it warmed up. It requested his personal password to continue.
He tapped them in slowly with one clumsy finger,

S H E E P, a £ sign and a smiley face.

His soulless and greedy eyes led his equally soulless and greedy mind to look out of the window and survey the land of peasants, all ready for fleecing. He snarled a few words at his secretary as she hurried in, looking flustered. 'Get your act together deary, I've got important friends visiting today. No mistakes, right? Smarten yourself up too, you look a mess, like you've been up all night.'
She forced a smile, looking after two small children and a sick husband was taking its toll on her and she'd had to pay through the nose to find a last-minute child minder so she could arrive early for work. She desperately needed to keep this job. 'Yes sir, of course sir. It's the mayor and head of chamber of commerce isn't it? I have everything organised for them, just as you asked.'
As she bustled off to prepare for his guests, he sneered under his breath, 'Dopey woman, no idea why I keep her.'

Let us now consider the successes of both these men.

One of them can find his way anywhere, in peace and calm, regardless of the weather, he is given food freely by those who care for him. He has no need of modern technology to get him though the day. He uses his mind creatively and is always willing to help others – he knows the meaning of gratitude and of empathy. He is rich in spirit and at peace with the world despite his various hardships. He lives in tune with the seasons. He is content with his cardboard box in the warm doorway of Cayman Buildings.

The other, has no friends except on social media, where pretence takes the place of honesty. He cannot find his way home without sat nav and is afraid to go out at night. No one makes him a dinner unless he pays for it. He must have holidays abroad in warm countries but no place he considers dirty. He has burglar alarms and cameras at his house. When not bragging on Facebook he watches TV. His success, if that is what you call it, comes from robbing old ladies of their pensions. (Perfectly legal, the small print does explain the risks.) He is despised by all who meet him. He has no soul. But his Ferrari tells the world he is successful.

What is your choice?
You'll hear your inner voice, but will you listen?
Of course not, you know better, don't you?

The welcomed stranger.

The tale of a young man's strange and supernatural adventure near Countisbury, where moor meets the sea.

Sam was a tall, strong young man in his early twenties; staunch defender of a fiercely independent and self-reliant nature, a trait he'd no doubt inherited from his Celtic ancestors.

Despite all his youth, strength and adventuring experience, as he approached from the Churchyard track, he was very happy to see signs of life and the early morning smoke rising from the chimney of the Inn, very happy indeed.

Though he was all night tired and hungry, he had a compelling tale to tell and tell it he must.

The landlord, an affable gentleman with a welcoming smile, observed him through the small casement windows as Sam crossed the road with determined gait and lengthening strides towards the Inn. The landlord slid the bolts and opened the heavy oak Inn door, a large long-haired black dog stood curious at his side.

'I'm sorry sir, we don't open until later…' The landlord's voice trailed off as an inner voice told him something strange was afoot, his dog backed away silently and deeper into the old Inn. 'Never you mind the time though sir, you come on in, come on in and sit yourself by the fire… We have some soup warming...'
Sam interrupted him, 'Can it wait a while? I must tell someone what happened to me last night. . . someone must believe me. . . well to be honest I'm not certain what really happened at all, perhaps it was all a dream but then, how did I get here?'
'Here, sit you down there, sir,' reiterated the landlord, pointing to an upright wooden chair opposite an inglenook fireplace, the source of the smoke that had first welcomed Sam to Countisbury. The landlord carefully placed a fresh dry log and poked the fire thoughtfully; he asked, 'So what's your name then sir, and what brings you to our door so early this winter's morning?'
'I'm Sam, Samuel Richmond, I should have been here last night. . . I've bed and breakfast booked here. . .' Sam forced a smile and a pretend laugh, 'too late for the bed I suppose but I'd love a breakfast. . . but only when I've told you what happened first.'
The landlord nodded, held his hand up as if to say, 'one moment', then called towards the kitchen and his wife, 'guest for breakfast dear, make it a big one.' His wife poked her head through the open doorway by the bar, smiled, nodded in acknowledgement and disappeared again. 'You'll not be disappointed Mr. Richmond,' the landlord assured, 'so how is it you didn't arrive last night then?'
'Yesterday I was visiting friends over at Yenworthy Cottage, they're writers you know, well Robert is, and his wife Beth is an archaeologist with a big university somewhere up north. They'd rented the cottage for six months, she's

researching some old myths and legends about Viking raids along the Devonian coast and Robert is writing a book on the same sort of thing; he's calling it Dragon's Lair or was it Wolf's Lair. . . can't remember exactly, it's all made up stuff that he writes. . . but interesting none the less. I'd had a great day with them, an interesting couple, passionate about their work. . . particularly Beth who couldn't wait to show me some old human bones she had recently unearthed, she obviously didn't consider it disturbing the peace of the dead. . . it was just science to her. I stayed for a relaxed and pleasant lunch then we had a short walk to look at the sea. I was leaving it a bit late to get here by then and they told me I should stay overnight with them and walk here the next day in good light. But I didn't listen, I don't like to let people down and it's not more than a few miles along the coastal tracks. I collected my small overnight bag, nothing special in it and certainly nothing to equip me for the night that was to confront me and my sanity. Then I said my goodbyes to them, nearly for good too as it happened. I can't say I wasn't warned you know, they both said more than once I should be watchful for the sea mist coming in before dark and how dangerous it was along the combe edges. I told 'em straight, 'don't you be worrying about me, I'll be fine, and such a stroll in the park won't be a problem for me.' Well, I set off at a goodly pace along the wooded track towards the sea, all was going well, few ups and downs as you'll know but going okay; the track was fairly clear to follow and I couldn't see it being a problem to arrive here either before or just after dusk.

'I'd walked about an hour or more when it happened; in the blink of an eye the mist fell on me from all sides, as if it had been waiting in hiding just for me, I couldn't see much at all, I lost sight of the track, in fact it was almost as though it vanished in front of my eyes, as if it wasn't there in the first place. I was committed by then; it was as bad or maybe worse to try and go back to Yenworthy. . . I have to confess I was filled with much regret and I'm not ashamed to say, a little fear, for the darkening night was cold and the mist was already eating into my bones. I knew well enough to keep away from the cliff edges and that I had perhaps three steep valleys to cross before I'd be out of the trees or come across the road. I was filled with such a sense of loss that it was as though nothing I knew existed any-more; my only proof of existence was a few feet of un-trod ground around me; No torch had I nor could I read my watch; I listened hard for the sound of the sea or of streams running seaward but the mist smothered all sound, I could hardly hear my own footfalls. I spoke loudly to myself, 'Sam you idiot,' I said, ''You have done for yourself, now damn well get yourself out of this mess, come on get me out of here.' God alone knows who I was talking to but talk I did. I knew I couldn't stay on the ridges but would have to drop down into a valley and up the other side. I thought that if trees could grow on the slopes then I could climb them too, it didn't work out like that, I made many small detours searching for invisible footholds with my blind feet while my cold hands grasped equally blindly for twigs or branches to keep my balance.

I was tiring quickly, and the damp was truly biting bone deep, I began to feel the cold of the already dead. I'd always said I didn't need the help or advice of others, that I could do it all on my own but now a new truth was thrust upon me. Half way up a steep and thicket strewn incline, my feet slipping on muddy slopes and thorns tearing at my clothes as if to hold me there, my legs began to fail and I thought to myself that this was the end of me; if they ever looked for or found my body they couldn't know the horrors that I felt last night. Then, as if by some magic, my feet found themselves on flat ground and I stood on a narrow ledge, my legs shaking a bit with exertion and adrenalin and me thinking I was losing my mind, hallucinating perhaps . . . but it was no illusion. . . there in front of me was a small stone and timber hut. . . and even better still, it was showing a light. With a fresh lease of life in body and in spirit I made my way to the hut and peered in through the wooden bars of a small glassless window; there was nobody in but a fire was burning in a simple earth hearth. I tried the door; it was primitive but opened well enough; I went in and sat on a bench like log near the fire and warmed my hands. . . oh, heaven it was to feel the mist dry out from my clothes and bones. I was sure that whoever lived there would return soon and I mentally prepared a little speech of thanks, apologies and the like that befits having entered someone's home uninvited. Though time seemed almost alien in that place, I glanced at my watch in the firelight; I cursed, it seemed to have stopped and it was a treasured gift from my long-lost father. I put another log on the fire. . . there was a small stack near the bench within easy reach and a larger stack over by the far wall to my left. I sat in relative peace and calm with my speech in mind. . . the door opened and all my plans went out the window as I observed the owner of the hut standing in the doorway. He was shorter than us but stocky with one or two big scars on his bearded face, his hair nearly obscured his piercing eyes with a fringe that looked slightly reddish in the fire light, his clothes were simple and looked like he'd made them for himself from whatever he could find in the woods. He wore a stout leather belt which held an ancient looking axe at his side, his hand was on the axe shaft and his thumb caressed the curved blade. My speech had gone, not just what to say but the ability to say it too, I was gripped with fear. He came into the hut and closed the door, all the while looking in my direction and then he sat opposite me on a similar log bench to the one I was on. Still thumbing the axe blade, he stared, almost as though he knew something that I did not, straight into my eyes. The only sound was my own breath and heartbeat. The fire began to die down and the room become darker, he gestured to me with his head and eyes to put another log on the fire, which I did so very carefully. God, I was tired, I have no idea what time it was or how long I'd been in the hut. I dared not sleep, I had to stay awake. The fire died down yet again and soon all the spare wood was used; I scraped together a few bits of bark and twigs and threw them on the fire, which seemed as pleased as I to see the dancing flames warm the room. . . but soon they too were gone. As the hut cooled again, I went to stand and fetch a log from the other stack by the wall, as I did so, that stocky little man reacted sharply and gripped the axe handle as though to tell me to stay where I was . . . or else. . . or else I might die? Only God knows that answer. Now and then the fatigue of exhaustion closed my unwilling eyes, which would then be startled wide open by my fears, only to see the apparition still before me, his own ever wakeful and watchful eyes staring straight into mine. Try as I might I could not keep my eyes open and must have slipped into a deep and desperate sleep, and now, this is the strangest of all things, when I finally awoke to a chilly but mist free dawn, the strange man had gone, so had the fire, the logs and the hut, all gone. I stood on the flat ledge and looked around in bewilderment. There, where the second log stack had been and which my intimidating and forbidding host had stopped me from reaching, there was nothing but space, a sheer drop to rocks and a stream far below. I would have fallen to my death; had I stepped there in the night for firewood, my broken body would have been meat for the rat, the fox and the raven.

Once the light of day had frightened the mist into the shadows, I could so easily see my way forward and it wasn't so long before the path became clear all the way to the Inn. I left behind me on that flat ledge, thin grass mounds that still tell the world where walls once stood and perhaps, who knows, it was not so long ago. I also left behind me eternal gratitude for a life saved; my own.'
The landlord's wife called through that breakfast was ready and was to be had in the lower dining room. As Sam tucked into a hearty fried breakfast, the landlord suggested, 'Your room is booked till midday, why not have a rest and stay for a pub lunch before moving on.'
The welcomed stranger was a welcomed guest once more. Sam nodded in agreement and glanced at his watch. . . he looked up and smiled. . . it was working again.

Author's note; I've revisited the Inn many a time and never heard the landlord speak again of that night, nor did Sam ever tell his tale to any other living soul. Sam left the Inn shortly after lunch and long before dark. He was not to be heard of again in these parts. Only you and whoever it is that inhabits the unearthly world of the sea mist knows the truth. If I may be so bold, I suggest, if you know what's good for you, you will neither tell what you know, nor venture out when the sea mist threatens the night. Better you stay in and read a book by the inglenook... You don't have to heed my advice.

**

'Experience is one thing you can't get for nothing'
Oscar Wilde

**

Fagus' workshop; the story.

(Note for reader. Fagus was a searcher for the great mystical secrets and at one point morphed into a puppet of a carpenter. However, he retained the essence of life and living).

This is a long story, in fact, the longest of all, and could indeed entertain you for a lifetime, or maybe more than one...........

In the old Beech copse, moss clad stones mapped out the ground of an ancient building. The stones and the tall trees welcomed the group of tired walkers; they who had trod the Western Highlands in search of freedom and the chance to meet their soul on the path. She who was one with trees and animals beat gently the drum, 'bom,' 'bom,' 'bom.' Each found a place of solitude from each other but company with the trees. 'Bom,' 'bom,' 'bom,' slowly, softly the drumbeat reached out to the falling autumn leaves. The taller of the group, and not yet as insightful as others, sat on two flat stones he had heaped to make a comfortable seat. 'Bom,' 'bom,' 'bom,' and the thinking mind was fading, like the sound itself into the distance, and the knowing, feeling inner mind became more alive, and alive to the great moss clad Beech Tree to his right.

As earthly surroundings faded, he became aware that a moss-covered arched door had opened in the tree and the diminutive figure of Fagus beckoned him. Inside it was roomy and well-lit with firefly and glow-worm lanterns, it was warm and dry with an earth floor and a large central walnut table on which Fagus poured two cups of tea. 'A rare thing this,' Fagus said, 'Not much walnut of this age left any more. One of the best things I've ever salvaged from man's above earth destruction. Still, enough said of that. How did you get here?'

The tall traveller eased his bones with a stretch and said, 'I have come far, from beyond the Great Bog Territories, raging torrents, and climbed the great hills where one can fly across the valleys.'
Fagus smiled, 'A brave journey my friend, did you come alone?'
After a sip of tea and a longing look at some ginger cake that Fagus had just placed on the table he replied, 'No, we are five, though not here all together. Our guide is patient and strong like a lioness, and such is her power that no bog or hill could bar her way; it is she that led us to your door. The location of the key, unknowingly hidden inside our very selves, was given to us by her friend, a joyful little woodland fairy we know as Maggie. She teases the secrets from our souls and communes with rocks and trees and they with her.'
Another sip of tea and a good chunk of ginger cake later, he continued, 'Also one of five is a friend and fellow traveller but she is one who has journeyed afar and in other times methinks. While others sleep, she walks the dark as quiet as starlight and guards the resting with her compassion. But enough of us,' said the traveller, 'How have you been keeping, I heard that the old house in Bedford is now empty and what are you doing in this hollow tree?'
'Aha,' said Fagus, chuckling to himself, 'This is my workshop. You remember of course that I was a carpenter in a former life; well, I continue my work in this one. When the old house was sold the puppets were sent to new masters, but I was lucky when the postman failed to notice my parcel fall from his bicycle not far from here and the house to which I was to be confined in slavery, as all puppets are. Didn't you know why trees are hollow? It's because we take the wood and make beautiful things with it. If we're good at our job, we can get to the great trees before man.'

Curious to know how this was possible, the traveller asked, 'Then where do all the shavings go, and where are the beautiful things?' 'Well,' Fagus replied, 'You in the upper world have discovered that atoms consist mostly of vast amounts of empty space, but you didn't know this until you desired and knew how to look, so it is down here, the great void, another dimension, an alternate wavelength, the abyss, Valhalla, call it what you will, for it matters not, only that it is so. It is in this space Earth's great treasures lay.' Again, a broad grin spread across Fagus' face, 'I think it is now safe to tell you, for you have begun to open your heart to the 'knowing' and in any event when you tell others, as you surely will, even if asked not to, they'll never believe you, and that is why we are safe down here, for only those who truly care will ever truly know.'

An excitement coursed through the traveller's body like a ghost was trying to occupy it. 'At last,' he thought, 'I'm going to be told the great secrets of life.'

'Not so fast,' said Fagus reading his mind, 'I can show you the way, but it is only your own effort that will take you on the path, step by step and one foot in front of the other. No one can walk it for you, for then it would only have value for them alone and not for you.'

The traveller mused on these words and thought earlier of the trek to Glomach Falls where mountain water dived unhesitant 350 feet into the valley below, a magnificent and awe-inspiring sight, but for the eyes to see this at all, their feet had to carry them there.

'Now!' Fagus said seriously, 'Come,' and he beckoned to the side of a buttress like inner support of the tree to reveal a set of steps. 'These steps,' confided Fagus 'are the steps to the infinite space below ground where all Earth's treasures are stored.'

'But I can only see one step,' exclaimed the traveller.

'The first step is one of *'fear'* and stops you seeing others,' comforted Fagus, 'Here, take my hand and your fear will be lessened.'

He took the open hand, and it was true, he was not quite so afraid, though he realised that the steps were so narrow that sometimes it would have to be single file, and would the fear return? Indeed, once the fear had subsided, the other steps down were easier to see.

Fagus led the way, carrying a lantern just bright enough to see a few steps at a time. 'Be warned,' cautioned Fagus, 'Concentrate your whole being on one step at a time, do not let your eyes or your mind wander to those that may be in the future, any slip and you may fall into the abyss and for ever be in a dark place. There without the knowledge to find the light that frightens away the demons of fear and despair.

Our traveller took the first step, banging his head on a little wooden sign hanging from ivy string above the narrow doorway. Though the sign was in some ancient script he found he could read the message, 'Without risk you are chained to your past.'

'Mind your head' Fagus warned belatedly, 'Now remember, you must feel the step you are on, not rooted in the past or dreaming of a future that may not come, every part of you should be in the 'now,' and trying to absorb the essence of the one step through the very soles of your feet.' 'Thinking has no place down here, only feeling.' 'Now, let me see, what it is the next one is about ... aha .... of course ... *Faith.* Now Faith is believing in something that you cannot prove but that you accept exists, you may not have seen the proof, but others have, and in the great connective consciousness they will reach out to you and transfer belief by their presence alone. Just like the blackbird that can sing its heart out even while the dawn is still dark. Don't be confused, for later you will find a step for acceptance and one for belief and one for understanding and. . . yes the last step will be .....? ... we will both know what it is when you find it.'

The traveller absorbed *'Faith'* into his being, how could he deny faith otherwise he could not be here. Were not faith and overcoming fear connected? Come to think of it weren't all the steps connected? He hoped so, in more ways than one, for he could not see what held them up.

Fagus, seemingly now losing his endless patience, snapped, 'What have I told you about looking forward and here you are thinking and not feeling and to cap it all using words from other steps like *'hope'* and *'connection.'* There will be a place for anticipation when you're actually on its step.' Fagus continued, 'Just stop your talking for once and listen and feel, let me tell you what it is you need to know.'

'Phew, snappy little so and so,' the traveller thought and then realised that he'd done it again. He took a deep breath and began to try and sense the meaning of the step.

'There are a couple of quick steps here old friend, quite easy to take in,' Fagus kindly assured the traveller, feeling somewhat guilty for his little outburst; Though he did think that at times it could be justified where life and death were in the balance. 'This one is '*Value*' and *'being valued.'* In the great scheme of the Cosmos what is it that we touched in life on which we would put a high price? You must feel this for yourself. .... And what of being valued? Do we need it?' Fagus paused a long pause, 'Well done old friend, you sense it right, if it was done for the right reason, we have no need to experience being valued for it.'

They moved down the steps into an ever-deepening sense of darkness, though the occasional glint of quartz crystal in the earth walls reminded him of the bright stars in an indigo sky. It made the traveller realise you could 'see' remote things without going beyond where you stood.

That brief feeling went as Fagus told him, 'Rest again here on the step of *'accomplishment,'* and for a short while you may reflect on the feelings you have felt. ……….. Pay heed now for the path does not always go so easily, there may be danger ahead. Carefully place the feet on each step without stumble, for that will take your mind and disturb your journey. A bit like stubbing your toe, your mind is in the toe and all feelings relate only to that and leaving little space for other, better, feelings to enter your being. Therefore, walk carefully and with mindfulness or the treasure of the Earth stored in the great under-space of the infinite will never be yours. How often have you come to understand something but cannot recall by which route you came to it? Well, the step is the same, having trod the step it is hard to imagine how you arrived or indeed that you were not always there.

Down, down, and down, step by step, knees tightening with tension, but senses more alive than ever, warmth and tingling in the hands and feet, downwards they went.

'Whoa!' shouts Fagus, with what appeared to be a tiny gloating and knowing smile. 'Watch out for this one, it was put in by mistake, so they say, and is difficult to remove, so they say. Many a time you'll tread this step and without true awareness, not realise you are there.'

'Damn,' thought the traveller, 'That 'Ego' step felt so good, it had me fooled for something substantial like ……' He couldn't think of anything it was exactly like, he was beginning to learn how subtle were the changes in feeling, perhaps dear reader, you can come up with an answer when you tread this step yourself.

On the step of 'questioning' Fagus allowed the traveller to speak again. 'I'll tell when it's okay or not,' Fagus said.

The traveller inquired, 'Will this path lead to the *Great Truth*?'

Fagus laughed a friendly little laugh, 'Why, no, there is no 'one truth', only 'a truth', just as there will never be certainty, you must just do the very best you can in all circumstances, to be the truth and not seek it for it is not out there beyond self to be found.'

Down, down, down, the space underground seemingly now so vast. Fagus, like some people can, picked up on his feeling and said 'We have touched on this before, but we are all mostly space, this was known to the ancients long before scientists discovered what they called the atom and discovered a tiny planet surrounded by comparatively massive space, and little things with no mass at all charging round the edges like crazy. Some feel that travelling the steps allows us into that dimension where space, true nothingness, exists in the forever now. Some people can see images or colours that others cannot, and this is a similar idea, though not at the same level; however, it fits the principle of entry to another dimension and therefore awareness of a different wavelength. Perhaps for a moment they have unknowingly trod some steps, with their relaxed mind crossing into the subconscious. The subconscious of course knows all but keeps the secret until the step is trod, then, if there is mindfulness to access the secret, it is revealed. It's what you humans call inspiration or sometimes, rashly, enlightenment. Of course, there are sadly too many that have embraced the dark pleasures like the Ego we met earlier.

The traveller interjected, forgetting his earlier resolve, and said, 'Perhaps they've not had such a noble, all knowing, angel spirit like you to guide them through their own inadequacies.'

Fagus replied with a chuckle, 'Of course, you are right, I am wonderful.'

He laughed again, they both laughed, the infinite space heard and echoed their laughter, and they were on the step of *'humour'* and it felt good. .... Laughter stopped as suddenly as it started and a feeling of foreboding filled the traveller, for he had sensed what Fagus was about to say about the next step.

'You'll love this one,' Fagus said, with only half a smile left, 'This narrow, rickety one is 'trust.' When you step out on to this one, you'll feel like you might fall, and the abyss below seems to look into you and draw you down. Trust may only be a small step, but a huge one in terms of where it can take you, if you know what I mean. Try not to lean or use your hands, stay upright, it's the best way.'

The traveller did have trust, he trusted Fagus, but he also trusted his instinct too, and that thin wobbly step looked like it should not be trusted. How deceiving appearances can be. He searched his soul for the lesson gained on the step of 'fear' and made his move. How glad he was that he had trusted, for he now felt more secure than ever before in his life. He stretched out his arms wide into the emptiness and with palms facing downwards to meet the uprising energy of the void he felt that he could not fall, for how can one that flies ever fall, he knew what it was to be the eagle.

'Come on,' urged Fagus, 'let's keep moving, so many more to go. Of course, you know that even great Masters are still learning till the day they die, and if the path is too hard for you, you can always turn back; trouble is if you do, you will return to a world where you always get what you always got. It's up to you, and this is where to do it .... *Decision.*'

It was an easy and comfortable step, made so because it was taken with no thought but feeling, ninety-nine per cent correct is our instinct, we just don't listen to it. Everything in the traveller's body told him it was right to continue, for he'd gained so much in so little time compared to the years of struggle and sacrifices which had previously brought him little. 'Next step now,' he thought, and he knew already what it was, he was becoming more sensitive. It was the *'thinking'* step. He whispered to Fagus, so as not to break the rules, and just in case someone or something else was listening, 'Thinking step Fagus, …. thinking destroys feeling … thinking takes a long time but understanding and feeling they come like magic in an instant.'

Fagus knew he now could relax more, for the traveller would soon be able to find his own way, and though he would always remember the guide, he would safely walk his own path into a brighter future.

But not just yet, and he led the traveller down, down, down, through the feeling steps. The step of *'now'*, where he reminded the traveller of earlier words of 'not forward, not back, but the step you are on,' and how most accidents are the result of an out of now experience, like walking into a lamp post for example. (The traveller wondered how Fagus could have known, for he had done this very thing – more than once as it would happen!) Yogis and the like experiment with the 'now' and touch the essence of knowing, often with breath technique.' Fagus had explained, 'breathe out and hold it out, until forced to breathe it in, that space between is the closest you can truly feel to a now moment, for nothing but that moment has any significance, not past, not future, but only now.'

'Now,' said Fagus, 'remember I told you we would come to *'anticipation'* all in good time, well here it is and now you may look forward.'

Pleased to have arrived where he was allowed a look to the future, the traveller anticipated the final step. Would it be enlightenment, or happiness, perhaps just being, or would it be to return to the beginning and know it for the first time?

He found he could anticipate the step but not what it would bring.
Fagus eased his torment and said, ' Don't try to work out what the final step is, you won't know it until you arrive, and in the same way you'll find a disappointment in not being able to share your discovery with others. It will mean nothing to them; you waste your breath, for you cannot walk their steps for them. Your conscious mind can never know when all the steps are trod, just as you cannot know the steps of others, for they too will be different, and our journey may end before the path is run.'
They moved on to the step of *'storytelling,'* oh how the traveller wanted to stay here, desperate to tell of 'The Princess and the China Bell' with its new happy ending, perhaps you'll hear it when you are on this step, but there was no time to linger, just time to know this step existed, many great writers and readers too, are trapped on this step and are happy enough to be there.
'No time for that now,' said Fagus, 'I want you to spend more time with this one, for it reveals much more than it conceals if you know how to see. The traveller stepped forward eagerly but was held back by a firm hand, 'Careful old chap,' warned Fagus, 'We will sit on this step together with our feet firmly on the step below it, the step of *'awakening'* and the step we sit on is the step of *'dreaming.'* Remember well these words, 'wake now or forever stay asleep,' and when you sense the sign to wake make sure you act, for it has great purpose. The sign may be a voice or a vision or sometimes an urgent sounding knock, knock, knock. Make sure you wake!'
The traveller did not need to be told twice about this warning; he had in the past ignored such things until a fearful apparition was sent to stand in his home to make sure he paid attention. He looked straight in Fagus' eyes and said

with deadly conviction, 'Don't worry Fagus, I'll not be staying asleep!'
Trouble is with dreams, is you can't tell what is real or not, nor how long the dreamtime kept your consciousness, you might vision an epic, but it took only seconds of waking time, or perhaps the other way round. The dream world has immense power that often will not transfer to the waking world. In dreams there are questions and answers too of great intellect and intricacy which are beyond the wit of the woken mind that dreamed them. Songs may be sung with beautiful words the like of which are yet to be written, and colours so bright and clear that even the finest stained-glass window cannot surpass. As the sub conscious shuffles the cards of places, people, and deeds, we can have no inkling of the hand to be dealt.
There is no doubting when to wake as you physically feel or hear the signal, the only question is, how important it is to you! No knocking on windows or doors this time, no gentle ghost like shaking of the feet, but a gentle 'bom,' 'bom' , 'bom' in the distance. The traveller was wide awake now and Fagus next to him, just sitting expressionless, being the watcher.
'Well?' asked Fagus, 'what did you see, eyes closed or not in your dream?'
'Was I asleep for long?' inquired the traveller.
Fagus confided, 'It's not important, old friend, it's the message that counts, not how long it took to arrive. The dream may have lasted but a split second and it might take you a day to describe. That should give you a sense of the immense power of the subconscious when it is allowed to operate in the now. So, let's hear your dream and when you have finished you will have arrived at the next new step.'
'Strewth!' exclaimed the traveller, 'where to start? There was so much, so much colour, I could feel the weather and

hear the bird song. I'm sorry if I miss bits out, but I'll do my best.' He continued, 'We had just taken a step, one you warned me of earlier for thinking ahead but said we'd come to eventually, *'connection'*. I stood alone, but not lonely, at an ancient burial site of some 4,000 years, and which was bounded by Beech trees, huge stone mounds marked the spot where an ancient was lain to rest by his fellows in respect and honour. His body and tomb, salted with again the quartz crystals, aligned to the Sun of the Winter Solstice. Each tomb too had a circle of standing stones, one of which I placed a hand either side to see if palm to palm energy could penetrate the rock ...... and it did too. In this special place a feeling came to me that my soul was connected with all other souls, for the spark of life is from a universal source. I felt wonder for those ancients that possessed a knowing, long since lost by modern man, but I could only feel the energy of self and that of the gentle rain splashed wind that blew. It came to me that some of us will ever sense nothing significant at such a place and others will ever feel the presence. This presence may be the pulse of Mother Earth or sometimes a travelling soul on the low road beneath. Souls on the low road would often confide their secrets to the trees, the *connectors* of earth with the heavens, and oft times humans will confide in a tree and oft times too, the tree with them, and so the folk lore lives on that trees have wisdom. One of the great Beeches silently called me to sit at its feet; it was much like the one we are now below. As the thinking mind began to fade and the watching mind gain in presence, I saw an eye with my closed eyes and knew for the first time that the eyes we see are fleeting glimpses of the watcher inside, and sometimes other watchers from other parts of the great universal soul consciousness come as well, for they too must watch. There was something about the number of steps was the same as number of stones on the burial mound, I think, but am not too sure about it now. If only stones could talk, we could find out.'

The traveller seemed to be dreaming again, for he sensed Fagus had gone, he heard a sound like a door closing behind him forever, and the soft 'bom,' 'bom,' 'bom,' came gently on the breeze to his ears, and the dappled shade of the copse met his eyes, and he was no longer sitting on the step of dreams but on the little stone seat he had made earlier.

'Time to head back now,' said the guide, 'not many steps left before we are home once more, and back at our beginning.'

I could tell you more, but I've said too much already, shhhsh… listen …. listen carefully ….. Did you not hear a knocking just then.........................?

Salix Caprea October 2005

**

'Do not seek to follow in the footsteps of the wise, seek what they sought.'

**

A dream of times

My mind is filled with time gone by,
a place I never knew.
And visions, open in my mind,
of then, and me and you.

Of times gone by, we may have known,
a truth within us wakes,
and when we dream, how we were there,
to *there,* our souls it takes.

In harbour thronged, our masted ships,
were readied for the sea.
Those left behind, wrung hands with hope,
alone upon the quay.

As heroes sailed, to far off lands,
many tears were shed,
for noble hearts, they loved so much,
soon, numbered in the dead.

Why should I care, my mind to fill,
with heartfelt loss at sea.
Perhaps it is, that we've come back,
from then, yes, you and me.

The Portal

A tale about a group of spiritualists who take it just one step too far.

It was agreed; they had three months to prepare for a journey of a lifetime.

The seven ladies were part of a spiritualist circle, which met once a month in search of enlightenment and they had an exciting new plan; a plan for the summer solstice like no other. Well, no other that had been practised for several hundred years for sure.

'I have developed a meditation plan which we all must follow to the letter. Each of us must be proficient in connecting with both the path and with each other for it to work.'

They were all on the edge of their seats, as Hazel explained further. 'The old manuscript found in a Dartmoor barn some hundred and twenty years ago and left to me by my dear late aunt has been transcribed by the archivist at Truro records office. Along with the map, we are told all we need to know about opening the portal, the gateway, to the other side. I cannot emphasise how important it is to practice our collective meditation and develop our discipline to the highest order. Now, Jill has something to tell you. Jill, please.'

Jill stood with ease from her seat and spoke of the practicalities. She was a keen hill walker, which suited her for the task of guiding all of them safely across some difficult, and rarely visited territory. '*Breus Entrans*, is the old Cornish name, it's not on ordnance survey but is on the manuscript map. Old wives' tales say it is known as Doom Tor and it boasts a group of minor standing stones, seven in all. Once again there are no modern records of this stone circle, possibly because it is notoriously awkward to reach and archaeologists have plenty more important sites that offer easier access.'

Jill looked around the room, everybody was engrossed; this was going to be the culmination of a magical and life changing journey they had sworn to take. Hazel nodded encouragingly at Jill, and she continued, 'seven of us, seven stones and the seventh hour. . .'a murmur around the room was quieted by a serious frown. . . 'Yes ladies, seven in the morning. We need to be there and ready at the seventh hour. I have arranged B&B for all of us together, about 6 miles from the site. We'll need an early night and a very early start. Here's a list of suggested, better think compulsory, items you'll need to wear and take. The weather should be okay, but we won't risk it. A dry spring will mean the mire in *Breus Golans* should be passable with minimal risk. So please, all pray for no rain, ladies.'

They all worked hard to prepare for the journey, a journey both physical and spiritual. They hired a minibus for the 20th June and met at Hazel's house with all the stuff they needed. The weather was perfect as they set out for the B&B, a delightful and remote farmhouse run by a psychic animal healer and her farmer husband. Extra camp beds had been placed in as many rooms as possible to accommodate the chattering excited group of soul seekers. They all enjoyed an evening meal of carefully chosen foods, some picked from the moors, some from the farm garden and all generously provided by the hosts. They had all agreed to no alcohol, much to some disappointments. Still, they were definitely on a high without a drop of the hard stuff. Except for Maggie, at 35 the youngest of the group, she'd smuggled a bottle of vanilla flavoured gin along with some cheap doughnuts in her rucksack. Maggie was ever the rebel.

'We're up at 5, girls, so no chatting all night. Chamomile tea and then we turn in for a good rest so we can make the most of this rarest of opportunities to view the great portal of eternity.' Hazel looked around the room until she received a nod from each of the group.

There would be no phone signal up on the moor so Mary took advantage of the farm's satellite connection to update her social media – until about two in the morning. Time just flew, it was so absorbing, like going through a time portal itself. She wasn't aware of her body or time as she silently tapped out her important messages into the ether.

Just as bad were Patsy and Jenny, who were sharing a room together. They always had plenty to say and that's what they did most of the night. They weren't tired at all, the excitement of the trip, the food, the farm and its psychic occupant, the plan to see the great spirit gate . . . all these things served to keep them quietly engrossed. While they gossiped, dawn was stealthily creeping closer to the eastern moors.

For all the ladies, whether they'd slept much or not, it still came as a surprise as doors were knocked and a lively voice called, 'Up ladies, time for breakfast. Come on, up and at it, come on, no dilly dallying.' Jill was relishing her position as walk leader; it reminded her of her youth and the army cadets she had joined - just for the fun of it.

Bleary eyed and not looking like they were fully conscious, except for Hazel and the now indomitable Jill, they sat around the farmhouse table in unusual silence, holding their mugs of herbal tea.

Hazel tapped her mug with the spoon and the room went even quieter. 'Solstice time is five am but our appointment with destiny is at seven am. The manuscript explains the delay as being akin to a high tide following the full moon and not arriving simultaneously. We have two-and-a-bit hours to turn up at the stones; Jill tells me that the last part of the trek is across pathless moorland and we must be extremely careful where we put our feet. There is no mobile phone signal out on the moor, so any trouble is going to be all ours to sort out. Still, that's how it was for the ancients and in part, it may raise our own awareness levels to advantage. We will see. Now, Jill has a few words to say.'

They all looked across at Jill. 'We have about four miles of reasonably easy going, old farm tracks and the like, before we take on the open trackless moor. I suggest we keep as quiet as possible, keep the talking to a minimum. Once we reach the pathless section, I would like everyone in single file. Each person places their foot in the exact place of the previous footstep. You will find this way of travelling very meditative in its own right and it is the way of the ancient tribes whereby an unknown number of people only ever left one set of footprints. For us there are added benefits, one, the leader, me, will be finding the best route from experience and two, you'll like this one, any ticks waiting for a feed will be on me, not you!'

For some it brought a smile, from others a look of horror, they hadn't considered ticks, bogs and the potential for death, they'd had a rose-tinted image of a grassy walk in the sunshine like going on a summer picnic. Soon they would be tested. Today they would all be tested.

Shortly after, and suitably attired, they gathered in the farm yard and with lots of smiles and 'see you soon' to the farmer and his wife, they set off with the slowly rising sun at their backs, their long shadows rushing ahead of them keen to reach the stones first.

'Not so sure we'll be seeing them all again, got a funny feeling about this,' said the thoughtful psychic to her husband.

He joked with her, 'you worry too much, you've never been right yet. Come on, we've work to do before they're all back having discovered nothing but blisters and ticks and they'll be desperate for their dinners.'

Jill had been so right about the absorbing and meditative effect of walking in silence in a single line; Each concentrating on the previous footstep, like looking into the future but a future that was safe because your friend had already been there. Even Maggie was able to keep the faith, despite her shorter legs and plumper physique, 'heavy bones,' she always told others, 'just heavy bones.' Hazel stayed at the back, lost in thought for the untested ritual ahead; such was the terrible responsibility that began dawning on her.

The small hill of *Breus Entrans* was set in a shallow, bracken and grass filled valley. However, the prevailing wind had thankfully kept vegetation to a minimum on its summit. The stones were smaller than they had anticipated but there they were - all seven in a perfect circle and a gap or entrance where the eighth would have perfected the pattern. The group maintained their silence and walking in line until they were right next to the stones themselves. The sun was higher now and already warming to their backs. It took Hazel a while to tear herself out of the silence which now firmly gripped her and the others, 'Well done Jill, that was truly awesome, I've never experienced such a feeling before, well done you. Ladies, please take your places on the inside of the circle and in front of a stone. Rucksacks and stuff from your pockets all to be left outside the circle. Start with Jill on the left of the entrance, then Jenny, Patsy and Maggie - in the order we practised at the hall. I shall be on the last stone by the gap. We have ten minutes left before the witching hour.' An expression Hazel was immediately sorry she had used, 'why on earth did I say that?' she scolded herself.

They took their places at the stones, each facing the centre of the circle where they imagined the portal must be. Beyond the centre each had a friend and a stone opposite, all but one, who faced the empty space where the eighth stone presumably once may have been.

The light breeze stopped, lifeless, sound fell silent, only Hazel's soft tones could be heard, before they too would fall into the unknown abyss of space and time.

'Eyes closed and down, hands on centre, imagine finding the path that leads to the underworld, follow the path until you find a gateway, when we all reach that gateway we will feel the connection between us and see and feel the ring of energy we create in this sacred place. Remember, do not step through the portal that appears, just look to see what is on the other side and later we will share what we saw. Let us begin with a gentle chant for seven breaths, then seven silent breaths as we set out on the hallowed path. Let us begin. . . .'

Though some of the ladies were imbued with greater skills, their connectivity after the tribal walk had strengthened their bond enormously and it was not long before they were all in a deep meditative state. Each unthinking mind became the observer of the external, of that not born of thought at all; each not knowing or caring what the other was seeing. As they struggled to complete the circle across the gap of the eighth stone, they saw a shape appear, human in frame yet without definition, reminiscent of a fuzzy grey aura. The figure, or whatever it was, completed the circle just as the seventh hour took its place in the enduring passing of the ages. The sensations were electrifying but none could awaken, so deep had they travelled into the underworld of their own imaginings. It was only afterwards that they would come to understand that each and every one had seen the same thing – in precise detail.

At this point, all normal vision or interpretation of images was lost, the figures and the stones melded into the same indeterminable but present grey shapes. A shape began to cross the circle, across to the eighth place and the waiting grey entity. The two shapes left the circle together and disappeared. That was where the portal to the other side had been, and yet none of the ladies had been able to see through to the other side as planned. As suddenly as the shapes vanished, the spell of the sacred place was broken and the ladies were out of the dream world, back in real time to hear the endings of what to most of them was best described like a fading wail, not dissimilar to the last note of a wolf howling. Then silence, before the breeze blew again off the moors and the sunshine warmed their bodies.

Eyes wide open in the bright sunshine they each looked directly across at their partners, all except for Maggie, as it had been her that was opposite the gateway. Maggie's slumped body was resting against her stone.

'Oh God no,' moaned Hazel, 'she's fainted.'

'Or been supping her gin,' said another.

'Come on,' ordered Jill. Being the first aider and guide on the moors, she had a pang of guilt about their joking, 'give me a hand to check her out.'

Jill knew as soon as she touched Maggie's arm that she had not fainted, she was dead. 'Quick, we need to lay her flat . . . come on Hazel help me, the rest of you stand back out of the way.'

In stunned silence they stood back as Jill desperately attempted to bring Maggie back with emergency resuscitation. Jill knew in her heart of hearts it was a waste of time, but it was her accepted duty to try . . . even if it was for the benefit of the group to know at least they tried.

Hazel spoke quietly to Jill, 'It's no use Jill, she's gone. We need to think of getting off the moor now. Take the fittest of the group straight back to the farm, inform the authorities, the rest of us will cover her up and stay by her side until help comes.'

Jill reluctantly agreed and set off with three others as quickly as the ground would allow.

Three hours later, the sound of a helicopter filled the air, finally whining to a halt as it landed some two hundred yards away. Paramedics confirmed the situation, strongly suspecting a heart condition after the overweight patient had trekked over such wild moorland and they explained what was happening next. Maggie's body would be flown to the hospital for a doctor's signature and to maintain some dignity for the deceased. The remainder of the group was to be picked up by the moors rescue team, probably by Land-rover within the hour.

The rest is just detail.

After a very bumpy drive back to the farmhouse, they all spent a couple of hours consoling each other around the kitchen table.

The coroner's verdict was death by misadventure caused by a presumed heart attack following a strenuous walk on the moors.

Though each of the ladies suspected differently, they kept to the coroner's version. After all, who would believe otherwise? They had businesses to run and lives to lead that depended upon credibility. But they would always know deep down that what they saw was indeed real, Maggie's soul had crossed to the other side before her time, she'd always been a rebel.

Hazel was never to speak to others of her own deep insights, born of that fateful day - that the aura is a visible manifestation of life force, the soul does not reside within the brain but is symbiotic with aura. Usually the energy takes three days to leave a body on death. Death being the permanent departure of the aura. Hazel considered that perhaps shamans and yogis experienced out of body events while their auras temporarily went walk about, but in Maggie's case, her spirit or soul was called by the gatekeeper to pass through to the other side and her life force left in the twinkling of an eye, visibly crossing the stone circle to enter the portal to eternity. Hazel knew that she could never share this awareness with others, as it flew in the face of the beliefs of so many influential and self-involved people. It remains her uncomfortable secret to this day.

In the vain hope that her spirit will join their circle once more, every solstice the group still remember their friend Maggie, just as every solstice her soul joins countless ancients at the *Breus* stone circle to watch the sun-rise, and to pray for a reincarnation that may never arrive.

Postscript:- Breus -judgement entrans – gateway golans – valley Many an old wives' tale has an ancient truth, Doom Tor was no misnomer.

A copy of the manuscript still occupies a place in the archives at Truro, my advice is, leave it there.

The Journey of Hisato Khalid.

Born in London to a Japanese mother and Egyptian father.

Still honouring their own cultures, his loving parents brought Hisato up to embrace western society and adopt English as his first language. As a happy young child, he would often peacefully drift to sleep listening to his mother's storytelling, which without fail ended, *'and they all lived happy ever after.'*

The abiding memory that came with those childhood stories was to remain with Hisato for the rest of his life. He was a bright child, studied well and achieved excellent results at a prestigious university, where he studied philosophy and ancient history. To the joy of his aging parents, Hisato married an attractive young woman whose parents were wealthy entrepreneurs. She had an eye for material gains and made the most of her position in life to accumulate substantial wealth. Hisato was more spiritually inclined, believing that we can never truly own anything; we merely borrow it while we live. His views made no impact upon what he perceived as his wife's obsessive behaviour with financial gain. A big house, social standing and an interesting and clever husband led to ever more success and no room for children. For Hisato this was not the dream life he'd desired from childhood. Then, after his parents died, he knew it was time to move on.

He'd imagined his parents would live forever. After all, didn't the fairy stories promise this? He took little with him but a few necessities and a change of clothing. With a reasonable bank balance of his own and passport in hand, he set out for the lands of his ancestors. There he hoped to find the answers to immortality that abounded in eastern mythology. First stop, Cairo, then on to Luxor, where his Egyptian parentage, smattering of Arabic and extensive knowledge of ancient history made him a most welcome guest among the local people. He bonded well with boatman Mustafa Mohamed and spent several weeks staying at the family home. They were good days, good company, fine weather, simple healthy food, and a chance to meet genuine minded seers of ancient mythology. But even the guides working the valley of Kings only had superficial knowledge and it soon became apparent that what Hisato was discovering, as interesting as it might be, was not taking him towards the edge of immortality. Mustapha and his family begged Hisato to stay. Why not? He could settle there, marry a fine and devoted wife and enjoy a long and happy life in Egypt. But such a life was not long enough to fulfil Hisato's dream. Many a tear was shed at the airport for his parting, as the aircraft took off for an interconnecting flight to Japan. Perhaps the spiritual city of Kyoto would bring him the answers he sought?

Once more, Hisato soon made friends by his humble ways, his knowledge of the ancients and the Japanese language which his mother had taught him. Hisato seemed frustrated at every turn; Kyoto had become superficially spiritual to attract tourist dollars. Hisato already knew as much as any of the priests, monks and scholars of their day and the only gain, was meeting with relatives of his mother. They felt blessed by his arrival; they could not have been more attentive and kinder to him. Old Uncle Morihiro, as Hisato knew him, made him welcome in his own home and soon secretly dreamed of marrying Hisato off to a beautiful Japanese woman and there, in the village, they would all live happily ever after, all family and friends together.

One night, as Hisato sat with Uncle Morihiro, he told him of his dreams to realise immortality, just as the ancient Gods had done. Uncle was deeply saddened by the conversation.

Being a deep-thinking philosopher himself, he had found no reason to believe in the possibilities of immortality.
'Hisato, my dear boy,' he said with great affection, 'only the Gods are immortal and they, only so, while they live in the minds of our children and in their children. It is the destiny of man to die. Don't waste a good life by trying to avoid that which is inevitable, for indeed it is.'
But Hisato was **not** sure death was inevitable, there **must** be a way, if only he could find it. He was irritated that the very root of his beliefs, in the lands of his ancestors, failed to provide the answers he sought. He was by now short of money, having spent it on gurus, monks, and mystics, but he had enough for one more flight. Hisato had already trawled the finest libraries and private collections for manuscripts that might help his quest. He had once read a quite plausible report of a Hermitage of Immortality near an obscure Tibetan/Mongolian border. Here would lay the answer, of this he was sure. Yes, this would be the place.
Once more, a happy family was to be saddened by his parting. With much begging and wringing of hands they watched him leave. Part of them died, for he'd taken a piece of their life away with him.
The journey to the Hermitage was long, much longer and harder than he ever imagined it could be. With his money soon gone, he fell on charity, begging lifts from drovers and other travelling folk. Much of it though, he walked. As the weeks wore on, his clothes were rags, his feet blistered through worn shoes and his joints ached with the sorrowful hunger for rest. In truth, this was a lonely, painful road and its only saving grace was his belief that, at the end, the secret of immortality awaited him.
Eventually, Hisato came within grasp of his destination and a villager pointed towards the distant greenery of a small valley amidst an otherwise barren and stony landscape. It

took Hisato a whole day to arrive. By then the sun had dropped behind a mountain peak and he felt the cold bite into his bones. In front of him was a humble stone hovel showing thin wisps of smoke from a dwindling fire. The hermit welcomed him in. It was hard to tell who looked the more ancient, as both had suffered much in search of their respective desires. Hisato was surprised to see how frail the Hermit appeared and was obviously not a candidate for immortality. Weakened by the dust of his road and demoralised by this final disappointment, Hisato collapsed exhausted on the cold earthen floor. With the last remnant of his own life the Hermit eased Hisato's body onto the cot and sheltered him with sack cloth. Now all alone and in the dark, Hisato was just conscious when death came for him and tapped on the doorway of his soul.
Hisato's search was over.

Postscript:

Hisato means - 'long lived', Khalid means - 'immortal'.
His name and his upbringing, like a moth to a flame, enticed him towards an enchanting lamp that he would never see lit.

**

Gateway to reflection.

Thomas Worthington, a devoted explorer and sincere mystic, sat deep in thought in the cafe garden at Avebury Stone circle.
He wasn't to wait long before his deliberations were interrupted by a loud and familiar voice, 'there you are, Tom

old pal, long time no see,' continuing, as he held his hand out in friendship, 'why have you dragged me all the way to Wiltshire just for a cup of tea?'

'Hi, Ken dear friend, it's because these nearby megalithic stones offer us a means to see our lives from an alternate point of view. They were built as gateways to the other side. But let's order some more tea, then I'll share my latest news with you.'

The waitress brought fresh tea and left the two men to talk in peace in the secluded corner they had chosen by the wisteria.

'I'm leaving, Ken, going for good, so likely this will be our last meeting as I doubt you will decide to travel the same path yourself. But before we part, there is something that I believe I have discovered and of all people, I want to share it with you.

Ken was intrigued, though Tom had always spoken in riddles of a higher plain than Ken ever visited in his mind.

'I've worked it out Ken, we don't exist alone on this earth.'

'You're dead right Tom, there's the waitress and that old couple by the gate . . . '

'I knew you'd be hard work Ken, but what I tell you will transform your view of life and death.'

'Whoa, now there's two opposites for you!'

'Ah, don't you be so sure Ken, in life there is always a tiny bit of death, so logically, in death there will remain a tiny bit of life . . . in some form or other. You are right, they are opposites, but opposites in harmony, not conflict. Ever heard the saying, 'if the end is part of a story then death is part of life'?'

Ken shook his head and smiled before lifting his cup.

Tom reached out and stopped him, 'take your teacup, it has an outside and an inside, two opposites that are joined in harmony, right? The valuable thing about the whole cup is the hole in the middle – the empty space, which is the very source of its usefulness, its power if you like.'

'Well, it would be if you let my arm go and let me drink some. But I do see what you mean.'

'So, Ken, you'll concede my point that everything must have an opposite in order to exist. For example, noise and quiet or happiness and sadness. If there was no sorrow in life, then joy would cease to exist. Change is required in order to register a judgement.'

'Yes Tom, I concede that point, without two sides to a coin, or a sheet of paper, neither could exist.'

'Have you ever looked into a mirror and really explored what you see, or think you see?'

'Only that I have more wrinkles now and less hair.' Ken was the constant joker, but Tom was an ever-unyielding teacher.

'Deeper than that, have you ever stared intently at your third eye?' Tom pointed to a place on his forehead, 'if you do, the chances are that you will observe fleeting images of other people, often relatives, parents, uncles, grandparents . . . but I digress, it is something else I wanted to reveal. Where is the image you see in the mirror? It's as far behind it as you are in front . . .'

Ken lifted his cup, unopposed this time, 'Yes, I know that, remembered it from school. So what? Are you saying that the image is our opposite? Like from another dimension?'

'Not exactly, but you are correct to say they are a form of opposites either side of the glass – a mirror image. Often people find a mirror image photograph is more pleasing, more comforting. I can only tell you that at the interface of the two opposites, two things are happening. One, there is nothing and I mean nothing there, it is a timeless void. Two, the opposites exist in perfect harmony. . . hand in hand if you like. This middle place is the essence of all life, it is where the alchemy of magic is manifested. It is all powerful without doing anything. It is also the portal or gateway to the other side ... the side we agreed must exist for anything to exist. Place your consciousness there and you may be in the presence of that which allows you to exist, for **you are** only because, **it is**.'

By now Ken had drunk too much tea and overtaxed his mind with Tom's bizarre philosophy. 'Back in a minute, must water the horse.'

When Ken returned, refreshed and now willing to have it explained in terms he might grasp, Tom was nowhere to be seen. 'Excuse me miss. Did you see where Mr Worthington went?'

'Yes sir, he paid the bill, said something about all debts been paid and walked out into the stone circle sir. When I returned with his change, he'd vanished. Just like one of them magic tricks on telly sir.'

Every year on that day Ken would return to Avebury, always hoping Tom would have returned from wherever he'd been. Ken was never brave enough to try the mirror and find his ancestors, nor to place his consciousness in the stone circle.

But he often wondered if he would ever meet the opposite that was out there somewhere . . . and keeping him alive.

**

ADVENTURE, CAMERARDERIE, SACRIFICE

The Fog.

A mountain rescue somewhere in the Scottish mountains, on one foggy December night.

Inside the loch-side village hall all was bright and warm yet, outside, it was like another world, a world of darkness, chill and fog, thick fog.

Inside, laughter and shouting filled the air; the buffet table was weighted down; it was a special night that night; special for one man. Tonight, they were celebrating the retirement of old Tam McInnes, thirty years he'd served the mountain rescue, and served with distinction too, but it was time for younger hands to grasp the nettle. His popularity was evident by the numbers that filled the hall; many others were simply prevented from being there by an impenetrable fog that shrouded the mountains and valleys north of Glen Katrine

Around the hall, small groups stood with drinks in hands, reminiscing, prophesying, or even both. Drinks were drunk and stories told, some funny some sad. In a small group by the door one pretty young girl engaged her audience, and embarrassed her boyfriend, himself a prospective candidate to join the team, by telling how they'd been out walking, and he'd decided to show off his climbing skills instead of going through a nearby field gate. He'd negotiated the stone wall all right but sadly for him not the cattle trough the other side. There was much laughing and slapping of his back. Though she'd been sworn to secrecy, that too, was something that had conveniently slipped her mind, along with the number of vodkas she'd had.

At the far end of the hall there was a different mood; new members of the team were listening to Big Jimmy, the long serving village bobby; 'aye,' he said solemnly, 'I've witnessed many an incident come to an end, both the good and the bad, and it's many a widow and orphan I've had to tell. That's why you boys must do your duty and save the sorrow.' He knew he'd oft times made his 'white lies' as he knocked their doors .... 'it was all over very quickly .... he wouldn't have known what was happening .... he didn't feel a thing' ... .' But he knew the end had oft been fearful and seemingly, endlessly merciless, that pain and despair were their abiding companions as they waited ... even hoped for death .... nay, not good ... not good. 'we'll be counting on yees t' save they lost souls and bring 'em back safe and sound ... we'll be counting on yees.' He stopped abruptly and turned away from their gaze, saying he was off for another sandwich, but in truth simply didn't want them to see the tear in his eye ..... it just wasn't done you know.

To the skirl of the pipes and a rousing rendition of 'Flower of Scotland' by all present, Tam was led to the small stage at the far end of the hall. There the local president of the Mountain Rescue Association waited long for the applause, whistling, and cheering to subside. He had many a tale to tell of Tam's exploits ... some of them told him in whispers of embarrassing moments, some of bloody-minded heroism ... speeches were often boring but this one was going to be good ... this was a great night for someone special. The president had hardly started when his next breath was interrupted by the hall doorway opening and admitting both fog and a shawled lady looking for her son ... 'the polis have phoned laddie,' she said, ' there's a farmer missing over yon Ben.'

There was a steady murmur throughout, and the president had his chance to at least say something of use .... 'all those on call please to the hall doorway to sort yourselves out, the rest of us down this end and keep it quiet please.'

Silence came quick, as it does to those who know its value.

There appeared to be some concerned discussion going on with the team members of the mountain rescue, and retired or not, old Tam McInnes wasn't going to keep his nose out. To gather a full team was going to take a desperately long time due to the dense fog; also, there was snow and bitter weather on the tops, so speed was essential. The lost farmer, known by many of the team, and now known as 'the casualty' to depersonalise the issue, farmed beyond the hills above the village. His farm could be accessed by road around the mountains, but it was a long way around .... too long for comfort. Tam interrupted the group, who listened intently to a man they had grown to respect immensely over the years, 'I suggest that you make up a small team out of whoever lives in the village itself, take the Land Rover from base as far as the track up the valley will allow and make your way on foot to the casualty's last known position. As time permits the rest of the volunteers can take what transport they can and travel by road. I know it'll be a long journey for them, but it seems best to me ... what say you?' The murmur of agreement confirmed the plan. 'So, how many of you can be ready in a few minutes from the village?' Tam asked. Six hands went up. Tam surveyed the expectant faces, 'Christine, you lead the team, you know the valley well enough, even in this soup, ... Robert, go to base and prepare the transport and gear for them, don't forget the radios and spare lamps and you can pick up the rest of the team on your way back through the village.'

No sooner was it said than they were gone, ... gone into an eerie fog hushed unknown.

As planned, each volunteer, dressed for the terrain and the weather, complete with rucksack of equipment and provisions, was collected by the team's Land Rover in the main street. 'All aboard that's coming aboard,' called Bob selecting four-wheel drive and low ratio.

'Can't you find some more gears in this thing Bob; I've got somewhere to go next weekend!' said a nameless voice from the back.

The Land Rover crawled out of the village and along the old farm track towards the valley head. They knew Bob was doing his best but it was in their nature to temper the seriousness of their task with the deft and often dour touch of highland humour ..... 'Come on Bob, any slower and we might as well get out and walk.' Bob said nothing and the Land Rover staggered on in the sightless mist, lurching from pothole to pothole, ...

'Here you are you ungrateful lot, this is as far as I can take you. Now hurry up and get out as I've still a pint and dram waiting for me, ... have fun,' laughed Bob.

'The way you drive Bob we'll be back before you ... aye, and with the casualty too,' continued Bob's antagonist.

Soon through the field gate and steadily onward they heard the departing vehicle disappear into the all-pervading and stifling mist. Then the only sound was a little heavy breathing as the track turned steeply upward and the steady crump of boots on moving stones. No one spoke, the leader led and the led followed.

Unusually for mountain rescue this group was being led by a woman, Chris by name, a lion-hearted little woman of great strength and much experience. She'd lived and worked in the surrounding valley and hills for more years than she cared to tell. Though she knew the terrain like the back of her hand, she knew also that this fog was going to test her; the team however, implicitly trusted her judgement.

The five climbed a stile over a stone wall, their boots landing softly on grass and heather the other side. All was eerily quiet as the fog deadened all sound, all except the sound of breathing and the light swish of waterproofs.

'Mind your step ... small ditch here to cross,' she called back. Each team member repeated the message to the one behind.

A soggy squelching sound of boot into boggy ground accompanied by the mumbling of a curse, brought a smile and light chuckle to all but the last team member who was now enthused with gratitude for his bog covered gaiters.

An hour into their climb and they were leaving behind all trace of pathways and landmarks, Chris stopped the team, 'take a breather, I'm going to set the compass, let's have another lamp here please.'

Chris had a choice of routes; one, a long way around and following the contours, or a shorter more direct way that wasn't without the risk and challenge of one or two short climbs. Chris allowed herself a moment to consider what Tam would have done.

'Damn it,' she thought, 'I'm not Tam, it's down to me now, must follow my own intuition.' Chris called the team to the map, it was important that everyone knew the plan, 'we're going this way ... it'll save us an hour.' No one questioned her decision; trust was a byword in the survival business.

'I'm all for that,' said Dave, mostly known as 'smiley' by his pals, and now sporting one bog-stained leg, 'Bob must be halfway back to his beer by now ... I'm looking forward to

beating him to it.' Despite their situation, their fog-soaked clothes, and dewed eyebrows; the team gave a little cheer ... then just as quickly were quiet again.
'Come on team,' urged Chris, 'we're on our own in all this, no helicopter flying, and any other teams will be many hours behind us.' Chris had never seen fog as bad, almost as if the Gods had sent it to mark Tam's retirement ... one thing for sure it would enter the realm of myths and legends in the village.
They must first cross a stretch of featureless heather moor and Chris sent Smiley off in front on her compass bearing. Before losing sight of him the rest of the team would follow, to repeat the process time and again. Slow it may be, but better safe than sorry as the route they were taking had some severe slopes ahead and they must arrive in the right place to avoid them.
'Spot on Chris,' shouted back Smiley as he reached a flat and spacious ledge that separated the upper and lower slope.
A sense of excitement ran through the team, the elation of carrying out a perfect navigation on such a night gave them all a feeling of power and achievement. ... but the night was not yet over. In such a small team, each and every one of them was essential, one fails, the team fails, tonight they must not fail, for they, a mere handful of volunteers, could be all that held the line between life and death for the lost farmer.
Now standing on wet snow, the team gathered around Chris, and a deft hand wiped clean the misted map case; from their right-hand side they could hear the faint sound of falling water. The nearby falls plummet some hundred and eighty feet, and when the snows melt, they are truly magnificent, but tonight the fog concealed its beauty .... misty spray frozen in space, magical ice structures shaped by nature's artist festooned the ravine side Rowans, ... it was

all out there in the fog and the night ... but not for them to see.

Chris pointed to the route on the map, 'up this slope, mostly steep but with peat and heather, then we meet the rocky ridge rising up to our left ... no doubt covered in the same snow as we have here; keep close when we reach the ridge, we must find the easiest way through.' The soft slope was steeper than they would have liked, the sort of slope that is easier to go up than down, and this one wasn't easy going up, many a time boots were kicked into soft ground for a toe hold and hands grabbed lumps of heather for support. As they climbed, each of them living out their own struggle, the air became colder; the fog was beginning to freeze, and the ground was hardening as they reached the snow-clad rocks of the ridge. Chris and three others made it to the top edge of the ridge, but where was Smiley? In fact, he wasn't far away, only a few feet below them, he'd taken a slightly different way but hearing the teams voices so close had believed he was in their footsteps; .... but he wasn't, he'd gone up a narrow but steep snow-clad gully and was now faced with a large smooth boulder, chest height that barred his way; Rock each side of him was like that in front, all worn smooth by centuries, his only foothold just under the base of the obstructing rock so that his body was being pushed backwards. Smiley knew he was in a dangerous spot as he fearfully scrabbled for a good hand hold, but the time worn rock denied him; if he slipped, he would be unable to stop himself sliding back down the slope to an even bigger drop beneath.

A concerned voice broke the silence, 'Come on Smiley, what you doing, having a leak?' called one of his mates from above.

'Just coming, nearly there,' Smiley called back hiding his fear in his words and the fog.

Somehow Smiley's elbow had found something to push on and in doing so he was able to raise himself up enough to put his body weight over and not under the rock, as it had been since he first became frozen by circumstance. Smiley's legs were shaking a bit as he joined the team, 'okay, made it,' he said putting on a false tone of comfort, 'how the hell did you all get past that snow gully rock ... I'm taller than all you, and I struggled .... well, a little bit anyway.'
'What rock?' they said in unison, 'we came this way,' so pointing towards a simple open climb.
'Oh,' murmured Smiley, and said no more .... But thought a lot!
'Okay, team, said Chris, drawing them together again to look at the map, 'we follow the ridge to the summit then drop down the slope on the other side, picking up the stone wall about here,' pointing to her chosen start point for the search, 'we'll follow the wall north west and back towards the farm and see what we can find on the way.' She turned to Smiley, now you are nearly back to normal, get on the radio, and give them our current position and status ..... no need to tell them about your ditch or your rock.'
Even Smiley had to laugh, nothing got by Chris .... that's why they followed her.
As the fog froze to their eyebrows and their boots made a unified crunching sound on the crisp snow, they descended from the ridge summit. 'Message sent Chris, reply is that they are only just getting a back-up team together with transport now,' said Smiley having jogged quickly by the others to be at Chris' side. It was a good half mile to the wall, they were aiming high so as to be sure of picking up the gateway shown on the map on the way down, no need to use the technique they used earlier, this was all open sheep grazing land in the summer. Boot prints in the snow,

disappearing into a dark and claustrophobic past, showed that they were keeping a good line.

'Wheesht! Listen .... all quiet!' commanded Chris.

They all stood silent, their lamps creating reluctant rays of light into the all-pervading fog, they could all hear it .... no doubt about it ... the sound of an idling diesel engine .... 'sounds like we've found someone's Land Rover,' said Smiley quietly. Mountain rescue never counted their chickens before they hatched, they never knew what they would find, but all the while must keep enough strength to make it home again … never easy.

'This way,' called Chris, 'we'll head straight for it and if abandoned we'll look for tracks ... wait till we get there before radioing in a message ... let's see what we've got first.'

Their pace and hearts quickened to the task and it was not long before the shape of a Land Rover tilted over to one corner loomed out of the mist, like a whale from the deep.

The side lights and cab light were on and there behind the wheel looking right as rain sat George the farmer. He'd had a fright earlier when trying to return home; he'd lost a wheel into a dip near the wall, then trying to extricate it had twisted his ankle. He'd liberally used hill farmer language to bewail his predicament .. not that was going to help him ... and he'd resigned himself to a long wait till morning.

Well, the fright he'd had earlier was to pale into insignificance compared with the almost heart stopping fright he had as his tediously unchanging view through misted up windows suddenly filled with lights and strange faces .... with just their eyes visible. What a relief it was as he heard a familiar voice, 'what are you doing sleeping out here George, your wife wants you back home ......'

'By jings it's you lassie, you gave me a fright Chris, I thought they'd come for me at last,' George smiled

‘So, George, what is your situation, can you walk?’ asked Chris through the now open door. George explained in hill farmer terms that if he could walk, he'd already be home in front of his dinner by now. Chris was pleased they'd found the old boy alive and reasonably well, ‘Smiley, get on the radio and tell them back at base, 'casualty located, minor injuries, team and casualty making its way to Low Ben Farm, will contact by landline on arrival, ETA approximately thirty minutes.’ ‘Now George, you’re a bit of a lump for us few to carry you down to the farm … we’ll have to drag you down ….’ Chris said with a wry smile, just visible to George through the fog. A quick glance in the back of the Land Rover revealed the makings of a sledge of sorts; using the team's fold up stretcher and some canvas sheeting the team soon had it made and had George well wrapped up with almost anything to spare and the odd 'space blanket’ thrown in. With four corners of the canvas gripped by a team member each and Chris leading the way .... not without frequent advice from George it has to be said .... the sledge made easy going over the hardened snow.

With George's encouragement, for he'd not eaten in a while, and advice given on the best way down the fields, they were knocking on the farm door in just over twenty minutes. After the initial shock it was a merry welcome to all the team ... and a sharp word to her daft old husband too ..... outdoor clothes off and warming in the back scullery while a phone call was made to stand down all other teams and soon hot plates full of egg, bacon and chips weighed down the farmhouse table .... no need to rush back ..... nothing to rush back for.

Lizzie, George's wife, poured the tea and thanked the team, ‘tonight,’ she said, ‘is a night for one special person, and with a tear of joy in her eye turned to Chris and said, ‘May God bless you for bringing my man back from the hills, only

someone special could have done this thing, thank you Chris.' There was a loud cheer from the team and the clink of a bottle as George unusually voluntarily dug out his best whisky ...... there was no rush anymore.
Beyond the hills, way down by the loch, they still celebrated the retirement of their honoured guest, Tam, once mountain rescue leader.
In a wee fog bound highland farmhouse somewhere in the mountains they celebrated the birth of a new one.

**

'Faith is the bird that feels the light when the dawn is still dark.' Unknown

**

The Phoebe-Marie

August 1878.
Genny's Cove, a village on England's Atlantic coast.

Sea birds were ominous in their unusual silence, and like the lone man in seafaring clothes at the end of the quay, seemed spellbound by the changing sky. A weathered hand touched his shoulder and disturbed his dreaming. Turning slowly, he shared a knowing smile and a greeting with William, his lifelong friend. The wind off the sea grew colder by the hour; no boats would set out that day.

Walking back along the quayside towards the fishing fleet beached at low tide, they met others near the harbour steps, all eyes fixed towards the horizon. Andrew and William turned to look. A gust of wind flapped their collars, voices fading as the wind howled in their ears. There, far out to sea on a northerly tack, were sails.

For a while, a squall hid the ship from view. 'She's closer inshore already Andrew, I can't say I like the look of that; no, not at all,' William's voice, uneasy.

Andrew nodded thoughtfully, this was a coastline he knew well, from hard won experience.

Together they watched a while longer, until a new bitterness in the wind and the threat of heavy rain drove them to seek shelter.

*

Aboard the ketch, *Auckland*, Captain Sam Harvey faced a dilemma. On board was the ship's elderly owner, John Lightfoot Esq., and his family. Intended to be a treat from the owner for his grandchildren, all were now sick with sea and fear. None had expected such terrifying weather. Had he not been ordered otherwise by the owner, a rich and powerful man, though fully ignorant of the sea, the captain would have sailed far from shore and waited out the storm. His only other choice was to find anchorage in a sheltered bay along the coast, yet on this rocky seashore, safe harbours were few. Studying the charts, he found a bay whose southern edge would give shelter. Influenced by a dictatorial owner, the Captain gave orders to sail for Yenisbury Bay. A bay with no safe beach, their anchor *must* hold. A reluctant crew set to, making way for the line of white water which separates sea from cliff. Once past the point of no return, the bay became their abiding hope, but the wind strengthened and drove them shoreward towards a hostile coastline never shy of death.

At Genny's Cove, Andrew chopped logs at his cottage, readying the winter's wood supply, his wife Elizabeth prepared food in the kitchen. When the roof tiles started to rattle, Andrew walked through the house picking up his coat on the way. Elizabeth said nothing, for she knew where he was going. The same place he always went when the weather was bad. Cloth cap tight on his head, and collar up, he strode purposefully along the narrow village street, his fisherman's boots strangely quiet on the tanned stone cobbles. When Andrew arrived at the boat house, he found the rear door already open. He approached slowly to stand in the doorway. He heard voices and stopped to listen.

'Large axe; check it's sharp. Hatchets, two, and sharp, throwing lines, under the seats, three spare oars and the anchor. . ' At that point William spotted Andrew in the doorway, 'I knew you'd be down here Andrew.'

First, acknowledging his friend with a raised hand, 'You helping your uncle William out then David? You'll not go wrong listening to him.'

An hour later, the heavy hoof beats of a farm horse clattered on the cobbles outside. 'Thank God you're already here. You've heard the news then?' The farmer was breathless, but they understood well enough. 'I was fetching sheep off the south foreland by Yenisbury Bay, there's a ship in trouble. One mast looks broken to me and she's close by the rocks already. . . I saw people on deck. . . '

A change of mood swept away all pleasantries.

'William. Put up a maroon and raise a crew, David, open the front doors then help with the launch,' and seeing the eager look on David's face, added, 'but you'll not be coming with us.'

Andrew turned to prepare for action and spread open the sea chart, his mind racing. A heart stopping boom shook the village. It wasn't long before volunteers filled the boathouse. With wind and tide running the way it was, this voyage would test the strongest crew. Andrew, their trusted coxswain, walked among them picking a dozen men with a firm hand to each chosen shoulder. As horses and ropes were prepared for the launch, Andrew gathered the chosen ones about the sea chart, 'Dis-masted vessel in Yenisbury Bay,' Andrew paused, while a murmur of dismay came from his crew. 'She's already on, or close to the rocks, tide is on the flood and the wind unfavourable to say the least. Her crew has been seen on deck.'

*

On board the half-wrecked ketch in Yenisbury Bay, the sailors sensed their fate. They were realistic about any chance of survival as the pounding sea met jagged rocks. Death might reach out its unwelcome hand and touch them at any minute and the creaking of ship's timbers and flapping of tattered sails had long driven terror into the poor children's hearts.

*

Phoebe-Marie's crew and helpers rallied their strength and launched into a sea of wild white horses driven ashore under an ever-menacing sky. Andrew had picked his strongest crew well and as he called upon them to pull together, he steered them beyond the worst of the inshore waves.

*

On board the ketch, a watery grave might beckon but Captain Sam Harvey continued to reassure his passengers that all would be well. He could only hope that their end would come quick and clean, though a desperate yearning for salvation would haunt them all to the very end. If the ketch survived intact, she might be stranded by the outgoing tide. Then they might all walk along the shoreline to safety. But such a hope was like the drowning man clinging to straws. The '*Auckland'* looked unlikely to last until the tide had ebbed.

*

As for our valiant lifeboat, now some distance from shore, many a time wind and wave contrived to capsize her as the storm met her beam on. Yet the skill of the coxswain and the strength of her crew prevailed again and again. It was more than two miles to Yenisbury Bay, with the storm pushing them ever closer to sea cliffs that rise a thousand feet or more. 'Set the for'ard sail, we'll take advantage of this wind where we can. Two men raised the mast and set the sail, an astonishing feat as the small boat was buffeted mercilessly by the elements. Spray stung their hands and faces; their clothes were soaked in sweat. Water swilled about their feet as the self-drainers struggled to keep up.

'There she is! I see her, off the starboard quarter. Take courage lads and save something for the journey home,' Andrew shouted, steering with one hand, and pointing with another.

As the lifeboat edged ever closer, Andrew made his plan.

The *Auckland* was indeed dis-masted, sails shredded and her rigging a tangled mess in the foam. She was pinned to the rocks by the wind and the rising tide. However, Andrew

could see a little slack water by her bows. 'That's where we'll take them off,' he thought, then called for the sail to be lowered and mast stowed.
'Put up a flare Jack, let them know we are here.' With all the skill of a master mariner, Andrew picked his spot to turn, anchor and line up, drifting *Phoebe-Marie* stern first towards the ketch.

*

From the stern rail of the *Auckland*, Captain Harvey and his first mate watched through spray stung eyes as the lifeboat crew reduced oars and paid out the anchor line. It seemed to take forever, as though time itself had stopped to watch the spectacle.
Once at anchor and no longer making way, the *Phoebe-Marie* pitched and rolled with every wave. Andrew pointed to the bows of the *Auckland* with outstretched arm.
As of one mind, Captain and mate made their way forward, gathering the crew as they went. Captain Harvey shouted into the cabin, 'Be of good cheer sir, we may still be saved. . . lifeboat coming. Stay below, not safe yet.'

*

As the *Phoebe-Marie* slowly came alongside, Andrew organised his rescue party, some used oars to keep her from striking the hull, and others prepared the throwing lines. 'Prepare to take a line on board,' Andrew hollered above the noise of sea on rocks, and then more quietly to his crew, 'standby to cut lines if need be, we've got this far, we'll not be dragged down with her if she moves.'
Captain Harvey's crew set about with renewed vigour to secure the throwing line, and despite numbed hands, the knots were tied with skill, 'All secure Cap'n, all secure.' Captain Harvey immediately ordered a rope ladder over the side.

Andrew determined to board the *Auckland* and assess the situation for himself. On a rising wave he reached out for the rope ladder and began to climb, the wave nearly sweeping him out to sea. Helped over the ship's rail by eager hands Andrew was soon on deck. A handshake with the captain, an exchange of names and damage to *Auckland* was quickly assessed.

Taking the captain to one side, 'We can take ten Sam,' he confided, 'and no promise we can make it back for the rest of you.'

Sam nodded solemnly, the nod of a man preparing for his own funeral. An honourable man, he knew he must stay with his ship, 'You choose then Andrew, for I cannot.'

Choosing was not so much a hardship for Andrew; he'd done it many a time before. Andrew surveyed the pleading eyes of the crew; no one wants to die, not like this. He chose six strong sailors who could help his own crew with rowing and the woman with her three terrified young children, but the elderly gentleman looked like he'd seen most of his days already and his survival was questionable. 'Right Sam, put the chosen men on board the *Phoebe-Marie* then we'll help the woman and children aboard ourselves.

While the waves battered the creaking ketch steadily towards her inevitable submission and hanging with one arm from the rope ladder, Andrew lowered the three children one by one to the waiting arms of his crew. Their mother was already weakened by her ordeal and as the lifeboat rose and fell, the frightened children watched in horror as she lost her grip on the swaying ladder. Andrew reached out and caught her with almost superhuman effort. She was helped aboard to sit centre of *Phoebe-Marie* with her children huddled around her. It wasn't without a price to pay, Andrew had felt something tear in his shoulder, and it wasn't his coat. He was in pain already as his crew pulled him strongly towards them and into relative safety. Certainly, Andrew didn't want a fuss; his crew looked to him for leadership as well as seamanship. He would just have to steer with one arm, that's all.

From the rail of the ketch, the forsaken remnants of the crew watched as the life-or-death struggle played out before their eyes. When the *Phoebe-Marie* left the slack water by the *Auckland's* bows she met breaking waves that sought to beat her against the ship's hull. Suddenly, like gun shots, two oars were broken, their splintered remains quickly lost to the deep. Above the noise of the wind that drove white horses to their untimely death on the rocks, they could hear Andrew's commanding voice, 'heave, men, heave on that line. Oars together now. . . pull men, pull.'

Slowly but surely, the *Phoebe-Marie* made progress, anchor aboard, they were at last heading for home.

Andrew looked southwards towards Genny's Cove but all he saw was white water and spray. It seemed, row and die or stay and die, though such men gave up only when their hearts stopped beating.

Meeting the wind head on, the lifeboat crew pulled hard on the oars in silent unison, the mark of a disciplined crew. Adrenalin gradually drained from Andrew's body, replaced by pain in his damaged shoulder. Steeling himself, he braced his body against the tiller and set his eyes on a course for home. Against rising waves and blinding spindrift Andrew guided his gallant crew, reading the waves and seeking every advantage. The crew, with backs to a hungry sea, timed their stroke with the man in front and listened for their coxswain's orders.

They'd already lost sight of the *Auckland,* and only home filled their thoughts. Blistered hands hauled away at heavy oars while death hunted them close by in the deep. When a man began to tire and a chance came, he changed him for one of the sailors he'd rescued. An unwarranted sense of guilt made the crew reluctant to give up their place, ashamed to meet the eyes of their comrades. Then, once at rest, sweat and sea water cooled quickly and brought a shiver to their bones. Little by little, the *Phoebe-Marie* and her precious cargo made progress against wind and tide. A remarkable feat of strength and courage that few would have ever thought possible.

Yet another half hour and Genny's Cove was just visible. Now was not the time to relax, now was the time to redouble efforts. Whatever the cost, there must be no mistakes.

'Land ho, off port quarter. . . home in sight,' Andrew cried. The news gave the crew renewed strength.

Genny's Cove lookouts had already seen the coloured speck appearing and disappearing in the distant waves. Willing villagers prepared to receive the boat into harbour and the boat house was ready with blankets, dry clothes, and food.

Finally, *Phoebe-Marie* was rowed safely into the relative calm of the harbour to welcoming shouts from the villagers. Safe home and on dry land, the relief of the crew was immense. The deep indeed, had failed to claim them.

Fresh volunteers secured *Phoebe-Marie* to the quayside, while the rescued mother and her children were comforted in the boat house.

Andrew, however, was already planning the next mission. . . his clear orders calling for replacement oars and an additional anchor and line. As the exhausted crew dragged themselves off to the boathouse, fresh legged volunteers busied themselves with returning the lifeboat to sea readiness.

Andrew disguised his pain, as he too made his way to the boathouse. He sensed he was the only one who might make the repeat journey with any chance of success; lives depended on him and his leadership.

'**Quiet** please! **It's not over**,' Andrew shouted, bringing an instant hush to the gathered crowd. All eyes were on him. It seemed that hardly a breath was taken, 'we must go again, and soon, for she'll not take much more of this sea. Volunteers only, step forward, this will not be easy, make no mistake. None from the last trip, no one can row this sea twice. I'll take anyone who can pull a decent oar. Yes, you, you and you, get rigged for sea and wait by the boat. . . alright David, you can make up the numbers, but you must row like the devil is after you, for he most certainly will be.' David nodded with a sense of pride in his heart that he was now among the chosen, picked up a life vest and joined the others on the quayside. Andrew saw the worried look in William's eyes.

Perhaps Andrew was pinning his hopes on the weather abating and making life easier, for he'd picked his strongest crew for the first run and now look at them . . . keen in spirit but drained in body. Once again, he called the crew to action as the lifeboat cleared the calm water and met the wild sea, 'Oars together now. . . pull men, pull.' Soon she was lost from sight in the spray, somewhere out there upon the deep.

Of those left ashore, some went to work or home to rest, others stayed at the boat house, those that did, cheered themselves with the success of an amazing rescue. While they eagerly awaited the lookout's cry that the *Phoebe-Marie* was homeward bound again, as of one mind, they talked of the strength of their fine boat and the men who served.

After two or more anxious hours, hoof beats of a farm horse clattered on the cobbles outside the boathouse. William stood and in tangible silence, walked outside. . .

Now I must tell you, we have already stayed too long.

It's time we left the villagers of Genny's Cove to their own fate, whatever that may be.

The village fades from our sight, but our hearing lingers long enough and before it is gone forever, we hear the impatient stamp of horseshoes on cobbles and a familiar farmer's voice calling to William . . . 'I've something for you. . .' a gust of wind howls and it is difficult to hear clearly, then a lull and we hear William exclaim with great joy and a hint of curiosity, 'David! David my boy, it's you. How. . .?'
'Uncle, all is well, we saved them all. . . beached on next cove along, resting crew. . . skipper said he'd never hear the last of it if he didn't send me back to you with the news.'

On 12th September1878, young David Trescothick received the RNLI silver medal for gallantry. He never missed another shout, and on Andrew's retirement took over the role of Coxswain. None were prouder than his uncle William. The lifeboat station was closed in 1926 but his medal remains on display in the small village museum.

**

The love of life - Louisa.

(Inspired by the lifeboat, Louisa of Lynmouth, in the late 19th century, when lifeboats were launched by man and horse and were rowed to the scene.)

Wild calls for help, bring with them fear;
maroons, they wake the night.
Calls, to men both brave and strong
and bound by hope, not fright.
The crew is picked, the orders clear,
the coxswain shares his plan.
She's launched into the pounding surf,
as only lifeboats can.

'Pull hard my crew,' the coxswain shouts,
'Pull hard for distant sail.
Through wind and wave and darkness,
I vow that we'll not fail.'
Back at the quay, the helpers stand.
When will the storm abate?
To welcome heroes home again,
their fearful hearts must wait.

Upon the ship the children cry,
the tattered sails cry too.
Their captain tired, he's given up,
not so, the lifeboat crew.
'Set off a flare,' the coxswain says;
'Twas done without a fuss.
As dark turned bright, the captain prayed,
'God's angels come for us.'

Then voices called, from out the dark,
'You're saved, now come aboard,'
but robbed of prize and sacrifice,
the angry sea, it roared.
The ropes were thrown, and grapnel fast,
ship's timber, it did grip.
With failing hands and racing hearts
they stumbled from their ship.

As one by one they made their way,
each felt the need to rush.
The sea, it wants to hurry too,
Louisa's hull to crush.
They sigh relief and comfort seek,
all huddled on the deck.
With spirits high and bent to oars,
they leave the sinking wreck.

Now turned for shore and distant lights,
oh, still so far from home
and homeward bound, they have to race,
white horses, and the foam.
The waves rise high and troughs sink deep,
the elements do rave,
determined not to let them go,
but put them in their grave.

That coxswain strong had other thoughts;
he'd seen it all before.
'Our good Louisa lifeboat,
will take us to the shore.'
While sound of surf at base of cliff,
bid the storm run free,
to know if they can make it home,
they pray; as so might we.

Above picture extracted from a painting by the brilliant marine artist Mark Myers RMSA

**

Photo by author, Tyne Cot, Ypres.

Never to come home.

1917 France.

The call for help, was loud and clear,
I could not stand and look.
I joined a queue, that showed no fear,
to serve, an oath I took.

At training camp, they fed us well,
though discipline was firm.
Our orders came - in line we fell,
'Tomorrow - it's our turn'.

Off to the front, we marched next day.
Arrived with blistered feet.
'Twas then that hell, it came our way,
the shrapnel, gas, the sleet.

Now even if you said I can,
I could not now, home go.
For t'would appear, that I had ran
in shame before the foe.

Our staunch resolve, it will not fold,
we've lifelong friendships built,
should I desert my comrades bold
I'd sicken with such guilt.

Upon a stone, let others know,
About, what we did give.
How from these trenches, we must go,
to die, so they shall live.

But now we stand, with guns in hand,
too late to make amends.
I'll find my peace in *no man's land,*
and lie beside my friends.

Cambrin Cemetery, battle of the Somme, France.

The War to end all wars –

(And for so many, it did just that.)

Are we as sad, as he once was,
to see his friends all killed,
to sing the hymns and utter prayers
as grave on grave was filled?

In trenches foreign, far from home,
he laboured night and day.
And with the gas came nightmares,
he prayed could go away.

So very rarely, leave it came,
for home, and part this strife,
to new mown hay and roses
and marry, his new wife.

By special licence they were wed,
dismay they yet must bear.
The telegram it said quite clear,
'Recall to duty, there.'

A farewell hug, a kiss goodbye,
so sad to go away.
But duty calls, to send our friend
once more into the fray.

Back, where blood of man and horse,
flowed red into the ground,
all through that mud they marched as one,
until their peace was found.

**

One stormy night –
Lynmouth Devon 12th January 1899.

That stormy night – we watched them leave.
Their plan, it touched our hearts.
What they attempt, hard to believe,
but here, our story starts.

As winter cruel, their bones did chill,
'Make haste!' the coxswain bid.
In few short steps, they met the hill,
where moonless path was hid.

Those distant miles, we all did know,
but we did silence keep.
O'er moor and hill in gale and snow,
they'd strive, while children, sleep.

One mile, four hours, to Countisb'ry,
Inn's refuge next the moor,
not one of them, could disagree,
the easy choice, for sure.

Some cold and beaten, must head home,
the crew though, still advance.
For ship adrift, in wave and foam,
may still be saved, perchance.

By night and sleet, frail road obscured,
like trackless moorland waste.
Pained heroes all, fierce cold endured,
in silence, they made haste.

Those desperate men must doubt, it's said,
but hope, still filled their soul,
'gainst mud, and blood - four horses dead,
the rescue, stayed their goal.

Then, ten miles on, at Porlock hill,
exhausted, sure, they'd be.
While thoughts of home, can test their will,
from duty - none were free.

Once on the beach at Porlock Weir,
high tide, floods in again,
yet boat is launched, and scorning fear,
makes way, through spray and rain.

Daring, 'gainst such stormy weather,
through tempest, all did row,
'tis now, they'll live or die together,
and we might never know.

No news came home, to cheer us all,
our village drowned in sadness.
While out at sea, the Forrest Hall,
a rescue, born of madness.

Oh, such brave crew, the tales they'll tell.
How, when, by moorland track,
they fought their way, through gates of hell,
then safe, by sea, came back.

**

One stormy night - we watched them go. . .
into a moonless, stormy winter nightmare.

Set close by the rocky seashore, nestling below hills that rise steeply to bleak moorland, is Lynmouth and our home. The road to the east is no more than a narrow mud and stone track with an unguarded drop on one side to the sea, fit only for cart horses and an occasional coach. The tiny harbour floods twice daily under one of the highest tides in the world and all this day long the village has been battered and soaked by a relentless north westerly gale. It's seven o'clock in the evening on Thursday, January the twelfth 1899 and the Lifeboat Louisa rests in the boat house on her carriage. The tide is at full height and the gale already swept a wild sea over the harbour wall and into the lower houses. The cold already hurts and feels below zero, everyone shelters inside, waiting out the great storm. None can remember such as this. In the lamp light of the tiny post office, the telegraph clatters urgently into action before falling silent, another victim to the storm. The postmaster holds the ominous message with trembling hands. It's a call for help – a ship in distress and a desperate crew in need of aid. No other boat along that coast is located better for a launch than the Louisa. Despite the roar of sea and wind, the unmistakeable boom of a signal rocket shakes the air above the village, a sudden flash of light illuminates the empty streets. Like everyone else, you run to the boat house, eyes half closed against the driving rain. The maroon summons the village to action, the crew needs help to launch. With a fierce wind tearing at your already soaked clothes, you stop in horror, shocked by the impossibility facing the crew. Great waves carry rocks from the beach and crash into the street over the low harbour wall; neither man nor beast could ever survive a launch in such a maelstrom. You join the crowd in the boathouse, aware of the warmth of shelter so cruelly denied to those now lost out at sea. Your father is among the chosen crew, you see a tear in his eye, you have never seen this before, he is your hero and many a time has set out to sea risking all for strangers in need. But tonight, is different, tonight they are helpless. Through an open doorway you turn to look seawards, far away through the spray and gloom you watch, as a distant distress rocket falls to its own untimely death. What can be done? How can they, brave men all, stand idly by while their fellows drown, the shame, the helplessness? These men know the sea and know the risks, yet duty and honour run like the blood in their veins. Suddenly, a commanding shout cuts the air. You stand quietly, safe amongst the now hushed and waiting crowd. It's the coxswain, leader of the crew. Highly respected, they would follow him through the gates of hell. He calls out, 'We'll launch beyond Gore Point at Porlock Weir. We'll take our chances there.' It is a long way. You know full well their first obstacle, for on a fine summer day, you've climbed Countisbury Hill on the east bound track yourself. Without any burden, it still took you nearly an hour. Beyond Countisbury lies eleven miles of unrelenting, exposed moor and the infamous hill that twists its tortuous way down to Porlock. Only then, can the exhausted crew of Louisa attempt a launch and row out with already blistered hands and aching backs to search an unknown darkness in Porlock Bay. You are not alone in thinking it impossible, but that is their choice, certain death or the impossible. They choose the latter. The call quickly went up for horses, rope and lanterns, and even the doubters became inspired. Men, women, and children scurry to prepare the lifeboat for its journey. Many of them, along with the horses, climb that hill, stumbling painfully, hauling and heaving as their feet slip and slide on mud and stones. The wind extinguishes already dim lanterns, almost impossible to re-light in the gusts and rain. The rain turns to sleet, the cold increases. Even in such cold, they sweat, a sweat that cools rapidly should they rest for even a few moments, chilling the body to the bone. They disappeared from sight after about an hour; just a faint twinkling of a dim lantern in the far darkness before nothing but blackness remained. We know not, if everyone will make their way back home safely and of those who do, they will be changed forever. It will be a long wait. We, who did not take this amazing journey, will never understand nor dream of what, they who went, endured. The pain of cold is not felt by reading words, nor is the sadness of slipping harness from a dead horse, dying for the cause, its body unceremoniously dragged to one side, because other things now matter more. Through the long hours of night and through the next day we wait, not knowing who of family and friend will return. Shoulder to shoulder, we will wait together, you and me. We will prevail, it's what we do.

**

'They also serve who only stand and wait.'
John Milton, on his blindness

The Inn on Countisbury Hill at the time.

The Resolute Coxswain.

(A lifeboat rescue story like no other.)

Old George Millar was a popular grocer in the little fishing village. His shop, with its worn boarded floor and evocative smells of package free food and spices, was like a place that time had left behind. Now in his eightieth year, kindly George Millar still served, driven on by a secret he'd kept for fifty years, and compelled by conscience never to give up.

George straightened the frayed collar of his soft and comfortable shop coat, returned to the wooden counter and added freshly cut cheese to the contents of his customer's cotton shopping bag. 'There you go, young Andrew, you'll not be short of something for tea now and just the job for a snack after a call out. Has the boat been busy lately?'

Andrew, with his several years' experience at sea, was second coxswain for the village's all-weather lifeboat. It was a job he loved dearly and, like many of his forebears, always felt he was born to it. 'No, nothing much happened this week, Mr. Millar, just a shout to surfers who were taken along the shore by the rip tide. Just as well that it's quiet too, this being early March, the skipper is away for a week's training in Dorset, possibly a new boat coming our way later in the year is my guess. Mind you, the weather forecast is not good for later today. Rapidly strengthening winds with a cold front from the east they say, that'll keep the surfers on shore, even the wild ones.'

'And indoors in some nice warm hostelry no doubt,' smiled the affable old shopkeeper, 'and who could blame them?' Then his face darkened, and the smile disappeared, 'Of course, I knew your grandfather Robert well. A dreadfully sad day it was when we lost him. He was a first-rate coxswain and a good man truly. When the alarm beckoned him to sea for some poor soul in need, you never found him wanting, he wouldn't give up until he found them you know. Might be what cost him so dear in the end.' George was staring intently at an empty space in the shop as though looking in disbelief at a wild but empty ocean, to this day still looking frantically for some sign of a life that was already long extinguished. 'It was a day much like this one Andrew, I tell you, just like this one.' George Millar often repeated his sad tale, forgetting he'd told it so many times before. From that day on, he'd lived racked with a sense of guilt and a haunting memory from which this old man seemed never to be free.

Andrew always humoured him, never letting on. They all knew how George Millar had punished himself all these years, 'I don't remember him, Mr. Millar, I'm sad to say he died before I was old enough. Dad has told me many a tale of his exploits though, so I feel that I do know him. We have a few photographs of course and I almost see him before me when dad tells his stories. I suppose his tales are born of truth, duty and tragedy and as such, they'll always carry something of the spirit with them, something undying. They're stories that will live forever.'

Both stood humbly quiet for a minute or more, their shared silence suddenly broken by a rapid bleeping. Instinctively Andrew slipped the pager from his belt and read the message. . . it simply said, 'launch all-weather boat.'

'Must go Mr. Millar, we've got a shout, keep my groceries for me, see you later,' and with that, the old shop door rattled closed and he was gone.

'Stay safe boy, stay safe,' muttered George. He knew only too well what might be waiting for his brave friends in the gathering storm. A gust of wind beat at his shop door. George Millar sighed. Picking up the bag to place it in the fridge, he muttered to himself, 'A day just like this, just like this.'

Andrew was not first to arrive at the lifeboat station, the mechanic was already there and dressed. Engine running, the tractor was parked on the slipway with the transfer boat waiting on its trailer.

'Local boat called it in Andrew, it's the *Anne-Clare,* crew of three, one man overboard, half mile off the west point of Anchor Rocks, they have fishing gear out and retrieving it now,' he shouted, pointing to a sheet of paper he held out towards Andrew.

Andrew lifted a hand in silent acknowledgement and entered the locker room to collect his dry suit and life jacket. 'Fishing gear out,' he thought, 'that'll slow them down, no wonder they've called for us.'

Andrew knew Mark the skipper of the *Anne-Clare* quite well, they'd been to school together and some of Mark's family had also served on the village's earlier lifeboats, *Princess Dauntless* and the *Jocelyn.* It was a sad *Princess Dauntless* that had slunk home from the sea without his grandfather all those years before.

Andrew shook himself out of such thoughts and called for a crew of six from the rapidly gathering volunteers. Integrity and a common purpose overriding any personal desires or fears, it was not long before the chosen few were afloat and motoring out in the transfer boat to the deep-water channel. There, like a straining dog on a leash, the Tamar-class lifeboat rocked impatiently in the waves as though eager to be slipped from her mooring.

They faced a spring tide, running strong and rising fast at nearly half flood. Conditions that meant the ocean currents around Anchor Rocks would be even more dangerous than usual. They were going to have to hurry, the weather would undoubtedly worsen.

By the time the crew were pulling themselves aboard the lifeboat, the bustling cloud had already thickened overhead, and a cold wind sprang up from the east, a woeful harbinger of rain. As the crew hurried efficiently about their various tasks, the boat's great diesel engines roared into life like a rudely awakened giant. As it was untied and readied to return to the slipway and safety, the impatient transfer boat bumped roughly against the lifeboat's deep blue hull. Even in the estuary there was a rapidly rising swell.

'Shore boat's away, Cox,' called the deck crew as the navigator took his place and prepared his sea charts for the journey.

'Standby to let go mooring!' Andrew eased the throttles forward to slacken the shackle tension.

'Free for'ard,' came the snappy reply above the strengthening wind. As the boat cleared the buoy and started out along the estuary, the mechanic busied himself with the radio. 'Coastguard, coastguard, coastguard, this is lifeboat *Dauntless II,* crew of six, now at sea and mobile to man overboard, fishing vessel *Anne-Clare,* Anchor Rocks, over.'

It was a five-mile run to the incident, a tough five miles that first took them out into the bay and then North to the rocky promontory called Anchor Point. An Atlantic ground swell added to wave heights, peaking around ten feet or more, limiting their speed to about fifteen knots. Maybe a twenty- or thirty-minute journey and every one of them a living hell for their friend lost at sea.

'*Anne-Clare, Anne-Clare, Anne-Clare,* this is the lifeboat, *Dauntless II,* at sea and on course for your last position, are you receiving, over?'

Meanwhile, the lifeboat left the relative calm of the estuary and began to hit the open sea beyond the sand bar. Andrew steered a course with port bow to the waves, it might lessen the crew's discomfort. Visibility was reduced by spray that topped the waves like the flowing manes of the sea's wild white horses. Wind beating against tide created over-falls and spindrift on the crests of deep green waves. A translucent deep green, a beautiful captivating colour that enticed, and commanded attention. Then came the eagerly awaited reply. '*Dauntless II, Dauntless II, Dauntless II,* this is the fishing vessel *Anne-Clare,* good to hear your voice. We have our fishing gear all aboard now, visibility poor and worsening. Bob Harkness went overboard about fifteen minutes ago. The only good news is that he was wearing foul-weather gear and lifejacket at the time. With only two of us left on board we are unable to search for him with any degree of safety.'

Most of the lifeboat crew knew Bob Harkness; a likeable young man with a family and many friends in the local community. Andrew spoke resolutely and quietly to his mechanic and navigator, 'Find his exact position now, then see what the current might have done with young Bob since their first call. Let Mark know, we won't let him down, soon be there, then his keen eyes were back on the green and white of a wild and growing sea that stretched away into an uncertain future.

Meanwhile, old George Millar looked pensively out of his shop window at the changing sky, 'Just like today,' he mumbled, his thoughts far away. Head down and shuffling his weary feet slowly across the seemingly rolling floorboards, it might as well have been yesterday, it was all so clear to him. He leant forward to press his hands on the counter edge just as forty years before he'd pressed them on the storm-soaked rail of the *Princess Dauntless.* 'Some fool in a cabin cruiser – no right to be out there! Damn the idiot!' He paused from his brief anger and was aware of being back in his shop, the wind rattling the door as if to wake him from his recurring nightmare. But he was soon at sea again, raging green waves with spindrift that conspired to rob any lost souls of rescue. Eventually, they had come across the hapless small boat by sheer luck. She was starting to founder, rolling more and more, deeper and deeper. To all the crew, brave indeed as they were, it looked a certain lost cause. But Robert, their coxswain would have none of it, resolute he was, he would never give up, never. Neither could he bring himself to ask anyone to do what he wouldn't do himself. 'George,' he'd said, 'here, take the helm.' With George now at the controls, Robert made his way to the rail and, with an almost beyond human effort, boarded the stricken vessel. For a moment the crew saw his intense eyes and keen hands earnestly searching for any sign of life. Then suddenly that silly damned boat rolled hard on a wave and capsized. Not long after that, she slid bow first deep from sight.

George was overwhelmed by the haunting memories he'd carried alone for too many years, aware that he must finally tell what he knew, someone must hear his tale. 'Oh, we searched, and we searched for our beloved coxswain until fuel and us was near exhausted. I swear on my life I saw him once, in a deep, fleeting trough, still wearing his sou'wester and high enough in the water to see his life vest. Oh, I shouted and pointed but it was only I could see him. He was waving us away - gesturing for us to leave him in that watery hell and go home. I'll never know the truth of it. His image haunts me to this day, a day just like this.

Some there were that praised him for his bravery and some there were that cursed him for the very same, leaving us like he did. His body was never found and to this day the sea still has him. Our dear Robert is still out there somewhere.'

Putting on his coat and hat, George Millar left the shop, locked the door and slowly made his way to a place he once knew so well, the lifeboat station by the old quayside. He tucked in his scarf, turned up his collar and wiped a tear from his eye with a worn sleeve. How could he ever forget?

*

'There she is, off the port bow!' Came the lookout's cry as the *Anne-Clare* came into sight. Andrew was decisive, 'Radio to Mark to hold his course and speed steady, we're coming close alongside, make ready the crew to move up to the flying bridge.' At the same time, he dropped a few revolutions off the powerful engines and deftly brought *Dauntless II* around to run parallel and on the windward side of the rolling fishing vessel. They were close enough to shout across and gather useful information, enough to initiate a search pattern that gave them at least some small prospect of locating the lost fisherman.

High up from the lifeboat's flying bridge, all eyes scanned the chaos of a boiling sea. All were eager and ready to shout and point the moment they found young Bob.

Motoring on above an insatiable deep, the valiant crew's rescue boat pitched and rolled steeply on a wild sea of deep green. It was as though Neptune himself was vigorously shaking his cloak. At fifteen minutes gone, the navigator voiced grave concerns, 'Look, Andrew, we've near enough completed the official search pattern and we're edging closer all the while to the submerged rocks off the Point. As we have wind over tide, I think the current may have taken him closer to shore, but the wind will have moved the *Anne-Clare* relatively further out to sea. We won't have much time.'

With time and tide in a deadly race against them, Andrew decided on a couple of sweeps closer inshore and nearer the treacherous submerged rocks off the Point, then failing that, they would be obliged to repeat the already unsuccessful standard search pattern.

It was not going well at all. Visibility was already appalling. Nothing found inshore, they began to motor seawards again, when suddenly, Andrew caught a glimpse of someone in the water, he began to shout, 'We have him!' but went deathly quiet when he realised this was not their friend Bob. No, this man was older, wearing clothing from a bye-gone age . . . and, under an old sou'wester, his face shared a knowing smile. The old man in the water was pointing insistently and resolutely towards the next wave. Then he was gone. Andrew said nothing about his vision to the crew. Regardless of the cold logic that would have ignored the apparition's instruction, his soul made him look where he'd been told. Sure enough, as they crested the next wave, there in the trough was the lost fisherman. The shout went up in preparation to gather him safely on board.

Poor Bob Harkness had been in the water for what seemed to him an eternity. Spray stinging his face, fingers numbed to useless, cold biting deep into the bones of his body - he did not expect to survive. He knew any chance of being found in such a chaotic sea was against all the odds, it was a risk they all accepted when they took such work. Pulling his knees up to conserve what little heat he had left, alone and afraid, he waited for the end to come. His heart had already sunk nearly an hour before, when he'd tumbled overboard, watching helplessly as the *Anne-Clare* motored away into the waves without him. Now, finally he'd succumbed to a strange quietness - just waiting for the deep to swallow him up.

Bob was completely unaware of the lifeboat's presence and its gentle, beam-on approach from behind him. That is, until he thought he heard, 'Come on dopey, we haven't got all day you know.' To begin with he ignored the voice, for earlier he thought he'd already seen and heard things out there, sharing with him the nearby sea. Somewhat unnerving it was. As his body sank into another wave trough, something told him he was not alone. Like an old friend's voice calling to him on the wind. Then the voice came again, only louder, 'Oi! Don't you want a lift home then Bob? You'll go all wrinkly if you stay out here much longer!'

A shivering Bob flailed his cold, tired arms and legs weakly to turn around. Thank you, God, he was saved. Smiling friendly faces, arms reaching out, and the rescue sling already in the water for him, saved. Tonight, he would dine with his wife and children about him and not with Davy Jones. Soon, secure on board and being treated for exposure, he smiled thankfully as he could feel the powerful diesel

engines carrying them like a caring father would his small child, safely away from danger.
Still on emergency channel 16, the mechanic radioed their success to the coastguard and conveyed a welcome message to the fishing vessel.
Dauntless II, now making way with the tide, managed an easy seventeen knots. They were all going home; every single one of them.
Even as they moored *Dauntless II* to the deep channel buoy, the shore boat was alongside. Bob Harkness would be taken away first to a waiting ambulance and despite his emotional protestations, attend the County Hospital for the mandatory checkup.
After closing down, checking fuel and securing the lifeboat, Andrew and his brave volunteers were also ferried ashore.
As he walked into the station, the first man Andrew met was old George Millar, 'Hi Mr. Millar, what brings you down here? You brought my groceries?'
'I had to come. It was a day just like this when we lost your grandfather. I never told anyone before,' he said gesturing Andrew away to one side for privacy, 'but I thought I saw him in the water that day you know, waving us away, I can still see him now, like as though he'll pop into my shop any day... He was never one to give up, and yet we came home safe without him, we left him behind, we lost him to the deep.'
'Never you mind Mr. Millar, you're a special man yourself, we all think we see things in the sea, in fact I believe I saw him myself today. He showed me where to find our Bob

Harkness when all seemed lost for certain. Funny, he looked just like my dad described, had a smile on his face too he did. He never did give up, did he? Perhaps his spirit is still out there looking for souls to save.' Andrew touched the old man's shoulder gently with a strong hand, 'Best we tell no one else though, eh Mr. Millar, best we keep it to ourselves, or else they'll be locking us both up! I'll get out of this wet gear and walk back with you to the shop, collect my tea things.'

At last our old friend George finally understood the truth of the apparition he saw that fateful day so long ago. One lost soul was grief enough for the village to bare but an entire crew lost on a fool's errand would be a pointless tragedy. Robert's resolute and abiding spirit had urged George to take the crew safe home, to live, and serve again.

At long last George Millar's own soul could once more rest in peace.

He smiled and knew, 'There'll never be another day like this, no, never like this one.'

Everybody out!

A disused military base,
somewhere in the United States about 1964

'So, it wouldn't matter if we set fire to it as well then?'
'No Robert, the entire range of buildings need demolishing anyway. It's a derelict and the military want it cleared by next year. Like you suggest, it would make an ideal venue for a firefighting exercise. Then simply leave it to burn afterwards. That'll greatly reduce our clearance costs.' Daniel O'Holland the local airfield commandant, slapped the palm of his hand conclusively on his desk and smiled across at the elderly but highly enthusiastic fire fighter before him. 'I'll arrange for you to have security clearance to inspect the building. Come up with a plan and a date and let me know. I'll even ask what's left of the airfield crew if they'd care to join you.'
The building was ideal for training, real training, none of that namby-pamby synthetic smoke. The genuine article, something the fire crews could truly learn from and probably talk about for the rest of their lives.
As our kindly Robert Nelson thoughtfully surveyed the mostly timber structure, he took note of the two mezzanine floors and the maze of corridors with side rooms of different sizes. Perfect! Many windows were boarded up, making the rooms dark. Even better! There were four or five access doors from the airfield side but all those near the perimeter fence appeared to have been nailed shut, probably to deter trespassers. Robert marked on his plans where he would place the fire cribs and considered that he might light them sequentially to create a developing fire situation. that would make the attending crews think dynamically. . . and work hard.

Preparations went well, and on the day, Robert had three pumping companies, two ladder units and a heavy rescue vehicle lined up at the airfield entrance. To maximise the benefits to service personnel, several extra crew from the stations had made their way by private cars. The command post was to be with the incoming local captain at his own vehicle, where he would be overseen by an area chief, only there as an observer.

This was a big day for Robert, if anything, the crowning glory of all his years in the fire service. He lit the first crib and waited. Oh, so slowly to begin with, the paper and wooden pallets began to take hold, then faster and faster. Fire can accelerate at an amazing speed and easily catch people unawares . . . and it often did. As the flames began to lick the ceiling and the smoke drop down the walls to partly hide the doors, Robert stepped out, picked his way down the corridor, and made the first radio call from his car. Now it was all up to them. As the sound of engines and sirens broke the airfield silence, Robert returned, ready to light more cribs. The great plan was afoot.

On arrival, the captain allocated two entry points one each for a pump crew and kept the third back for water supplies. Crews from the ladder units were also set to work on running hose and securing water to the firefighting pumps. Four men, all wearing compressed air breathing apparatus, would be sent into each of the two selected entry points, two at the front to locate the fires and extinguish them, backed up by the two others who worked separately to help lift the heavy charged hose around corners and deeper into the building. It wasn't long before the first fire was located, found more by feeling the heat than seeing, they hit the base of the fire with the jet and immediately felt a hot blanket of steam push through their clothing to their skin. 'Down, down,' the branch man screamed. They both hit the floor and thanked god the steam did not follow them. Lying low, with hot gases escaping over their heads, they hit the fire again. 'Something's not right . . . the fire should be out, it's only a crib with pallets.' Their second mistake . . . for the building was now on fire; the ceiling had been breached and fire was rapidly spreading unseen throughout the roof void. Heavy smoke was now pouring out of the eaves and soffits at the front of the building. Clearly now, the roof needed ventilating before a flashover could occur. The delayed ladder crews were quickly withdrawn from water duties and instructed to axe-cut holes in the roof to release smoke and heat. Water supplies were already a serious problem, as airfield requirements had eased, the mains pressure had been reduced or at some hydrants been disconnected all together. Everybody was working like the devil. . . they had friends inside that inferno. Lives were at risk and it was a game no more.

Inside the building, conditions were deteriorating fast, the first crew we followed in our story, were now cut off by the fire, which had dropped down with a collapsed ceiling into their escape corridor, the hose was burned through, cutting off their own supply and severely reducing pressure to the other crew of four. The second crew heard the stifled shouts for help and two of them left their hose to go and assist. The two remaining were then forced by surrounding flames to abandon their worthless hose and follow it along and back to their entry point, where they joined the chaos outside, as men ran hither and thither, fetching and carrying, calling for help. The six left inside, were breathing heavily and keeping low, their air would not last for ever and worse still they could see flecks of flame appearing in the black smoke that rolled along the corridor ceiling towards them. 'This way.' 'No, this way.' 'The back exits are locked, this way to the front.' So came their muffled shouts as the roar of the fire conspired to deafen them.

Confusion reigned, with no hose to follow to safety, they argued angrily with each other at a junction in the main corridor. It was essential they escaped now or for sure they would die a horrible death in there. Panic set in, and, despite their training, they split up, four went one way and two another.

Outside, the area chief was as shocked as anyone else at the speed and severity of the fire. He had taken over command and called for assistance and ambulances as a matter of urgency. They were joined by three military officers who had knowledge of the building layout. They began to send small teams in with hoses, positioned just inside the doorways to try and preserve a rescue path for their colleagues inside. They could only hope, lack of breathing apparatus and fire severity had robbed them of all chance of a rescue party.

At last, at the far end of the building our two weary but thankful firefighters burst out into the daylight, immediately pulling off their face masks and gulping down cool fresh air. Having had only a brief respite they walked amongst the spaghetti of hoses and running men, to the command post. There they hoped to meet up with their colleagues.

They were nowhere to be seen.

The building was becoming an inferno, hot gases ready to explode into flame, the ladder crews had been forced to abandon the roof as being far too dangerous, parts of it in imminent collapse. Through the holes they had made, smoke and flame vented under great pressure, the rising plume of black smoke clearly visible for miles.

He had seen enough, 'Everybody out!' screamed the commander, 'everybody out!'

Spurred on by the evacuation signal of deafening whistle blasts, crews withdrew from the doorways and were quickly beaten away from the building by the intensity. Radiated heat was igniting anything in its reach, even exposed hair on the firefighter's heads. Suddenly, one by one, the lost hose crew appeared, stumbling, and crouched as if drunk, trying to move away from the middle doorway as a burning ceiling fell and followed them outside. Immediately half a dozen brave souls ran forward, shielding their heads with their hands, to grab their colleagues and half drag them to safety. Once on the sheltered side of one of the pumping engines, they sat down and removed their face masks, the air in their cylinders almost down to the last gasp.
The fireground commander was relieved beyond belief but now must mitigate any more damage. 'Appliances and crews to be moved to safety and a roll call carried out. Nothing we can do here anymore, let the blasted place burn.'

Sometime later, 'Roll call carried out sir, all personnel accounted for and all equipment made up ... apart from what we lost inside sir.'
'Yes, yes, well done, it could have been a lot worse. We have all learned a valuable lesson today. I can see we must change our procedures; we must know who is in and who is out. we cannot let this happen again. Oh, by the way, tell me, whose car is that, still left over there by the perimeter fence?'
'Oh, that's our old station Captain, Robert Nelson's motor, sir. It was already there when we first arrived.'

Based on a true and tragic event.

**

The Maroon

A lifeboat adventure story.

Some few years past now and a cold mid-December; 'twas a deathly dark and stormy night; a heavy fist thumped hard on the coxswain's cottage door; and thumped again, and thumped again, though almost drowned out by clattering rain, howling wind, the roaring sea, and a roll of thunder.

The coxswain, well respected in the village and popularly known as 'old Bob', was not a man to dilly dally, and in his heart of hearts he'd had a feeling this would happen. His door soon opened, spilling light into the foreboding gloom and there it fell on the rain drenched faces of two … no … three men.

No need to ask what was wanted, their presence said it all; the nearest, an old fisherman called Dave, gasping for breath shouted, 'Yacht … big one… off sand bar ….. looks like she's in … big trouble…!'

Without a word spoken, old Bob threw on his big coat, pulled the door closed behind him and all four hurried along the narrow, cobbled street into the enveloping darkness and towards the lifeboat station. No words exchanged, but many a thought ran through their minds, 'tide's in', 'wind's nor easterly, off the sea', 'will we get a crew?' 'Can we launch in this messy sea?' 'Whose is she?' 'what the hell's she doing out there in this storm?'

A stabbing flash of lightning reflected brightly off the rain lashed cobbles and lit up an old stray dog cowering in the half shelter of some cottage steps. The village seemed deserted, windows closed and shuttered against the relentless rain.

They were soon at the station; breathless, they went about their tasks in silence, each knew what they must do. Lights flickered on all over the station, the radio crackled into life, and the coxswain went to look at the slipway – now almost hidden by crashing waves. 'Not enough crew', he shouted, 'get a maroon off!', and under his breath muttered, 'and God help us too'. He'd never seen such a raging sea this side of the sand bar before.

He knew his duty, as had his late father, he must try and save the terrified souls on the stricken yacht, but as the mighty thud of the maroon shaking the night sky awoke the village, he knew he could soon be sending men, good men, to their deaths.

Three long, agonising, minutes passed by before crew started to arrive; the first to run in through the now open station doors had more bad news, 'Sid, the mechanic, not coming ... I saw him .... He's slipped and done his shoulder ....Damnation, what a night!'

With the odd tweak of their waterproofs to make them comfortable, if that could ever be possible, they gathered at the stern of their stalwart old lifeboat.

'Right lads', shouted the coxswain, 'I don't need to tell you what this storm means to those who are out in it, but I'm not picking the crew tonight; Volunteers only this trip.'

To a man they all stepped forward. Old Bob knew they must be afeared, for so was he, only an idiot would have no fear of a cruel raging sea like tonight's. He felt immense pride in his comrades, but this was a time for clear thinking, not emotion.

Old Bob stepped forward and placing a strong hand on one man's shoulder he said, 'not you lad, not you ... you stay at station ... look after everything for our return'.

The man, father of three young boys, was filled with guilt that he was not to go, but knew the coxswain's word was law, and how happy his wife would be that he had not gone to sea – like any of the crew's families would have been, that night of all nights.

Six men manned the lifeboat that fateful night and all six doubted that they'd see the morrow as the aptly named '*Princess Dauntless*' ran down the slip just as fast as a big wave came in to meet her.

It was one mighty breath-taking crash, every one lurched forward, there'd be a few bruises later if they survived, the wave seemed to swallow the boat whole. The Coxswain gunned the powerful diesel engines …. He must clear the slip and surrounding rocks before the next wave hit and pushed them back.

They were away, ….. but only God knew how they would ever return.

The young family man, spared by old Bob, was joined by four or five others who had braved the storm. A storm which was now occasionally hurling swathes of hand numbing sleet at the village; temperatures were tumbling. The volunteers left at station busied themselves, there would be little sleep that night, wet clothes went to the drying room, floors were mopped, doors closed and VHF radio set on the emergency coast guard channel. Someone put the big kettle on the gas and set some chunky white mugs out on the table … extra mugs were lined up for the returning crew.

How long those mugs were to sit there waiting, no one could ever tell…. They were lined up in view of the sea through the upstairs window as if waiting, if mugs had feelings they waited with patience and hope.

While the base crew were warm and safe in a station that was built strong to withstand a storm of the century, the lifeboat crew and their boat were taking a beating from breaking waves as they closed on the sand bar, they were truly in a storm of the century, a cutting wind drove sleet and heavy sea spray into the strained faces of the deck crew as they struggled to see any sign of the stricken yacht or its crew.

'No sign skip, no sign yet', shouted one of the crew above the noisy roar of the sea, the howl of the wind and the racing diesel engines.

Without turning from his task of steering a safe path through the boiling sea the Coxswain replied, 'If she's here, we must be close ... back on deck ...... and for God's sake hang on!'

Often on a trip out to an incident the crew would have time to reflect on life and chat to each other – not so this time – every breath, every heartbeat, every cell of their bodies was focussed on each and every eventful moment as it came rushing from nowhere and raced by them, as did the sea, into a darkening past. The next moment could be their last – they were in the firm grip of a merciless storm.

In the cabin, the coxswain's second in command wrestled with compass, charts and clock as he desperately tried to keep track of position. While still too much dark cold sea washed over the decks the coxswain also wrestled, not only with the wheel trying to read the waves, but he wrestled with his conscience. Old Bob felt for the deck-hands, and allowed himself a moment to wonder if he'd made the right decision. They were all facing death out there and still no sign of the stricken vessel; had she sunk? Was she even really out there? How much longer could they stand this punishment? How would they communicate – coastguard had confirmed this yacht had no radio.

Then, just as they crested a wave, there, in the trough, lit up by the powerful search lights from the lifeboat, there she was; About a forty-footer, sails tattered and with lines and rigging not only strewn on deck but trailing into the sea; No lights showing, no sign of life, the powerful floods and search lights from *'Princess Dauntless'* scoured every visible inch of the heaving yacht – nothing.

With one eye on the moving sea and the other on the tortured yacht, old Bob came alongside as close as he dared;

tough as it was their lifeboat could still be damaged and debris in the water choke her engines; no other boats covered this area and with air-sea rescue helicopters grounded – any rescue was up to them – just a handful of men and their 'dauntless' vessel.

'No sign of life – no response', shouts a crew member through the open cabin door.

'Damn, damn, damn,' thought the coxswain, 'as if it wasn't bad enough'. It was one thing to risk life to save life but here they could risk all to find no one on board. Finding a body in this maelstrom of a sea would be without hope or sense, they would be lost for sure. 'Damn, damn, damn', he thought, and while he fought the sea from the wheel, he called most of the crew to the inboard cabin, leaving only the searchlight crew up top.

As they gathered, soaked, tired and battered, the Coxswain, always tenacious to the last, said, 'One last chance lads, one last chance .... we'll board her, search her, and if no luck we'll head up coast and look for shelter. ...... You know I don't like asking you, but we need a volunteer, we need someone agile, young and strong.'

They all, to a man, turned to look at Dave's son, Jim, no doubt the strongest among them. Jim sensed there was no escape from this, better to volunteer, that's after all what they did; put their lives on the line to protect others from the perils of the sea. 'What's the plan? I'll go,' Jim said, clearly and calmly. A couple of good slaps on the back from the crew and the Coxswain explained, 'Be on the port beam, I'll come alongside her from above as we drop down a trough, ... you'll not have long but you should be able to drop on to her deck. As soon as you've gone, I'll pull away and hold off. We'll pick you up the same way, but we'll come in beneath the yacht and on our starboard side. We'll watch for you all the time; the sea shall not have you. A couple of you go with him to help safely clear the rail. If it looks impossible ... well ...' his voice trailed off, there was nothing left to say really.

As the coxswain began to ease the lifeboat into position, he caught a glimpse of the boarding crew through the port side window, they struggled for balance on the heaving deck and were buffeted by the wind, but he could see they were ready and clipped to their safety lines. At last, the right sort of wave came along, fairly clean it was and big, and, like toys moved by a child's hand, he put *'Princess Dauntless'* alongside with but a foot between them. He saw Jim launch himself beyond the safety rail and then could see no more, with a deft touch he pulled away from the stricken vessel. There was a thumbs up from the deck crew and he knew Jim had made it. The deck crew watched intently as Jim gamely fought his way to the rear hatch of the listing yacht, twice he disappeared from sight, the tension unbearable, and then they could see his lamp moving about inside the cabin. A breaking wave nearly rolled the yacht right over, but she recovered, it seemed like forever, one wave came and then another, breaking more frequently now as they closed on more shallows. Another glimpse of the brave Jim at the fore cabin and then again, nothing. It seemed a lifetime was passing by and hope was fading, but suddenly Jim was up on deck signalling that the vessel was empty ... no one on board.

Now the struggle to get him back.

'Jim says it's all clear, and he wants to go home!' came the shout into the coxswain's ears. He took a moment to glance over his shoulder and with a smile shouted back, 'stand to then, and let's go fetch him.'

As Jim found a vantage point on the stricken yacht he breathed a sigh of relief ..... at last, he was out in the open air and not in a floating coffin where half the time he didn't know which way was up. He had stumbled and fell the length of the yacht, in places water up to his boots, in places up to his neck, there was no sign of life, but he'd looked for a body too; he had groped and floundered in the dark water for anything solid and come up with a number of cushions and clothing. He was glad he was out ..... 'now, where's my lift home,' he muttered through shivering lips.

The yacht teetered on the crest of a wave, rolled a little then started to drop down, beam on, ... his heart skipped a beat ... there in the surrounding darkness, a bright jewel of hope, there she was moving in below ... beautiful to see .... *'Princess Dauntless'*, with all deck lights bright and deck crew waving, Jim could see two comrades ready by the safety rail they had prepared. His comrades stood ready to catch him, come what may.

It was looking good, he prepared to jump, but the sea was not finished with him yet, just as Jim committed his body to that leap of faith, the crest of the wave had broken, dropping heavily on to the yacht; the yacht listed sharply away from the lifeboat and Jim missed his footing, his desperate fingers clawed at the lifeboat's safety line and his comrades were quickly on him with strong hands to draw him to safety. First, he felt their determined power as they began like giants to heave him on board... then he felt the sickening pain as the yacht rolled back and crushed one leg between the boats. The Coxswain heard the scream both in his ears and in his heart; a gap appeared between the boats and Jim's semi-conscious body was dragged unceremoniously into the cabin. The coxswain cleared the sinking yacht, called for a bearing for the estuary and fixed his eyes, body and soul on the sea ahead; he must get them home safely. An hour later, they were in calmer waters, on shore they were welcomed by the blue lights of a waiting ambulance. The crew did their best first aid but by the look of the leg it was not going to be a comfortable transfer.

'You'll be ok' ... ' see you at the station' .... 'see you in the pub,' came the farewells from the crew.
It was a good few months before Jim was back in the village, his dad drove him down to the station, but he wanted to walk in unaided. He limped into the familiar faces of all his comrades, picking up on some trivial banter on the way … 'Oy, Jim, when you gonna bring them waterproofs back?' …… … 'All right for some, we have to work for a living' … but there, sure enough, on the table was his mug ... 'come on', said the Coxswain, 'let's fill this up with something stronger than tea.' As Jim moved forward to pick up his mug, he saw next to it was a little blue box ... 'that's yours', shouted one of the crew. Jim picked it up, carefully he opened the hinged lid, and there nestling on velvet was a Silver medal, he read the words quietly to himself, it simply said *'For Gallantry'*.
Tea, banter and a little rum flowed, and they celebrated Jim's final return from that little adventure they had shared and endured; they were all back together, comrades all..
'**Quiet!**' shouted old Bob, the room went suddenly silent... the radio crackled yet again, ... 'Mayday, mayday ......this is ……..'

While good men live there'll be no end to this story …
Few have more courage than they.

**

HUMOUR

Christmas Dinner - The Invitation.

It seemed impolite, not to accept the old couple's invitation, to join them for Christmas dinner. Many years of living alone had made him resigned to doing his usual thing but for a change he thought he'd take up their kindly offer, despite only having met them at the bus stop the day before.

He arrived as requested, just before mid-day. The old man, Bert, opened the door to him and with a squint into the brightness of normal daylight, grudgingly accepted the chocolates and wine and stood to one side. He was met by a mixture of strange odours, the overriding one emanating from the kitchen was a distinct burnt smell.

'Come on through,' said Bert, 'keep the warmth in. We don't open our windows till May, last year it wasn't till June. No, keep yer shoes on . . . or her damn dog will 'ave 'em else.'

As his eyes slowly accustomed to the semi gloom he was glad he'd kept them on, the living room floor was littered with things the dog had encountered in the months and even years gone by. Bert used a stained, slippered foot to slide a full cat litter tray under a coffee table. 'Sit yerself down, make yerself comfortable, I'll go and tell herself you've arrived.'

He carefully chose the only chair that wasn't cluttered and sat down. He noted the décor, the like of which he'd not seen since his great uncle had passed away. As he heard a toilet flush somewhere in the house, a large, long haired and unkempt brown dog rushed into the room and shoved its wet nose straight into his groin. As he struggled to push the excited animal away, herself came into the room holding out a wet hand to shake his.

'Bert,' she scolded, 'you should have told him not to sit there.' As he stood from the chair, his backside felt a little damp. Herself continued, 'his damn cat wet itself there yesterday.' She brushed her hand over the now warm dampness, 'not to worry, nearly dry now. Come on through, sit at the table.'

'Bert! For God's sake, don't let the dog do that, it's disgusting at dinner time.'

He was beginning to regret coming, life was better at home, still, perhaps the dinner would be good, I mean they couldn't have reached that age on bad food. 'You're worrying over nothing,' he told himself as he squeezed by the dog that had now transferred its full attention to twenty quid's worth of M&S chocolates which it eagerly bolted down, complete with wrappers.

What a relief, he needn't have worried, the table was set with bright clean cutlery and crockery. 'I bet they have a dish washer out back,' he thought, thinking further that it was an appliance he had long admired though never bought.

'You sit yourself at the head of the table dear . . . Bert! Throw that damn cat out into the garden.' Herself's tone softened and continued, 'I've already had to change the menu once today, the blessed thing mauled and gummed about the chicken breast I'd taken out of the freezer, try as I might, just couldn't save it I'm afraid . . . we've got sausages now. I take it you like sausages?'

Well, this was going to be one novel Christmas dinner, one he'd never dreamed of and nor likely would anyone else.

'Yes, sausages will be fine, are they beef or pork?' he enquired, in as matter of fact tone as he could muster.
'Neither I think,' herself replied, brushing something indescribable off of her apron, 'we got a job lot off a traveller last year, he said they were venison. Could be or could be rabbit or perhaps even cat . . .' She laughed. 'Pity they didn't take Bert's old Fluffy at the same time.'
Candles lit in the table centre added a festive feel to the place, as well as a little warmth and were a welcome insurance against darkness should the electricity meter run out.
It was quite a posh set up with the food in large bowls from which you served yourself. 'Don't be shy, get stuck in,' she said, slapping Bert's hand, 'let the gentleman go first, you wait your turn.'
Carefully, trying to take from the middles, he selected small portions of what transpired to be margarine and turnip mash, last year's de-frozen Brussels sprouts, a dark green cabbage with the most un-chewable leaves he'd ever encountered and some small roasted potatoes, which actually seemed the best bet there, so he took extras. Bert smiled with pride as he watched his guest load up on roast potatoes, he'd dug them himself. Free they were, growing wild down by the sewage outfall. Must have been dumped at some time then self-propagated from then on. Easy to dig they were too.
Herself lifted the lid on an old, enamelled casserole dish to expose several burnt sausages. 'They're nice and well cooked, you can never be too careful with sausages I say,' she put three on his plate, three for Bert and two for herself, saving one for the dog later. 'I told Bert to put them in the fridge but thick that he is, he left them out in a warm kitchen overnight. . . I knew I should have done it myself.' She concluded her verbal assassination with a sigh.

As he ate those bits he'd chosen for his plate and that looked almost edible and hacked the burnt crust off the curious tasting sausages, he felt his right foot becoming wet. His first thought was the cat had somehow sneaked back in but looking down, saw that it was the half retching dog, an excess of anticipatory drool flowing steadily from open, chocolate covered jaws onto his socks and best suede shoes. As he thought deeply about the foolishness of accepting this invite, he was shaken out of his mindful solitude by herself saying loudly, 'Eat up, there's plenty more, and I've made my own Christmas pudding, Bert even found some loose change in his pocket to put in there, so if you are lucky you could be going home with more than you came with.'

He felt his tummy rumble and watched as a large flea performed a double somersault on the way from dog to damp sock. 'Yes,' he thought, 'I'm sure you are right there.'

He looked at his watch and with pretence shock, yelled, 'Oh dear, I'm so sorry, is that the time, I just remembered I have to be home for a very important phone call. I'm sorry to dash off - it was really nice, thank you.'

'Would you like me to make up a doggy bag for your tea?' Herself asked kindly.

When he graciously declined, she scraped the remaining bits of sausage onto Bert's plate and then placed it on the floor in front of an apparently ravenous brown dog, which in turn was probably feeding a couple of well-established tape worms. As he stood in the doorway he watched in stunned silence as herself picked up the now spotlessly clean plate from the floor and placed it back on the table. 'There,' she said, 'clean as a whistle and did you know, a dog's saliva is antibacterial. Almost better than a dishwasher Bert says . . and a lot cheaper.'

As he waved his goodbyes to an already closing door he wondered if the doctor's surgery might be running an emergency service, now all he had to do was make it back home and find out.

Happy Christmas, and by the way, what are you doing for dinner?

**

The loaned caravan.

The Ponsonbys were affable people. Kind to strangers, they were a family for all seasons, attuned to nurturing the best of humanity. They were steady in their outlook and clear in their resolve. They decided to lend their superb, state-of-the-art, caravan, a Maximus Excelsior Deluxe, complete with high end model Range Rover, to the unemployed Smith family down the road. Tom 'typhoid' Smith and his family were over the moon and appeared extremely pleased with the offer.

Exactly a week later, the vehicle and caravan were returned, timely, just as promised and parked on the Ponsonby's grand driveway. A note left on the cracked windscreen, thanked them for such a great time. Apparently, they had taken the opportunity to tour the country's traveller sites looking for Tom's relatives.

The Ponsonbys examined their pride and joy in horror, a dead squirrel was jammed in the radiator grill, just next to some graffiti which said, 'get off the road tosser.' Though the cupboards were empty, the toilet was full, and the body of a badger was wedged in the wheel arch on the near side. The

bin was full of rabbit skins and one of the best saucepans containing a mouldering chicken carcass. Graffiti seemed to be a family hobby and poorly developed art form as the limit seemed to be, 'Smiths woz here!'
As the Ponsonbys walked back to the house, heads down in despair, they failed to notice that the wheels on the Range Rover had been exchanged for some old worn-out ones– nor did they notice the police van across the road checking out a vehicle seen leaving the scene of several burglaries.

The Ponsonbys remained affable – their psychotherapist said it was best that way.

**

The Hitchhiker

Pete hadn't planned on driving far but was certainly going to make the most of a dry sunny day and the pleasurable smooth running of this immaculate classic BMW.
'What a car,' he thought as he settled comfortably into the white leather upholstery and listened to the alluring purr of the three-litre engine at a steady thirty miles per hour, 'absolute luxury.' His eyes keenly surveyed the interior at all the switches, buttons, lights and screens that only God and BMW knew were for.
Suddenly his peripheral vision glimpsed movement in front and Pete instinctively hammered on the brakes, coming to a halt only a breath away from sending some old lady to Valhalla.
Pete pressed the button that opened a window so as to apologise but it was too late, she had already pulled the door open and thrown her walking stick and handbag into the

seat well and climbed in after them. 'Thank you young man for stopping, I've been thumbing a lift for ages.'
There didn't seem much Pete could do or say about it now and after all, he owed her something after nearly running her over.
'You need to put your seat belt on.'
'Eh? What's that dear?' she squinted quizzically in his direction.
'Seatbelt!' He shouted, flexing his own to show what he meant.
'Damned new-fangled thing that, how do you work it?' she asked.
Pete leaned across, took the belt and clipped it in place, noticing as he did so that his new passenger smelled of a mixture of peppermint and urine. Still, she wouldn't be in the car for long, what damage could she possibly do?
'Where to then?' Pete enquired.
'Taunton,' came the reply, 'I'm trying to catch my grandson, he's taking our dog to the vet.'
'Taunton?!' Pete looked at his watch then the fuel gauge and back again, both were warning him he'd be on the limits of his ability. Still, if he got on with it, the BMW was a fast car, and he could just make it back to Bideford in time. He'd just have been away longer than expected . . . that's all.
A short while later and after a few miles with windows open and speeding as fast as he dare, the old lady pointed and screamed, 'there he is, there he is, my grandson with our dog Satan. Oh quick, toot! toot! and stop for him.' Then turning towards Pete with her false teeth loose and a modicum of spittle spray, 'He must have missed the bus, or spent the fare in the bookies. He's a naughty boy that Nathan.'
It was quickly becoming a bad day for Pete, but he felt the guilt of obligation to help this trio of helpless souls, one he'd nearly run over, another a penniless addict and the last, a

sick and innocent animal. If he didn't stop, it would look like he was abducting the old lady against her wishes and he was already in enough trouble as it was.

Pete drew the gleaming BMW alongside the boy, who seemed to be an inebriated twenty-fivish thug, and his dog, a large white boxer come mongrel beast, which seemed quite reluctant to be with the boy at all.

'Watcha Gran,' slurred Nathan, using his boot to push the door wide open to the limit of its hinges, throwing Satan on to the back seat and joining him. Safety pins and zips on his jeans noisily scoring the white leather in a most unsightly way.

As Pete now proceeded with even greater hurry towards Taunton, he noticed in the rear-view mirror Nathan emptying his pockets, obviously in search of something urgent. Among the debris were some scraps of paper, betting slips no doubt, a well-used filthy looking cloth, a switch blade and some small plastic bags containing white powder, one of which Satan promptly swallowed without it even touching the sides. Satan's spontaneous eating habits earned him a hefty smack on the head and an earful of choice expletives, some of which Pete had never heard before. It seemed obvious to Pete where the bus fare had gone . . . and no doubt any vet's fee too.

Pete thought to be sociable and asked, 'What's wrong with the dog? Looks fine to me.'

'Na mate, poxy thing has the runs all the time and when not doing that spends its time throwing up. We reckon it's 'cos of what he finds to eat when we let him out at night.'

Satan, by now feeling the effects of the white powder had shoved his head between the front seats and was breathing heavily into Pete's ear while staring vacantly at the road ahead. A foul-smelling drool was hanging from Satan's chops and swaying gently with every bend or bump in the road, that is, until it finally dropped off, on to the handbrake lever.

About the same time as Nathan had asked why on earth Pete was driving them to Taunton when the vet was back there ten miles in Tawstock, Pete had to slow for a sheep loose on the road. As he eased the once pristine BMW past the oblivious sheep, Satan took his chances and leapt through the open window. Shocked by the combined screams from Nathan and his Gran, Pete braked hard and stopped. Nathan was out first having carefully avoided the puréed contents of Satan's bowels that now decorated the back seat along with Nathan's discarded pocket contents. His Gran was next out, her handbag catching in the chrome door handle and ripping it off. 'Stay there,' she yelled.

But Pete accelerated hard and the doors slammed half shut. After a short way down the road, he spun the car around to head for home. As he approached his former hitchhikers, he was shocked to see that Satan was on the sheep in a drug crazed frenzy of passion with Nathan's gran beating him mercilessly with her walking stick . . . something the dog appeared to be enjoying.

As Pete approached, Nathan's gran spotted him and realising she now needed a lift home, tried to flag him down. This time Pete wasn't stopping, even if it meant life in prison for manslaughter. Gran's stick was waving him down but succeeded only in hitting the wing mirror and leaving it hanging by a couple of wires, the rubber end of her stick then scored a long black line into the paintwork like a badly done go faster stripe. Pete dared not look in the mirror but if he had, he would have seen Satan throw up, then take a bite out of Nathan's leg before jumping the fence into a field of drug induced dreams – and a whole flock of pretty sheep. Meanwhile Gran was busy flagging down a naïve looking tourist's caravan with French number plates.

Pete drove the car home, not his own home of course but to the chap who collected classic cars and who had let him borrow his prize BMW only that morning for a short trip down the road to the supermarket and back.
Pete hoped he wouldn't be too angry as he was now running much later than expected.

**

Flight of the Great Goose

Kevin was the leader,
great leader of the geese.
He had his missus with him,
she was called Denise.

Kevin said, 'it's getting cold,
it's time we're in the air.'
His missus said, 'I like it here.
this really isn't fair'

'Do as you're told,' he said,
'for I am *he,* in charge.'
She'd surely have to toe the line,
if she, was not so large.

At last, he had his way.
Denise agreed to go.
'Okay you bolshy gander,
I'll follow with the flow.'

High above the tundra snow,
Kevin was in heaven.
With eyelids shut, he dreamed away,
of a lake in Devon.

Didn't hear the warning shout,
he didn't feel a thing.
Now he's going home again,
upon a Jumbo's wing.

Denise, she could not tarry,
no wish, to be kept late.
Now she'd lost her Kevin,
she'd find another mate.

**

Peggy Davis and the Dog in the Park.

Peggy Davis, age eighty-six, was a sweet little old lady who wouldn't say, 'Boo' to a goose and had never once carried out any unkind act. She'd been brought up that way by the ailing parents who she had cared for most of her adult life. Peggy had reluctantly remained a spinster, having sacrificed many fine opportunities for the sake of duty. Now, at last she was free.

She was never one to gossip or complain and only her doctor knew of how she suffered daily with arthritis in her knees and ankles. However, it never stopped her visiting the park to feed her beloved ducks, and today was one such day.

It was warm and sunny as she set out for the park, stopping on the way to pet a stray cat that followed her for a while and then to smile at a child in a push chair. Peggy was wearing a pleasing and comfortable blue dress embroidered with flowers and which she had only the day before, bought from a charity shop. Most of her clothes came from charity shops, in part because of her meagre pension but more so because she'd always supported good causes, and not infrequently to her own detriment.

With a bag of expensive duck food in one hand and her walking stick in the other, Peggy entered through the park gates, carefully picking her unsteady way along the path between some bushes and the grass slope that ran down to the pond.

Peggy stopped a while to catch her breath and rest her knees. While she did so, she watched a much younger lady, perhaps in her forties, throwing a stick for a big curly haired dog, like a cross between a Lurcher and a Poodle. It was so amusing, and the dog was obviously very excited and enjoying the game of .... throw, run, fetch, over and over again. The young woman seemed to be tiring of the game though. 'Perhaps the poor dear has had enough and wants to go home,' thought Peggy kindly.

So, as to speak with her, Peggy took a few more steps closer, just as the woman made a huge and seemingly desperate throw of the stick. It inadvertently landed in the pond, scattering the waiting ducks, that were already gathered for Peggy and the bag of treats.

Now that Peggy was closer to the other woman, the dog was delighted to see a new willing playmate and ran to her, dropped the stick at her feet and shook its not insignificant bulk with a frenzied vigour, flicking stinking pond water, fleas and probably tics all over her clean dress.

'Oh dear, what a naughty doggy,' said the young woman, stepping back quickly out of range of residual spray.

More than naughty, thought Peggy, but she had no wish to offend anyone, a habit of her lifetime, it just wasn't her way. At this moment, the dog picked up the scent of duck treats and launched itself skywards on its back legs, muddy front paws making new patterns on Peggy's chest. She staggered back a little but despite the brutal arthritic pain she held her ground to stay standing. Now, the dog's head was on a level with her own and the great slobbering tongue, that only a short while ago had tasted a rotting squirrel corpse in the bushes and licked its own privates with gusto was now engaging generously with Peggy's face.

'Oh my, he likes you lady,' said the younger woman, 'he's giving you lots of big doggy kisses.'

Peggy tried to push the dog's head away from hers but something tacky and disgusting came off the matted fur on to her hands. She could smell it from a mile away and was in no doubt that the overbearing creature must have had a penchant for rolling in the unmentionable.

With the duck treat bag now torn from her hands, Peggy's new friend devoured the contents like there was no tomorrow... including the paper bag and, as an impromptu thank you to Peggy, the dog clamped on to her body in a fit of passion. She was too frail to escape.

The younger woman looked on awe struck and not without a little gratitude that such amorous attention was not being directed her way, 'Oh, you seem to have made a friend for life there lady, he really has taken to you.'

After his justifiably exhausting work out, the dog stood between them panting heavily and choking a little on some dry duck treat that had earlier gone down the wrong way.

'My, what a strong dog he is,' observed Peggy. Continuing politely, without wishing to cause anyone offence, 'Have you had him long?'

Looking on in bemusement at the bedraggled and abused old lady, she replied, 'Oh, he's not mine my lovely, no idea where he came from, I was only throwing his stick for him. It seems to have got him over excited. Well must be off now, I'm meeting my husband in the park café then shopping for a new dress. Bye, bye dear.' And with that, she turned and walked away.

She hadn't taken many steps before, in the ambient tranquillity of the park, she heard a surprised yelp from an even more surprised dog, as Peggy's arthritic right foot sought justice and with appropriate force, connected with the dog's rear end.

Peggy Davis was never to be the same again.

'Hello there, chuck us a stick then …. Go on….'

A curious train of events

As he ran down the platform, he quickly checked his mobile phone for messages. He cursed silently and remembered how he'd meant to charge the battery at work. He leapt up the carriage steps and hurried through the train to find a seat, something he'd done a thousand times before, and he was always lucky. Lady luck smiled on him again and he took the empty window seat with a contented grin. He glanced at his watch, a treasured Rolex wedding gift from his wife's well to do parents, it was five minutes past six, precisely. The train set off and as he watched the station disappear behind him, he listened to the familiar click clack of iron wheels over the points. 'What a comfortable way to travel,' he thought as his eye caught the poor sops in the traffic queue at the A5 roundabout. 'What idiots,' he thought. It was only then that he felt a sudden crushing blow to his chest, as though he'd been hit by a speeding truck. He shouldn't be on this train. . . he'd used his wife's car today ready for travelling to her friend's wedding tomorrow. Worse still, he was now sitting on a train with no ticket and little money in his pocket.

He must return to work for his wife's car, she would be furious if they missed her best friend's wedding. He planned to jump off at the first stop and immediately take the next train back.

He prayed in his newly sweat soaked suit, that the inspector would not arrive before he could leave and prepared himself to walk carriage to carriage to delay such an unfortunate meeting.

He emptied his pockets, fumbling under the pressure to see just what he had with him. Car keys, a few coins, a works biro, only borrowed of course, his almost empty wallet, with several supermarket loyalty cards, one credit card, a crumpled fiver, and of course his useless mobile phone. The next station was approaching fast, as was the ticket inspector. Once again lady luck favoured him, and he escaped just in time. There was a rare public telephone box at the station, and he thought he might just find time to call his wife before his return train was due. They were always five minutes late anyway. You could always rely on that.

He eyed the graffiti, the grunged up earpiece, the tacky advert cards, inserted his last few coins, and dialled his home number. The phone rang and rang and rang, he stared intently down the track, watching for the imminent inbound train, then back at the adverts, some of them he realised were quite well designed.

Eventually, 'Hello, who is it?'

'It's me dearest, can't stop, just a quick one to let you know I've had to work late at the office, something really important came up, but I'll be there don't worry, just get my best suit out and other stuff ready for when I arrive, and we'll be off. . . . '

'Hello?' came an annoyed female voice. 'Hello, is there any one there? Hello, hello, hello!'

'Yes dearest, it's me, I'll be late home . . .' there was an audible clunk as the line went dead but not before he'd heard his furious wife utter the words, 'perverts, weirdos'.

He took down one of the nicer adverts and scribbled a hasty note about wedding presents on the blank reverse then popped it into his pocket. His train was already at the platform.

About twenty minutes later, another glance at his watch told him he was doing okay, all would be well, after all he was always lucky. They called him that in the office. He walked hurriedly to his workplace where he was once again hit by a proverbial speeding truck. The car park gates were closed and locked! He rushed to the front entrance, almost

knocking down a lady of the night in his hurry. 'Steady dear,' she shouted after him, 'you'll have a heart attack.'
He briefly considered the possibilities of her prediction while hammering on the glass door. 'Of course! It's Friday . . . all locked up for the weekend.'
An elderly gentleman in an ill-fitting security outfit cautiously approached the glass, 'we're closed, come back Monday,' he shouted as though the listener might also be deaf.
'I work here, I need my car from the car park . . . I'm in a hurry.'
'Sorry, I don't have a key for the car lot and in any case, I don't know who you are.'
He reached for his wallet to show this part time bumptious clown who he was and that he really worked there. But his wallet was missing. 'Oh no, God no. I've left it on the damned train.' All he had in that pocket was his advert card which he now noted said, 'This is your lucky day, call Mabel etc'.
The old fellow shouted again through the glass, 'phone that number,' and pointed to the office number above the door. 'Someone might be able to help you. Sorry.' He turned and shuffled back to his tea and sandwiches.
Now he was truly stuffed, no money, no phone, no car, no railway ticket and the way it was going, soon to be, no wife, home or job either.
The lady of the night was still close by, striking an appropriate pose by the railings. He quickly approached her with a new and more desperate plan beginning to take shape, he might yet save the day. 'Excuse me lady, do you think you can help me?'
She smiled, 'I'm sure I can ducky, what is it you fancy tonight?'

'Can I use your phone, it really is important, but I'm afraid I have no money.'

She eyed his Rolex and judged that he was fibbing about money and handed him her mobile. He quickly tapped in the works number and lifted the phone to his ear, he stifled a sneeze as some white powder went up his nose from the phone screen, which he then wiped clean with his palm and listened again. 'You are through to Bloggins and Bashum accountants. I'm afraid the office is closed until Monday at nine am. In case of emergencies call ... a long number ... which he scribbled with great difficulty on the back of his lucky day card. 'Please, can I just make one more call?'

'Go ahead ducky, I don't pay no bills for it anyway, knock yourself out.'

With fumbling fingers, he tapped out the new number and for some strange reason discovered he was beginning to lightheadedly enjoy this experience, 'how odd,' he thought. The phone was answered, and he began to speak, explaining his predicament as quickly as he could, but the idiot at the other end kept talking over him. He paused to listen. 'We value your call and will answer as soon as possible, you are in a queue. If you would prefer, please visit our web site and leave a message on the contact page or attend our office which is open from nine am on Monday.' Then some nice music, followed by, 'you are number 27 in the queue, we value your custom etc etc.'

He angrily stabbed his finger on the off button and threw the phone over the fence before realising, it wasn't his.

He altered his plan, as best he could manage, in his newly experienced drug infused state, 'how would you like to earn a Rolex watch lady? Do you have any friends that can break into the car park here ...? I've got keys.'

She signalled to someone in the dark and soon an old white van pulled up alongside. 'I think you'd better come along with us,' and with that, he was bundled by a couple of heavies unceremoniously into the back of the vehicle.

When he did not arrive home by eleven that evening, his wife called the police. His wallet had already been returned to her by a transport officer from the local station, so she suspected something bad might have happened. It was worse than bad. It was confirmed. He had been arrested in London that very evening on suspicion of consorting with prostitutes, namely one Mabel, conspiring to breaking and entering for the purpose of auto theft, damage to police property - one mobile phone, causing a public nuisance by hammering on glass doors and using a Rolex watch to bribe an undercover police officer to engage in criminal activity, oh, and he was also being done for cocaine possession. His luck though had held out with the railway and he was never charged with fare avoidance.

His wife took a taxi to the wedding, spent an hour or so with her best friend discussing her impending divorce, starting yet another interesting train of events in the rich tapestry of life.

Of course, it was too difficult for him to contest the divorce proceedings successfully from Parkhurst prison, where the old lags affectionately knew him as 'Lucky'.

Kovidd, a cousin from China arrives
(another covid 2020 tale)

Mabel Finnegan was a not unattractive single lady in her late fifties. She lived in the end bungalow of Doom Close, a cul-de-sac on the edge of the village. Her nearest neighbours being a property under restoration and a holiday home owned by a rich family from London. Mabel was slightly deaf, slightly short sighted and just a tad absent minded. Of course, she would strenuously deny any of these scurrilous views.

Just before the neighbouring builders put up extensive metal scaffolding, Mabel had caught a snippet of news on the TV about some deadly virus, made by the Chinese in Halfords and distributed by travel companies using cruise ships. Before her reception was completely cut out by even more metal scaffolding, an association she failed to make, she caught the news reader's words, 'Stay indoors, do not go out for fourteen weeks . . . ' then bzzzzz, phut, meeeeep, her TV fuzzed out and her mobile phone lost signal.

'Damn,' she thought, 'The Chinese have nobbled the TV people already.' She looked out of her front window in time to see the scaffolders run to their truck and drive off at speed. Mabel was oblivious to it being Friday evening and the big rugby match was being screened in the sports bar in town.

'God speed,' she said quietly to herself, making the sign of the cross and praying for those brave men in yellow jackets that must have been out checking that everyone was safe indoors.

Mabel turned off the buzzing TV, threw her mobile in the kitchen drawer and went to check the fridge, freezer, and cupboards. She vaguely remembered a public information film about nuclear war and filled her bath with cold water. 'Just in case the Chinese cut me off,' she thought.

While the lights still worked, she found a pen and wrote on the calendar, marking off the fourteen weeks of quarantine. 'Hell,' she thought, 'I'll miss Wimbledon!'

As time went on, Mabel's habits changed dramatically but she soon settled into her new routine. Rising with the light of day and sleeping at the call of night she would daily, safe behind the glass, look out of each of her windows to view the world beyond. There wasn't much to look at mind you, though she enjoyed watching the crocus, daffodils and bluebells come and go, followed by the neighbour's plum tree blossom. The foxgloves came and went with the buzzing of bees and the vegetation started to reclaim the earth.

One week a postman arrived, it was a cold day, and he had a scarf across his face. His gloved hands pushed some junk mail through the letter box, and he was gone. Donning a pair of yellow marigold gloves, Mabel took the papers through to the kitchen and disinfected them in the microwave. The staples sparked and caused a small fire, but Mabel thought better that than dead. One day she spotted a large cat walking the garden fence and as she was down to her last tin of corned beef, she wondered what cat tasted like – she could use an old tuna tin to lure it indoors.

While Mabel was becoming a seasoned survivalist, the rest of the known world was fine. By two and a half months, her bin was heaped high, she'd not had a bath and she'd successfully reknitted a favourite sweater seven times.

2020, the year cousin Kovidd visited from China was to be like no other, especially for Mabel Finnegan.

**

The Dinner Party.

It was a special day for the County's unofficial food guide group. They had mostly met via face-book and trip advisor, where they had a reputation for the most savage and vociferous 'honesty' about the qualities of the various pubs they invaded, I mean visited. Today, there were only fourteen of them, should be easy enough for the pub, pah, pub, it had the nerve to call itself an Inn and it had changed names a few times too. Remember Windscale? They changed their name too, after the radiation leak. Most of the members had partners of varying attachments, seemed more respectable that way and who knows they might get lucky. The men were predominantly either office workers retired on incompetence grounds or failed Masonic applicants, both of which promoted a desire for revenge and to re-establish their sense of deserved power of which they had been so unjustly robbed. Some of the women used to work the counters of Woolworths before it closed down. Anyway, they arrived and pulled into the car park, pompously parking with little consideration for others but spread out to allow an easy and thoughtless swing of their own car doors into unobstructed space. They started to make notes as they walked towards the main road which separated them from their victim . . . the affable and kindly Landlord of the Stag and Hounds.

'Car park untidy; needs fresh gravel.' 'Poor view of Church, trees in way.'

'Don't like the colour of the walls.' 'Needs a woodshed ... and not on the main road.' 'Motorcycle came by too quick.' 'Weather inclement, too windy and cold, looks like it rains here.' 'Hill too steep.' The Inn was already down to a two star and they hadn't opened the front door yet.

Inside, the happy staff were busying themselves in preparation for their famous Sunday lunches. The landlord noticed the hotel entrance door was ajar, left the bar and went to close it, it seemed stuck, then he realised it was being held by a plump little woman smelling of lavender and possibly something like onions. He stepped back to allow the customers through, some did, and he retreated to the bar where he could best be of service. About four actually came that way into the bar area. While the plump one held the hotel entrance door open to the moorland weather and peered into what must have seemed like mist or darkness to her squinting eyes, the remainder of the group entered by the proper Inn door and stood in a mess of people that prevented it being opened by anyone else. Still, who cares, they were all accounted for. Still, the plump one, who must have had a managerial position in Woolworths, stared out into the cold, a light drizzle having made the glass of her spectacles look like bathroom glazing.
The chair of the group, a struck off solicitor, but that's a secret, stepped forward to the bar, peering from a distance into the welcoming eyes of the landlord. (He would have stood closer, but rotundness prevented him.) 'You'll be expecting us, we booked lunches for eight but there are fourteen of us, I'm sure you won't mind, it looks like you could do with some decent custom,' he said looking around the room at a tall bald chap with a red wine and roast dinner, he shifted the obvious plumb in his mouth and spoke again, 'right my good man, show us your best tables.'
'Oh no, no, they won't do, they really won't, what about over there, you can move those tables around so we can all sit together, there's a good little man.'
The landlord was a fair but firm man but none the less he decided to oblige the group this once. With some assistance

from his likeable and hardworking staff pulled from other tasks, he rearranged the tables.

'We'll order from here,' shouted a rather uncouth woman who was obviously with the rotund ex solicitor and at one time probably loosely employed on the Woolworths sweets counter until being dismissed for sucking the chocolate off the Brazils.

The landlord thought for a moment then agreed; as, to be honest, it would be better if they stayed away from the bar.

'I'll be back in a moment,' he said bumping into the wet plump one who had only just realised she was on her own at the door.

More notes were made, furious scribblings, in more than one sense of the word; 'Very poor table layout, no thought for decent sized parties,' 'Rather draughty, felt like a door was open somewhere, thoughtless,' 'ghastly décor and there was a hole in the carpet too,' 'horrible black curly haired dog tried to get past me into the pub, had to use my foot to keep it out, obviously some half-baked nutter's dog,' 'we seem to be waiting a long time for service, don't they know who we are?'

The plump one threw her wet coat over a piece of polished furniture; it shouldn't matter as it all looked like it came from Oxfam anyway. She managed to squeeze herself into an empty chair near one corner.

'Where's the landlord?' demanded the ex-solicitor.

'He's busy with some other customers at the moment, can I take your orders for drinks please, if you are ready,' smiled the young barmaid.

'Just tap water for me,' 'Make that three,' 'no, four'. 'A bottle of Red and nothing from South America or Eastern Europe if you don't mind.' 'a babysham,' 'a J2O, what flavours have you got? No, I don't like those, make it a lager instead.' Make that five tap waters,' 'I'll change the lager for a

Guinness, is it extra cold?' 'A gin and tonic … not the cheap tonic, if you only have that I'll have a rum and coke, but not diet coke, if you only have that I'll have a pernod and blackcurrant.' 'two local beers here, and three white wines, as long as they're not warm or come from Germany.' 'scotch on the rocks here, and none of that imported crap.'

There you go dear and have one on us,' said the ex-solicitor, eyes like hands running over her body.

'Thank you kindly sir but I'm fine, I'll take your order through and return to take your food orders,' with that she turned and left … even thought about keeping on walking … out the door and all the way home, but she didn't.

'Ah, waiter, at last some service,' pomped the ringleader of the gang to the landlord, who had saved his young barmaid from the maddening crowd and put his own life and reputation on the line instead.

The landlord ignored any comments, smiled, and asked if they were ready to order. Three people spoke at once and continued to do so until they had finished. He picked up odd words from each person, 'no lobster on menu,' 'meat pie homemade,' 'just a salad with side order chips', 'what's in gravy,' etc.

'Okay, let's start again, from this end, one at a time please.'

The landlord's comments were greeted with looks of thunder, it reminded them of when they were at work, they'd been treated just the same, no respect for their own brilliant offerings. However, they complied . . . their day would come as sure as Satan lives in hell.

'Roast dinner, pork but only if the pig died happily, two yorkshires and extra roast potatoes, and none of that burnt pig fat and skin you try and fob off as crackling.'

One down thirteen to go, the pub would be closing before he can sort this lot out.

'Next.'

'Isn't there a specials board I can look at, I don't much fancy your printed menu, oh, hang on, yes, I see now, er . . . . . er . . . . . what do you think, shall I have the baked potato with cheese? . . . er or perhaps tuna, . . . yes that's it, tuna baked potato. No changed my mind I'll have the cheese. But only if it's French cheddar.' She was previously employed in a police control room . . . until her dithering caused such protests from all ranks that she was retired on ill health and a huge pension, of which she was careful in spending . . . very careful.

'Next please.'

'Six roast dinners at this end, all beef.'

At last, a sensible order. But . . .

'No parsnip on two of them Peas instead of cauliflower on one, and no gravy on two of them, are they new or old potatoes? Doesn't matter, no potatoes on one.'

The order was interrupted by a thin bespectacled man jumping up and shouting a muffled expletive of unknown origin. The cause of his agitation slowly straightened up in her chair . . . the plump one had inadvertently interfered with his groin as she'd groped about under the table for her handbag. Totally oblivious of her actions and their effect, she began to order her dinner, 'vegan roast for me dear,' she said squinting at the boar's head wall trophy having mistaken it for the waiter.

The landlord simply recorded 'veggie dinner,' it occurred to him that one with awareness such as hers must have disabled the connection between taste buds and brain by now.

'Next,'

'Have you taken my order yet?' enquired a confused and strangely dressed lady in the middle, it also looked like she was confused while finding clothes for her day out. She couldn't remember what day out and indeed, looking

around the table, she wasn't quite sure who half the people were . . . 'must be someone's birthday,' she thought.
'No madam, what would you like?' smiled the rapidly tiring landlord.
'Don't you have any menus dear?' she responded, on the assumption that the waitress was very tall for a woman and poor girl was nearly bald.
'That's a menu you are holding madam, why don't I recommend something or perhaps one of your friends will help.'
They all knew better and either stared out of the window or a very interesting crack in the plaster. 'The roast dinners are good madam, perhaps a small portion would suit,' the landlord held his pen at the ready.
'Can't you get on with it man, I'm waiting for my dinner, must have ordered it an hour ago by now, and make sure your half portion for Miss Memory here isn't charged at full price. We're pensioners you know. Not made of money like some,' growled the ex-solicitor peering intently and accusingly under his eyebrows. God he'd like to see this man in a dock in front of him. . . there'd be no slap dash dilly dally faffing about then.
As the landlord turned towards the kitchen, staring at his scribbled note, even more furious scribbling was going on behind him from the pub guide contingent. He thought he heard, 'I think I'll change my mind . . . er. . . .' but he pretended he hadn't heard. 'They probably won't remember what they ordered anyway,' he mumbled, not even sure if he'd actually got all fourteen of the little darling's orders.

Furious notes from the group, with conferring, now the idiot had gone.
'Waitress unsuitable, too tall, bald and with a deep voice . . . puts you off your dinner,' Waiter completely confused about

what he has or hasn't got on the menu.' 'Off putting whiskered dark-haired bloke continually staring at me', wrote the plump one mistaking the boar's head trophy for a man and the tablecloth for her notebook. 'The presence of dogs can be off putting when they search for crumbs under the table,' 'the presence of dogs touching your legs under the table was a welcome change from the usual pub visits,' (from a lady in her 50's who had joined hoping to meet her soul mate, however it would be more likely to meet a cell mate with this bunch). 'Ceiling's too low, not enough light,' 'ceilings too high, too bright, needs more subtle romantic lighting,' 'not enough attention to when a man's glass is empty, should be shot,' (guess who.)

It all went very well, and their comments are available on trip advisor.

The landlord they say is on holiday . . . they won't say where, until the doctor says he can come home.

**

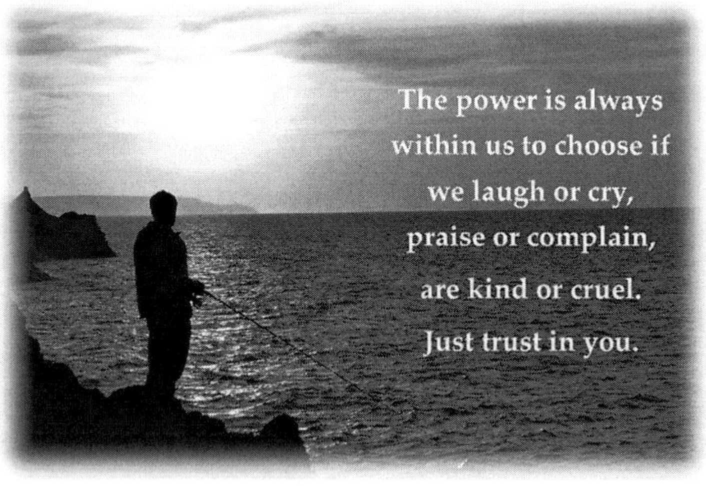

Publishing a Biography.

(Eavesdropping on a meeting between a publisher and hopeful author.)

'Well, I've read your manuscript – not bad – needs a bit of tidying - some sentences too wordy and some with appalling grammar. Mavis, our tame editor and a cross between Dickens and an Orang-utan with typing skills, will knock it into shape for you. We'll deduct her wages out of yours. Easily done, our accounts people are real wizards, ex tax office folks.

Smiling inanely, 'Thank you, I didn't realise how easy it was to be published with such a reputable company.'

'Whoa, don't jump the gun, hold your horses a bit, the chickens haven't hatched yet. Your story is good, well, alright, workable. However, the biography part is complete tosh. For starters, what made you pick such a stupid name?'

Surprised, 'But, that is my name. I just wrote the truth.'

'Truth? Truth? For God's sake, they don't want the truth. They want gossip, intrigue, mystery, heroes and above all an author they can believe in, a real someone – you know, like a soap actor or a convicted politician. Let's sort your bio out while I have you in the office.'

With that, Montague Falcon de Chevalier took out his old Woolworth's biro and began to write. 'What about, 'Sherpa Cameron,' illegitimate son of an Earl and a Tibetan peasant. That has a nice ring to it.'

'No, I don't think that would be right at all,' the author replied, still somewhat shocked at a top publisher not wanting the truth.

'Okay, okay, what about Peregrine Gainsborough, descendant of the famous painter, your parents are Cornish farmers distantly related to Tess of the Durbavilles.'

Verging on indignant, 'No, no, I couldn't be party to that. . '

Brutally interrupting, 'Look, if you want that book seen in the light of day and read by anyone other than you and your mother, you're going to have to start listening to me.' With that, an irate Montague threw a few new books on the desk. 'Look,' he said, pointing a stubby finger at each cover in turn, 'Sexual secrets of Freemasonry, by Babs Malone – the inside story by the wife of a leading mason who was accidentally killed during a frenzied ritual, they reckon that to produce such depraved and graphic detail she must have been present. There were surprisingly no prosecutions. Or this – Games in the Second House, an exposé by Lord Butterfield, real name John Smith from a council estate in Islington. Or this – Sir Edmund Hilary – Nazi Spy, by Abraham Goldsmith, real name Bob Jones a failed trade unionist who'd never made good of anything in his life. And this brilliant piece of modern literature, How to have everything you ever wanted, by Sir Archibald Smythe-Flannigan. A self-proclaimed millionaire whose advice is sought by great leaders from around the globe. In truth, the man is a compulsive liar and there not being a shred of evidence to back up any of his claims. He uses a pseudonym so he can't be traced in Who's Who or google. In reality he's an old lag currently doing 15 years for swindling funds from orphanages. Now do you see?'

Drained of any resolve to resist further, 'I suppose I must accede to your professional integrity – will you please advise me?'

'That's better. We'll call you. . . Zeus Maximus, infamous author of the dark arts. Don't worry, we can seed the internet with the name and various untraceable rumours. Father?'

'Er what do you mean, 'father'?

'Your father dopey, who was he?'

'He was simple cobbler, his mum died young and he fought in the Second World War, that's it really, no one special …

Oh, he did guard Balmoral Castle once when he was in an Anti-Aircraft company of the Artillery.'

'Mmm, okay – let's see, brilliant author inherits wisdom of his father, his whole life coloured by the presence of an unsung war hero. Zeus' father, who we cannot name for legal reasons, was born into poverty and orphaned along with his siblings at an early age. Sent to work aged fourteen, five years later he was first in line to volunteer to serve king and country against the fascist hordes that were sweeping Europe. He was selected for secondment to a crack Anti-Aircraft unit to protect royalty at Balmoral Castle. It was later rumoured that the aristocratic elite had fraternised liberally with young soldiers. This may explain why so many were transferred to other regiments and sent in on D Day, conceivably to purge witnesses to the infamous 'Balmoral affair.' Changing his name again on return to Blighty he became a successful and self-made leather goods industrialist. He never spoke openly of his loves and trials in life but in this enlightening book, Zeus Maximus reveals all he knows and more, shedding long awaited light on the eccentric social past of Great Britain. That'll do for a start – Mavis will knock it about a bit – should make a best seller – we can easily buy a few prestigious awards for it and enter it into our own competitions where we can guarantee you coming first. Nothing to it really if you just have the will to face the truth.'

M. F. de C. 2016

**

Mr and Mrs Karavana take a well-earned break.

Any other breakages were purely incidental.

It was early summer and already some of the nation's schools had broken for holidays. For once the British weather forecast was unusually optimistic.

It was on a hot and sunny Friday afternoon. Having left his Hampshire home a few hours before, (*address withheld for security reasons*), Silas Ebenezer Karavana, Rotarian and Retired Accountant, trundled his car, his wife, Brunhilda Adolfina Karavana and their posh, state of the art caravan along a charmingly winding and unfettered west country road.

'Oh, look at the lovely views dear,' he said leaning forward and to his left to have a look at a steep wooded valley.

She slapped her crossword magazine down onto her lap, 'never you mind the views ... you just watch where you are going .... Plenty of time for views when we arrive,' she glared at him over her glasses. Once Silas' satisfactorily admonished eyes were back on the empty road in front she continued in a more conciliatory tone, 'How lucky we are with the roads, you would have thought that people would have wanted to take advantage of such a nice weekend.'

They did .... oh, indeed they did and, moving so very slowly south westerly, a few hundred of them languished in the exhaust of the Karavana's old under powered petrol engined Ford, unable to safely overtake the Karavana's latest proud acquisition, a wide frame, 30-foot caravan, which Silas and Brunhilda called home from time to time, the manufacturer's called 'Viking Marauder III,' and most motorists called 'that which may not be written.'

Silas couldn't see any of the following hordes mind you, as he had forgotten to fit the wide plastic clip-on mirrors, you know, the special ones for humanity impoverished caravan, horse and boat towers … otherwise all they see behind them is their own trailer; funnily enough they'd remembered a half pint of milk from the fridge, a half bottle of tomato sauce from the cupboard and two urns of dog ashes that they planned to scatter on a nice little tourist beach they knew of, but they were at the end of their street when he'd noticed the missing mirrors. Brunhilda abruptly put his mind at rest, 'You don't need those silly things, and we're not going back now, what would the neighbours think.' Not that they had cared much for their neighbour's thinking while their caravan blotted out the Sun and view as it pressed against their fence for most of the year. Anyway, Silas had heard at the Grubstaker Caravan AGM they only used those mirrors to count cars in hope of entering The Guinness Book of Records for longest tailback; currently held by a chap in his eighties who towed a travelling dog kennel with his mobility scooter through the Lake District one Bank Holiday.... so rumour had it.

'I suppose you are right yet again dear, after all it's only a few hours' drive, then we're parked up for a couple of weeks, I don't suppose they'd make any difference,' he agreed; 'Compromise is always best,' he thought.

'Dozy clod,' she thought back.

As the tedious miles wore on relentlessly, every now and then in a demented semi-conscious fit of desperation some rabid lunatic would scorch by on the wrong side of the road and disappear in seconds into the distance in a cloud of burning oil, fuel, and rubber. 'Absolute nutters,' Brunhilda fumed, 'they should be shot and prosecuted.' ... and that indeed was the order in which she foresaw the punishment .... 'where are the police when you want them, I say,' she continued, having a mock cough over the diesel particulates left suspended in the still air trapped between the roadside hedges and trees. Meanwhile, at a junction some two miles back, an officer of the law continued to wait for the convoy to pass or someone to let him out. As sure as eggs is eggs this was not going to happen, as most drivers, complete with car crammed with luggage, screaming children, nagging wife, snoring mother-in-law, and a dog with head out of window wondering why its cheeks and ears weren't flapping in the breeze, had been in the queue long enough to have been soul numbingly stripped of all humanity and good will.

Some of the trailing drivers were doing okay; there were the Yogis that saw every small delay as a chance to practice breathing meditations and Mudra hand shapes while holding the wheel, and there were those that had something unpleasant waiting at the end of their journey, who, if anything, hoped their journey would never end, or workmen who were counting the overtime payment at every tick of the clock or the dull of wit who were happily listening to a repeat four hour radio show about knitting on St Kilda in the 1600's narrated in Glaswegian American on the world service..

Those drivers that were most certainly not doing okay were those with business appointments, those with pregnancies on their mind, either concluding one or starting one, those with dinners already cooking in a pre-timed oven, those with travel sick children in competition with the family dog as to who could bring up the most, and scoring points for inconvenience ... like the passenger's lap or the driver's neck, then there were those whose ability to control their bladder was fading with increasing pain and diminishing muscle strength.

Where the hell could they stop, if they ever found a parking spot, they'd never leave it again and if they did stop a thousand laughing or 'must look but be disgusted' faces would be watching them as the doomed cavalcade droned on by.

It was some of them that took life, opportunity and bladder in hands as they squinted already glazed eyes westwards into the blindingly bright setting Sun, changed down a couple of gears and prayed that they would be met around the bend with an empty road and not a herd of sheep or tractor as they gunned their engines in a panic that befitted those about to die of an imminent ruptured bladder.

Further back down the winding road, behind the oblivious and content Karavanas, was a trail of debris and destruction, both material and human. There were poor drivers who couldn't afford a service, nor the AA either, half parked on a scrap of grass verge with steam issuing from radiator and ears alike ... just a little more speed would have cooled their engine ... just a tiny bit more... not much to ask from life. There were sporadic minor bumps as distraught and distracted drivers nudged the car in front, driven by someone in a similar state. Luckily, the only deaths were to insurance no claim bonuses. 'Can we keep the police out of this mate, I just can't take any more points on the licence, damn this awful road, what on earth is causing the jam, ... I bet when we get there there'll be nothing in sight.'

Three cars back a budding and promising holiday relationship was ending abruptly and prematurely and five cars back a surprise divorce was being worked out. Two cars in front and the bloke was making plans to have the family dog re-homed when the holiday was finished .... unless it drowned at sea or something similarly fortuitous before then. Anxieties over the little pointy thing that told them fuel was nearly all gone triggered angina and migraines among more of the unlucky wretches that day .... 'I told you to get petrol at the supermarket, but you wouldn't listen, would you .... Oh no, you always know best, don't you ... now look at the state we're in … I'm not pushing this car again …. you did the same in 1962 when we were courting … my mum said you weren't that bright then either, don't know why I married you …now I need a wee.'

Picking up on that thought, Silas had bought himself a little unit advertised in *'Non-Stop Caravanning For Middle Englanders.'* It was a bargain, only £29.95, with chain attached screw top bung and made of recycled plastic in camouflage green. Although they had a loo in the caravan the Karavanas much preferred to use other people's and in any event when Silas had stopped in the past he'd been most annoyed to find that the empty road he once enjoyed had suddenly become busy ... and no one would ever let him back into the traffic ... 'miserable wretches,' he'd thought, 'have they no soul?'

Well, it wouldn't happen now, not with this new equipment, 'excuse me my lovely, would you pass me the Wall-mart 'Weelief' unit please dear,' he asked nicely as he slowed the vehicle to fiddle with his trouser zip. Although Brunhilda found the process somewhat lower class she realised that it was more prudent for their slow towed vehicle to remain mobile and not leave the road; she herself abstained from drinking for twelve hours before a drive but old dozy had finished off a carton of sell by date reduced orange juice at the house. A quick change down a gear to relieve the again struggling engine and Silas urinated satisfyingly at about thirty miles per hour while the convoy slowed to a steady twenty-five. The system worked well, but then he had been practising quite a lot from his armchair in front of the telly; Brunhilda fortunately for him was blissfully unaware of such activities and imagined that this was Silas' first time. 'Impressive,' she said grudgingly placing the warm 'Weelief' unit on the floor behind his seat. Silas didn't hear her, he was too busy trying to drive around a tight left hander with knee against the wheel and to do up his zip without damaging something precious in the process, .. to him it was any way. It would be a fair assumption that at least a hundred people behind him would have bought expensive tickets to see it torn off by a galloping horse.

'Here's our turning Silas, next on the left, only 5 miles to Dawdler's Paradise caravan Park now,' she beamed. Nearby undergrowth, recently promoted to overgrowth, nearly hid the little sign that said, 'B 666 Stragglers Combe.' Silas was almost sorry to leave the main road, he'd enjoyed the little jaunt, and he'd been counting the cat's eyes and calculating how many to the mile and comparing it with other journeys he'd made. It was a sort of hobby of his, that and mentally calculating fuel consumption.

The liberated traffic sped on past with hell bent acceleration and intention, yet, retaining enough control to glare down the leafy lane with avowed hatred at the back end of the receding Viking Marauder III and make a mental note of the registration **ASB01BS** as they passed by the B 666 junction and the partially hidden sign that said, *'Unsuitable for HGV vehicles or trailers.'*

On the main road south, the population of the next village had enjoyed a somewhat quieter day than usual and could not believe their eyes when this massive convoy drove in like refugees fleeing from a disaster, many seeking toilets... just locked 5 minutes before ... and food and drink from the local shop closed for at least ten.

In the upstairs back room, unaware and beyond sight of his locked shop door, the local grocer was just sitting down to a frugal tea and confessing to his wife, 'a bad day today dear, only sold a tin of beans and a pasty to old Mrs whatsername from the corner, otherwise no passing trade at all .... who'd have thought it on a fine day like this.' His wife turned on the 6 o'clock news to see if there had been an accident or road works.

Outside, a few drowsy hypoglycaemic motorists struggled to control their cars, families and eyelids.

Meanwhile, with his caravan touching the hedges both sides of the road; Silas was feeling a lot more comfortable and asked Brunhilda for a sandwich. He felt a lot less comfortable when Brunhilda asked sarcastically, 'and have we washed our hands then?'

'Still,' she thought, 'it'll save throwing it away later,' and moving the dog ash urns from near her feet where they'd once sat when alive she found the pink Tupperware box, ripped off the lid and pulled out a sandwich with the same hand as had been all round the Weelief bottle earlier, … 'there you are then, be it on your head if you die on holiday of some awful disease ... here's the last chicken sandwich .... it's a bit warm ... been in the Sun, ... watch you don't drop bits all over the car, I'm not cleaning it on holiday you know.' As it thwacked heavily into his open left hand the energy rippled through the fat in his body all the way to his gripping right hand and via the steering wheel it finally manifested as a frightening slewing of the caravan which for some 20 yards began to collect clumps of West Country flora and fauna from both roadside banks. 'Eyes on road … eyes on road, not your sandwich,' she snapped, thinking, 'dimwit!'

'Soon be there dear,' he mumbled, much to her disgust through a mixture of warm dried chicken, whole meal seeded bread and saliva, 'and I negotiated a good discount from the owner, Mrs MacGreedy.'

'Well, you'd better not have negotiated us into a place next to the bins and toilets again,' Brunhilda warned as she picked up her book to read again, as, at 10 to15 miles an hour, it could be some while, especially as the milk tanker

they had met in front was having to reverse. Silas didn't say any more about discounts ... he realised he was in a bit of trouble now .... mind you not as much as the tanker driver who was still trying to find a farm entrance refuge in his mirrors ... proper mirrors too ....
Brunhilda thumbed the pages of her book for her place .... aha .. there it was, a page on Rhubarb and vodka crumble recipes. It was a book written by Dennis Thatcher on the use of alcohol in everyday recipes ... absolutely fascinating what could be achieved .... how to ferment jams for optimum strength ..... Guinness pies, with options to add meat to taste .... Port and Sambuca roulade ..... Newcastle brown, cheese and herb, pancakes.... mmm that Dennis knew how to cook. Dennis and his wife Margaret were their favourite people, in fact swinging about on the caravan wall was a photo of them both, and not only that the Karavanas had named their late miniature Boxer dogs after them.
They'd both died reasonably close to old age but somewhat mysteriously suddenly .... Silas put it down to them being fed one of Dennis' Recipe dinners by accident .... but he wasn't going to tell Brunhilda that ..... she thought that after they staggered about in the garden and slumped down quietly that they had just been tired then later died peacefully of old age in their sleep. Silas liked it that way as it was his Schnapps and chocolate fudge cake with Ouzo custard they'd eaten. It wasn't his fault; he'd just popped it down by the patio chair while he used the Weelief unit.
At last Dawdler's Paradise was in sight and that nice Mrs MacGreedy was waiting for them at the gate with arms akimbo. As she waved them through the leaning and bramble covered gateway, she shouted through the window, 'You must be Mr Karavana,' she said, ignoring Brunhilda completely, 'you're first on the right, next to the toilet block as you arranged. Electric goes off at nine thirty

and back on for eight in the morning. Anything else, see me at the house tomorrow, goodnight, sleep well.'

There was a bird silencing and brooding pre-war atmosphere as Silas reversed the caravan into the allotted place just a few yards from the toilet block and waste bins, in the process nearly knocking some chap over that was emptying his chemical toilet into a nearby open sump. Silas made a mental note not to walk round that side of the caravan in the dark. He was pleased with his parking as he'd done it all on his own without Brunhilda's help, or her blessing for that matter.

For the next few days, the proximity of the block was to be a blessing in disguise for Silas, as the chicken sandwich seemed to carry out Brunhilda's desire for retribution to be visited on the house of Silas, well on his body at least. After a few days of hanging around the caravan … just in case …. Silas had begun to browse the for sale section of *'Non Stop Caravanning For Middle Englanders,'* 'mmm,' he read and thought quietly to himself, 'caravans for sale, my, I'm pleased with the knock down price I got, even if the cupboard units look like they don't belong in this size van, mind you, look at some of these foreign ones, still a couple of thousand more … ah, the Australian Bonza Croc Mk II and the South African Ridgeback Dominator weren't bad value, nor was the vintage Mk1 Buzzard Scavenger … a real beauty in its day' …. Silas quickly became fascinated by the extensive section on secondhand toilets and accessories … 'mmm .. quality second hand rear seat commode conversion, fits most Fords.' He was beginning to wonder if they could deliver it to Dawdler's in time for the trip back. As it happened, he was better, if not thinner after a week.

They could certainly have picked a better day than the Saturday to scatter the ashes of Denny and Maggie on the beach. It wasn't how they imagined it would be …. they'd thought a quiet dignified little private ceremony and then sprinkle the ashes along the shoreline. However, the wind had got up and a big gust had distributed the remains of their beloved pets across a crowded beach. As the Karavanas made a swift exit, many a small child was asking what the little black bits on their sandwiches were, and young ladies rushed into the sea to wash off dead dog residue that was mottling their suntan lotion, several people sneezed, including an elderly gent with a big nose all over the bare backs of some teenage lager drinkers. Luckily for them … and dare I say it, the Karavaners too …. no one knew …... until now.

How had the Karavana's earlier victims faired? Not so well I'm afraid, some had gone home early, others stuck it out hardly speaking to each other after the frenzied and uncontrolled breakout of abuse caused by such a frustrating journey. 'Never mind dear, we'll pack up early morning and set off home tomorrow, we'll soon be home and the kids will have their friends, your mum can go home, you can put your feet up and I'll take the dog to the pub … it will be fine, you'll see, back to normality.' So, after their two weeks holiday in the sunny south west the family loaded everything into the car, including sheep tics collected by the dog and some seashells and a couple of dead crabs collected by the children. The parents weren't aware about these extra passengers, not yet anyway, and they set off home ready to enjoy their journey.

Unfortunately, at this juncture Mrs Macgreedy was pushing tax free £5 pound notes into her tartan apron pocket as she was waving goodbye to her guests; Silas cut the corner a bit sharply and bramble scratched the van as he pulled out of Dawdler's gateway, now they, with fresh sandwiches and the comforting presence of an empty Weelief bottle, were on their way home to Hampshire ... and only 5 miles to the main road and the homeward bound family. Not far at all. 'Now look at what you've done to my nice caravan, you were in too much of a rush, showing off to that woman, you needn't think that you're going to drive like a maniac all the way home .... you're going to take it steady ... I'm going to read my book,' informed Brunhilda Adolfina Karavana.

Perhaps you know them? Perhaps you've been behind them ... perhaps you are them !

**

**

The Joy of Cycling.

Narwhal Bliss OBE was in his late fifties and had retired early on a banker's pension. Worn out by the pressures of a luxurious city life he had moved with his wife to rural Devon, a land of hills, trees and narrow lanes. He'd also taken up cycling. A state-of-the-art racing bicycle and embarrassingly tight fitting and wasp like yellow and black racing lycra outfit had set him back about three and a half thousand pounds. Fortunately, he couldn't be recognised when wearing his helmet, goggles and gossamer silk pollen-filtering scarf. This was the only reason his wife let him out. Lucinda found it an abhorrent almost disgusting sight and sought solace in gin and cream tea sessions at the country club with her friends. All had similar stories to tell.

It was 11.45 Friday morning and Narwhal Bliss was out for a ride, not too far, perhaps twelve miles or so. He chose the narrow coastal road for its fine woodlands, its twisting, bend filled treasures, high hedges and pretty flowers that leaned out across the tarmac. As he wobbled along slowly he felt the gentle breeze pass by, his helmet camera recording everything so he could play it back to his wife in the evening and his ears and mind filled with the sound of taped whale music. Bliss by name and Bliss was what he was having. The road was his, not a soul in sight, except for an occasional vehicle travelling in the opposite direction. Some of them seemed to wave at him – he smiled and nodded back. How foolish people were, not to be out enjoying the countryside and this fine weather, still, it meant the road was his, all his.

Five yards behind the euphoric Narwhal, an old Devon farmer sat patiently in crawler gear listening to his catch-up box set of The Archers, a few yards behind him was the full muck spreading bowser he was towing. At least a hundred vehicles had now joined the procession. Some would gladly have turned around and aborted their journey. This was not such a road. About halfway back, a policeman had time to leave his car and book a woman for using her mobile phone. The fact that she was a midwife trying to organise alternative assistance for an imminent home birth, cut no ice with the policeman, whose bladder was likely to rupture if he didn't get relief soon. Two cars behind them and Bob Lovalot realised he would never get his girlfriend home before her husband was back from morning rugby training and he was already in trouble with his own wife for not remembering something she thought he should have – whatever it was. Life looked like a change was in the wind. Also in the wind, was the rich farmyard aroma from the muck spreader, suitably aided by the fact it had sprung a leak. Two children on their way to school after a doctor's appointment threw up out of the back windows of a brand-new Audi, their mother's screams clearly audible above the hooting of horns, abuse and engine revvings.

'Oooooeeeeoooowww, oooieeow,' howled Narwhal as he sang along with the whale tape. He thought about stopping in a small and rare lay-by but changed his mind at the last minute; after all, what was the point on such a fine day. He pedalled a little harder to see if he could catch up with a squirrel that was sitting on the road up ahead, peacefully scratching an ear with its foot. Narwhal glanced down at the electronic device on the handlebars, he didn't understand any of it, except the speed and that was in some foreign thing, not miles per hour, ah, eight, excellent, he was doing eight somethings. This pleased him, eight was nice number. He turned up the volume of his whale music, smiled and thought deeply about the number eight. How beautiful it was, its sound, its shape, its mathematical importance, chess boards have them, two to the power of three was eight. Though he wasn't completely sure about that as banking wasn't about maths as far as he remembered. Still eight was a lovely number.

Far behind him was a different sort of eight, in fact it sounded similar but began with an 'H.' Nobody could overtake safely, too risky with the tractor and trailer taking up so much room, even a deranged youth on fizzy drinks and driving his dad's Subaru decided it was a move too far.

Somewhere in a nearby town a judge was signing the arrest warrant for a young man stuck in car 74 and who had set off early so as not to miss his court appearance. An irate homeowner was phoning around for another plumber and no, he didn't care what it cost, as long as the ba****td turned up on time. A dog had been left in the house too long, desperate to get out, it had urinated profusely on the best carpet and taken out its frustrations on the antique chair legs, splinters costing about fifty quid a time mixed with a rabid saliva as the pet took its revenge. The dog's oblivious owner turned to her friend in car 53 and said, 'oh dear, little Flufkins will be waiting for me, probably sitting by the door waiting patiently for his mummy to come home.' Her friend, who was a cat lover anyway, simply drawled a long expressionless 'yeees,' and stared out of the window at the unmoving scenery.

Narwhal's mind began to roam to food. He'd recently read about a muscle building bean curd and marmite sandwich in his cycling magazine, 'Cycling Supremos, magazine for the gifted elite,' time to cycle back and try it out. With only half an unsighted glance behind him, Narwhal briefly flicked out his right arm, grabbed the bars again and slowly wobbled around to face his journey home.

His goggles were slightly steamed and in any event his spectacles couldn't be worn at the same time, so they weren't. He could see well enough for his own needs and was now amazed at the number of vehicles out on the road since he'd started out, how glad he was that he was turning for home. He certainly wouldn't want to get caught up in all that traffic. The stench of overheating cars, diesel, petrol and some awful smell he'd never experienced in the City affronted his nostrils. Thank God he'd got a bike. As he passed by the now mostly stationary collection of motor vehicles he smiled and nodded back at those who seemed to be waving at him. 'Ah,' he thought, blessed are the cyclists, for they shall inherit the roads. See how loved we are.'

Narwhal waved, smiled, and wobbled his way home, passing motorists exchanging accident details, motorists calling the AA for help, motorists in open war with their neighbours, partners, wives, children and a happy looking policeman watching from the other side of a hedge.

Narwhal switched on his second favourite cycling tape, 'Zoo animals in slumber,' and to the sound of a snoring Galapagos tortoise, he dreamed of his sandwich and blissfully pedalled home.

Where would he go tomorrow?

No cyclists, squirrels or any other living creatures were harmed in the making of this story.

**

Vacancies at Mrs Grimsworthy's

Mrs Flora Grimsworthy, or 'iffy' to her friends, had plans to run Ferret's Holt guesthouse ever since being widowed some five years earlier. She needed an income without having to work for it – and a B&B seemed to tick all the boxes. Her late husband, Theodore Grimsworthy had succumbed to a bout of typhoid, finally traced to a tin of contaminated corned beef. They say that Flora had previously seen the government warnings but was reluctant to waste the large catering size tin, procured from the local market at a very reasonable price. It looked alright, smelled alright and according to her husband at teatime, it had tasted alright. They buried him two weeks later. The family dog, a vicious Jack Russell, called Lucretia after Theodore's mother, effortlessly finished off the remainder in one sitting.

A cobwebbed board hangs above the kitchen doorway, proclaiming, **'waste not want not'**. It was a motto that widow 'iffy' was forced to live by, even more than ever, especially once the authorities found out that Theodore was dead and cancelled his benefits. The claimant's recovery officer sent to deal with the substantial overpayments had decided on the doorstep that it was not worthwhile pursuing a prosecution . . . and certainly not worthwhile him confronting the toothy slavering dog from hell that guarded the entrance. The guest house was born.

Flora allowed young Nathan, the drug dealer from down the lane, to grow cannabis in her overgrown back garden and in return he used his computer to advertise her guest house. Now, Nathan had an imaginative turn of skill when it came to enhancing the guest house's image. Many people who booked, were quite surprised on arrival that the swimming pool and games room didn't exist and obviously never had. Quite often, as there were no nearby alternatives, they were forced to stay . . . almost like being kidnapped . . . against both their will and better judgement.

Flora made an art out of controlling her guests' daytime activities, they were encouraged, regardless of the weather to vacate the premises during the day. The presence of a rather plump but still vicious Lucretia begging at their breakfast table was an added incentive to follow house rules. How to cook sausages was not a skill that Flora had ever come close to mastering over the years, but her guests never left any, so she assumed they liked them half done. Lucretia's plumpness of course was a result of a never-ending supply of half cooked sausages, donated by often highly suspicious and nervous guests.

Once Flora had seen her guests safely off the premises, she would set to work doing all those onerous chores that such an establishment demands. It was soon apparent that her washing machine would not last as long as the advert had promised her . . .'forever'. Flora came up with an innovative plan. She would move guests' dirty towels from room to room so that they would see the new colours and believe fresh ones had been supplied, still damp from washing and fragranced thoughtfully with aftershave. In fact, fresh towels every day had earned her good points on trip advisor. Another neat trick, which she'd read in a magazine somewhere, was, not to change the sheets, but lightly run a hot iron over them so they looked unslept in. Along with a liberal spraying of cheap lavender scented disinfectant in the bathrooms, this saved her hours of unnecessary housework. Occasionally, Lucretia would have a snooze and a drool on a guest's bed, even Flora daren't tell him off, (yes, you did read that right, Lucretia was a 'him' dog) it was easy to fix, Flora had thought this one out for herself . . . by turning over and also reversing the cover, Flora could use the same duvet

cover four times without washing. Saved a fortune in washing powder.
To deter guests enjoying the guest lounge, which looked nothing like Nathan's brochure, not having a sea view or herd of red deer looking through the window, marble fire surround or otters playing in the lake, Flora had carefully decorated the room with discouraging horrors. A nasty looking stain on the carpet, a partially furless stuffed cat with one eye missing, a pair of dentures picked up at a charity shop poking out from under a cushion, a portrait of Maggie Thatcher giving a two-finger victory salute, grey net curtains and an odd smell that was equally unidentifiable and repulsive at the same time. Her hard work had paid off and no one ever spent more than the briefest moment exploring the guest lounge.
Flora 'iffy' Grimsworthy cordially invites you for a glorious stay at Ferret's Holt country guest house, cash only, includes breakfast. Contact Nathan at w,w,w,ferretsholt.hash

It might well be okay there now, as Lucretia has recently gone to join Theodore and his mother. I'm also told that guests have truly enjoyed the chocolate brownies made fresh on the premises. Comments on trip advisor claimed that they tasted 'euphoric' and had made the stay 'so much more pleasurable'.

**

The meeting.

Ever been confronted by someone you think you should know, but just cannot place them? You will!

The number 21A bus drew abruptly to a halt, two elderly ladies slowly met at the open door, one to dismount and one to board. However, as they both stood on the sun warmed pavement their eyes met briefly, and just long enough to spark some distant recognition. . . surely, they knew each other. Their pupils had briefly dilated as one peered through her rose-tinted glasses and the other over the top of her bifocals, triggering a reminiscence response in their brains; Brains that were now racing overtime to remember who the other was, before being beaten to it.

The bus driver, already running late, closed the doors and left.

Neither of them noticed its going, they had stuff to talk about. Each knew they must ask probing questions until a suitable clue emerged in the quest to identify their friendly stranger.

Lovely to see you again, how long has it been? Came the smile from behind the Rose-tinted specs.

Must be ages now, I can't remember. How have you been keeping?

Not so bad since catching a bout of dengue in South Africa . . . a rather difficult time.

Oh, how lovely, that's some sort of antelope, isn't it? Was it a difficult place to be for you there?

Not so much for me, but Bob being mauled to death by baboon troupe was quite shocking to watch. I have it on video, I'll show you one day.

I don't remember your husband's name, was it Robert then?

Oh God no, Clarence was serving six years in the scrubs for embezzlement at that time. Don't you remember, Bob was

my miniature poodle, he died defending my handbag after a baboon stole it for the contents.
Can't say as I remember him now. Tell me, do you still live in the old place?
Yes, and you?
How are the children? All grown up I suppose now.
David is doing really well after dropping out of school with no qualifications and is now manager of a high-class dancing studio in Thailand. You'll remember Mavis of course; she was killed in a hot air balloon accident in Bolivia. How is your family these days?
Both mum and dad are passed away now, and my civil partner Imogen left me. It was heart breaking because she took custody of Cyril and moved to Cuba.
Oh, how sad for you, does Cyril keep in touch?
Oh, poor Cyril, no, being a Burmese long haired cat, he can't write. But I bet he'd love to, all the same. I still keep tins of the luxury cat food, Fishycrap, in my cupboard, just in case he makes his way home on his own. Have you any pets now?
Not anymore. Since my neighbour attacked and ate another resident's gerbils, all pets are banned at the home. But we do still feed the pigeons in the park.
Oh, which park is that then?
The one we used to play in as children, you know, the one with the swings. By the way, did you go to the same school as Miriam Tufty?
No, I don't think so, did you?
No, but I saw in the local paper she died recently, quite suddenly.
Shame, heart attack?
Run over by a bus it said. Talking of buses, here comes your bus now. I suppose I must be getting home myself. Lovely to see you again, you really must pop by for a coffee some day and we can chat about old times. If you remind me, I'll

dig out the video of Bob with the baboons, the scenery is stunning.

The lady with rose tinted specs climbed aboard the 21A and continued a journey she didn't want, while the lady with the bifocals, squinted after the disappearing bus before remembering she should have been on it.
Still, next time she meets her dear old friend, they will have lots to talk about.
Whoever she was . . .

**

Reggie and Betty's stay in America

Betty had always wanted to visit the land of the free and the home of the brave. Now, there she was, and having a good close-up view of their interesting legal system.
It had started reasonably well. The flight had been pleasant enough until Reggie had a couple of bouts of air sickness and a panic attack about the type of aircraft they were on . . . a new Boeing 737 max jetliner or something. Must have been a good plane though because he said it had been in the news a lot lately. Poor old Reggie's sparsely distributed luck abandoned him again at LA airport, his case must have brushed against a drug smuggler's luggage and become contaminated. Betty took photos of the drug dog playing with its toy while Reggie was tazered and handcuffed; all a bit of a shock for an arthritic seventy-year-old with a pacemaker and who now twitches uncontrollably whenever

he sees a pair of rubber gloves. Still, those nice policemen gave them both a coffee each and shared selfies with them as they were released via a service exit.

It was still pleasantly warm outside despite it now being two am. There was only one taxi left at the rank, so they availed themselves of both it and the driver's advice for a hotel. They had missed their connecting sleeper train and would need to rearrange for the following day.

The fact that the new train ticket cost them twice as much as the earlier booking and with no refund from the missed trip, seemed quite inconsequential after the trauma of their disturbing night at Hotel Cukaracha (Hotel Cockroach). The hotel was frequented by the local ladies of the night, was a transit camp for asylum seekers, breakfast looked like it was a warmed-up meal deal from the bin of a neighbouring Macdoodles and they'd spent a sleepless night on rubber sheets scratching at whatever small creatures infested the darkness.

The same smiling taxi driver took them to the station via a lengthy scenic route, as he explained, 'we have loadsa time before youra traina leaves.' They arrived at the huge station with a minute to spare, losing one suitcase in the process of boarding. Not to worry though as it was the one the drug dog had taken a fancy to, and they wanted no repeat of such holiday trauma.

The general plan was to travel north to Seattle, because Betty had liked the film of the same name, then go south east to Missouri, because an old neighbour had a friend who once lived there. Disturbingly they were now playing it by ear, because they simply hadn't realised just how big a place the states were.

They made it to Seattle but it didn't look like anything from Betty's film, still, they visited where the native Indians had once lived happily for 4,000 years and the bare land where forests once flourished before the logging industry took over. Their guide, cheap at $40 an hour, (I mean a dollar is only about 20 pence isn't it?) took them to a back-street parking lot where she showed them a home-made plaque, commemorating the foolhardy bravery of some executed English patriot in the glorious war for Independence. They would have been mugged in the nearby street but for the fact they had no money on them and looked like they had suffered enough already. On only day four, Reggie made a rare decision, based partly on his own over confidence and general dislike for what he'd already endured in America. He decided to take charge and hire his own car and drive to the places on Betty's list. What could possibly go wrong eh? The still jet lagged, and traumatised Reggie was high on vitamin pills and strong coffee when he hired his vehicle, the fact that it was a pickup truck with a seemingly innocuous 'skunks and democrats should be shot' on the rear screen, did not seem to bother him. It was cheap and comfortable to sit in and Betty was quite pleased because a truck like this was in a film she liked with Bronson, or was it Heston? McQueen? Well, someone famous anyway.

Thanks to the wide, well maintained roads, Reggie found that driving an automatic wasn't so bad and after a few hundred miles he became used to vehicles passing him on either side. Although the occasional tooting and rude gesturing from some drivers was a little annoying and at least twice, Betty had to reprimand him for trying to return them. 'Hands on the wheel Reggie, hands on the wheel and watch the road,' she'd say, then get back to studying her new Californian cookbook, the pages on variants of hash brownies were already well thumbed.

Reggie was pleased they were on a major road because he was totally confused by the way Americans used four-way crossings, it seemed so odd that first there had priority regardless of direction of travel. He had also been glad of the pickup's good brakes. They had proved particularly useful. After about a thousand miles, three tank fills and an earlier giant all-day breakfast, seemingly cooked for a family of eight, Betty screamed out loud, 'here, here, turn off here.'

'Where, where?' he shouted back.

'There, there,' she screamed pointing to a small turnoff leading to an even smaller road, 'it's Sundance, Wyoming. It will be like the film, Botch Cassidy and the Sundance Kiss. Oooh, it's so exciting. . . . mind that car Reggie, he's on the wrong side of the road. Yankee idiot!' she screamed out of her car window, trying her best to emulate her newly learned American gestures.

They'd gone a few tense miles down the narrow road when Betty, having recovered her composure, noticed something.

'Reggie, I think they want you to stop.'

'Who does?

'**They** do. The police behind us with blue lights and waving at us.'

Reggie did what he would have done at home, pulled in to let them pass, after all it couldn't be **him** they wanted, could it?

Well, they didn't pass, they just parked up behind him, now with all sirens in full wail mode. Two heavily built (a polite euphemism on the author's part) officers of the law both pointing some sort of weapons in his direction, approached Reggie's pickup, screaming, 'Show us your hands, show us your hands.'

'What did they say dear?' Reggie asked his wife.

'They said you should wear those damned hearing aids for once!' she yelled, now eyeball to eyeball with her annoyingly too often deaf husband.

As Reggie took his foot off the brake pedal the automatic gearbox decided to do what they always do, the pickup crept forward. This incensed the officers even more . . . it could mean they would have to run back to their squad car and risk a heart attack. They were now shouting all manner of confusing instructions at Reggie, 'get out of the vehicle, lie down, kneel, show us your hands, walk backwards, throw the keys out the window.'

'I wish they'd make their minds up, I wonder what they want.'

Reggie was about to find out as he was pepper sprayed and dragged from his car, 'Spread 'em you thug, hands on the bonnet now, keep them out of your pockets. Do as you're told. Murph, keep an eye on his old lady.'

Murph waddled around the vehicle to the passenger side, noticing a bag of wraps on the backseat as he went. 'Okay lady, what's with the drugs then? Dealing, are we?'

'Drugs? Oh, you mean those herbal things. We got them off a nice young man back at the last diner. He said they were good for headaches and Reggie, that's my husband over there collapsed on the bonnet, is blind as a bat since he lost his glasses yesterday and was having the most awful headaches. Terrible things headaches aren't they . . .' She would have continued but was helped forcefully out of the vehicle to join Reggie at the front.

Betty could see that Reggie was sniffling and snotty with the effects of pepper spray and reached into her handbag for a tissue. She didn't get far as she was instantly dropped by Murph's tazer. Amused at the peculiar way she had convulsed and collapsed in a crumpled heap, Murph hid a smile and said to his partner in justice, 'Okay, Buster, I got her covered, she was going for something in her bag. I'll cuff the old girl then radio in for a tow truck and the drug squad.'

It would all be on their dash camera as evidence, the dopey woman had reached for a weapon (allegedly) and for the safety of the honourable and public-spirited officer's protection she had to be neutralised. Murph rolled Betty over with his foot and clamped the Acme Mk8 restraint enforcers on her wrists as tight as they would go. 'Small wrists, Buster, small wrists. Watch him, watch him, he's coming around again.'

Not for long he wasn't, as Buster gave his tazer an outing. Reggie didn't mind, it dulled the pain of his arthritis and took his mind off trying to breathe.

They had a good view from the back seat of the police car as they entered town but only Betty could read the big welcome signs. One was for the Skunk Fanciers Society's annual best of breed show and the other was the annual dinner for democrat enthusiasts of The Wyoming State Psychiatric Clinic. She would have taken a photo, but her camera had been confiscated. Later, some of her photos would star as exhibits for the prosecution, an honour that gave her mixed emotions.

On arrival at the police station, the officers now had the problem of shifting their prisoners from car to cells and one of Reggie's Acme restraint enforcers had slipped off his wrist making him more dangerous. It took four plump, sorry burly, officers to remove the almost comatose arthritic pensioner from the vehicle. He was pinned to the ground by a twenty stone officer who repeatedly screamed at him to stop resisting . . . all caught on CCTV for evidence. 'You filthy limey drug mule stop resisting,' he screamed as he tried to wrench Reggie's arm behind his back. Even a rudimentary knowledge of anatomy or even his own personal experience should have clearly informed the officer that his prisoner's arm could never reach his back from that direction.

After all their recent suffering, a night in the cells proved quite relaxing and the bedding bench and ensuite facilities were far better than at Hotel Cukaracha. It was also free.
After being seen by a doctor, photographed naked, fingerprinted and fed a breakfast of pancakes and coffee, all recorded for supporting evidence, the unhappy couple were ready to meet the judge, clear up all the misunderstanding and get on their way, they wouldn't even press charges of false arrest. All they wanted was to complete their holiday of a lifetime and on which they had invested their life savings to visit the land of the free and the home of the brave

The courthouse was only next door and by ten in the morning they were escorted in chains to their place of persecution – I mean, prosecution - Buster took the lead with Reggie limping along behind him, followed by Betty and Murph. As they began the climb the few steps to the place where the guilty stood, Reggie's arthritic right knee gave way and he fell forward, he reached out and grabbed whatever was in front of him. Reggie's flailing and desperate hands took as firm a grasp as they could on Buster's gun belt . . . Buster froze, stuck his hands in the air and pleaded for mercy. There was a bang, Buster wet himself and Reggie fell to the ground tazered. 'Got him, got the swine trying to disarm an officer,' yelled Murph, hoping if he said it loud enough some small reward or commendation might come his way. After a few moments of confusion and embarrassment they finally got Reggie into the dock where he stood dazed and slumped forward.
A squeaky angry voice screamed out, 'stand up straight man, stand up and look at me when I'm speaking, for god's sake you snivelling coward stand up!'
With the hand chains connected to the leg irons the only way Reggie could straighten his back was by bending his knees

and he wasn't going to last long like that. He gave it a try though and looked up at a red-faced judge with traces of white powder under his nose and a pretty animal badge on his lapel. . . a small black and white animal with a bushy stand up tail!

'We'll teach you filthy foreign scum to bring drugs into our beloved country. The state will generously attempt to find someone willing to defend you if you cannot afford an attorney. I have other more important things to do today and then am on holiday for a month. The dopey looking woman is dismissed on bail of thirty dollars if she has that much, it looks like she hasn't a clue what she was doing but that wretched spaced-out drug dealing animal is remanded for two months. That should be plenty of time to ensure a conviction by the state prosecution.'

'See you at dinner,' called Betty to Reggie as they were led away in different directions. She didn't, nor for supper either . . . even if they had one in Wyoming State Penitentiary.

There was only one lawyer in the state that was willing to take Reggie's case and he'd have done it for nothing if he had to. Bob Lincoln JD LLM was a rabid republican and had old scores to settle with that poison dwarf, recovering alcoholic specimen that dared call himself a judge. Yes, judge Arnie Benedict had once sentenced Bob's uncle to three months for organising a charity skunk hunt in aid of the Trump campaign. The judge, however, was desperate to be seen to do well, he needed to prove himself a pillar of society and staunch defender of justice. Sending this foreign drug dealer down for a few years would go a long way to buy votes for the next municipal election of officers. It promised to be a challenging trial but a trial with only one deserving outcome. Justice must be served.

The couple sold their lovely house in Kent with all its contents at a knock down price to Grabbit and Runn, Estate agents London WW1. The dollar was highly buoyant against the pound and a few more thousand were lost in exchange rates and transfer fees but it was enough to keep Betty in a hostel and pay Mr Lincoln his fee.

Once the Judge was back from his subsidised holiday at the Nancy Pelosi Happy Park, California, the trial began. The judge dragged his feet at every turn, he wanted to capitalise on the press coverage for maximum effect.

The local rag, The Sundance Kryer, (Yes, that's how they spelled it) ran a daily update.

'Police Officer Murph in tears as he recalls the arrest. He sobbed, 'I just wanted to go home safe to my lonely old grandmother who I care for in my off-duty time, but my brave colleague and I had to face down a vicious drug crazed maniac that tried first to run from us then resisted arrest. I'm sorry, it's been too much for me.' The judge gave him the day off to recover from the trauma and the trial was adjourned for the day at ten past ten in the morning. New update tomorrow, 'Buster to spill the beans.'

After 3 months, Betty's travel visa ran out and she was deported ... the good news being, deportation flights are free.

As their hire car was detained by the prosecution and the anti-democrat sticker used as an exhibit, the hire charges kept accruing and Reggie was charged with grand theft auto. The hire company are currently pursuing Betty's extradition from the UK.

Bob Lincoln was disbarred and spent the rest of his life in a secure psychiatric unit funded by the Democratic Party of USA where he was treated for a rare form of anti-establishment psychosis.

Murph and Buster were both promoted and awarded State Citations for Bravery above and beyond the call of duty.
Reggie was found innocent of all drug related charges but found guilty of failing to obey a lawful order by an officer of the law, attempting to flee the scene, resisting arrest, assault on an officer in an attempt to take a lethal weapon, and contempt of court for not standing straight when the judge passed sentence, (he'd actually fainted from shock).
Reggie was given 5 years in the state penitentiary. He settled in well, treating his arthritis with homemade drugs manufactured in the prison kitchen and landing a plum job in the prison library teaching the inmates English as a Foreign Language. He proved popular with the prisoners who all seemed to be ex gun club republican supporters and skunk haters.

The UK Foreign Office stated that all that could be done was being done to bring Reggie home to his loving wife Betty, who was living in a one bedroomed flat on social handouts in a rough suburb of Wolverhampton.

Reggie was much better off in the land of the free and the home of the brave … Wyoming State Penitentiary.

**

'Virus – what virus?'

Retired road sweeper, Fred Bloggs, had won the lottery big time and it gave him the chance to buy a beautiful Georgian mansion with its own grounds, lake, stables, and servants. It also found him a wife - or rather she found him. She didn't much care for the name Bloggs, as it seemed overly common for a lady of her station – a new station that is, her old one being Euston – so she called herself Lady Marjoram Phorbes. Yes, you did read that right. Mabel, her real name, wasn't that bright. However, she was quite attractive for someone approximately forty and Fred was an easy-going type.

He liked his beer and telly, and my goodness what a telly he had bought himself, more like a cinema screen. He had hoped to start his own beer brewing kit too until his wife put a stop to it, saying that it would make the house smell funny.

Fred was watching a report on the rising death tolls with the new Covid 19 virus on the TV, when his wife stood in front of him and said, 'what a load of rubbish you watch, I'm off out, the roads are clear at the moment and I'm taking the Jag into town. There's a nice dress in M&S and they're open because they sell food. I won't be long, unless I find a wine bar open afterwards. And do stop dropping crisps down the back of my new sofa!'

'You shouldn't be going out on non-essential journeys, the government wan ….'

'Stuff the government, what do they know about anything. If you were less dopey, you'd realise that.' She shoved Fred's credit card into her purse and left for the car in one of her moods.

Fred turned the TV off and wandered towards the kitchen to see what cook was preparing for tea. Through the window he heard the double crump of a nearby shotgun and a shout from his gamekeeper of 'got you, you beauty.'

'Could be pheasant next week for dinner with luck,' thought Fred, 'or perhaps we'll have some trout from the lake.' He reminded himself to check with the head gardener on how the walled vegetable garden was progressing with fresh produce. They were quite self-sufficient at the mansion, they even had their own spring water and a backup electricity generator, the staff all lived on site. It was an oasis of security against the killer virus and yet his wife was out there putting all their lives at risk …. For a dress. She'd have nowhere to hang it anyway as all her wardrobes were packed to the gunnels.

Fred never noticed that his wife hadn't returned home that night. They were to have separate rooms once married, as she'd told him that's what posh people do. She had only slept with him before she persuaded him to tie the knot, but after that, she somehow seemed to lose interest. He'd tried the interconnecting door a few times, but it seemed stuck. 'One day,' he thought, 'I'll have the handyman take the door off and fix it.' Breakfast came and went, as did lunch and dinner and still no sign of the Jag and its belligerent driver. Fred was watching a replay of Chelsea against some foreign team when the maid came in and said, 'telephone for you sir, it's the police. Will you take it here or in the library?'

Pressing pause on the TV remote, Fred smiled and said, 'I'll take it here dear, thank you.'

'Fred Bloggs speaking, can I help you?'

There was a momentary pause at the other end, then a questioning voice answered. 'I'm so sorry sir I was trying to contact Mr Phorbes, it's important sir, city police matter.'

'Phorbes is my wife's chosen name officer, I am her husband god help me, has she been speeding again?'

'I'm afraid it is much worse than that sir, can I ask you to sit down. We would normally call around and speak perso….'

'Yes, yes, officer I understand, we are all self-isolating here, it was only that my wife felt there was something essential she had to fetch from town, please carry on officer.'
'Ah yes, she managed to buy the item sir, a rather fetching red dress, which she was wearing when we stopped her for the third time today for taking unnecessary journeys. She was a little unlucky with the last officer, he was one of those who had been happily retired and was drafted back in. They said if he didn't, he would lose some of his pension … then they stuck him on a 12-hour shift in a busy part of town. Trouble is she looked down on him, blew cigarette smoke in his face, called him a pleb and a servant of the people and didn't he know who she was etc. Well as he'd only got a few minutes of shift left before he could go back for his first meal of the day at the temporary police hostel tent, he arrested her and called for armed backup and the van. Your car is safe sir, it's in the police pound, it'll be fifty quid to release it but as it's not an essential journey sir I'd leave it there. They're doing a discounted storage rate of a tenner a day while the emergency is on, can't say fairer than that eh sir?
Fred fiddled impatiently with the remote, the screen was freeze-framed just before it looked like his team might score, 'so what about my wife then officer, what have you done with her now?'
'Ah, I was coming to that sir, it's why I called. The desk sergeant was not best pleased when she turned up in front of him, all red faced, and coughing like a good 'un, she was. She is now in the local hospital … you can't visit her sir it's all quarantined. Because of her, we've now lost three officers from custody, the custody sergeant, the custody suite, a police dog and two vehicles for isolation and deep clean. The superintendent is hopping mad, because he'd been on duty all day and wanted to go home to be with his new wife, now he'll be sorting this all night instead. He was going to throw

the book at her … could have got her two to three years I reckon but the doctor said not to waste time as the prognosis was not favourable.'

Fred was a simple man of few words and none of them as long as those just used by the officer. 'In plain English officer, what does that mean please?'

'Afraid that's the bad news I 'm calling about sir, I'm afraid she may not make the morning. The hospital will keep you informed. Don't worry about prosecution sir, we've dropped all charges, you won't hear from us again. Have a good evening sir.'

The phone clicked dead. Fred handed it back to the maid, who always enjoyed listening in, 'thanks dear, can you let cook know we probably will be permanently one less for meals … oh and ask her nicely if she'd knock up a few chips for me … oh and a bottle of beer … that corona one will do. No need for a glass.' Fred flicked the play button and in a few moments the household knew that Chelsea had scored. 'Yes, yes, yes, yahoo!'

Lady Marjoram Phorbes nee Mabel Smith, formally of flat 2a Calcutta Square Euston passed away in the early hours and was despatched according to new government rules on mass cremations. Like all the others too, she wore a fetching black numbered body bag in place of the essential red dress.

Fred Bloggs survived the entire emergency by staying in isolation with all the happy well-fed staff. He eventually married the cook, who said she like sleeping with him and he could have beer and chips anytime he liked.

**

SUPERNATURAL

The Pub Ghost.

'What a night,' tired landlord said,
in the darkness, by his bed.
'Few others have such busy life,'
he mumbled, to his sleeping wife.

All was hushed and all was still,
at the inn, upon the hill.
A noise downstairs, he sensed a wrong,
as fire was stoked by someone strong.

As into darkness, he did stare,
He told himself, 'but no one's there!'
For in the Inn, 'tween moor and sea,
every guest, in bed, they be.

Footfalls, on old stairs, came slow,
fear, within his soul, did grow.
Steady creaking of the floor,
God save him now, t'was at his door.

Door swung open, wife's voice said,
'The fire is banked; I've come to bed.'
If stood the one, he'd married fair,
Then who is that? That's lying there!

**

Harry's rescue.

Dave's feelings were more than a little hurt as he recalled his wife Beth wagging a finger at him from the kitchen doorway at home saying, and not without a touch of inherited venom in her voice, 'If you don't go to mother's seventieth, I will be, and I won't be coming back!' He knew she meant it too; she'd been the love of his life but was quite difficult to live with for sure. However, he didn't want to lose his home and family and so it was, that one autumn Friday afternoon they arrived at the cosy but fateful hotel on the south coast. The family had clubbed together in a haphazardly unequal way to pay for the special event. Dave suspected that his share was considerably more than his brother-in-law Nathan's. Nathan, an astute and manipulative man, was almost as mean as his mother and had been named after a frequently friendly local butcher.

Beth and Dave enjoyed a reasonably friendly evening on their own, as they had travelled down a day earlier than the rest of the party. Their room was pleasant and comfortable but without a sea view, as those rooms were reserved for Beth's mother and company. As they settled into the plush bed and put out the lights, Beth warned Dave once more of the consequences of alienating her mother, 'Don't you dare be rude and don't you dare wander off and leave the party. We're only here to give mum a good time for her special birthday.' Both room and mood plunged into an even deeper darkness. Dave mumbled his agreement and turned over with some sadness. He couldn't stand the mother-in-law, he could hardly choke the words out to even speak to her, he certainly never called her 'mum' or even by her first name. He called her Mrs Briarley on the odd occasion he was obliged to converse. Dave was fully aware that his mother-in-law was of the opinion that he was a useless, weird and unpleasant object that would have been better off being put down at birth. She hadn't attended their wedding, had written Dave specifically out of her will and refused to acknowledge Dave and Beth's three now grown-up children. None of that bothered Dave as he doubted if she had any money to leave and her absence from his life was a blessed and possibly divine intervention – to his way of thinking anyway.

In general, Dave interacted well with most people, he liked chatting to the landlady at breakfast, he enjoyed greeting people in the street and always had sound advice for his children on the odd occasion they might distain to listen. Beth had few friends but wasn't too bothered, they were mostly idiots out there anyway, and especially the man she regretted ever marrying.

The family, various attached partners and their children arrived midday and after a brief exchange of obligatory greetings, went to their rooms to rest. At least that's what they said they were doing.

Dave was at a loose end, he'd read all the hotel's newspapers, perused the paintings on the wall, mulled over the menus a few times and stared out of the window at the sea. And he knew worse was to come. He returned to his hotel room where he found Beth sitting on the bed, filing her nails over his pillow, and preparing for the party. 'For God's sake, stop moping about, why don't you do something useful for a change,' she exclaimed, having been quite happy with her own company.

'I think I'll go out for a walk along the beach,' Dave said, almost as though asking permission. He suffered a little from a self-esteem issue.

'Right, that's it, all my family here and you want to go for a walk on the beach, that's charming isn't it?' she retorted, 'Well go then and be back well before the dinner, you be back by four, or else.'

Dave wondered, as he turned the door handle, what the 'or else' might be, but was left in no doubt when Beth assured him, 'If you're not back for mum's party then you'll be dying a lonely old man!'

As Dave wandered left along the beach and away from the hotel and edge of town, those words played on his mind, in fact he would never forget them, not to his dying day. He just couldn't understand how someone could even think such things, he didn't want to be lonely at all, let alone die in that way.

The further Dave walked from town the more he began to relax, the sea air, the autumn sunshine, gulls calling him to admire how well they flew, small sandstone cliffs and a sailing boat far out at sea . . . all compounded to make life so much better, so much happier. Dave checked his watch, plenty of time, he could go another half hour at least before turning back. Just up in front and around a small promontory, he spotted what looked like 1940s war time defences. 'Worth a look, this,' Dave thought, 'this is interesting.' It seemed like there may also have been a small landing pier at some time, though the sea had brought the once proud and staunch metal framework in a tangle to its knees. There was a recent chain link fence with a sign attached, **'MoD Property. NO ENTRY. DANGER.**

However, there was an easy gap in the fence near the cliff face and it looked like people had made a habit of passing through, 'Perhaps fishermen,' thought Dave as he stood unashamed and excited on forbidden ground. 'This is more like it,' Dave chuckled to himself, 'knocks the socks off sitting down to dinner with the mother-in-law.'

Back at the hotel, the family was beginning to assemble in the lounge. Pretentious greetings intermingled with handfuls of free nuts and canapés.

'Like a flock of vultures they are dear,' confided the landlady's husband. He was sharply rebuked, 'Shhh if they hear you say something like that, they could easily write us bad reviews, they seem that sort. You be on your best behaviour and take them some more nuts out. . . I'm helping the cook now with the meal preparations. Oh, and the nice chap who came last night with his wife has gone for a walk along the sea front, said he'd be back before four, keep an eye out for him, poor man.'

By now, a new self-empowered Dave had drifted off into childhood dreams and memories and was exploring the remains of reinforced concrete and twisted metal, all of which were unsighted from the town . . . 'and for good reason no doubt,' thought Dave.

The green sea algae had made Dave's new playground more slippery than ice. Disaster was inevitable and not slow in arriving.

'You stupid, stupid man,' his self-admonition a mixture of grief and annoyance. . . instead of looking where he was going, he'd glanced at his watch. . . he'd fell, twisting his ankle into the bargain. 'Idiot, idiot, idiot,' he said with more than a wince of pain, looking at his only good clothes covered in sand.

'Oh well, nothing for it but brush myself down and limp straight back to face the music I suppose,' but his foot had slipped between the rusty metal lattice and he couldn't pull it back. The more Dave panicked the worse it became, the injury was already beginning to swell his ankle and making extrication nigh on impossible. What was he to do? He was more in fear of his domineering wife's retribution than the more imminent disaster of drowning, a fate incidentally, which did not cross his mind for some minutes. Drowning? Dave looked about him, the tide was out, yes, but it would be coming back. Even if he could sit up, he was still below the seaweed that had made its home on the old pier stanchions . . . if he didn't get out, he would drown, he was trapped and going to drown. . . slowly and inexorably. Dave panicked even more and began to shout, even scream, for help. He paused to listen hopefully for a reply, surely there must be others out here, fishermen, dog walkers and the like . . . the only sound that came back to his eager ears was the distant soft swoosh of gentle waves on sand and the hungry cry of a seagull looking for something dead or dying on the beach. He checked his pockets. . . his wallet, car keys, a creased-up hotel menu and his mobile phone! 'Thank you God, thank you,' beamed a relieved Dave. His fingers fumbled to turn it on, it seemed to be working and there was still life in the battery. He decided to contact the hotel, he really must speak to his wife first. . . she would understand. Then he'd call the emergency services, the coastguard would be best, perhaps the fire-brigade too, and why not an ambulance because that ankle didn't look too good, possibly broken, certainly ligaments gone. Dave used the number on the hotel menu to dial, he had to try twice as his fingers were shaking so much. . . he put the receiver to his ears and waited . . . nothing. He looked at the phone screen, 'no signal.' Dave could have wept, no blasted signal, the one time in his life when he really needed the phone and there was no signal! He tied again and again, trying different positions, holding the phone high, holding it next to the steel work . . . none of it made any difference. Dave tried to sit up so that he could reach his ankle but the angle his foot was pinned meant that his knee would not allow it. There was still plenty of time, the tide would surely take several hours, I mean it only comes in once a day doesn't it? Help would arrive from the hotel long before that. He called out loudly again.

Meanwhile the Briarley clan were gathering in the lounge in preparation for their celebratory dining experience. The guest of honour, a paradoxical accolade, circulated importantly and in her time-honoured fashion badmouthed the rest of the population, particularly her dear daughter's repugnant wastrel husband, who she was quite pleased to note was missing . . . 'With a bit of luck been run over somewhere,' she thought with no smile.

A young and pleasant waitress appeared at the dining room door, 'If you would like, you can all be seated, and we can serve you drinks at the table. Please come though when you are ready.' Slowly the family wandered into the dining room and looked for their name cards, strategically planned so that Mrs Briarley's favourites sat opposite and next to her, with those she openly detested to the far edges of her vision. It wasn't long before Dave's absence was noticed due to the empty chair at the door end of the table. Mrs Briarley took this as an intended personal insult, my goodness she'd like to see him suffer, her hands twitched as if gripping him by his throat. 'Where is he then Beth, drunk, lost, asleep? Or have you come to your senses and left him at last. It's what I would have done a long time ago.' Some of the clan mumbled their conditioned approval, while others, fiddling with their napkins, kept an embarrassed silence, not wishing to be embroiled in the usual vitriol before having what they hoped would be a pleasant and digestible dinner.

Far away, along the beach and out of sight, Dave's mood swung wildly, from exhausted, resigned peace, tinged with hope of imminent rescue, (perhaps the phone had worked after all - it could be being traced and located as he lay there), to a sobbing helpless despair and desperation. The thought crossed his mind that a nearby broken bottle was almost within reach; one good effort and it would be in his hands, along with his own destiny. When the tide was closing in and no sign of rescue in sight, he could cut off his foot at the ankle – or failing that – finish his life quickly with the broken glass to his throat.

Just as Dave was choosing his own dreadful destiny on the remote and deserted beach, so the Briarley family were choosing their favourite starters in the warm Georgian dining room of Hotel Astraea. *(Goddess of justice and innocence).*

Dave's voice was beginning to fail, and the adrenalin wear off, he shivered without noticing and his mind wandered into a daydream, to a place where he felt no pain. He was startled awake by a voice from somewhere behind him, a man's voice, calm, strong and confident, 'Hello, old chap, you seem to be in a bit of bother. Perhaps I can help.' And, as he moved closer into Dave's sight, 'my name's Harry, I'm from around here, spend a great deal of time at this old Royal Engineers pier myself you know, fascinating place.'

Dave thought of the worn path by the hole in the fence and put two and two together. 'Strewth, you made me jump Harry, so good to see another soul down here, I feared I was alone. I slipped and my ankle's stuck in the lattice work, it'll need cutting free I think.'

Harry carefully inspected the trapped ankle with an almost clinical interest, as though he was no stranger to such things, and then sat down close by Dave on a fallen steel girder. He spoke comfortingly with calmness and authority, 'you're not wrong there Dave, the authorities will have to bring some equipment to cut the steel. Meanwhile, try and relax the best you can, there's nothing more you can do about it. I'll stay with you all the way, so don't you worry about a thing.' Looking straight into Dave's half-closed eyes, Harry lent forward, elbows on knees and concluded, 'You won't be the first that's done this. . . and I somehow doubt you'll be the last.' He smiled a little and gave a short reassuring laugh, but none the less, Dave sensed an overwhelming empathy coming from Harry. Dave felt a warm sense of comfort flow over him, washing away all his fears, thank God he was saved. Harry's kind and somehow authoritative voice put him at ease, at peace. Dave looked at his rescuer with more than a hint of hero worship. Harry was a little shorter and younger than Dave but was powerfully built. Dave wouldn't be surprised if Harry was in the military in some capacity. Certainly, despite the horror of the situation Harry was taking it all in his stride, like he'd been there, seen that and done that all before. Dave felt blessed indeed that Harry had turned up, it was obvious now that the situation would be resolved satisfactorily and naturally.

Back at the Hotel there were blessings too. . . mostly for the size of the main course portions. The waitress noted that Dave's chair was still empty, 'Are we still waiting for someone? Shall I keep some of the servings back in case they turn up late?' She asked with a smile.

Beth started to speak but was beaten to it by her mother, 'No, you can clear away the place setting, he won't be joining us. We're here to have a good time, not worry about some waster with no manners.' One of his nieces, a kindly girl of good disposition towards him tried Dave's mobile number, perhaps she could send a covert warning of what was happening at the hotel, but only the messaging service kicked in, Dave was not answering wherever he was. They returned to the jolly matter of fine food and plenty of it, 'Good job Dave paid his share up front Beth dear,' confided her mother with a knowing, some might say patronizing look, 'You've wasted half your life on him, whatever was wrong with that nice boy you went out with before, whatever his name was?'

'I told him to be back mother, he's so uncaring and selfish, I hope it doesn't spoil your party,' Beth replied, already making private, vengeful plans for Dave's unhappy future. She would see he suffered for as long as he lived for this embarrassment.

Harry looked across at Dave and smiled kindly, 'Don't worry Dave, all will be well in the end, you'll see, just have courage. Far beyond his ability to understand why, Dave watched calmly as short, soft waves began to wash over Harry's feet. Dave was given comfort and strength by Harry's stoic resolution in the face of danger, that and the fact Dave had already exhausted himself with his earlier exertions. The onset of hypothermia was dulling some of his senses and the sea water that began gently lapping over his own feet seemed warm and agreeable, even welcoming.

At the hotel, puddings were being served to already stuffed stomachs, most of which were looking forward to a lie down on their beds for the afternoon. Beth was amazed at how much her mother could pack away, 'She was certainly a special woman, one to be admired,' Beth thought quietly.

'Hey! There's still money in the kitty . . . special coffees all round eh waitress,' shouted Nathan as small bits of fudge cake decorated the tablecloth in front of him - A grand end to a party.

At the beach, Dave thought of the party that he'd missed. He'd always been grateful for a good dinner and he was sorry he'd failed his wife and children by not being there for them. He imagined what Beth's mother would be saying about him . . . then he dismissed such negative thoughts. They just didn't seem appropriate for the moment and they certainly wouldn't help the situation. Warming soft waves gently lifted then covered more of his body now. Harry still sat on the nearby girder, water up to his waist but remaining

resolute, still strong and with a compassionate yet empowering smile.
Dave was to feel no more pain from his trapped ankle and with his earlier plan for the broken glass long forgotten, he fell peacefully into his final sleep under the gentle rising water.

Postscript.

After being alerted by the landlady of Hotel Astraea, the authorities found and recovered Dave's body. It was the second time they had been to the old MoD site that year. Harry was quite right in what he'd said, and they had to use cutting equipment to free Dave's leg too.
Beth had left the car and all Dave's belongings at the hotel and travelled home with one of her children and her mother. They excitedly discussed divorce plans all the way. It was only when, a week later, a police officer called that Beth found out Dave's lifeless body had been found on the beach.
'Don't distress yourself too much, he wouldn't have known anything about it,' they said, 'it would have been over very quickly, he wouldn't have suffered,' they said.
Beth's mother smiled, now at last, she could move in with her daughter and be looked after properly.
Dave sat with Harry beyond the fence on forbidden ground, they sat together on the girder chatting happily about old times when life was good and they watched with curiosity as twice each day the sea would cover them like a blanket, like the Gods covering a sleeping child from the cold.
At last, Harry was no longer alone. Perhaps one day someone else will join their party because they will always be there, waiting.

**

'He who dies while he lives
shall not die when he dies.'

**

It's an ill wind and the collector.
(A covid 2020 tale)

Locked in an unchanging expression of surprise, a young man in his twenties sat motionless and staring through the barred attic window. A pretty young woman with long auburn hair was brought to his side and joined him, adding her own bewildered gaze down to the empty streets below.
The undertaker took a step back and, still slightly high on the fresh aroma of embalming fluid, admired the new additions to his collection. He smiled and inwardly gave thanks to recent events and the chance to bury some carefully selected empty coffins.
His wife called from two floors below, 'Telephone beloved – yet another covid client I'm afraid.'
'Coming dearest, be there in a moment.' He locked the attic door and patted the key in his pocket. Smiling broadly, he descended the stairs and thought, 'God, I just love my work.'

I cannot divulge where this gentleman plies his trade, you must just hope it is nowhere near you … or that he by chance dies before you do. Sweet dreams.

**

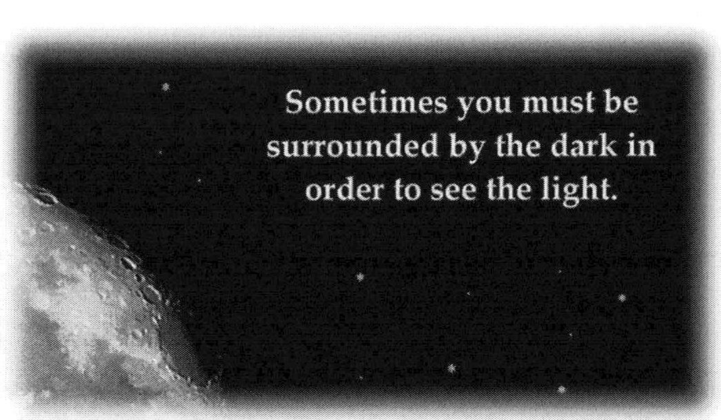

A Winter's Night on Irsha Street.

Comfortingly back home in my contemporary kitchen, doors locked tight and electric lights all on, ... I sit with my elbows resting on my old pine table, its enduring strength a reassuring prop to my insecurities. My much-loved table, despite its many sufferings, it has stood the test of time. I feel the warmth from the log fire sending out its comforting glow across the room, the burning wood crackling a song of the forest, accompanied by a hushed but harmonious howling as air is drawn through small iron vents. Both the table and fire somehow seem to connect me to the past, with happy memories of days that were for me, perhaps not as durable. I pick up a notebook and begin to write for you, though my senses are still somewhat puzzled by the events that occurred during a visit I made earlier this evening to a little place called Irsha Street.

Irsha, almost a place that time has forgotten, was a quaint little street in a remote old fishing village. Irsha is long and narrow, with only a car width road and no pavements; many small alley ways disappear left and right into a darkness that has dwelled for centuries between the houses, some paths disappear inland towards the hill and some out towards the sea. The houses on one side of Irsha stand elevated from the sea on a cliff like stone sea wall. Lower down, even closer to the sea, once stood other old seafarer's houses, but these had failed to endure tide and time and stand no more; no trace remains, as if they never were.

As I write this, something is telling me that I am not entirely alone in this outwardly empty kitchen, something gently touches the crown of my head as if to say they know what I am doing, ... perhaps a warning, but there is no sense of dread, not this time, just a presence that has joined me from where, I know not, and nor why.

In any event, alone or accompanied, I'll still share with you of my visit.

'Call in for a cup of tea sometime,' Joe had said.

So, on this wet winter's night, as occasional drizzle drifted here and there dropping gentle rain on the rugged Devon coast, I thought it time I accepted his kind offer.

I left my car in the poorly lit and deserted quayside car park, put on my long black overcoat, and adjusted my scarf and woolly hat against the damp. As I walked alongside the waterfront railings and into the darkness towards Irsha, pinpoints of coloured light brightened the gloom far across the bay; warnings to sailors of sandbars and rocks; sparkling beacons distant in a dark foreboding sea. As I entered Irsha Street the wind dropped and all became hushed, even my shoes on the tarmac were strangely silent, as were the many houses I passed on either side. The street itself was deserted; and seemingly so were most of the houses, only one or two showed a light, and even then, no one was to be seen through the glass, I didn't like to peer inside for fear of someone looking out only to be disturbed by such ill-mannered intrusion.

Directions and landmarks, I'd been given, soon led me to the house I sought; it was pleasantly easy to find in fact.

It was dark in Irsha except for the few dim street lights that sporadically lit the narrow roadway; a roadway wet from earlier rain that evening. There was a light on in the house and I could clearly see through the window I had found the right place; my host was sitting in a large chair in the far-left corner of what appeared surprisingly to be quite a large room. I soon found the door and knocked.

I didn't have to wait long before the door opened, and a smiling face greeted me.

'Come on in,' Joe said, 'come on through.'

I bowed my head through the low doorway and entered.

Once inside, I found the house was much larger than I had anticipated, I previously thought that they were all small two up two down cottages along Irsha. As is so often the case, what we think we see isn't what we think it is. There's many a surprise in life for us, all about what we thought we saw. The entrance lobby and first room through which we walked was unlit, except for light coming through an opening to the next room, but I could still see the beamed ceiling, tasteful furniture and paintings. Underfoot I felt the cold and uneven flags of the 16th stone floor. We moved through the opening into a similarly presented room. My host, a worldly wise, stocky and affable man of some years was talking to someone that I could not see. It all became clear as he ushered me through another low opening to yet more rooms at the back, and there was the lady of the house, the partner to his conversation, quietly making tea. She was a pleasantly positive and talkative lady who invited me to remove my coat and sit a while and 'did I want sugar in my tea'?

'That's a relief,' I thought, at least he's not talking to imaginary people; or worse still, something else of which my mind would rather stay in ignorance.

It was a large and interesting back room, with a central inglenook fireplace complete with old ironmongery for hanging meat and cooking pots. All around were misshapen ancient walls, on which paintings of seascapes and sailing ships hung as testimony to a maritime past, and floors that leaned this way and that in no particular manner. As my tea slowly went cold in my hands my host's conversation continued absorbingly, with tales of smugglers, murders, secret tunnels and of footsteps heard crossing the wooden floors of the empty rooms above. Joe spoke quietly of these things in the manner of a man that knew the truth of this world.

Once an old inn, both the building and its contents smacked of another age. It was almost as though I had gone back in time, as though the energy left by the past was still present and willing to show itself. The conversation led me to sense that I too might 'see', 'hear' or 'feel' the past. After tea I was shown around the labyrinth of rooms and stairs of all shapes in which many a hiding place could remain a secret for all times. I stood on steps where once stood the murdered excise officer and I walked the floor over which many a contraband barrel had rolled, I looked to the walls and floors, beyond which lay secret places and hidden history, in part I felt that my soul saw more than my eyes.

How often have we glimpsed something from the corner of our eye but when we look again there is nothing there … or was there? The child that plays with imaginary friends, or sees something in the night, is soon put right by the knowing and fearful adult. ….. 'best not to look … no, no, don't look, … don't tell me any more … there's nothing there …. Go to sleep, close your eyes.'

Whose eyes is it that were really closed?

Another cup of tea and the invisible hours had passed us by, as though they never were ....
I picked up my nearly finished tea ... the cup was cold to my touch ......'Gosh, is that the time?' I said, glancing at the digital watch on my wrist, 'I really must be away home and leave you in peace; thank you so much for your timeless hospitality, most interesting,' ... and, reflecting upon their revelations, thinking privately, 'and almost beyond belief too.'
I bid farewell and re-crossed the 16th Century stones to the door with Joe, the gentleman of the house. He too seemed timeless, as though he were part of the fabric of the old Inn himself, at one with the hostelry, attuned to the heartbeat of the house that held so many secrets.
Buttoning my long dark overcoat, it seemed to fit me better than when I'd arrived, I somehow felt taller, more comfortable and stronger, as though younger now, almost like being someone else. I stepped into the rain damped narrow street, the old Inn door closing quietly behind me.
I began a silent, contemplative walk eastwards along the hushed and still deserted Irsha. My mind wandered to the events of the evening, then I glimpsed something from the corner of my eye; something large that loomed out of the darkness. My eyes slowly accustomed to the night and a faint breeze carried the smell of salt air to my nostrils and the creaking of timbers and rigging to my ears .... as the darkness was eased apart by shifting clouds a faint moonlight revealed an ancient ship of two masts riding newly at anchor in the deep-water channel, rolling so gently in harmony with the tireless estuary waves, her sails furled, ... I thought I saw movement on deck, thought I saw the swing of the hurricane lamp, ... and then nature drew its curtain of clouds once more to hide the moon and I was left with a darkness within a darkness and the sound of water

lapping the rocks. A previously unknown knowing came into my head, she was a Brigantine, yes, that's what she was, a Brigantine, two masted and shallow draft .... and not long home from sea too.

If she was truly there or not, now I cannot say, but that night I knew exactly where she was, how tall, how rigged and all such detail that could be seen and told.

All was made more real by the clearly audible, slow soporific swoosh of gentle waves lapping the shore in slow rhythm, with the pauses between almost as though the sea were holding its breath.

As I passed by the little slipway, I sensed three men, short and stocky, wearing mufflers and caps, heaving their fully laden row boat further up the stone slip, for the tide was still not yet passed to the ebb. I did not linger to watch, but somehow intuition told me what they were doing; contraband. How thankful I was now that I had left the house when I did, this was no place for the faint hearted and those men would not be best pleased to be discovered.

The spectre of a long gone past began to haunt Irsha, and I edged nearer the middle of the empty street for safety. I walked on quietly not wishing to disturb what was happening, yet slightly fearful and knowing I could no longer turn back, it was as if I had entered the sorcerer's cave and now fear to wake him.

Irsha is long and narrow but this night it seemed ever more so, time seemed confused in some way, the street, like time, never seeming to end. Then something walked alongside me, I became aware of two men, who though strongly built seemed of a desperately nervous disposition; their nailed boots trod not on tarmac but on rutted stones and there was a fleeting whiff of rotting vegetation and sewage in the air as if it lay in the street. They walked in a greater darkness than I. It would appear, that the men did not see me, or if they did, I meant nothing to them. Nothing I saw seemed to see me, a cloak of timely invisibility covered me, though at times I feared it would not.

I became aware of the untidy ramshackle quay side with its frames, boxes and nets and the river beyond as though there were now no houses between me and they.

I walked on and on, passing some small houses that seemed no more than pauper's hovels and into one of which both men vanished. It was as though they never were, except that the sound of their voices lingered on, it was the last thing to pass ... a curse it was, 'twas press gangs working the town that they cursed, ... then their voices followed them into their greater silence, and Irsha was quiet again.

Driven by an unexpected and short-lived gust of wind some smoke drifted across the street; the smell of wood smoke filled the air and my now heightened senses. I moved on, still slow and in a silence, sensing, as I passed by, places born of centuries past itself, the shivers, the hunger, the fear, a sense of little expectation from life but to survive, a sense of those waiting in vain but always in hope of a loved son's return from the sea.

I walked out of Irsha and towards the Church and its graveyard. There, no doubt, we might find our ghosts'

ageing bones, but so often the poor can leave no markers except in our hearts. We may still be touched by their troubled spirits even today if we did but take notice. Somehow transformed by my journey into Irsha, words of noble poetry and stories of the soul sprang eagerly to mind, and those words triggered feelings. Not unlike hearing songs or stories that can fill us all with feelings. Feelings as if we were still there, like when we were young; feelings that connect us to our own past and even to our own ancestors and a knowing what they must have done and felt …. For in part, we are them. In our mind we can belong to a different place and time … even if for a brief while, for a glimpse is all we need in order to 'know' ….. You must have been there yourself; you must have felt this in your own being sometime, somewhere. …….

Irsha was well behind me now and I carried only memories with me towards the live music that came from the local pub. To my left a glint of Moonlight, which had evaded the clouds, crossed the river to the streetlights of Instow.

The pub was full of friendly people enjoying the warmth of drink and music, the bar was full of life. Warm applause greeted the rag tag and bobtail group of musicians as the song ended, leaving me with residual feelings ….. feelings that were trapped briefly in time past …. Once again, I felt the strength of my youth and the courage of my forebears, my mind had transcended time and distance if only for a while. I ordered a Guinness from the bar and I reflected on an old saying, 'if the end is part of the story, then death is a part of living,' …. Perhaps we will 'live on' somehow too. …..

'The end of anything is never a stopping point;
It is merely the doorway to new discoveries.'

Well met, on a bridge to the other side.

A fading summer Sun had hushed the land to sleep. High up on the old bridge that spanned the tributary, a clumsily dressed, thin young man in his early thirties stood wide awake in stillness. Transfixed like a rabbit caught in headlights; eyes captivated by the swirling torrent far below; a torrent that rushed on unquestioningly in its blind search for the ocean's dark but welcoming shroud. By two in the morning all was graveyard quiet and he was still there, lost in thought, the air was warm, and his frayed T shirt and old trousers were all he needed that night, or any night . . . his body and soul braced forlorn on the wrong side of the railings.

Suddenly a voice shattered the silence and with it went any peace he might have had. The young man nearly jumped out of his skin, for he'd not seen or heard a soul for three hours or more. 'Steady on mate,' said the voice, 'didn't mean to make you jump.' The young man gripped the railings even more tightly with both hands, pulling his back firm against the bars, his mind now in turmoil, for he'd hoped to end it all alone.

There was something of an Aussie twang to the voice from the dark; its owner came closer, stopped a few feet away, rested his folded arms on the parapet and continued talking as though finding a walker, never mind an erstwhile jumper on the bridge at this God forsaken hour, was quite a normal occurrence.

'So, what you doing here then, young fellah? Sure is a lovely night and what a beautiful view you've got yourself here. Betcha that river's full of life down there, them crabs and fishes don't sleep at night yer know.'

The young man didn't know what to say, in fact he didn't want to say anything; he just wanted this bloke to clear off to whence he'd came. He'd been content with his prior misery. However, curiosity had the better of him and he sensed a non-judgemental calm from his surprise visitor, 'Crumbs, you made me jump, no pun intended, what on earth are you doing here at this hour?'

'Well young fellah, I could ask you the same, but me, I'm what you might call of no fixed abode, a gentleman of the road, homeless if you like. It's not so bad you understand, though it was before, loads of things went wrong before, lost the missus and kids, parents died, injured at work ... in the army I was you know. Oh, they paid me off all right, but pound notes were no compensation nor cure for my ills back then.'

'So, what brings you to this road, this bridge, tonight then?' the apprentice jumper asked again.

'Oh, dunno really, just going with feelings, always follow the good feelings I say. When you walk with a smile on your face, you'll always get some coming back your way. It just felt right to go further south, more rural, nicer people; chance of a few jobs on a farm or something. Food in the hedgerows, berries and the like – yeah, that's about it really – just feelings and as it was a warm night, I thought I'd take advantage of the cooler air and quiet road. Then I met you, nature watching from your fine perch on my bridge.'

'Sorry about that,' said the reticent jumper, who somehow felt empathy for the ex-soldier and his losses in life. He realised that somewhere, way back, we're all linked together one way or another. In fact, this happy tramp had suffered far more than he ever had himself, 'You never thought of ending it all then?' he enquired.

'Yeah mate, I thought about it but when I got there some young fellah had nicked my spot – you gonna be long?' the jovial tramp's smile could just be made out in the moonlight.

For some peculiar reason, perhaps contagion, it appeared funny to the would-be jumper and he smiled back, 'Oh yeah, good one, very droll,' he said. The strange thing was, the thoughts that drove his racked body to the bridge were changing and as the thoughts changed so did his feelings. In fact, the tramp was right, it was a beautiful view, it was a great night, the moon smiled down on a land at peace with itself and he, for that moment felt part of that. What had possessed him to ever want to throw such beauty away? 'I'm coming back over,' said the reformed jumper.

'No mate, stay there, you'll be fine, in fact, I'll join you over there – that little bit of fear, the adrenalin rush just spices life up a bit at times, makes you feel more alive than ever – come on, shift over a bit, give us a hand.'

The pair of them nattered away for ages, like two long lost pals reunited.

Interspersed with tales from down under, of joys and woes, the gentleman of the road implanted his wisdom and set the seeds of hope and resolution in his young friend's mind; he'd given him a gentle push – in the right direction. Good thoughts began to bring the young man good feelings and they filled his very soul and body.

'Well, I reckon I'll thank you kindly for all your help and wisdom and be on my way home now, for tomorrow I have much to begin.' So saying, the young man clambered roadside of the railings, his body and spirit lightened from the burdens he'd earlier carried to the bridge. It was as though he'd dropped them into the swirling depths below to be lost forever. He was now free and felt it, like somehow, he'd paid off some long outstanding debt at last.

'So long mate, I'm gonna stay a while longer, before I make my way to the other side. You be good, you think happy, feel happy, and don't waste yer life ...live it well.'

As the young, now rehabilitated, jumper reached the end of the bridge he suddenly realised he didn't even know this saviour's name, he turned and started to shout his question but there was no point in finishing the sentence, the kindly stranger had already gone. 'Oh well,' he thought, 'After his good deed tonight I hope at last he finds somewhere to rest in peace, he's obviously decided not to wait any longer on the bridge after all.'

That young man went home, made a better life, repaid that good deed a thousand times over and never forgot his friend the tramp, well met on the bridge to the other side. He resolved to share his story with anyone who would listen, just like he had listened that fateful night so many years ago.

And now you have heard it. I must leave you now, for there are others waiting in the darkness, on bridges they built for themselves.

If you would only look, you will find joy on every path.

No matter how dark it seems.

**

'After the long slumber of ignorance,
a single word can change a man forever.'
Nan Guo Zi

**

'It is required of every man,' the ghost returned,
'that the spirit within him should walk abroad among his fellow-men, and travel far and wide; and, if that spirit goes not forth in life, it is condemned to do so after death.'
Charles Dickens

**

'So do we pass the ghosts that haunt us later in our lives; they sit undramatically by the roadside like poor beggars, and we see them only from the corners of our eyes, if we see them at all. The idea that they have been waiting there for us rarely crosses our minds. Yet they do wait, and when we have passed, they gather up their bundles of memory and fall in behind, treading in our footsteps and catching up, little by little.' *Stephen King*

**

Uncle Robert's Magic Carpet.

Little Sophie was adamant; she was **not** going to stay with her great aunt and uncle for a whole two weeks while her mother was away on some silly training thing for work.
'But you'll love it there Sophie, I always did when I was young. Uncle Robert and Auntie Florence are really kind people and it's not for very long.'

Nothing seemed to change Sophie's mind, 'I'll stay here on my own then mum, and Mrs what's-er-name next door can keep an eye on me.'
'No Sophie, that won't do at all, you are far too young, and Mrs Gracie is too old. Poor dear must be ninety. We must sort this out soon, today would be good as I have already written to them. Aunt and uncle live in the most wonderful old cabin up in the mountains, fresh air, good food, why, they even had horses when I was there, my favourite was a big friendly white one called . . . ' Sophie interrupted, 'Horses? They have horses? Will they let me ride them?'
Sophie's mum saw a glimmer of hope, this sudden change of mind was a blessing. 'Oh, I'm sure they will, and you can take their old dog for walks in the forest too,' she said keenly, hoping the dog might still be alive, after all, that was twenty years ago.
'I'll put you on the bus and give you a note for the driver to let you off at the right place and Aunt Florence will be waiting there for you.'
'Okay mum, but if there are no horses I'm coming home on the next bus.'
True to their word, the driver dropped Sophie off at a remote countryside bus stop and Aunt Florence was patiently waiting for her. Sophie liked her immediately. 'Isn't it quiet here Auntie . . . where is the car?'
'Ah, a car, yes, we had one of those contraptions a long time ago Sophie, but now we just look after ourselves up here in the mountains. Come along, give me your bag and we'll take a nice walk home through the woods. It's not far, about two miles, that's all.'
'Two miles!' thought Sophie, that's like forever. I don't even walk to school and that's only around the corner.'

The walk turned out to be very pleasant and not tiring at all as they walked on a carpet of soft pine needles and dry leaves. Sunshine lit the ground between the trees and in the distance a woodpecker could be heard making a home in some unlucky tree. Squirrels, curious to see who was walking through their forest, popped their heads around branches to watch. By the time Sophie reached the cabin she was already looking for the next adventure.

As soon as he heard their happy chatter arriving, Uncle Robert stopped digging in the vegetable garden and waved wildly, so pleased he was to see them. 'Hello my dear Sophie. My, how you have grown, you must be ten years old by now. . .' Sophie interrupted, 'actually, I'm eleven now uncle, or will be next month.'

They went into the house and showed Sophie to her room, 'Your mum stayed in here too you know. She liked it because the window looks out over the paddock. We had lots of horses then.'

Sophie's heart dropped. No horses? 'Have you no horses now then auntie?' she enquired, hardly able to hide her disappointment.

'Just the one now dear, a great big friendly white horse called . . . ' Sophie interrupted again, 'I see him, I see him, there, by the fence looking this way. Do you think he knows I am here Aunt?'

Aunt Florence laughed, 'he sure will, once you feed him a carrot or two. Go with uncle while I prepare the dinner. Not too long now, you'll need to calm down before bedtime. Not too long Robert, and not too many carrots either!'

Over the next few days Sophie enjoyed the pleasures of the countryside. In between picking berries, helping in the kitchen, and feeding the chickens, she played happily in the nearby woods. Instead of seeing animals on television she saw them for real and was always being amused by the squirrels that visited the gardens. But most of all, Sophie liked the friendly old horse. Sometimes Uncle Robert would sit her high up on his back, he seemed to like Sophie being there. He only walked slowly and never too far, for he was indeed quite old now. Uncle Robert told Sophie not to become too fond of the old horse as he was likely to be going the same way as the others had, possibly while Sophie was staying at the cabin. Sophie wasn't quite sure what to make of this but every morning when she woke; the old horse was peering at her window from the paddock. Perhaps dreaming of when he was young or perhaps just waiting patiently for another carrot.

Sophie's next favourite thing was sitting on the colourful rug in front of the log fire after supper, when aunt and uncle would tell her stories, stories about her mum, life in the mountains and their travels when they were younger. One night, Uncle Robert was to tell Sophie about the carpet she loved to sit on, it was a magic carpet. 'Well so the old gentleman told us when we bought it in a marketplace in the ancient city of Thebes,' confided Uncle Robert, with a glance towards the window to make sure no one else was there. 'We made instant friends with the shopkeeper. Mustapha Mohamed was his name. It was the only magic carpet he had ever seen in his entire life, but he'd not been able to find the secret which made it work. He said that it would be up to us to find the key that unlocked the magic.'

Sophie was spellbound, 'Have you tried abracadabra? Or open sesame? She asked, watching the rug very carefully as she spoke.

Her aunt Florence laughed, yes dear, we've tried them all, and in the end, we gave up. We only have Mustapha's word that it is a magic carpet and whether it is or is not, we've had it so long now it's become part of the family. See, it still has

all the bright colours and there are no holes in it anywhere, it's just like when we first had it.'
Evenings could be cold in the mountains and snow was always expected at this time of year. Tonight, could be the night. 'Well, time for bed Sophie but before you go, I have some sad news about your old friend out in the paddock. We are not wealthy people Sophie, and the time has come to send our old horse to another place. Possibly a man may arrive tomorrow to collect him.'
Sophie was terribly upset as she went to bed; she wished her mum was there, she would know what to do. Even though it was late, Sophie was still wide awake when she heard her aunt and uncle go to bed. They were soon snoring happily. Sophie looked out of her window, the snow had stopped and by the light of a full moon Sophie could see the old horse looking at her from over his fence. She saw him shiver with cold and shake off a little snow from his mane. She must do something; she could not rest until she had. Then Sophie had a wonderful idea. Tiptoeing in bare feet, she crept through the house and picked up the carpet from in front of the fire, how warm and dry it felt. Still in bare feet she crossed the snowy ground to the paddock and managed to climb onto the fence with the carpet in her arms. It was cold outside, but nothing was going to stop such a kind deed for this beloved animal. The feeble old horse moved shivering alongside the fence as though knowing he was about to have a warm coat. Soon the carpet was comforting him across his back. Little did Sophie realise that the key to the magic carpet was not in words at all but in actions of unselfish kindness. After all these years the carpet began to work its magic again, the old white horse was changing before Sophie's eyes, becoming more white, taller and muscles began to cover his old bones. He was young again, young, strong and no longer cold. But more! He was no longer just an old horse but a splendid

unicorn! Sophie watched in amazement as the unicorn shook off the carpet, took two steps forward and rose into the air, it was flying, flying over the paddock fence and away into the distant moonlit mountains. Sophie gathered the magic carpet in her arms, brushed the snow off and returned it to the warm fireplace where it would dry off overnight. Sophie didn't feel the cold anymore and was soon in bed and fast asleep.

Sophie was still snugly asleep when she was suddenly woken by shouting outside her window. It was Uncle Robert, he had discovered the old horse was missing, 'Florence, Florence, the horse has gone, come quick, look!'

Sophie quickly dressed in warm clothes and rushed outside to join them.

'Well I never, Florence. That old horse could never jump this fence and the gate is still locked.'

'That's not all Robert, look, there are no hoof prints in the snow outside the paddock. How could he possibly have got out? The man was coming to collect him today too, what on earth can we say to him?'

Sophie wasn't sure if it had all been a dream, but she chose to tell what she knew anyway, 'He just turned into a unicorn and flew across the mountains over that way,' she said pointing excitedly.

Aunt Florence gently brushed her hand over Sophie's hair, 'Bless you my dear child, what a lovely idea.'

'Yes,' said Uncle Robert, 'what an imagination they have eh? Well, it's a mystery to me. Let's have breakfast and see if we can find out how he escaped later.'

They never did find out. Only Sophie knew . . . and now you of course.

**

'If you believe in me, I'll believe in you,' said the unicorn.

Mo's Dream.

It had been a tragic and frankly awful six months for Maureen, or Mo as her few close friends knew her. Mo's mother had died suddenly and without any warning only the day before Mo and her good husband, Alan, were to pay her a visit. Mo was a kindly lady in her early forties, same age as Alan, and the death of her mother at only sixty-two, was an unwelcome and devastating shock.

Mo was a precious only child and her steadfastly protective mum had always looked out for her wellbeing until they'd moved many miles away for Alan to find better employment. The joy of visiting, laden with gifts, photos and news to share, took a crushing blow when the neighbours explained what had happened.

When they entered her mum's house it was neat and tidy, even more so than normal. The best china tea set was laid out ready on the polished front room table. Sharing the table was an old shoe box containing her mum's 'little treasures', her grandmother's wedding ring, her father's military medals, lots of photos of Mo as a child and a miscellany of buttons, tickets and postcards. There too, lay a writing pad opened ready on the first page; alongside, a simple but pleasing silver fountain pen, a gift from Mo, with black ink and broad nib; however, the page was blank, not a mark, just blank. Alan and Mo often wondered what the empty page would have told them. If only they had gone the day before, if only her mum had written the note, if only, if only. . .

Following this sad event, Alan was kept busy with his work, and Mo, with sorting her mum's estate, of which she was the sole and meagre beneficiary; her mother had been as poor in material possessions as she had been rich in emotional and spiritual matters.

Mo had many sleepless nights, thinking, dreaming, worrying, grieving and every night questioning just what the letter would have said. Who was it to? Why didn't her mum start it? Why was she writing it and why was the little 'box of treasures' alongside? Were they connected?
Sleep came and went but the questions were always there, even in her dreams the questions came.
Mo even thought about visiting a medium or psychic or anybody that might be able to fill in the gaps. She kept putting it off though because Alan wasn't much of a believer in such strange goings on.
Then, one Thursday evening in September, on his return from work, Alan told her, 'right Mo, that's it, get your bags packed and dig your walking boots out of the under stairs cupboard. We are off on a little holiday.'
'Oh, that's a lovely thought Al, it really is,' she replied warmly, 'but I don't think I'm up to it... and you have work tomorrow... '
'Nope! Got the day off... and Monday too... we're going and that's that. It will do you good... get away from this place and feel some fresh sea air, eat some good country food and maybe take a few walks on the moors too,' said Alan confidently as he held his head up high and smiled a smile of satisfaction.
'Moors?' Mo enquired, 'Where are we going then?'
'Never you mind, it's a mystery, no, it's a surprise. Everything is booked, all taken care of, already paid for, you'll like it, you'll see. So, sort out your gear and we're off at the crack of dawn... OK, perhaps not quite that early... and we'll buy a nice breakfast somewhere on the way.'
So, it was to be, and on one fine early September Friday they arrived at Countisbury; it was about noon when Alan pulled into a large car park to the sound of city tyres on country stones.

‘Here we are Mo, we have arrived. . . our new home for the next three nights,’ announced an excited Alan, ‘let's grab our bags and register at the Inn then the afternoon is ours.’ Mo was temporarily excited too; she had forgotten all her troubles. . . just for a while that is. Alan saw her mood change quickly as Mo noticed the old church and graveyard beyond the car park, her thoughts returning to her mum and the letter she never wrote. ‘Come on, that's enough of that, old girl, this is a lovely happy place, somewhere new that we've not seen before, it will be a lovely holiday. Let's see what they have for lunch. . . anything you want you can have.’
Mo snapped out of her thoughts, ‘of course, I'm sorry Al, I should be more thoughtful of you too. Let's treat ourselves; you can have a steak if you like.’ So saying, she threw her rucksack over one shoulder, picked up her handbag and they crossed briskly over the deserted roadway to the Inn.
It was a warm reception that welcomed them to their new 'home'. They settled into their upstairs room, situated above a quiet part of the building and with fine views of open countryside and a blue sky decorated with small white clouds. ‘There, look at that,’ said Alan, ‘if God were to paint a picture then surely it would look like this. Come on, change of plan, let's have a light lunch and get out there amongst that lovely nature.’
‘OK, love, I'll catch you up, I just want to lay here for a moment and enjoy the peace and quiet after the journey,’ murmured Mo as she kicked her shoes off and reclined on the bed, her eyes almost closing as if to enjoy the peace the more.
‘Don't be too long...’’ replied Alan as he quietly closed the latched door behind him and softly descended the stairs to the bar area. The ground floor of the Inn was huge, very long with changes of levels and room widths; it looked to Alan as

though it may have been extended or altered many times; it added to the charm, it added mystery. Alan soon made friends and chatted to a couple of pleasant local characters in the bar downstairs. Meanwhile, upstairs, as though someone who loved her had sent it as a gift, a gentle sleep overcame Mo. . . and almost as quickly, she was visited by a strange dream. It was as though she had gone back in time and was sitting in a quiet corner of the Inn downstairs; the only light, the light of early morning, came in through some cobwebby windows to her right, wood smoke drifted from the open fire along an oak beamed ceiling and a smiling, plump faced, pretty girl in servants garb walked happily towards her from the far end of the long room; she was only a few feet away when the sound of a wagon and horses on the old earth and stone road outside reverberated through the Inn as though it really were there; It woke Mo with a start. Now wide awake, she listened intently to an unexpected and all-pervading silence, then glanced at her watch; she hurriedly slipped on her shoes and went in search of Alan.

'Ah, there you are love, the landlady has made us some sandwiches and suggested a fine short walk to the headland where we can eat them and look across the sea to Wales. How's that?' said a beaming Alan.

Mo began, 'I've just had a strange dream. . .'

She was quickly interrupted by Alan, 'come on Mo, we've had enough of dreams for a while, we're on holiday, let's enjoy our time here. . .' and so saying, picked up the neatly wrapped sandwiches and taking Mo by the arm led her to the Inn door and the bright outside world of a September Devon. Alan was going to do his utmost to help Mo out of the doldrums of the last six months; this was going to be a special holiday.

They walked through the churchyard and out to the headland. The landlady was right, it was a beautiful spot. They were blessed with warm sunshine, found a comfortable rock to sit on and were sheltered from a light breeze by a bank of gorse which still carried its alluring coconut scent. The sandwiches were excellent, and time disappeared, replaced by contentment. As the sunshine began to fade, their thoughts turned back to the warm Inn and its open fire. 'Al, let's look around the church on the way back, I'd like that,' she said, standing and stretching her arms with pleasure.

'Okay,' Alan replied, adding, 'we'll have a night in by the fire, there's a nice one in a back room, with settees by it, we'll have a meal and why not a few drinks. . . we'll just chill out and enjoy our time. . . Right, the church it is. . .'

As they walked quietly alongside the outer wall of the churchyard towards the little wooden gate, Mo had a flashback to her earlier dream, a little shiver ran down her spine, she put it down to the cooling air and didn't mention it to Alan, he didn't seem to want to know these things. They spent a while reading the gravestones and wondering at the disparity of lifespan, there were those who made their eighties and some who never saw their first year out. 'Disease, probably,' intimated Alan, 'simple diseases we can treat now, were killers then. How lucky we are to know all what we do these days.'

That evening they enjoyed a lovely meal, found one of the Inn's many quiet and secluded corners and played some of the board games the Inn kept for guests. They played until Alan realised that perhaps he wasn't used to drinking so much and started losing both plot as well as games. 'I'm off to bed love,' slurred Alan knocking his legs against the low table they had been using.

'Okay dear, I'll be up shortly, I might see if I can get a hot chocolate,' Mo replied.

When Mo returned from the bar with her hot chocolate, she was surprised to see another guest sitting there, a pleasant old lady with a motherly look to her. 'Oh, I'm sorry,' said Mo turning to go.

'You do no such thing my dear, you sit ee here, I be Grace Elworthy and I'm not one to turn you away,' Grace gestured reassuringly and smiled warmly.

Taking a seat opposite, Mo said considerately, 'I should leave you in peace really.'

'Ar, dear, we're all looking to find that,' Grace replied softly.

'I'm sure I've heard that name before somewhere,' quizzed Mo.

'It's an old name round these parts, perhaps someone in the Inn mentioned it,' suggested Grace.

It was the beginning of a long and heartfelt conversation during which Mo told her all about her mum, the letter, Alan's work and how he was treating her to this special holiday.

'What a dear old soul,' thought Mo as she later climbed the stairs to bed, 'I feel so much better now.'

Later that night, Mo had the dream again, she saw the same girl with the mop cap walking towards her from the far end of the long room. . . it seemed she walked with real purpose but still smiling happily. . . then something quite strange happened, Mo became the girl in the dream; it was most odd, there were times when she felt that she was awake enough to tell herself it was a dream... most odd, most real, she felt awake, the dream world and the waking world seemed in confusion. Mo, now the servant girl, actually felt herself opening the Inn door, a different door to the one she knew as Mo the guest, she stepped outside and down two steps onto an earth and stone roadway. It was early morning in the dream and to her right, in front of a small barn and stable, was a young man preparing horses for a wagon. He had harness in hand but none the less lifted his cap and smiled coyly at her... Mo felt herself responding, this young man was the love of her life.

Up to then Mo hadn't taken notice of the iron pot she was carrying but now she did, for it slipped heavily from her hand and clattered loudly on the stones where it fell. The horses were spooked, they became increasingly more skittish and the young man struggled to calm them, he couldn't hold them both and one made off, bolting straight down the road and directly at Mo. Mo was frozen with fear, transfixed to the spot, the sound of hooves and the desperate cries of the young man filled her ears all in distorted slow time. The last thing she heard was the horse's frenzied breath and the last thing she saw was the sky vanishing into blackness. Mo sat bolt upright in bed with sweat pouring from her brow, her body surging with adrenalin, her breathing rapid and her hands trembling. Mo turned to Alan to wake him... tell him all about it. Mo stopped, looked at Alan snoring peacefully and resolved she would keep this silly dream to herself. Poor Alan had had so much grief since her mum died, he deserved this special holiday and he certainly didn't deserve being woken up at three in the morning by his crazy wife.

It was well over an hour before Mo slept again, there were no more such dreams. Still, she was up early in the morning and with questions to ask. She pulled the duvet around her sleeping Alan's shoulders and quietly crept downstairs in search of breakfast. . . and some answers too.

Mo was too early for breakfast, so she found a quiet corner in which to think on the nightmare of last night. She was so lost in thought she didn't notice her new found friend and confidante, the little old lady Grace, join her at the table.

'Good morning, dear,' said Grace quietly.

'Oh, hello Grace. . . not sure it's all that good mind you. . . I had a nightmare last night. . . saw a young lady die in an accident with a horse. . . right outside that door it was. . . brrr. . .,' shuddered Mo.

'Don't you worry about things like that dear, all such things can be explained, I've not been about all these years without taking an interest in such matters. . .' Grace paused for a moment, and then continued, 'I'll tell you all about it later, I think I hear your husband coming and you should enjoy each other's company without some old lady hanging around with you. Look for me when you have some quiet time and I'll tell you all.' Grace stood quietly with ease and left. Mo was just thinking how well Grace walked for an old lady of her age when. . .

'Morning Mo, crikey, what a night that was. . . I shan't be drinking as much today. . . how did you sleep?. . . come on, I think breakfast is ready through the back room. . .' Alan pointed animatedly in the direction of breakfast and gestured with the other hand for Mo to join him.

Alan and Mo sat opposite each other at the pine table, breakfast was brought in by the landlord himself, he placed the plates gently and asked if there was anything else. 'No, we're fine, thanks, 'said Alan. The landlord turned to leave, 'No, wait a minute please,' said Mo, holding her knife and fork at the ready, can I ask you a question?' The landlord nodded thoughtfully, and Mo continued, 'Tell me, do you have ghosts here? Do you know anything about a young woman, probably a servant who was killed by a horse outside your very door?'

The landlord smiled and said, 'Ghosts? I can't say as I've seen any here, we've been here a few years now. Sometimes the locals speak of such things, but I think the spirits are mainly in the bottles or in the customers. . . mind you, occasionally I'll hear the odd noise. . . but that's to be expected with an old creaky building like this one. . . even the wind howls by the door frame when it blows from the north,' he paused and thoughtfully put his hand under his chin, then continued, 'I have done lots of research on the building and its occupants and never come across any death of a young woman. . . I mustn't keep you; your breakfast will get cold.' He bowed his head slightly, turned and left for the kitchen.

Alan hadn't been listening that intently but asked, 'Wow, what was that all about then?' Mo didn't want to disturb Alan about her dream; he needed this holiday probably more than she.

'Oh, nothing really love, I just get the feeling that we are not alone here sometimes.'

'You're right, we're not,' said Alan sternly, 'we're being watched as we speak.' This was most unusual for Alan to take such things so seriously and it surprised Mo, even startled her a little. Alan continued, 'See, over there? I see eyes; watching us from by the doorway?' Mo hardly dared to turn her head to look. 'I reckon he's after one of these sausages!' Alan laughed and was back to his normal self as Mo turned to see the big black dog who lived at the Inn staring intently not at her but at the table and its contents.

She had to laugh herself, she needed to lighten up, she'd made something out of nothing. . . time to forget it and finish breakfast. 'What shall we do today then Al,' Mo smiled, 'take that dog for a walk?' They both laughed. . . it was a special holiday after all.

'There's a lovely old lady called Grace who's staying here, you must meet her sometime, she's a real angel, great to chat to about life,' confided Mo.

'Yes, there are some wonderful people around here. I was chatting with a couple of locals at the bar and they told me that there's a spectacular geological fault called the Valley of the Rocks. They told me how to get there and that it was worth the effort. . . but not to miss the Sunday lunchtime here. . . they said the Inn is renowned for its excellent Sunday lunches, they said there are people who come twenty miles just for the dinner. I do just love a Sunday roast,' said Alan looking wistfully into the future. . . almost certainly at a Sunday lunch.

'Okay, Valley of the Rocks, here we come. We'll go soon and walk off the breakfast before you restock with lunch. I sometimes wonder if anything else but food occupies your mind. Come on, teeth cleaned and boots on, let's be having you,' she chuckled to herself, threw her paper napkin remonstratively onto her empty plate and went to prepare herself for the next adventure.

The couple enjoyed a bracing walk in the Valley of the Rocks. It was a little colder than they expected, as much of the path didn't see the Sun until afternoon. None the less it was exhilarating, and they took a few photos of Castle Rock and the odd wild goat or two to take home for the album. They were pleased to return to the warmth of the Inn and even more pleased with the roast dinner. As the Sunday lunchtime diners started to thin out and go home, Alan and Mo enjoyed a few drinks and chatted with a local farmer and his wife. God, life was good on holiday, if not quite so good for farming; hedge cutting, ploughing and storing the winter feed, all needed doing. Alan enjoyed hearing of the practicalities of life on the moors. . . and enjoyed the fact they weren't his to worry about. . . God, life was good on holiday. As the last of the customers left the Inn for home, the tables were cleared and wiped by staff before they too disappeared into the kitchen. Suddenly all was quiet as the grave and Alan was struck by a bout of tiredness, 'must have been all that talk of work on the farm,' he told Mo.

'More like that big dinner and the few drinks that followed,' laughed Mo, 'why don't you go and lie down for a bit, I'll stay down here and read a while. . . I've seen a nice book on short stories about somewhere; it has a nice red cover with a table, a candle and a letter, looks interesting. Off you go, I'm fine.'

Good as the book might be it was not why Mo wanted to stay in the bar, she hoped that Grace might still be at the Inn; Mo had noticed that Grace wasn't one for crowds; in fact she'd noticed that Grace even avoided Alan, despite Mo desperately wanting him to meet her. As Mo searched and rounded one of the quiet corners of the long room, she almost bumped into Grace coming the other way, 'Oh, hello,' they both said in unison just like twins.

'Well, my dear, now there's no one about to listen to our conversation so I reckons I can tell you what you wanted to know. Let's sit by the inglenook, it be warmer there for ee. No one will come back in the bar until later this afternoon. They have their own dinners now and forty winks after,' said Grace with a wink of her own. 'About your dreams; they were more than dreams. . . sometimes they are you know. . . I sense I can tell you these things; it is your time to know. You saw the girl, well young woman really, because you were seeking something beyond your own living world. Your mind was open and receptive, that's how she could share with you her own experiences. It happened long ago, she was an orphan, only known by the name of Hannah. In fact, she was about twenty-three or four when she was killed, not so long before she was due to marry. I reckon that would be about 1892.

As you said, she was chubby faced, happy girl with a great purpose in life; she never fulfilled it and her spirit stays here trying to complete that which can never be.

The stable lad never stopped loving her and he never married another. . . he's buried over in the churchyard across the road, though not near Hannah; she was a pauper you see and buried in common ground with no marker. He has a grave marker, even if it is much worn and hard to find now but his spirit was content with what he had done in life with his sacrifice and dedication to Hannah, so his spirit has moved on. Your mum has moved on too, she was content with life, she could see you were happy and that was her purpose in life, just to see her daughter happy. I think this holiday was as much her idea as it was Alan's. He was suddenly inspired to act. . . a seed was planted in his mind and grew in his heart. I also think that seeing Hannah is also a message just for you. . . many might feel her presence but precious few will ever see her as you have done. . . It's a message that tells you there is somewhere else to go beyond death. Those who have fulfilled their purpose in life simply move on and those that have yet to do so struggle to find a way to join them. In consequence they can relive their demise over and over, trying to find a way of atonement, trying to find redemption, a way out of the spiritual prison their own mind has created. I also think that Hannah had a message for you too. . . about being happy. Hannah didn't question about her parent's life or death, she lived her orphan life as best she could, as happy as she could. For all her problems she was a happy girl. There is the answer you seek, be happy. It is what your mother would have written had she the time. Your mum sent you this message, this special holiday, today of all days you can be happy again. I've said too much I'm sure, I must leave you now to think. . . and smile. . . I must go; I have other things to attend to now. Perhaps I'll see you before you leave.'

Mo so wanted to hug that dear little old lady that had befriended her so kindly but it didn't seem appropriate at the time, she'd catch her later. Mo was at peace, the peace she had sought for months. With a smile on her face and a skip in her step she went in search of Alan. . . wake him and take him out for a walk to clear the cobwebs. . . or perhaps just quietly lay down beside him and sleep a happy dreamless sleep.

Come Monday afternoon the car was running well, almost as though it knew it was on the way home and the Autumn Sun shone brightly all around. The road was quiet, the car was quiet and Alan drove slowly so as to enjoy the experience, he felt good, all was well with the world, a beautiful world. Deep wooded combes gave way to undulating hills and views of the Somerset levels; he took the view in like taking a long and welcome breath.

'That was a great little holiday, wasn't it, Mo,' said Alan rhetorically, 'and we didn't think once about your mum's letter either; I wonder what she would have written.'

Mo reached out and touched his hand, 'sometimes there are no answers; sometimes you don't need the questions either; we might never know but our soul will.' She smiled a contented smile and looked out of the window to enjoy the rest of her journey; as she did so, her mind wandered back to the last few minutes at the Inn. . . Alan was carrying their bags out to the car, when Mo looked for Grace one more time, she was not to be found in all her usual haunts but Mo did find the landlord checking the bar stock, 'thank you so much for a wonderful holiday,' she'd said, 'can you tell me where I can find Grace, she helped me so much and I want to say goodbye.'

'Grace?' enquired the landlord, always willing to help if he could.

'Yes, that's her, Grace Elworthy, lovely old lady that's been staying here for the last few days.'

The landlord had put down the dust cloth and bottle, slowly turned with a puzzled look on his face to look Mo in the eyes and said, 'But Maureen, you and Alan were our only guests this weekend, no one else is staying here.'

**

'No argument is so convincing as is the evidence of your own eyes.'

**

The writer – all souls day.

From childhood, Susan Richmond had one abiding ambition, – to be a writer. However, life had conspired to keep her dream out of reach, that is, until today.

Today was All Souls Day and she decided to write a story in honour of her parents, both of whom had been talented writers. Her father was an eminent archaeology professor and author of many great historical novels. Susie's mother was more of a children's storyteller - skilled with the sort of beautiful bedtime stories that forever remained treasured childhood memories.

Tragically, both parents lost their lives in a house fire while Susie was away at university. She would have been nineteen back then, some thirty years ago. The fire officer's report to the coroner had indicated that her mother was probably dead long before her father had entered the burning building in a desperate attempt to rescue her. A futile but brave effort that would cost Susie both of her parents.

Susie had tried writing stories many times before, but any worthwhile tale always proved beyond her.

'None the less, today's the day,' she vowed, 'of all my days this is it. This evening, the magic will begin.'

She'd heard somewhere that a ritualistic scene setting was the key that opened the door to great stories. Such rituals placed the writer's spirit somewhere unworldly, somewhere between heaven and earth, in a twilight zone where souls could exchange ideas.

During the day, she tidied the house until all her jobs were complete and out of mind. She then lay resting on her sofa, listening to Tibetan chants on a CD she'd come across by accident in a charity shop. She waited quietly for evening to arrive.

Susie placed a cushion on one of the kitchen chairs and a small electric lamp on the table. The house was otherwise shrouded in darkness. Then Susie brought out a lavender scented candle, a mug of herbal tea, a glass of red wine, some white copier paper, and her best fountain pen with spare ink. She sat comfortably, satisfied that the ritual was as good as it gets, her back warmed by an open log fire. Across the table, she observed her own reflection in a dark kitchen window. As Susie stared thoughtlessly at her own reflection it amused her to see glimpses of her mother and her grandmother looking back. These brief apparitions pleased her as she remembered those kind people. Susie smiled to herself, took a sip of wine and picked up her pen.

The clock on the wall tick tocked its sleepy song, the full moon showed itself briefly from behind the clouds and the world journeyed on relentlessly.

'Oh no, not again,' she sighed, realising that all she'd done was stare at the white paper. The paper, without judgement or emotion, simply stared back, as it had already done for the last ten minutes.

Anxiously, she stared wide-eyed into an unhelpful gloom and begged the heavens for help. Anyone's Gods would do, ancestors, angels, even the devil himself if they could only release her imprisoned spirit.

Then it arrived, a joyful spark of inspiration. She didn't need anyone's help after all. Indigo ink flowed freely from her pen, though not quick enough for the wonderful ideas that crowded into her mind. She was almost in tears with the hurry to scribble one thought down before the next one pushed it aside. Her pen frenziedly scrawled across page after page. The scented candle flickered benevolently as she reached out for a sip of tea. The fire at her back reminded her of sitting on her mother's lap and the warmth of her body while some enchanting story lured her into the strange world of dreams.

Susie's father had told her more than once, 'a story must always have a grain of truth, like the grain of sand in an oyster from which something beautiful will grow.'

Her own grain of truth right now was about never giving up hope, that everything must be possible if you only apply yourself wholeheartedly into the venture, for it is belief itself that gives rise to real power.

Reflections looked lovingly on from the windowpane, the soft light from the table lamp and perfume from the candle flame effortlessly carried Susie's hand across the paper – a masterpiece in the making. In beautiful script, the writer's spirit indelibly crafted the essence of story in her mind – it was no longer a mystery. Her father's words again whispered to her soul, 'Never try and possess something, for it will in turn, imprison you.'

At last, she'd made it. She was completely at one with her story, a mistress of her own destiny. The story was good. No, better than good. It was exceptional and very few alive today could compete with its brilliance. It was a prize winner for sure. Totally original, with heroine, mystery, danger and eternal hope, it was all she'd dreamed of, ever since she could remember.

Finally, she put down the pen and felt her body relax. Then, the strangest thing, she sensed her father standing behind her, hands light and kindly on her shoulders, like when helping with her homework as a child. His voice, filled with reassurance, 'There dear, it's not so difficult after all, is it?'

Susie was startled by a burning log falling in the fireplace and illuminating the room with its eerie light, her tea was cold, the candle nearly out.

She looked down to admire her work. Blank white paper looked back, still waiting.

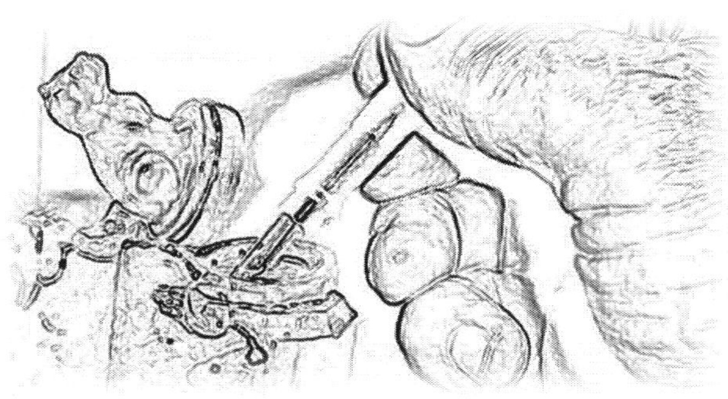

**

'Of ghosts, as it is with mirrors,
only on reflection will you know what might exist.'

**

Emily's Friend.

One misty September morning 1894 and it was just after seven in the little moor side cottage.
'If she's not ready soon, I won't be taking her to the mill with me,' George said to his wife, Victoria.
She smiled back and pointed to a small window that overlooked a narrow lane and the river beyond. 'Look there George, she's been waiting for you this last half hour. You know how she loves to visit the mill.'
George returned the smile, picked up the neatly packed lunch basket and replied, 'I know, I know. She's found a friend near the mill to play with.'

George reminded his wife that they might not be back till late, perhaps even after dark. . . but, 'everything would be fine.'

A cart hitched to two heavy horses stood in the lane ready to go. Shires they were, powerful, dependable, and hardworking creatures. George and daughter Emily, aged eight, climbed aboard and set off with a cheery wave. Soon they began the long climb that would take them through the wooded valley and on to the desolate moors.

The colours were already changing with the season and the autumn Sun shone warm and bright. The horses plodded steadily onwards, simply taking the moorland track in their stride. All was peaceful and happy. George whispered to Emily, 'Did you know, something is watching us from the hill to our left?' Emily peered at the hill, seeing nothing but bracken and gorse, then that something moved, and she saw it immediately. 'Oh, isn't he wonderful? He must be the finest stag on the entire moor.'

As the cart trundled on, Emily watched longingly as the great stag slowly faded into the distance. The great stag watched them go.

'Makes you wonder what else could be out there on the moor, just watching us as we go by, us not seeing, never even knowing,' said George, thoughtfully.

It made Emily think too and she edged closer on the wooden seat to her father's side.

As they neared their destination, the landscape began to change once more to wooded valleys. The mill was down at the very bottom of the valley and driven by waterpower from the small but fast flowing River Erle.

'Remember to keep away from the water, Emily. You must be . . .' George was interrupted before he could finish.

'Yes dad, I know. Be careful, stay away from the water and the machinery. I've been told a hundred times already,' said Emily with a hint of annoyance, 'my friend always warns me not to go anywhere near it.'

'Sensible friend that,' George thought, 'Emily seems to be aware of the danger; I'll not mention it again.'

George drove the horses just past the mill building to a horse trough under a great beech tree where they were glad of the shade and cool drink.

'Come on Emily, let's go in and see the miller, then you can find your friend and play, while I help in the mill.' So saying, George lifted Emily down from the cart. They walked away hand in hand, leaving the sound of horses drinking and the shaking of heads and harness behind them.

'Perhaps I'll meet your friend this time Emily?' George asked.

'She'll probably turn up when all the old people are inside,' Emily replied with a dash of authority.

Emily and George entered the old stone building, where they were warmly greeted by the owner, a kindly man called Harry Baker, 'Welcome, George, good to see you again. . . and you too young Emily, how quickly you are growing up.'

'Right, Emily,' said George, 'we have business to attend to. Take the feed bag off the cart and give it to the horses, watch they don't stamp on your feet. Then you can play a while until call for you.'

The miller called after her, 'You keep away from the water young lady. You keep well away.' He sounded really stern. Not like him at all.

An hour or so later everything was ready for loading. George leaned his head out of the doorway to see where Emily had gone. She was sitting by a pile of logs talking to herself and giggling. He smiled to see his daughter playing so happily on her own. Obviously, her friend hadn't turned up that day. It was a shame.

'Come along now, Emily. We must be off home. We want to be off the moors long before sunset.'

As they prepared to leave, Harry Baker the kindly miller pressed a shiny new copper penny into Emily's hand, 'spend it wisely my dear.'

Emily thanked him and with a smile, stepped outside, looking down at her new treasure.

'Lovely girl, your daughter George, reminds me so much of my own.

As they drove the moorland track, George spoke with Emily about her friend who hadn't turned up that day.

'But she was there dad, Lizzie is always there, I suppose you just didn't see her,' Emily explained. 'Lizzie is a really happy girl, we're the same age and she's the miller's daughter. We always play by the logs and keep away from the water, which she doesn't like at all.'

George wasn't sure what to believe; perhaps it was just childish imagination. 'Children are like that,' George thought, as he peered about the surrounding moor, wondering what else was out there that he couldn't see but could still see him.

As the afternoon wore on, the air cooled and the mist began to return, Emily sat closer still to her father, he gently flicked the reins, and it wasn't long before they were off the moor. Great hooves clip clopped their way along the lane and the crunch of stones beneath the heavy iron rims of the cartwheels brought Victoria to the door to greet them with a smile. They were safely home before the darkness came and with much news to tell.

Back at the mill, work was finishing for the day. Dusk was fast approaching, and the miller struck a match to light a lantern. He stopped by the doorway and brushed dust from

a stone set in the wall. He smiled quietly with fond memories as he read the name in neatly carved letters, 'In loving memory of Lizzie Baker. . .' He brushed more dust away with his sleeve and now with a tear in his eye, read on.
.' . . age Eight years two months, drowned near this place, fourth September 1888.'

'So often the real truth is hidden by what we prefer to think.'

**

Meditation – one last journey.

Using meditation, Tom had found a way in which he could leave his pained and frail body behind in the hospital bed and visit the mountains he'd always loved. Once there, he was fit and strong, his breathing easy. His favourite journey was to walk from the wooded valley and beyond the tree line to the sun-bathed snow slopes above.
While enjoying his mountain walk one day, he was overwhelmed by an urge to know what lay the other side of the summit. He'd never ventured that far before and knew he must delve deeper and longer than ever. Deeper still into

the quiet of his inner consciousness he went, until at last, just a few more steps to take then he would be on the other side, a place he'd never been before. He knew he dare not stay long for soon it would be time to return to his wretched existence of pain and distress.

It was just after three in the afternoon and Doctor Gratton solemnly addressed grieving relatives gathered at Tom's bedside, 'I'm sorry to say we've lost him. We tried everything we could to bring him back but found no response. I'm afraid we were left with no alternative but to terminate and switch off the machine. He seems at peace now.'

They nodded in acceptance that Tom would no longer feel pain.

A stillness filled the room, much as he'd always found on his mountain.

**

'One thought alone can stop ten thousand.'

**

Last desperate grasp for fame.

Ever since leaving school, she'd wanted to write and write well, to please, to entertain, to enlighten. All too often her proud efforts were denigrated by the blindly opinionated, but she never once let go of her dream. Her soul burned with the desire to produce a literary masterpiece that none could, nor would ever dare, deny. . . a lasting and fitting epitaph to her life struggles and final triumph.

'One day,' she determined quietly and resolutely to herself, 'one day.'

Week in week out, year in year out, in respectful humility she applied herself to researching, thinking, scribbling and typing her short stories. Slowly changes came, in her style, in genre, in grammar and in composition, though few credited her efforts.

Eventually, as old age beckoned her more assertively, inspiration came at last, a 'light bulb' moment, a brilliant story like she'd never heard before. . . an original. The story burned like a bright light in her soul, illuminating all that was once hidden in darkness.

Soon after, in a secluded cliff top hut overlooking the ocean she was to find the perfect setting to entrust her mind's eye to the written word and finally reveal her true literary genius to the world. Life had never before felt like this. She was enchanted.

Keeping the dark wooden window shutters in place with the door open to sea and sky, her sanctuary wore the quiet cloak of a hermit's cave. It was ideal, only her, her pen, and her ideas. Even the little path outside remained peacefully quiet and un-walked all day. It was a most appropriate place to begin and end her story. A story that couldn't have been finished anywhere else.

With a simple, admirable character, succinct wording and indispensable description, her story was as good as any could ever pen. Her little hands struggled to make the pen move quickly enough over the paper. The spelling was rushed and flawed, but no matter, the story and its final twist transcended all criticism. No one would dare venture a word of disparagement over this one. Once typed up correctly at her leisure, it would be sent out to eagerly awaiting publishers. She knew it would be a success and they would fight over the rights like their lives depended upon it. At last, she would be known, be valued, she would be somebody, her name would live forever along with the Bronte sisters, Austen, Potter, and others. Her efforts and enduring faith in herself would finally be vindicated.

As the tide withdrew for the second time that day and dusk tentatively approached, her cramped fingers scrawled the final, spidery, inspirational line - a line exclusively sent her by the Gods.

Now it just needed taking home to type. Pulse racing, her heart almost burst with excitement as she tore her story pages from the pad. She stood and walked to the door, a half step outside and, feeling dizzy, she paused momentarily. She reached out a hand for the shifting door frame.

'Silly me,' she thought, 'must have been sitting too long.'

The thought had hardly left her mind when she was struck by a thudding chest pain. Her left hand tightened to a fist, reluctantly crumpling her precious story. She was still conscious as her body hit the uneven slabs outside the hut and felt the cool of an evening breeze begin to blow.

Later, in the unattended moment of her passing, her hands twitched in one last desperate attempt to hold on, then relaxed and fell open.

A passing dog walker discovered her body next morning. Her literary gem, her epitaph, the proof of her worthiness was already scattered by the four winds into oblivion and, just like so much other litter, blown along the distant shoreline.

Only nature herself knows she was worthy of her own belief and yes, you're right, we don't even know her name.

Many a story is made and lost in such places.

BUREAUCRACIES AND POLITICS

A moorland tale of intrigue.

All names have been changed to protect the innocent, that being me, (protection from litigation, prosecution, kneecapping or simply being fed to the pigs.)

It wasn't so long ago, certainly in living memory, and in a land where the pace of life and the people who lived it seemed to have been left behind by civilisation itself. This story is inspired by a misplaced coroner's report, unfounded rumour and an isolated moor-land inn, we cannot say where. . . . it must remain yet another secret.

The press, particularly the rural press, *Moonraker's Weekly* and the magazine *Cull Monthly*, were full of subjective speculation as only the press can be, and the scattered moorland communities were rife with fervently bigoted rumour. Rumours without any basis in fact but none the less, they spread like bubonic plague, a series of Chinese whispers making them worse at each telling. Over garden walls, in the streets, the shops and pubs, everywhere rumours flourished. 'Of course, his wife will have to move house you know. She can't stay there, not now. I bet it was much worse than we can imagine. . . poor woman.' 'Yes, they say she must have known he was seeing them on a daily basis, probably calling out their names in his sleep; Must have been awful for her.' 'My God, I mean when did he go? Did he go at night? He always seemed to be around when we visited the Inn. He seemed like a nice bloke too, friendly chap he was.'

'Arr, that be his trouble, they'm reckons he were a bit too friendly they'm do.' 'Why, I'd heard he even had a portrait or a sculpture of one of his old acquaintances brazenly displayed on the pub wall.' 'Arr, no, it were the real thing, it was a real pig's head, nailed to the wall above the fireplace it were. . . girt big tusked thing, bold as brass he was.'

And so, the rumours went on and on and still to this day if you listen with a hush, you'll catch the whisperers at work whenever two moor-land people meet.

The coroner, one Doctor Remus Blenheim-Landrace Esq OBE, chairman of the local hunt committee and an internationally celebrated Cavy/Wallaby cross breeder, had concluded a misadventure verdict on the matter even before the matter had been investigated. He hadn't been interested in tittle tattle, well not publicly anyway, he dealt with evidence, hard evidence; he was a staunch right-wing defender of the law, as he interpreted the law anyway. Close friends of the good Doctor though, confided that he'd his own personal suspicions, about which he was bound by sacred oath not to disclose.

These are extracts from the personal diary of the court recorder, an elderly spinster with a vehement dislike of men. Miss Hades Vendetter always kept private notes as well as meticulous court records, that way she knew the truth could never be hidden. Sometimes she would feign deafness in order to humiliate a witness into repeating something she knew they'd rather not. 'Excuse me Coroner, could you ask farmer Cagey to repeat that bit about having a fondness for pigs himself, I couldn't hear through his mumblings, thank you coroner,' a hint of a snigger in her voice. The witness was then forced to face Miss Hades and repeat in loud clear words that yes, he was a pig fancier and proud of it. The police had confiscated a number of computers from drinkers at the pub, there was no denying it, the hard drives said it all, deleted files couldn't save them from forensics. Several farmers were questioned as to why they had googled for

things like, 'how to bed down your pigs,' 'what pigs need to keep them happy,' 'how to keep pigs quiet,' 'the dangers of making one pig your favourite,' 'nice names for pigs,' 'alcohol and pig behaviour,' 'pig breeding habits,' and so on. They came up with several lame and obviously conjured excuses like, 'breeding pigs for meat,' 'growing pigs on for market,' etc, one foolishly admitted to owning a potbellied pet. A senior Home Office Immigration official, Mr Ian Neptitude was contacted immediately as this pig was believed to be of Vietnamese origin and invoking even more scandal. There were a lot of people, high society people, who hoped the net wouldn't be spread too far and wanted the minimum of effort exerted in this tragic and obviously misunderstood case.
A top forensics scientist, Dr Joseph Scraghill PhD, JP, holder of People's Star of USSR, and a closet card carrying communist, had been given the investigation by accident. On the governor's desk two pieces of paper lay one over the other, one said, 'Do not employ this man on anything important.' The other piece of paper was instructions for an all-expenses paid 'holiday' trip to Exmoor on a job that 'didn't warrant close inspection under any circumstances.' Scraghill's name was inadvertently scribbled on the wrong one by a work experience girl from Bulgaria. Dr Scraghill couldn't understand why he'd been given such a plum job and looked upon it with scepticism and a great deal of suspicion, 'they'll have to get up earlier in the morning to catch me out,' he thought, planning the most detailed investigation since helping the KGB and the Stasi finding covert capitalist scum during his annual summer holiday trips to the old eastern block.
Well now he was in the witness box in front of Doctor Remus Blenheim-Landrace Esq OBE, a man to whom he instinctively took an intense proletariat dislike and if the

country was run his way, he would have had him shot at dawn, or earlier if at all possible.

The coroner hadn't got a clue who he had before him, he was half asleep and mentally writing his concluding speech, in a beautifully vague whitewash colour... 'Er, welcome Doctor, I understand that you are the so-called expert witness sent by Whitewash... I mean Whitehall.

'Not exactly Doctor,' glared Dr Scraghill as if looking along the sights of an AK47, 'I am the forensic scientist in charge of the investigation and will be giving you precise and definitive evidence relating to this bizarre suicide.' There was a gasp and shudder throughout the court and public gallery, from whence the occasional whiff of silage would flavour the air. Now the coroner was no longer half asleep but with eyes bulging out he stared disbelievingly at the perpetrator of such sordid lies about his friend and brotherhood associate, the deceased.

'We'll see about that Doctor, please proceed with your illusory suppositions,' said the coroner whose voice had suddenly reverted from his Devonian accent to one that was more often found in the dormitories of Eton, 'please proceed and with all due caution Doctor.' He wondered if his advantageous coroner powers extended to prison terms for despicable witnesses... or having him sectioned might be better, cleaner, clandestine, less paper trail, yes, the Doctor might enjoy seeing what it was like on the other side of the wire so to speak. Wouldn't do him any harm at all.

The coroner came out of his daydream just as the witness continued, . . . 'wire, yes wire was used in the most intriguingly clever manner for such a mundane man as a pub landlord, very clever. From what I have gathered the landlord was inclined to beer drinking binges with his pigs, who he apparently knew intimately by name... '

'Yes, yes, get on with it man, what about the wire. . . lots of folk around here drink with pigs, get on with the bit about the wire. Did he strangle himself with it?' demanded a very annoyed coroner, who'd not been so frustrated since he missed his turn with matron at public school. 'Get on with it!'

'Oh, touched a nerve here,' thought Scraghill, wondering if the coroner himself was implicated and ought to be investigated and secondly how long he could drag out his answer about the wire, 'Ah yes, the wire, I'll be coming to that all in good time,' he replied slowly. 'My own,' thought Scraghill with the smile of a man perusing Gulag plans for the English upper classes. 'His, the deceased's, relationship with his porky pals was about to come to an end, his wife had discovered about his drinking soirées and had made plans for Euthan Aziers Abbatoir Services to arrive prematurely. . . for all concerned as it happens. He determined to end it all cleverly so no one would suspect, but he didn't count on such a thorough investigation.'

'Yes, yes, man, get on with it,' twitched the coroner, worried his angina and piles would be aggravated by the tensions this oaf of a Doctor, if indeed he was a real one, was causing him, 'the wire, the wire.'

Miss Hades Vendetter made little personal notes by the side of everything that was said, this was one of the best inquests she'd been on since one of the pub customers bet that he could hang-glide off the cliffs using only a frame tent and some string. Some say he must have made it and flown to Wales, others that he faked it as a jest and was moving house anyway, yet others believed the evidence of an unidentified body found out at sea. *(Not an unusual occurrence during the Exmoor troubles they say.)*

'After plying his friends, I mean his pigs, with enough mature beer slops to drop an Ox or a stoker, and himself on imbibing sufficient anaesthetising quantities of quality local brewed ale, he threw himself into the deep mud of the pig pen, cleverly engaging his foot through the electric fence as he did so. The electric wire kept him safe from the pigs and allowed him to drift off into a peaceful but twitching stupor, eventually the batteries went flat, the pigs, like most blokes after a few beers were hungry and that was that. The only thing left was a booted foot on the outside of the fence, which I presume will find Christian burial at the conclusion of this inquest. I suspect that the landlord will be renewing his customers' acquaintance in the guise of the pub's Sunday roast dinners. My conclusion is guilty of suicide with collusion by his mates the pigs.'

Doctor Remus Blenheim-Landrace Esq OBE, chairman of the local hunt committee and an internationally celebrated Cavy/Wallaby cross breeder, smirked a secret brotherhood smirk as Dr Scraghill was taken away in a straight-jacket, screaming 'you wait till the revolution, you're first against the wall.' This statement was recorded by Miss Hades with glee and used in the psychiatric report, increasing doubt on the good doctor ever being released. The chief psychiatric nurse, R Arfbake OBE RCN, was an old fraternal associate of Dr Remus and had promised to see Scraghill had all the treatment he needed for long term correction. . . apparently, they had stored some early electrical equipment in the basement, and it still worked.

'Misadventure,' shouted the coroner, violently whacking the gavel down with an aristocratic relish as if eliminating some commy infiltrator from his own beloved version of society.

It was all over, the records were conveniently 'lost' somewhere in the 'files' and the local paper *Moonraker's Weekly*, edited by Mr Bertram 'Snooks' Wilberforce Junior OBE published a brief account of 'hero publican gives life to stop fanatical left wing pigs attacking village. The Coroner praised the publican who we cannot name for legal reasons and said that 'he would be sadly missed at the meetings and indeed at the pub. . . where you could still always count on a good Sunday dinner."

So, nobody knows, all except a little old lady called Miss Hades, and now you.

Best not tell, if you know what's good for you.

**

**

Dichotomy of a Brotherhood Bargain.

Nathan Sykes hunched his shoulders and stared thoughtfully into an empty beer glass in the *'Live and Let Live'* Inn, a spit and sawdust meeting place for the rough and ready lower classes. Big Jack Tyler, swarthy and rugged landlord, looked like he was born to run such a cut-throat establishment. 'So, Nathan, you been away on holiday these last six months then? Butlin's or her Majesty's place?'

'Rather not say, Tyler my friend. I been dealt some bad cards in life. I deserved better you know. Skilled bricklayer me, but you got to know the right people to get the right job. I tried for the Masonic club for years so I could make the right contacts, but they turned me away.'

'Well Nathan, if you're still interested, see that chap in the corner over there?' Tyler points to a dark corner of the pub. 'He's one of them funny handshake blokes. He might help. He's almost always alone, never seen him buy a drink yet neither.'

Nathan stared into the darkness, seeing no one. When he looked a second time, he could just make out a tall gentleman, smartly dressed in a long black coat. He decided he would give them one more try, after all, what had he to lose? 'Evening sir, may I join you?'

The gentleman, who had the appearance of an undertaker, nodded, and gestured with his hand.

Nathan took notice of the hand movement just in case it was one of the secrets he needed later. 'Is that a secret gesture sir?' he inquired with a smile, he was a cheeky rogue, despite a truly merciless criminal past.

'No, I'm merely pointing to the chair. But I guess from your question I might surmise the purpose of your attention. If you have a wish to join the brotherhood, then sit and tell me about yourself.'

Nathan spent the next hour selectively confessing his crimes and making excuses for previous rejections. Finally pleading for one more chance – in return for which, there was *nothing* he wasn't prepared to do.

The old gentleman made a gesture with his left hand and said, 'You may be in luck, one of the brothers has, er, moved on. You seem like just the one to take his place. Be here tomorrow night at the same time and I will take you to the chosen place. Do not be late. Do not tell a soul.' He reached out a hand, which Nathan took eagerly, studying every nuance of the grip. For who knows what is secret and what is not? The gentleman's hand was icy cold, 'Gor Blimey,' thought Nathan, 'that's what comes of sitting in a dark corner too long.' But he was too excited to think more on it. He must go home – no more robberies for him – he would be rich once he was in with that lot. Easy jobs, easy money. Once he was in, he'd show 'em, he'd teach them a lesson for rejecting him too. . . . He put on a kindly voice, 'Goodnight to you sir. . . Good night Tyler . . . .'

Next day, Nathan Sykes was a new man, something had changed in him.

'God, if ever there was one,' he thought, 'has brought me hope at last.' However, it was not to God, but to Tyler the landlord, he offered up thanks. He would always be indebted to him. Though he might not drink there anymore, not once he was a brother. As he walked through town, past St Paul's Church and into the busy market square by the river, he met a couple of the men he had begged for help in the years before, he smiled and nodded to them, gesturing with his hand like the gentleman had – just in case it was a sign. They smiled back and nodded too. Nathan spent a good hour in the sunshine amongst the market people, nodding, smiling, and gesturing. Perhaps it was all as simple as that . . . he looked forward with increasing relish to knowing more secrets.

The appointed hour was closing steadily, and darkness fell stealthily upon the town. Nathan had arrived early at the '*Live and let Live*' to fortify his nerves with a few beers. The old gent eventually appeared in the shadows of a side door and silently beckoned Nathan to join him. Soon they were hurrying along the pitiless narrow terraced streets towards the lane by the river, where the lodge had stood for some two hundred years. Nathan had many questions, but it was as much as he could do to keep up with the old man, who obviously wasn't in a talkative mood this time.

At the lodge entrance, the old gent explained to Nathan that this would be a turning point in his life. Now he must choose, either to go forward or return to whence he came. Whatever his choice, it was final, there being no second chance.

Nathan wasn't completely stupid, he reckoned this was simply one of the first tests. Well, he'd show them. 'Forward. It's time I had what I deserve. I'm ready.'

The old gent slowly rapped three times on the door, watched carefully by Nathan, who was absorbing all the secrets he could.

The door opened into a small vestibule with bare boarded floor and coat racks with a dozen or so old-fashioned cloaks and coats. The gent's cold hand on his back ushered Nathan inside. The door closed behind them and they were in darkness. When you've burgled a few homes, darkness is something you became used to, but Nathan had to dig deep to overcome a sense of foreboding, this was different.

The old gent spoke, 'may the light of those gone before, now shine.'

A weird glow appeared in the room, just enough to make out two figures, the gent and now one other, as though spirited in from nowhere. Desperate not to forget any of the secrets, especially this clever one on how to turn on the lights, Nathan was so intent on mentally repeating the words over and again, he hardly noticed the preparations for his initiation. He was past caring anyway, he didn't mind what happened as long as he learned the secrets to the life he desired, and so thoroughly deserved.

The gent spoke again, 'Nathan Sykes, with the power invested in me by those who went before, I will now lead you into the lodge to meet your fate. My advice is simple. Keep to the rules and obey all requests, no matter how strange they seem. You will be blindfolded throughout; this is for *your* protection. I now advise you most strongly, do not cheat, do not try to see. If you do, well, I'll leave it at that. You have been warned. You made your decision outside these doors. Now, you can only make the best of it.'

Nathan began to speak but was interrupted by a hand across his mouth, 'you will not speak out of turn, not where you are going. Stay silent. Do not worry. I will be here at the end to lead you back into town.'

It felt to Nathan that the ceremony went on for hours. He'd been led in and around what seemed like catacombs. Once, led down a spiral stairwell, the air had turned earthy, there was the damp smell of old lime. Someone had tried to disguise it with herb incense, but he'd been a bricklayer too long to be fooled by that. All manner of visions came to him as his mind compensated for loss of sight. He was filled with a sense that something was dead or dying in the surrounding blackness. Finally, the ceremony with all its rituals came to an end and he was accepted as one of them. Still in darkness, and not once had he dare test the old gent's words about cheating, each of the brothers offered up the secret grip, always exactly the same way and all of them with cold hands. Nathan thought that the place needed heating, all hanging about in the dark like that, no wonder they were cold. Once he'd been a few times he would suggest a fire of some sort, yes, that would do, what they needed was a jolly decent fire.

Thrilled with the night's proceedings and clutching as many secrets as he could carry in his head, Nathan was led back into town by the old gent. It was late, streetlamps were few and far between and a night mist had risen from the river. The old gent shook Nathan's trembling hand, Nathan responded as best he could. 'Remember,' said the old gent, 'there is no going back for you now, you are one of us. I will come and find you when it is time.'

Nathan shuddered at the gent's bony and icy grip and the tone of his words but put it down to damp night air.

'Thank you, sir, for opening the door for me. I look forward to your calling. Good night.'

Next day Nathan Sykes, newly born of the brotherhood, stepped into early morning sunshine, and set off to the marketplace to try out his new secrets. He was in luck, one of the gentlemen he'd met the other day was approaching. Nathan smiled, nodded, and held out his hand, quietly uttering a password. The man responded in kind and asked when and where Nathan had joined the fraternity. Nathan was over the moon. . . it worked. From now on everything was going to be different, oh, so different. 'Why, brother, were you not there last night at the lodge by the river? That was me being led around in the dark.'

Nathan paused as a puzzled expression spread over the man's face. He looked uneasy, even shocked.

'But brother Sykes, we have our new lodge now, behind the library in Harpur Street. The old one burned down, as it

happens, six months ago to the day. To be honest we only ever felt comfortable in numbers there, few could tolerate being alone. After the fire, the building was demolished and during excavations a number of bodies were found. They're still investigating of course, possibly an old plague pit but to tell the truth it's still a mystery. So, all joking aside, where did you join?'
Nathan had no time for further talk. He was on his way to the *'Live and let Live.'* There were questions needing answers.

Nathan Sykes was last seen late that same evening, walking quickly in the gathering darkness towards the lane by the river. A lamp lighter on his rounds reported that Mr Sykes looked agitated and seemed to be talking to himself, for there was no other with him.
The *'Live and let live'* was demolished to make way for the modern bus station that stands there today. The Lodge in its new home prospered more than ever. The building was a pleasure to enter, even in solitude and contemplation.

This strange tale of Nathan Sykes comes to us from the diary of the late Reverend Robert J Williams, incumbent of St Paul's Parish 1951 – 1958 and the last brother that Nathan was to meet in the cold light of day.

**

'Men occasionally stumble over the truth,
but most of them pick themselves up and hurry off
as if nothing has happened.'
Winston Churchill.

**

The world we live in, the world we create, is full of traps.

**

Your Government needs you.

(A one-way street - allegedly)

This work of fiction is not based on any persons living or dead and bears no resemblance either to the Government of the day or any broadcasting corporation, past or present or anything else you might imagine.

High up in a plush penthouse office suite of Broadcaster House, something rather more foul than normal was about to come home to roost.

'It's the Home Secretary on the line for you Sir Hugh, he insists that it is most urgent and highly confidential,' explained Bo, Sir Hugh's long overlooked and undervalued Personal Assistant.

'Put him through Ms Bo,' replied the totally unqualified Executive-in-Chief Sir Hugh 'Peregrine' Braggington Havalot, as he turned the volume down on his games console. He'd been blessed with inheriting the post when his step cousin, Lord Willy Hademdown the third, an unplanned product of selective inbreeding, died unexpectedly suddenly at a weekend grouse shoot on his boyfriend's 'not for profit' country estate.

Sir Hugh had earned the nick name 'Peregrine' due to his accent, purportedly aristocratic background, and the elevated position of his office from which he surveyed his prey far down below in the bustling metropolis. He knew nothing of this and to be honest, he knew nothing of very much at all.

The primly dressed, sixty-year-old Ms Bo, Boedica Flabergast, on the other hand was eminently qualified but had been actively ignored for any further promotion. Basically, she was too clever and always posed a potential threat to the dim witted who had normally found their own promotion surprisingly easy. Despite having unstintingly worked her little ice-blue cotton socks off for over forty years at the Corporation, she was now fated to work until sixty-seven before even being entitled to a pension. She had seen many a senior executive retired much younger on various and nefarious grounds, usually incompetence, and still receive an impressive life pension and a mind-boggling golden handshake. Something, along with the entire working population of the country, she could never fathom. Failure seemed to have its own peculiar rewards.

Oh, they had fobbed her off with their plausible excuses - when she was young and enthusiastic, they needed someone more experienced, more mature - when she was older and

more experienced they decided they needed someone younger, someone more daring, not institutionalised.
'Institutionalised?' To Boedica's keenly observant mind most of the senior staff at the Corporation should be sectioned and living in an institution and they soon would be too, if she ever had her way.
'Ah, Hugh, old boy,' came the Home Secretary's plum in the mouth Etonian voice, 'just thought I'd let you know about a new super bonus scheme we are pushing through the lobbies to advantage our finest and most loyal public servants such as your good self. Just thought I'd keep you in the loop for old time's sake, you know. Well, that's it old boy, you must come to dinner some time, bring the little woman if she insists. . . . Oh, I almost forgot, we need you to do the Government a small favour, keep us out of the news for a day or two . . . find something else, something exciting that doesn't mention the government at all, almost like we are on a different planet.'
Boedica controlled a snort and silently concurred that the Government might as well be on another planet for all the good they did. She then gently, with a skill that can only come with extensive practice, replaced the receiver. Forty years working among the gaily self-centred cunning of senior executives had taught her a good few tricks and her pension would be graciously enhanced by sales of her memoirs, an expose of the inept, corrupt and insane that ruled the country over four decades.
Sir Hugh slowly replaced the receiver, deep in thought about the important information that had just been shared with him and possibly him alone by the illustrious Home Secretary himself . . . bonuses eh? Super bonuses! Then he remembered that there was something else the Home Secretary had mentioned – ah yes, a good news story with no Government interference . . . or was it no Government

mention? No matter, Sir Hugh was a very powerful man, even if short of a full set of working neurons he had handfuls of old school chums who still maintained influential positions in the establishment and often in no small measure due to Sir Hugh's continuing mutual discretion.

As he pictured himself draped in plush ermine and dozing peacefully in the cosy ambience of the House of Lords, he pondered on the possibilities of the Government's dilemma . . . the one on which they didn't want any publicity.

'What could it be?' he wondered, mentally thumbing through a long list of as yet unpublicised possibilities, 'perhaps the clerical error that resulted in the long overdue and over budget new aircraft carrier, being named 'HMS Hopeless'? . . . or the old boy's network think tank pontificating on making being gay obligatory? . . . or worse still, having sold off the people's coal, oil, gas, water, forests, electricity, steel, fishing quotas and fracking rights under people's homes to foreign powers, (in order to fund foreign aid schemes and keep the USA congress contented by buying Trident), perhaps it was the latest draft treasury plans to tax the air we breathe. It would be funded by private finance initiatives and allow for generous shareholder dividends. There would be exceptions naturally. . . the dead of course, pensioners and people in comas would be on reduced rates while athletes and the like (the obese of the air breathing population) would pay a premium super rate. Mmm, could be any one of numerous faux pas,' muttered Sir Hugh as he picked up the telephone. As he lifted the receiver to his one good ear, he heard a slight noise, 'must get this phone looked at, always get a clicking on it, could be MI5,' he mumbled.

Ms Bo knew better!

'Get me Genghis, the news desk editor at once Ms Bo,' he snapped without even the faintest pretence of politeness.

Politeness wasn't something he needed in his high social circles where, like buzzards, they were immune from the riffraff far below. Sir Hugh's old schoolhouse tie, Buzzard House he was in, featured circling buzzards over an injured Wildebeest, symbolic of aspiring beyond the working-class masses, waiting until they are too weak to fight back.
'Please note that Genghis is only an inter departmental nick name Sir Hugh, you want David Carn . . . I'll put you through straight away,' thinking how popular her memoirs will eventually be with an entire assortment of people from named executives to unknown riff-raff, she smiled the smile she would have had long ago had life and the Corporation been more kind to her.
'Ah good, Carn, drop everything, put a hold on anything currently newsworthy about the Government and get yourself up here to my office . . . now!'
Sir Hugh had made a start, he put his games console in his desk drawer and stared at his office door impatiently, 'where was that idiot Carn?'
A cautious knock heralded the arrival of one David 'Genghis' Carn, a man sharing absolutely no characteristics with his namesake, a nervous twitchy sop like man whose indiscretions in the newsroom had been instrumental in his rapid promotion beyond his level of competence. Knowledge of his sexual adventures with various vegetables in the Corporation's staff canteen commanded total loyalty from him, whatever the task he was set. A big mortgage, his wife being a psychiatrist and the fear of some unpleasant years in a specially selected prison saw to that.
'Come on in Carn, come in, sit down and listen carefully,' shouted Sir Hugh, he'd never liked Carn . . . he'd gone to a state school like had that awful Bo woman. Sir Hugh was of the opinion that such factory fodder should never be trusted and must always be kept in their place.

Genghis sat timidly, crossing his legs, staring at Sir Hugh's vast empty desktop and fumbled with his fingers. 'Right, Carn, got a job for you, we need to run a great news story over the next few days that doesn't mention politicians or the government of the day. . . got it? said Sir Hugh, leaning forward and wiping little bits of talking spit off his highly polished Amazonian hardwood desk. He was fond of his desk, not likely to get another like this one. . . it being made from illegally sourced and virtually extinct timber.
'Th..th.. there's nothing m..m..much happening I'm afraid,' stammered a terrified Genghis, he'd never liked Sir Hugh and had a great distrust of anyone who didn't go to a proper school, a state school. God alone knows what went on in those hoity toity private establishments, and even God can't bear to look. Genghis feared being drawn into the Public-school elite circles . . . his wife's tales of Public-school related clients were enough to make him keep his distance . . . they weren't the sort of friends he wanted. 'What about something foreign? A sex scandal? Bank corruption?' continued Genghis.
Sir Hugh's white knuckled fist thumped the desk, 'I told you dopey, nothing to do with the Government. What's wrong with you man?' snarled the man in charge of the country's impartial face of freedom of the press. 'I have a plan of my own . . . the weather. People like to hear about the weather. Make it a snowstorm on its way. Get that incompetent weather bloke out of retirement and get him to tell the people about an impending Arctic storm that will paralyse the country. Do a news item on looking after the frail and buying in food while they still can. One day we do the warning, the next day we do the weather and on the third day we apologise. It won't be our fault; we'll blame the environment agency and the Met office, plus initiating a

grand public sacking of the idiot weatherman. There you are, easy, all sorted . . . now get on with it.'

'B..b..but Sir Hugh, the weather is fine, the only snow is in Scotland, some remote village somewhere in the Craggygorms or something. . . ' stuttered a confused Genghis. Even he knew this was a daft idea.

'You leave the met office and the EA to me; you'll soon have enough storm warnings to wallpaper the building. Get that pretty blonde reporter to go to wherever that snow is, you know the one I mean, the bimbo with the big boobs, everybody likes her. Send her with a select team in the Corporation Helicopter immediately and explain that her entire career depends on making this look like an ice age Armageddon. Go!'

His plan beginning to take shape and a couple of e-mails later, to contacts in the departments that would make it work, Sir Hugh reached for his calculator and began to work out his expenses for when he became a Lord. As he pondered over the cost of duck houses and business lunches in the Seychelles, the phone rang. It was that fool Genghis again, though Ms Bo always introduced him by his proper name and title, 'Yes, what is it now Carn,' snapped an impatient Sir Hugh as he watched his calculator time out and fade.

'It's the hell..hell..helicopter Sir Hugh. It's r..r..run out of airworthy service time, if you remember we c..c..cut its budget to allow for a bigger party this Christmas,' explained a reluctant David 'Genghis' Carn, listening intensely for the shot that would kill the messenger.

'Right, get this Carn and get it good. Tell the bloody pilot if he ever wants to work again then he's to fly the bloody thing to Scotland, tell him that! If the bloody thing crashes all the better, we'll have a better story than a bit of isolated snow... 'pretty, pregnant, single young reporter on drugs dies while running away with perverted drunken pilot in stolen helicopter etc' . . . but don't tell him that bit, dopey!' Sir Hugh slammed down the receiver and tried to retrieve his expenses data from the calculator.

Ms Boadica Flabbergast winced and held her ear as she slowly replaced the receiver. . . this was wonderful stuff; she could see chapter eleven of her book being read by Sir Hugh himself. . . as he served out at least ten years at her majesty's pleasure.

Meanwhile, somewhere deep in the Craggygorms at the little snowbound village of Glen Invergrumpy, the post lady was conveying a telegram to the sheep farmer who ran the airfield. 'Better move they sheep off the runway McTaggart, they'll no be long frae London by helicopter,' she advised.

McTaggart called into one of his barns where he allowed several East Europeans to live, in return for various labours and favours. . . they were a lot cheaper than locals for sure. Handing out shovels and with some hand signals of his own invention he soon had them clearing snow from the runway. A lot of it was swept into the cattle grid halfway along the airstrip, 'It'll take the bumps out of it for sure,' he thought, as he and his dog Wallace, a huge Rotweiller-Collie cross, (cross being a habitually operative word) drove the nervous and unbranded sheep into the worker's barn, 'save heating that, them sheep'll keep 'em warm for sure.' Wallace was fully trained, in what exactly, we may never know, but an English accent would trigger his hackles to rise and lips curl back in a terrifying display of well used bone crushers. He wasn't called Wallace for nothing.

The Corporation 'select' team consisted of Rob 'mad marine' Oakes, whose time in the SAS had seen him fly helicopters with a lot less than some silly airworthiness certificate; pretty blonde Samantha Wilfershore the sex symbol of the Corporation and who had created more unusable out-takes from interviews than anyone else in history; Nigel Yorner, a forty something divorcee from Cornwall on sound . . . and a fair variety of anti-depressants; finally young and spotty Skunk 'Spielberg' Harrison, the only cameraman willing to join the expedition and who had inherited a wild sense of adventure from his commune parents . . . that and a mild and intermittent dose of schizophrenia.

McTaggart had only just cleared his 'volunteers' off the runway and out of sight in their barn when the helicopter skimmed snow off the nearby hill and swept engine screaming into the valley at just over thistle height, Rob's eyes were open wide with excitement as he relived an attack on a mountain outpost he'd been somewhere in the world . . . he was never quite sure where it was, at one time he thought it might have been Wales. As he slewed the chopper into what looked like a hand brake turn and a dead stop the contents of the helicopter were thrown to one side . . . eyes all firmly closed with fear.

Before the rotors had stopped turning, Rob 'mad marine' Oakes had his platoon disembarked and running to the field perimeter complete with what little baggage they had for an over nighter. McTaggart directed them to his garden shed which doubled as the airfield customs and immigration terminal.

'Papers please,' he asked, holding out his hand, which received an arctic stare from Rob and a warm and pretty handshake from Samantha, 'Oh well, never mind the papers, we can always do that silly stuff later,' said the now grinning and newly besotted McTaggart. Skunk gave him a suspicious look but still managed to get a few frames shot . . . you never know when the ordinary will become the extra ordinary. *'Be prepared'* had been his motto ever since being thrown out of the boy scouts for selling naughty photos to his pals.

'You'll no doubt all be booked in at the village pub, just down the lane about half a mile. You can't miss it, it has an embalmed stuffed sheep for a swinging sign by the car park. . . it's called the Merry Shepherd, lovely place, peat fire, great whiskey . . . home grown as they say . . . nod nod. . . May see more of you in there later,' said McTaggart, still reluctant to take his eyes off Samantha.

Rob was already on his second pint when they joined him in the bar.

The landlady was also a McTaggart, second cousin by marriage it was alleged, a fine, burly but secretive woman who'd at one time held ambitions for the Olympic shot-put event but had unfortunately damaged her shoulder in a poaching accident while wrestling a full-grown stag to the ground.

Skunk checked his camera, yes, he'd also managed a few snapshots of the pub and its fearsome landlady. He was pleased with the footage already so far obtained, the crazed eyes of the demoniacal pilot, the staring eyes of McTaggart the airfield controller, the burning, fearsome crushing eyes of the landlady and lots of furtive glimpses of Samantha, 'yes it was going well,' he told his other self, who for a rare change was actually listening. The team settled in for the night, well fed on lamb stew and potatoes and well plied with spirits courtesy of some anonymous benefactor. Samantha retired early so as to try on her white leather one-piece ski suit and practice her lines in front of the mirror, a suspicious looking bit of furniture screwed to the wall of her bedroom. Farmer McTaggart watched with interest from the other side.

The rest of the team were watching the TV and hardly believing what was being said on the news. . . 'Amber alert across the country . . . only essential travel advised . . . check on old people. . . prepare for power failure, etc.' Having

flown over the entire country on the way to Glen Invergrumpy and seen not one single snowflake on the way, they wondered what on earth was going on.
'Perhaps it's a repeat,' said Nigel, '98% of transmissions are repeats . . . I reckon I've seen 'em all. Anyway, that's the weather geezer that got the sack for misinforming the nation about some great storm. Just shows . . . there's some glimmer of hope for all of us,' he concluded in a depressed and without any hope at all voice.

Back in London all was well. The retired weather idiot had been wheeled out and done his stuff. They'd told him it was a documentary about great weathermen of the 21st century; that, a free taxi ride, 200 quid cash in hand and a crate of stout was all he needed. He was going to be famous again and didn't he know it!
Sir Hugh had by now made all his necessary important and highly confidential phone calls, including one to the Home Secretary to tell him, 'Whatever it is you never asked me to do has been done. I'll say no more,' at the same time thinking, 'Actually I don't know any more . . . best kept that way I reckon. What you don't know, you can't be blamed for.' He'd also watched climatic Armageddon being prophesied on the main news which was followed by a genuine news flash about riots and food looting in two major cities, fuelled by panic about the impending great storm. Rival channels, fearing they had somehow missed something important, repeated the warnings without any corroborating evidence though still managed to over emphasise blame on the Corporation for causing the riots.
Sir Hugh smirked a Lordly smirk, it was better than he'd anticipated, the news was filled to the brim but without any mention of Government at all, a resounding success. He'd also naively asked Ms Bo to check over his expenses claims

which had taken him nearly all afternoon to create. She did check them. . . and then printed a photocopy for herself, 'Appendix Expenses Scandals,' she thought.

They all went to bed that night with a collection of their own dreams . . . none of them shared, Ms Bo was fighting off publishers and paparazzi and Sir Hugh, I mean Lord Hugh of Cambria, was making his maiden speech in a packed house of lords to rapturous applause from all sides. Ah, dreams eh?

It was fine morning that saw a bright Sun shining over the Merry Shepherd Pub and Rob 'mad marine' Oakes checking out the bruises on his arms, trophies from a late-night arm-wrestling competition with the landlady. Skunk had already been busy with his camera, including catching a furtive Farmer McTaggart tip toeing along the landing late last night. Skunk was determined that both of him would make it to the top one day . . . by some means or another, by tenacity, skill and innovation . . . or perhaps, just blackmail. Skunk also had some great infrared night shots of a light aircraft landing at the field and some posh looking geezers with brief cases and what appeared to be gorilla like bodyguards making their way down the lane to a big house at the far end of the village. Skunk never did do much sleeping.

Up at the big house, a large clandestine holiday property owned by the Government and used mainly by members of the cabinet for various deviant pleasures under the auspices of 'Wild Nature Adventures,' important discussions were afoot. The Home Secretary himself was there along with the Foreign Secretary, various civil servants, someone's old school chum, a cleaning lady in the basement sleeping off half the drinks cabinet and a few sheep fanciers. They were there to do a private and friendly deal with representatives from an oil rich ex-communist country with whom they were publicly definitely not friendly. It was essential to maintain secrecy, hence the 'request' to the Corporation for non-political news and so far all was going well, they were as oblivious to the Corporation team's presence at the Merry Shepherd, as the team were to the Government presence at the big house. The foreign representatives were reticent about speaking inside the house, they suspected listening devices and the like. . . the like of which they would have done had the tables been reversed. They insisted upon walking in the dry stone walled grounds of the big house. Anyway, they were used to the cold and took no small pleasure in seeing the port reddened faces of the home diplomats shivering in the weak sunshine.

Meanwhile back at the Merry Shepherd, it was breakfast time. As McTaggart the landlady dollopped out great ladles of salted porridge for each of her guests she attracted an admiring glance from Rob the mad marine and an understanding analytical gaze from Nigel who now felt he understood why she was built like she was. Skunk had already finished his bowlful in the time it took Samantha to wipe mirror clean the dirty spoon and peer into it at her reflection. Even in that she still looked alluringly pretty.

‘I take it ye'll all be having the Merry Shepherd's big yin,’ McTaggart the landlady asked, although it sounded more like a command.

‘And what's that when it's at home Ms McTaggart?’ asked a curious yet still sensibly cautious Nigel.

McTaggart pointed one of her huge sausage fingers at the menu board where it proclaimed, ‘Satisfaction guaranteed with the Merry Shepherd's Big One – full breakfast, 2 lamb chops, 3 bacon rashers, 3 eggs, homemade black pudding, chips and beans. £5.95.’

Samantha shuddered a little, count her out of that, she had a figure to watch.
The three men almost instinctively opted for the breakfast and contented themselves with watching someone else's figure. Nigel and Skunk watched Samantha's and Rob watched that fine feminine prop forward figure of a landlady, he'd not seen anyone built like that since stalking Silverbacks in western Africa.

Negotiations were progressing well, back in the chilly gardens of the big house, it wasn't only oil that lubricated, when it came to the wheels of government, money did that. . . usually lots of it and often to be found, or rather not found, in the bulging coffers of some offshore tax haven.
Senior negotiator, Vladimir Krushemovski, known as Vlad the impaler in government circles, walked close to the home secretary, known as the smiling assassin in foreign circles, 'as long as the people do not find out, all will be good. What about your famous investigative newspapers and their teams of illegal hackers? Are we safe?'
The Home Secretary smiled one of his now well publicised and practised smiles, 'they all have their price, they are more interested in making money than telling the truth. We keep them out of prison. . . they keep us out of the papers. They are loyal supporters and share a common dream . . . that of seeing their names in the new year's honours list.'
'Crikey ! What the hell . . .' interrupted the Foreign Secretary, grabbing the Home Secretary's shoulder and pointing towards a man about a hundred yards away on the other side of the wall. The intruder was also pointing with something they couldn't quite make out . . . their way.
In a flash the foreign bodyguards had knocked them all to the ground behind the wall. As they crawled out of sight through mud and goat droppings back to the house they

discussed how to deal with the situation. 'I can have MI5 find him and have him sectioned under the mental health act. . . whoever it is he won't ever bother us again,' cursed the Home Secretary, whose only previous experience at crawling had been first as a baby and later when he wanted the cabinet job.

Vladimir calmly, as though it wasn't at all his first experience in such matters, suggested that they let Big Otto deal with him, and they would drop the body out of their plane into the sea on their way home. Big Otto's eyes twitched, and he felt his pockets for the 9 mil. . . or should he perhaps use the bayonet. . . perhaps the garrotte? Ah, choices, choices, he loved them all.

Having returned to the house they dried their mud-covered knees by the fire and a touch more sanity ruled once more. After all, nobody knew they were here, it was a secret location and the media were already firmly in their pockets, along with their dirty hankies and some small change. They concluded that it was probably only one of the villagers out bird spotting. Yes, that was more like it, a lot of fuss over nothing. Documents and bank account details were exchanged, and the guests prepared as best they could for departure, phoning ahead to have clean clothes brought out to the plane on their return to the motherland. There was no desire to convey an image that the ambassadors had in any way been on their knees begging.

At the big house, they remained blissfully unaware of the Corporation's news team and talented film crew ensconced just a few hundred yards away in the Merry Shepherd.

The news team made their way back to the airfield where there was still at least a heap of snow, that is, all except Rob who'd stayed behind to help McTaggart the landlady who had promised him a look at her gun, gin trap and old bones collection. Skunk, with his amazing skills at special effects and making the camera lie, took some sweeping shots of a blizzard torn valley, then one of Samantha, sweeping along pristine white leather from foot to blue eyes. Samantha did her thing with the over the shoulder smile at the camera and rambled on in her soft seductive voice some inane drivel about snow and imminent Armadillos. No one would notice what she said anyway. While zooming in close for an eye shot, Skunk saw people running in the reflection, this was a money shot as they called it in the trade. This was the stuff that made good cameramen truly great. He would be investigating more when he had the chance. 'That's a wrap for now Sam,' said Skunk, 'how about sound Nigel, okay?'

'Eh? What's that?' asked Nigel, who for a sound man was rarely listening, 'Oh, yeah, lovely, lovely voice, and even got some sheep baaing in the distance makes it really rural.' As if Invergrumpy, one of the most remote places in the country, could be anything but.

'Right, all back to the pub ready for lunch and I'll send the edited copy back to base by satellite,' enthused a very hyper Skunk who not only had exciting plans but wondered if the satellite system actually stretched to the Craggygorms.

The reflection in Sam's eyes of people running had revealed the two cabinet ministers, a couple of civil servants and the foreign visitors making for McTaggart's alien holiday barn. They'd suddenly spotted the camera crew up at the airfield and decided that discretion was the better part of valour and certainly better than Big Otto's plan to eliminate them all, taking their bodies home to his brother's highly profitable organic pig farm.

They hid in the barn, in the quiet and the dark, not knowing much about who or what was in there. It was quiet but for the heavy breathing of nervous sheep and even more nervous illegal immigrants, some of whom thought they recognised Big Otto from wanted posters back home. On finding the coast was clear and covertly slipping Farmer McTaggart, the airfield controller, a wad of notes and a bottle of 80% proof special Vodka they made their way to the plane. Once airborne it slipped unnoticed under the radar and headed east. All had gone so well, and a hero's welcome was assured.

Not so long after all this had transpired, Sir Hugh was informed by David Carn that his snow Armageddon feature was ready to roll out on the main mid-day news, 'would he like to pop down to the newsroom to watch it go out?'

'Well done at last Carn, yes, I'm on my way down, if this works out there'll be a little in it for all of us,' smarmed a sneakily happy Sir Hugh, thinking and chuckling at the same time, 'yes, Ermine for me and a couple of years in Parkhurst for you.' He pushed his games console into the drawer and made his way to the lift.

Sir Hugh, David Carn and the news controllers gathered behind the glass that separated the news reader from outside interference. 'We've called in our top news broadcaster, one of the old school, great voice, very capable, can roll with the punches,' spoke the lead controller, being interrupted by an impatient Sir Hugh, 'yes, yes, just get on with it,' he said curtly, taking a note of the controller's name for the redundancy list he was working on.

The news credits rolled, and the camera zoomed in to the steady face of truth and sturdy voice of justice, Damian 'Benedict Arnold' Moronham, 'Welcome to the midday news. Today our main story is the chaos caused by the snowstorms that have swept and paralysed the country.' Damian couldn't hide a slight look of puzzlement on his face, 'what snow,' he thought, 'am I being set up here? Is it a, you've been framed sketch?' From this point on Damien's suspicions were going to influence what and how he spoke. 'We sent a news team to cover one of the worst hit areas in the country, the Craggygorms.' Again, Damien sensed something not quite right, I mean, where the hell were the Craggygorms when they were at home? 'But first we have some footage shot during last night's riots and food looting caused by a fear of shortages during the storm. Over to our outside broadcast team in one of our major cities.'

There followed a few minutes of burnt-out shops in seemingly snow free streets. The usual diatribe was wheeled out by the various factions of councillors, shopkeepers, police, the odd passer-by, and the occasional masked looter with name changed to protect his identity. It was nothing that Damien hadn't heard before, but where was the bloody snow?

Camera light back on Damien, he continued with no small amount of suspicion in his voice, 'thank you for that and now to our main feature with the lovely Samantha out in the snow in the popular tourist resort of Glen Invergrumpy, apparently the airport was only kept open by the heroic efforts of the residents using hand shovels . . . an amazing story, let's go to the report . . .'

As the footage sent by Skunk 'Spielberg' Harrison began to play, Damien's suspicions grew. If Glen Invergrumpy had an airport and was a tourist destination, then why in all his years had he not heard of it? He decided that he would go along with whatever the programmer wanted and consult legal advice later . . . it could be an earner for him.

'Ah, that's better,' said Sir Hugh turning to the big monitor and seeing a big picture of blizzards and that pretty blonde bimbo woman. He didn't care what she was droning on about, that leather ski suit was a nice touch though . . . then something horrible went inexplicably through his mind, not sure what had caused an image of a sheep hanging from a sign meant, he looked around at several other puzzled faces. It was the first of many semi subliminal messages that Skunk had inserted into the news piece. He had plans to be great one day, both of him. Scenes depicting snow, cattle grids, a helicopter, Samantha's pretty face and various bits of her anatomy dressed in white leather were interspersed with very brief glimpses of other things - Things like men looking over a wall then ducking down, a woman built like a gorilla and wearing a kilt, some mad crazed staring eyes, a grubby looking man that looked like a farmer and more. The images were only fleeting and never on long enough to clearly see who was who.

'What the hell is going on Carn,' snarled a by now fuming Sir Hugh.

Carn snapped some orders at the controllers, who quickly rewound their own copy and freeze framed the images. 'There's loads of them sir, looks like they run all the way through.'

'Bloody stop the thing man,' screamed Sir Hugh.

'No can do,' replied the bemused controller, 'we use computers to generate the signal, some clever bastard has built in some sort of override, we can't do anything but let it run its course then make some comment about technical errors. That's what we normally do.'

Damien had got the picture in more ways than one and began distancing himself from the report, despite the intermittent begging and threatening that was raging in his earpiece, 'We appear to be experiencing technical interference beyond our control.'

The report continued, transmitting to the nation and beyond. Then came a longer intermission, this time it stayed long enough to see who it was. 'God, isn't that the Home Secretary? Blurted out Carn as an image of a number of men all with mud on their knees standing amongst a flock of clearly disturbed sheep came up on screen. 'That's the Foreign Secretary too,' he continued.

'Perhaps that big bloke with the 9 mm pistol made them do it,' suggested the controller.

As their bulging disbelieving eyes became accustomed to the dark image of the barn it became apparent that the sick swine were performing to an audience, there being dozens of silent awe-struck faces staring on from the straw bales at the back of the barn.

'No wonder the Government wanted to be kept out of the news,' thought Sir Hugh as he made for home, he didn't want to get involved in this mess, time to take a short holiday.

Damien couldn't wait to make his way home too but not until he'd started a lawsuit to protect his image . . . and perhaps make a few bob on the way.

For three days the news was filled with speculation and denials, then lucky for the Government something else cropped up to take the attention. An Orang-utan had given birth to quadruplets in a laboratory experiment to solve the imminent extinction of the species. It was sponsored by the big Palm Oil conglomerate Grabitall Inc. Such wonderful news gave the Government a brief respite.

**

Addendum:-

A few months later, the Government was overthrown in a landslide victory for anyone but them.

Sir Hugh 'Peregrine' Braggington Havalot was retired on a huge bonus and elevated to the Lords by the incoming coalition. His hopes of sleeping in ermine and dreaming of expenses came true.

Ms Bo, Boedica Flabergast was offered a multi-million contract for the sole rights to her memoirs. As part of the conditions, she was to write more books from a cottage on the pretty island of St Kilda. None of her work ever saw light of day, nor did she.

Rob 'mad marine' Oakes moved to the Merry Shepherd to woo the landlady and lived happy ever after.

Nigel Yorner was over his depression, why should he be depressed once he'd seen what a total mess everyone else was in, he went on to be a successful stand-up comic doing the pubs and clubs of Landsovgrotty.

Skunk 'Spielberg' Harrison took up a fantastic offer to produce and direct an epic foreign film set in the east at an organic pig farm. He may be gone for some while.

Pretty blonde Samantha Wilfershore remained blissfully unaware of anything that was going on, anywhere, and was promoted to political editor of News Tripe the Corporation's flagship daily news magazine programme.

David 'Genghis' Carn was made redundant and once no longer associated with the Corporation was arrested, convicted, and now serving four years in Dartmoor.

McTaggart the farmer started a tourism business and made a small fortune from guided tours and cafes all run by very economical employees with foreign accents and wearing sheep costumes. A speciality trip was to spend a night in the infamous barn itself. A small gift shop sold miniature stuffed sheep pub signs, and lots of sheep oriented cheap gifts.

Wallace the Rotweiller-Collie cross found himself enjoying spells of the well-fed good life at a stud farm for the guard dog industry.

After the Government set up an interim inquiry into finding a panel to examine what should be the scope of any investigation, preferably taking so long that the guilty would have died of old age by then, the third inquiry decided it was too complex and should be considered for a public inquiry at the Home Secretary's discretion.

The disgraced Home Secretary and Foreign Secretary were both sentenced to ten years for various unmentionable crimes but simply served six months, just long enough to write a bestselling novel each before being released. They now work as substantially paid consultants to the new Government. Who knows, if they do well, they may be wearing ermine one day too. You'll often see them on the telly.

What did you get out of it?

**

'If you keep hanging on to who you were,
you'll never become who you might be.'

**

Value added. . . ?

It started with some seed, picked freely by dear Mrs Goodgrace, from a Hollyhock that overhung a public path. Lovingly collected and placed safely into a folded envelope the seeds were carried back home along with their new owner's benevolent dreams. . . then forgotten, misplaced in the shed for a year.

It was a pleasant surprise when the seeds turned up again, discovered by her helpful neighbour, Mr Kindly. 'Oh, you can have them,' she said, 'I meant to plant them then forgot, pity, they'd have been lovely.'

They all germinated, part of God's nature, the way of the universe you know, there was no charge, the rain came, and the seeds grew unhindered into fine plants nurtured by the Sun and a small pot of garden earth. 'Lovely, dear, but you have too many,' said his wife, Argusina Kindly, 'and I think they're just a bit too tall for our little garden.'

'All right love,' he replied, 'I'll not waste them, I'll give them to Mr Grubitout at the nursery, I'm sure he'll find a good home for them.'

**

Not so far away, at the posh end of the village, Mr and Mrs Havalot were in the process of having their garden landscaped by Mr Trimmings and Sons and, never having lifted a finger in the garden themselves, were taking his advice. He should be good as they had seen his old pick-up outside the 'big house,' owned by none other than, **the** Lucre El Dorado, banking consultant.

He'd 'do a good job,' Trimmings had said, and 'keep the price low for them as the Havalots were struggling to live on the rents from their Lucerne holiday flats, and what with the mooring costs at the yacht club too.'

**

'Just the very thing for you, Trimmings,' said Grubitout at the nursery sales counter, 'some fine Hollyhocks, mixed colours and only £6 a plant, I tell you what, I'll discount them at £5.50 for you, can't say fairer than that, a real steal as they say.'

'I'll take the lot, Grubitout,' replied Trimmings, eyeing the strong dark green foliage and beginnings of good stems – they'd flower this year with luck.

'Right, that's 20 plants at £5.50, er um, £110 plus VAT at 20%. . . dreadfully sorry about that, can't be escaped you know, we all have to pay . . . so that will be £132 if you please,' said Grubitout, not so much organically but more orgasmically as he rang the bell on the nursery till.

**

'All planted Mrs Havalot – I got you some real beauties, nursery grown, quality plants from Mr Grubitout's Establishment. . . Let's see now. . . that's £150 for the plants, real beauties, mixed colours he said, you won't find better anywhere I dare say. . . then only £50 labour, tell you what, you're nice people, make that just £45, as I like you. . . £150 plus £45 is er £195, plus that damned VAT at 20%. . the scourge of the nation that, still, we all have to pay it, can't be escaped . . . so that comes to £233 then please. Thanks for your business, call me back anytime,' smiled a very happy Mr Trimmings the landscaper.

Meanwhile out in the garden 20 free seedlings flourished in God's earth with free rain and free sunshine. Their added value would be the scented flowers that perfumed the air, the drop-in pollen café for the bees, no charge, no tax, and later the seed heads would feed winter hungry birds, free, no tax, their autumn leaves would fall and enrich the soil for free, no tax . . . such is the way of nature.

Some years later, as the Hollyhocks developed, they began to spread and overhang a garden wall, there to be spotted by that dear little old lady Mrs Goodgrace out walking with her granddaughter; She reached out and picked a few seeds. Carefully placing them in a folded envelope she said, 'I'll jolly well make sure I plant them this time, I bet they'll look lovely, come on, let's go home for tea and find some plant pots, I have some really pretty green ones I saved free from the rubbish tip.'

**

'Beware knowing the price of everything
and the value of nothing.'
Oscar Wilde

**

The Torrington Road Gibbet.

It was Doreen's first time in Bideford. She'd come to visit her old pen pal Pamela, who lived in a little terraced cottage on the hill beyond the police station. They first met through a little known spiritual organisation, an ancient collective for those with interests in 'the other worldly'.

It was early September and a pleasant evening about an hour before sunset when the two friends took a stroll by the riverbank and out along the Torrington road.

'What a strange place this is, and, if I didn't know better, I'd be frightened,' said Doreen.

'Well Dor, you're the one to know what's strange, what with your spirit dealings and all that... you've certainly always impressed me... I just don't know how you do it, I really don't,' replied Pam, still wondering just what was so strange.

'Fancy you still having one of those awful things here,' continued Doreen, pointing an accusing finger just down the road from the junction, 'there, look, on the left of the road.'

'I can't see anything Dor', said Pam peering over the top of her glasses and scouring the rising river mists for what strange thing could be out there.

Doreen didn't pause for breath, 'Well, I'll go to the foot of our stairs if it isn't a gibbet of all things... awful things they were too... and something tells me this one has a story to tell. Come on, let's go closer.'

Pam was happy enough to go along with this suggestion, after all it was still close to town, it was still light and Doreen was obviously on a mission; Doreen could 'see' many a thing that ordinary folk could not.

'Pam... did a highwayman once ply his evil trade along this road?' inquired Doreen.

'Never heard of one Dor, not that I know of anyway,' she replied slowly shaking her head in thought, then she went quiet as Doreen appeared to be listening to someone else.

'Is there anybody there?' Doreen asked calmly, 'Please come closer... what is it you want?'

Though it was a calm and warm evening, Pam felt a cold breeze by her ankles and something soft brushed her face; she could hear nothing but Doreen's murmured conversation and the light rumble of traffic crossing the old Long Bridge in the distance. After twenty minutes or so, Doreen was back in the present. Turning towards town she said, 'Come on Pamela, back to your house, and I'll tell you all... there's work for us to do here!'

They entered the house by the back door, 'Go on... what did you find out, Dor?'

'Kettle on first Pam, then, pen and paper and we'll sit at the kitchen table... there is much to tell...'

'His name was Tom. Though not sure how old he was, he thinks he was an orphan. He was probably about twenty-five years of age, a swarthy young man, scruffy and unkempt, with dark straggly hair. Locals called him 'Black Tom'. He'd been a runaway apprentice and could neither read nor write, something that no doubt contributed to his demise. He lived almost wild, surviving hand to mouth, begging from travellers on the Torrington road. Tom was befriended by the somewhat shrewd and outwardly benevolent landlord of an Inn, an Inn of ill repute some few miles between the two towns. Tom could often get a meal there for running errands or cleaning out the stables; sometimes he would sleep in them, despite the Inn being permeated by an apparent evil best avoided.

A blurry image came to me as he described the Inn, close by the river it was, a low, cob built building with a thatched roof, next to it leaned similarly built stables, there was a small carriage outside and about four or five horses, fine looking animals, not cart horses. Grey smoke came from a single chimney in the middle of the roof. I caught a glimpse of armed men running about, then the vision vanished into blackness and I found myself with Tom again, listening to his tale of woe. The Landlord was a powerfully built somewhat charismatic man called Rufus Hench, though that may not have been his real name.'

Pamela nodded an acknowledgement of the name and promptly made some notes.

Doreen continued, 'Rufus was very popular with travellers, always plying them generously with drink and meat and befriending them. In those far away days, many a traveller on that road would fall prey to some devious local highwayman and it wasn't unknown for a lone traveller never to finish their journey at all. The local magistrate and squire would often meet at the Inn to discuss their plans to catch this vicious local footpad.

Poor Tom cannot understand why it was him they beat, dragged away, tried and hanged. Rufus Hench had promised Tom he would put in a good word for him at the trial but in the event, he did not turn up and in consequence Tom stood alone, illiterate and defenceless against his accusers. Poor Tom's body was displayed on the gibbet we saw, as a severe warning to any would be thieves that came that way. After the hanging, the robberies stopped.'

Pamela finished making her notes and with an air of excitement proclaimed, 'Tomorrow Doreen, we'll go to our town library and see what we can dig up, I know the lady in there, I'll phone first so she can better help us.'

Later the next day, they climbed the few steps that entered the town library, 'Hi Pam... and you must be Doreen, Pam's friend, welcome,' said Rosey the reference librarian, 'after your phone call I had a good search of our archives... not

such good news I'm afraid, come on through to the back office and I'll show you what we have.'
They gathered around the desk upon which various documents, old and new were scattered.
'Right', said Rosey, 'the bad news. . . no record or even vague inference anywhere to an Inn on that road, no highwayman, no 'Black Tom' and no gibbet either and there's a reason for this. The good news is we have a lot on Rufus Hench. He was a very rich man who apparently came from London and commissioned a fine house to be built on the quay. According to the records we have, he came to the town just before the civil war. He appears to have been very popular and generous and soon became not only Mayor but also Customs and Excise Officer, in which capacity he served benevolently for fourteen years until he emigrated taking his wealth with him; after that he seems to have disappeared completely from public life. Unfortunately, there are very few records that survived from before Mayor Hench's time due to a fire only a few months after he was elected. Only the fire and any subsequent history remain on record. Sorry about that, perhaps your Tom the highwayman did exist, but now I'm afraid no one will ever know the truth.'
'I suspect in our hearts we already knew the answer Pam,' empathized Doreen as the pair left to walk soulfully up the High Street.
Perhaps one quiet day, if you're out along the Torrington Road as the mists are rising from the river you too might hear Black Tom's continuing plea for justice. . .

**

'And as a single leaf turns not yellow
but with the silent knowledge of the whole tree,
So, the wrong-doer cannot do wrong
without the hidden will of you all.'

Gibran (The Prophet)

Mrs Hoblingsgote – medical expert.

'Your favourite patient to see you doctor,' sighed the exasperated medical receptionist as she reported the third visit that week to Dr Hadenuff by Mrs Hipaemia Hoblingsgote.

'Send her through then, Miss Tattle, let's see what she has caught this time,' said the doctor, throwing an extra tranquiliser down his throat followed quickly by some experimental super juice on trial for mental disorders.

Mrs Hoblingsgote was the local hypochondriac; her Christian name had been adulterated by her very small circle of friends to 'Hypo' and she was well known throughout the county medical services. She'd been tested for anything from Dengue fever, rabies, osteo degeneration of brain tissue, green monkey disease and several other tropical diseases she'd read about either in the papers or any one of the several medical journals to which she subscribed.

Until the editors worked out that her qualifications were merely a figment of their own imaginations, they used to publish her letters and articles. Despite never having left the county except for a visit to London to see a hypnotherapy specialist, she was convinced that most sufferers of illness were being let down by the wilful misdiagnosis of medical practitioners under government orders to suppress the real truth. After her visit, the hypnotherapist retired on ill health and now runs a gerbil farm on an isolated Greek island.

'What is it today then Mrs Hoblingsgote? Bubonic plague?' the Doctor inwardly sneered with sarcasm while forcing his face to contort into the bedside smile he'd been taught at medical school, a valued skill that attracted the highest of marks in the practical exam, as he recalled.

'Ah, Doctor Hadenuff,' replied Mrs Hoblingsgote, in a dubious tone that questioned not only the doctor's sincerity but his qualification in anything medical, 'I'm feeling a pulse in the centre of my forehead and an examination of blood vessels and circulation that I conducted through Google (read God in her eyes) indicates this should not be possible. Either one of my veins has slipped or some flesh-eating creature with a pulse has burrowed into my skin.'

Dr Hadenuff sighed inwardly; he knew best not to argue directly as he'd been the subject of several reports to the medical council already. He picked up his stethoscope and walked around behind his patient, wondering how many years he'd get inside if he strangled her with it. Fortunately, the cognitive behavioural therapy on which he had been placed by desperate employers not wishing to inflict Mrs Hoblingsgote on anyone else in the practice, kicked in and he placed the listening end of the equipment on her forehead.

She turned sharply pulling it from his hand and shouting down it that it was cold and any doctor worth his salt would have warmed it first. By now the doctor wouldn't have heard a pulse even if there was one but he knew he must not give up, until she was satisfied with an answer, she would not leave his surgery. 'No pulse that I can find Mrs Hoblingsgote, show me how you found it yourself,' he said with pseudo pleasantness, a ploy that seemed to have worked in the past.

'Like this Doctor (read 'Dopey'),' she shouted as though he was deaf and thrusting her thumb into the middle of her forehead, her face silently asking the question, 'well, what have you got to say now then thicky?'

'Ah, Mrs Hoblingsgote, a common mistake,' adding very quickly so she couldn't take offence, 'even by members of skilled medical staff at times I'm told, there is a pulse in the thumb itself and that is what you feel when you press it

against your forehead (read, 'your thick skull you time wasting nit wit').
Mrs Hoblingsgote wasn't convinced, Google had never been wrong before, but she had to leave for an appointment with a Tarot reader before going on to the 'Pensioners against euthanasia' group of which she was a most active and vociferous chair. She'd probably report the doctor's incompetence later, unless of course the rampant dementia which she thought she'd had since childhood intervened. She thought she'd contracted it from a donkey bite when she was about twelve. The owner of the donkey sanctuary had reported the child's attack on his donkey to the RSPCA, but no charges were pressed.
After the meeting, Mrs Hoblingsgote donned her rucksack and jogged the two miles to the supermarket. While in there, looking for bargains at the in-store pharmacy, she ate three of the five pork pies she had purchased (well almost purchased anyway) a half of one of the cream cakes from the bakery, 'Mmm, chocolate éclairs . . . real cream . . . mmm,' she mumbled to herself through a mouthful of cake and drool, and had a swig of expensive pomegranate juice. (She considered putting it back on the shelf but noticed she was being watched by well-built security guard, 'fat git,' she thought, ' could do with going on a diet.'
She paid for her shopping; loaded what was left of it into the rucksack and jogged back home. As she walked up the driveway past her newly polished car, she looked at the disabled badge on the dash, thinking that it must be due for automatic renewal this month and it wouldn't be so long before her essential mobility car was up for replacement. She had thought about a Jaguar next time, but humility got the better of her and she set her heart on a BMW instead.
Shoving the last half of an éclair into her mouth she settled into her comfortable NHS orthopaedic chair and communed

with God, that is she hit the Google connect button, there were things afoot she must investigate. . . like that hopeless quack telling her there was a pulse in the thumb for a start. Mrs Hoblingsgote's computer held more medical information than the Lancet's archives and it was always willing to offer her more diseases to relish. She began to type in 'pu . . .' when it offered her the opportunity to read about pulmonary oedema. She did not hesitate and within minutes of reading the preface she was choking and coughing like she'd been gassed in the trenches. This was a hospital job for sure . . .

'Emergency, which service?' came the telephonist's reply.

Mrs Hoblingsgote gasped out with what seemed like a dying breath, 'Ambulance . . . gasp, wheeze, cough . . . another longer gasp.'

The novice telephonist put her through immediately to ambulance despatch. As the 'red' phone rang in ambulance control the electronic indicator informed the controller of the phone number being used . . . that too rang a bell. . . it was a number all too familiar to the ambulance service.

'Hello, you're through to ambulance control, name and telephone number please and what is the problem?' said old Chris, a veteran of the service for some thirty years.

Mrs Hoblingsgote was still taking in more information on her health problem from a link on the original article, she wheezed, coughed then went silent for a while before gasping out, 'urgent, pulmonary oedema, need urgent hospital treatment, need consultant in ....'

Under strict orders to comply with turn out times and thus satisfying attendance criteria for the government's big pre-election crackdown, Chris swung into action, 'Still at the old address Mrs Hoblingsgote?' A gasped 'yes' was all he needed to despatch the nearest ambulance to Nightingale Lodge, Bishop's Road. It didn't matter what sort of ambulance or who was on board, any old thing would do for the Nightingale Hypo as she was endearingly known, as long as it turned up and dropped her off at A&E and scored points for timeliness that is all that mattered. 'Ambulance on its way Mrs Hoblingsgote, just do the usual, be by the door with an overnight bag, toothbrush, nightie and the like, some coins for the hospital TV and a newspaper in the morning.'

As usual, Mrs Hoblingsgote was ready with her 'hospital gear' and even if she couldn't get to the door, all the emergency services knew the door key was kept under the flowerpot to the left. It wasn't long, ensconced as she was in her usual ward bed, before she was coughing herself into a frenzy in front of the consultant and disturbing a ward full of genuinely ailing souls. The Hospital staff might have found her a burden, but management almost looked forward to her visits as the turnaround was quick and it made their admittance to discharge statistics look remarkably good. Good statistics meant a proportionate bigger bonus, not that that is why they did the job of course.

Next day, assured by a nervous gathering of as many doctors as they could find, by several X- rays and a promise of the first scan when the new equipment was purchased and a large bag of various drugs, Mrs Hoblingsgote strolled jauntily out to the waiting ambulance.

'Pity we can't euthanize her,' mumbled one doctor clenching his knuckles and who'd not had a minute to deal with anyone else all night.

'Any chance of popping in the newsagents for my paper?' she enquired, 'I don't think I'll be able to get about much today.'

The ambulance crew obliged. You never knew when the clients would be sent a customer survey as to how they were treated, and Mrs Hoblingsgote was someone to be reckoned with . . . she'd already had two nurses, a doctor, a cafe waitress and a car park attendant struck off.

After a big fried breakfast and her yoga session she settled down in her chair to watch some medical videos she'd picked up cheap in a charity shop. They looked promising as they included footage of real operations and bore an 18+ rating.

The doorbell rang to the tune of 'The Sorcerer's Apprentice,' causing Mrs Hoblingsgote to leap to her feet then limp gracefully and with all the aplomb of an Oscar winning actress to her front door. She opened it carefully and showed a face wizened with pain to the caller.

'Morning Mrs Hoblingsgote, it's only me, Phillipa, the assistant at the village pharmacy. Can you spare me a minute?'

'Come on in dear, you'll have to excuse the mess, just can't do it these days what with my troubles and all,' she said with a mild croak and an exaggerated limp. 'What can I do for you?'

Phillipa put on her best smile and said, 'Mr Scribblings the pharmacist is in need of your help. The pharmacy has run out of two drugs, tri-pheno-di-benzoquack and baboonazipan, Mr Scriblings wondered if you have any spare that you could lend us until next week when a delivery is expected from Hong Kong.'

Mrs Hoblingsgote groaned and made a fuss about standing from her chair, 'this way dear,' and she led Phillipa through to her own kitchen come dispensary. Opening one of the big cupboards to an amazing selection of life saving drugs, some still experimental and some still unopened in original packaging, 'help yourself dear, but mind you replace them next week, you never know when they might be needed.'

Phillipa selected the required drugs and placed them in a cool bag she had brought with her. Meanwhile, Mrs

Hoblingsgote was reminiscing about previous pharmacists and counter staff, 'I knew your mother, dear, when she was at the pharmacy. Lovely lady, sorry to hear about her passing away, you look so much like her. . . lovely lady.'

Mrs Hoblingsgote had outlived several assistants, two pharmacists and the village postmaster. For such a frail and ill lady Mrs Hoblingsgote was managing extremely well, in fact, on her way to make medical history for surviving TB, scarlet fever, diphtheria, Ebola, black death and the virulent super bird flu mutation as well as numerous unknown diseases still being investigated.

'Bye bye Phillipa, nice to see you, must take my pills now and have a lie down before meals on wheels turn up,' she said with a limp wave goodbye from her front door.

'What a dear brave old lady,' thought Phillipa as she fought off the pain of her own debilitating arthritis while walking back to the pharmacy.

Mrs Hoblingsgote jogged jauntily upstairs to pack her suitcase; she'd been given a grant from a local charity to take a week's respite care at a private clinic in the Cotswolds but she'd managed to secretly exchange it for a bushcraft week on the moors. (When man-made drugs had been used up or were too expensive to give away, then she may have to turn to nature's healing ways and herbalism. This was a need-to-know mission).

Mrs Hoblingsgote was leading a double life if not a charmed one, though charm would not have been in the vocabulary of the myriad of health workers whose lives she had blighted and many of whom she had outlived, her cost to the NHS probably ran into millions especially when you took into account the ill health pensions and compensations paid out to those who crossed her hypochondriacal path.

However, to the University of Kurdlingstahn, she was a god send. As a senior consultant to the medical facility, she had been given an honorary doctorate and was the main link between the university department of medicine and the western world. She had designed and authorised many experiments on volunteers (read ethnic minorities and prisoners) in the development of her own theories on treating the anxious and depressed. She had several medical articles in her name but only in the Kurdlinstahny language, so ensuring anonymity.

A large bronze statue consisting of a recumbent goat and an elderly woman holding a stethoscope in one hand and a raised walking stick in the other, still adorns the main square of the capital city, Drugonia.

She is probably still alive and living in a town near you, you might know her, worse still, you might be her!

**

Prime Minister's Office ... who's calling please?

(A Covid 19 era story)

The truth is, they were now short staffed everywhere, including on the reception desk at number ten. A visiting rodent exterminator had inadvertently spread a new debilitating virus around the building. Many of the full-time and well briefed staff were subsequently quarantined, resulting in transfers from other, more obscure departments. The more unashamedly obscure the department, the more unaffected staff they had to offer. Still, they would cope, they were all dedicated civil servants, all signed up to the official secrets act and duty bound to preserve the incumbent government.

What more could you possibly ask?

And so, it transpired that the young and confusedly inexperienced Maisie Jane D'Urberville, fresh from filing documents in the Ministry of Unanswered Questions, was thrust into glorious stardom at the PM's very own telephone switch board.

From two metres away and mumbling incoherently through a mask, a senior aide with no knowledge of how anything really worked, explained her job to her. It doesn't matter what he actually **said**, what matters is what Maisie Jane thought she **heard**. This was training on the hoof so to speak, or on the mumble, if you will.

The phone rang, her first call, well the second, if you count calling her mum to say where she was. 'PM's office, can I help you?'

'Security here, name's Bob, I'm in the kitchen at the moment. Would you like a coffee? Milk? Sugar?'

'Er, yes please, milk no sugar, but if there's a nice biscuit going that would be lovely.'

Bob replied with a hush in his voice, (you can't be too careful who was listening in ... KGB, Mossad, CIA ... or worse, the PM himself), 'Bottom left drawer of your desk, you'll find the PM's private stash of Belgian biscuits ... the tin with *made in Belgium* scratched out. If you only take two or three, he won't notice ... he's not so good at counting and remembering simultaneously. Coffee with you in a minute or so. Bob, out.'

This was so exciting, she had only been there a few minutes and was already liaising with security, she wriggled in the comfy leather chair and reached for the biscuits. Sure enough, there they were, under a layer of Kitty Bat treats . . . '*made in China*' just legible under a felt tip crossing out.

Bob pushed the door open with his polished security boot and carried the drinks in with a flourish. Bob was a sweet old gentleman working out his few last weeks before retirement.

Bob had many tales to tell about working in number 10 and Maisie Jane was enthralled to hear all the inside gossip that you never read in the papers. 'Secrets, you know,' said Bob, 'mustn't tell anyone.' When the phone rang, he was just finishing the bit about the death of the first cat, said to have died peacefully in its old age while it slept after a good supper, in reality kicked down the stairs by a previous PM when he realised the cabinet were plotting against him. 'You'd better answer that dear,' said Bob to Maisie Jane who, with elbows on desk, was resting her head in her hands thinking about Larry the new number ten cat and if he too had heard this story, 'it could be important.'

'Oh, yes, thank you Bob. . . PM's office, who's calling please?'

A man with a deep voice and even deeper accent demanded to speak with, 'the idiot in charge.'

Maisie Jane remained calm and repeated her question as to who was calling.

'This is senior General Michalonavitchki Dzrastnychkovekia, from the Kremlin, now, the idiot if you please.'

Maisie scribbled down what she thought the caller's name was ... in a fashion . . . General Michael a vich something from ikea... and pressed the call button to the PM's phone. Good morning sir, Maisie here, I have General Mike o vichki from the Kremlin on line one for you.'

She heard a long sigh, 'get rid of him, tell him I'm not in all day ... tell him to leave a message and we'll get back to him. Does he sound angry?'

Maisie Jane confirmed the PM's suspicions, and he replaced the receiver with an even longer sigh.

I'm sorry General but he says he's not in all day but if you care to leave a message, we'll get back to you.' After listening to a torrent of poorly worded abuse, some of which she had never heard before, Maisie Jane cut in and politely said, 'That's very rude to shout like that, you'll only upset yourself, you shouldn't use bad language either. What would your mother say if she heard you? That really is so naughty.'

After a further prolonged and apoplectic tirade, this time in Russian, the phone went suddenly dead.

Maisie Jane nibbled a tasty chocolate biscuit, sipped her coffee, and settled back to await the next caller. This was easier than she thought, better than her old job and with an upgrade in salary too. She checked the other drawers with forensic interest, just in case. Security, you know.

The phone rang again but this time it was accompanied by a flashing red light, the ringing also sounded more urgent. 'PM's office, who's calling please?'

'Vice Admiral Hugo Horatio Blinkingsop-Smythe of the armed forces security council. Now, the PM, and be quick about it.'

Well Maisie Jane had learned her lesson from the previous bad tempered and rude caller. She also remembered what the PM had told her to say. 'I'm sorry the Prime minister is not in all day; leave a message and he'll get back to you.' She was still trying to scribble down the man's name .. admiral er hugatio blinking smith er . . . when the Vice Admiral exploded with language which was not becoming of a gentleman of his rank.

Maisie Jane interrupted him, 'That is so wicked, you should be ashamed of yourself, you would do well to take a leaf out of Bob's book.' She terminated the call and made some notes.

The Vice Admiral stared in disbelief at the telephone earpiece and wondered who the hell Bob was.
The PM was having a good day, by lunchtime he'd finished another chapter of his memoirs. So unusually quiet it had been, what with no calls, normally he was inundated with rubbish from heads of state, vultures from the media or more importantly party activists.
He wandered out into the reception office, Maisie Jane leapt to her feet and curtsied, 'good morning your lordship,' she smiled. The PM was rather taken aback, no one had ever been nice to him for years, not even his mother.
'Thank you so much my dear and good morning to you. You seem to be making an excellent job of it, keep up the good work. I'm off to the kitchen for lunch, would you like some?'
'No thank you sir, I have dolphin friendly tuna sandwiches with me.'
As the PM wondered how a dead tuna could be friends with a dolphin, he nodded his head and leant down to stroke Larry the cat who was purring with anticipation of a shared lunch from Maisie Jane's handbag.
As the PM left the room, he turned and with tongue in cheek, joked with the nice new girl. 'I'm off now, the country is in your hands, look after it well until I return.' He chuckled merrily to himself at his jest as his slippered feet meandered down the corridors of power ... and towards lunch. He reckoned he could eat a dolphin today never mind a tuna. This was a good day, one of the best.
Maisie Jane shared her tuna with the cat. What an incredible job, and such an honour to be put in charge on only her first day. She was about to phone her mum when the bells rang again. It was on the red phone this time. 'PM's office, how can I be of service?'
'This is General Worthingless-Coot of the combined services defence squad, the PM please and it is urgent.'

Maisie Jane brimmed with newly acquired confidence, this was all too easy this being in charge bit, 'What seems to be bothering you General?' She'd be good at this, she always read the agony aunt columns . . . and the stars for the day too. Today's, in the New Age Lost Hope Gazette, it had been all about an opportunity to make friends. As far as Maisie Jane was concerned it was coming true too.

The General sounded a bit perplexed but after checking that he had called the right number, continued, 'Something's upset the Russkis terribly, and their Baltic fleet is now in the channel on route this way. How do our people in charge think we should respond?'

Maisie Jane confirmed with the General, while he rummaged his drawers for more Valium, that by Russkis and Baltic fleet, the general meant a load of Russian sailors were coming to visit. 'Oh, how lovely. They have such a wonderful anthem, better than ours any day, and their girls are so pretty...'

'Yes, yes, yes,' interrupted the general, 'but what are we going to do? Should we send our fleet to meet them? I think we still have a couple of ships left and there's that old one moored in London by the bridge, we could tow it out.'

Maisie Jane was enthralled and considered the matter. She stroked Larry for inspiration and Larry responded. That was it, of course, friendship not warship!

'Okay General, we'll organise a big party for their admirals and generals on board the ship in London. Lay on a big spread, some vodka, they like that, and plenty of salady type things but not just leaf like stuff, proper Russian salads ... google them... send someone polite with a nice voice and a smart uniform on a small boat to greet them in the channel thing whatever that is and bring them in for a party.'

The General quickly drew his staff team together and issued orders with renewed gusto, he'd not had something so worthwhile to do for as long as he could remember. It was quite exciting, he wished he'd done it before. No one must know of this cunning plan, if his reading between the lines was correct, to capture all the Russian navy officers in one swoop and without a shot fired. My God, he could see a knighthood coming out of this. Google was checked, smart looking, and polite officers searched for, one who wasn't gay, military bands summoned, the guards regiment on standby as waiters and the police instructed to keep the roads open in case more vodka was urgently required. At last, the General was going to earn his pension. The might of the British military swung into action. Operation, 'Party' was a go!

Back at number ten, the door burst open and, shouting, 'no calls to be put through all afternoon,' the PM rushed through so quickly that Maisie Jane didn't have time to stand and curtsey, never mind pass on any messages. The PM's door closed with an emphatic thud and all was at peace again. A few moments later that nice man Bob called in with another cuppah and some more gossip. 'What's going on?' asked Maisie Jane.

'All hell's broke loose, it's pandemonium down there, chaos, everybody accusing each other. It's a frightening mess in the cabinet office.'

'Oh dear, it's nothing to do with the Russian fleet coming for tea is it?'

Bob looked at her quizzically, tilted his head to one side in thought then refocussed, 'no nothing like that,' pausing while he tried to make any sense at all of what the girl had said, 'no it's the cat's litter tray, someone has trod in it, knocked it over and then done a runner! The cleaning staff said it wasn't their cat, it was the PM's cat, so it was his job.

Crikey, they had to cancel a cabinet meeting over it. I'm off to see the cook, find out what more she knows. Bye dear.'

With that, Bob was gone, leaving Maisie Jane alone with her thoughts, the phones and Larry the purring pussy cat.

Next day, Maisie Jane was disappointed to find her chair retaken by the permanent secretary now back from lockdown, and so she returned to her old job filing unanswered questions.

Apart from some newspaper headlines about a new and excellent post-Brexit trade treaty with the Russian Federation, Maisie Jane was blissfully unaware of the consequences of her actions.

That very afternoon the PM had been gob smacked to receive a call from Vladimir himself, expressing his undying gratitude for the respect shown to his armed forces and promising an even bigger party in Russia for the PM and his innovative and charming military advisers. The PM hadn't a clue what he was on about but gladly reciprocated gushing praises to his new lifelong pal, the president of Russia. A few knighthoods were thrown about the services, the guards and bands were allocated a week's extra leave and the police confiscated the left-over Vodka for fingerprints . . . so the official requisition form said. Happy Russian sailors and special forces operatives were still being picked up in Soho for days afterwards, but it was not a problem as a Russian X class frigate had been left behind to wait for any stragglers. As the Russian fleet sailed north, they say the singing from the ships could be heard in Belgium . . . the place where the biscuits came from, allegedly.

Newspaper reporters, camped in droves outside their houses, were snapping at politicians for weeks after the worrying incident, demanding to know if the responsible party had been found and if they were going to apologise to the nation of cat lovers, who were all very upset and thinking of voting Liberal next time. Who knocked over the cat tray? An enquiry was demanded by a few treacherous backbenchers, an envious opposition and a raging incandescent SNP wanted a judicial review while the Welsh said it would never have happened in Wales. Northern Ireland wouldn't comment unless they were given a bigger budget.

When Bob retired, he threw away the boots and kept his secret.

**

'The greatest hazard in life is to risk nothing. By not risking you are chained by your certitudes, and are slaves, having forfeited your freedom. Only one who risks is free.'

Zen Osho

**

Man's meagre reward for delivering freedom ... but for who?

**

Not my funeral - but it could be yours.

A rainbow coloured, state of the art, funeral limousine stopped quietly outside, its EU badge of 48 stars surrounding a picture of a crematorium prominent on the bonnet. A young woman in an attractive short blue Ibiza style party dress alighted and with laptop in hand she approached the door.

'Bing Bong,' went the doorbell. Eventually the door was opened by an old man wearing comfortable 'sit about the house watching daytime TV' clothes. He peered into the light of day, 'Yes dear? Can I help you?'

'Oh, hello, I'm sorry about your sad news and we've come to pick up the dead body for the funeral. As you know,' she continued in a truly delightful eastern European accent, 'The EU department for standardised burials, cremations, and pension reduction initiatives, arranges everything. The mourners were all contacted by fazebrook or twitler and are waiting in the obligatory electric cars outside.'

'What's that to do with me?' asked the old fellow, fumbling for his glasses so he could have a better look at that party dress.

Ladvia, funeral representative and pension reduction technician, having inherited all the instincts and skills of her KGB grandfather, looked at her notes. 'You are Mr John Smith age 83 of 3 Botfly Avenue, New Hamburg, are you not?'

The old chap was getting some of his marbles together now and was used to dealing with cold callers, who incidentally were usually from the French Farmer's Benefits Association. That is, ever since double glazing and religious callers were banned by the EU Cult and Insurgency Eradication Programme. As a former trade union shop steward, he knew a thing or two about negotiating from strength.

'Well bits of that are correct, you've done well with the address dear, and the name is nearly right. You're ten years out with the age, I'm 93 and my name is Jim, Jim Smith. The other bit that you seem to have mistaken, is that I'm not actually dead yet.'

'Oh, dear, are you sure? It says here... look.... quite clearly, we are to pick up a body for immediate processing and despatch. All the documents are signed by the Strasburg Intelligence Unit, the crematorium fees have already been paid, interment documents completed, the mourners informed and ordered to attend and I'm afraid your old UK pension has been terminated and funds transferred to the Commission for Redistribution. There's nothing I can do; the EU will not compromise or renegotiate on this.'

'Be that as it may Miss, but I'm not dead and, old as I am, I will resist your offer of incineration with every sinew of my body. I'm stronger than I look you know.' Jim said defiantly as he leaned on the front door frame of his dilapidated one-bedroom council bungalow for support.

Ladvia realised there was indeed a mistake, a computer glitch no doubt, as ever since artificial intelligence was given the authority to run the department several similar errors had occurred. Luckily, some of the elderly people died of shock when the authorities called for their bodies and the self-fulfilling edict ensured that the funerals went ahead as planned. This Jim or John bloke looked like he might have a few years left in him - but not if she could help it. Rules are rules, (except in France where they had arranged a separate treaty to break them as necessary in return for handing over parts of Cornwall to Germany).

'Why don't we find you some nice clothes and take you for a ride in our delightful car. . . you can sit in the front with me.' Ladvia smiled a charming smile, the sort that Jim had only ever seen on the big screen, back when his eyesight was still functioning normally. However, he had a mind to go along with the invitation and nodded to Ladvia to enter. Jim enjoyed Ladvia's charming company as she rooted through his wardrobe looking for something suitable to be buried in. A quick wash and brush up and a loosely fitting old suit hanging on his shoulders and which he'd last worn some 40 years previous - when he was a few stone heavier. Now he looked the part of the requisite internment candidate.

Of course, none of the incumbent mourners recognised him or remembered what he looked like in order to confirm he was indeed the deceased because he'd moved to the South West over 50 years ago and had changed quite a bit. One of the mourners commented, 'My god, he's shrunk a lot, he was a six-footer when I knew him and look, he's grown hair . . . he was bald as a badger when I worked with him at the horse and donkey abattoir.'

Ladvia, like her Russian grandfather, didn't want to fail at the first hurdle, so Jim, coming along for the ride, would appease the throng of mourners who had travelled from as far as Australia to see him buried and hear the reading of his apparently substantial will. Rumour had it that he was worth millions and known to be generous. For many this was a funeral to die for. You just don't get many invites to funerals like this.

It's a long time since Jim had been out in a car ... a posh one like that anyway. She helped him into the front seat and gauged his health, there was still a chance if they play their cards right, they might be able to bury this chap anyway. ... whoever he was... at least the mourners can go home happy and the funeral directors have already paid the cremation fees by a deduction through the pension levy.

Ladvia tried everything she knew. She had the driver put the climate control on freeze and stopped off for a double cheeseburger and chips with chilli sauce for the intended deceased. She even resorted to fondling his knee, hoping for a heart attack. The trouble is, Jim was having the time of his life and thought happily to himself as he wiped his sweating brow with a cheap serviette, 'I really must get out more.'

Three times the driver had to drive by the crematorium, each time to a flurry of activity by the waiting Crematorium Executive Operatives First Class, all on EU minimum wage of 4 Euros an hour, and to the frustrated excitement of the following mourners. Three times they drove around the town, each time worse than the next for old Mr Corbun, who was feeling rather travel sick. He was travelling alone and had no family, in fact some of the other mourners had a suspicion he was a professional wake crasher and only in it for the free sandwiches.

Ladvia's earpiece crackled subversively into life. It was wonderful news and couldn't have come at a better time. It was Ahmed the Turkish driver of mourner's transport car three. 'Ms Ladvia, we have a body, Mr Corbun has choked on his vomit and none of the other passengers are willing to give mouth to mouth. Of course, I would, but section D of paragraph 2, part 1b of the EU burial operative's regulations forbids a driver to leave the controls of his vehicle while still in motion.' Ladvia smiled a smile of contentment as she revelled in completion of another demographical statistic and took her hand off Jim's sweaty knee.

'He can catch the bus home,' she thought.

The EU will have their funeral after all,
one way or another.

**

No one knows what is in your head –
even you cannot be sure! Can you?'

**

Judgement Day.

Gravel crunched under heavy boots as the incumbent vicar of St Judas strode mercilessly towards the Church door. He was toying with a sermon about liberating oneself from unnecessary debt. He was cross about the deep water some of his less discerning flock had gotten themselves into, with what appeared initially as insignificant short-term loans. As a result, the collection plate was suffering. 'Stupid people,' he thought to himself. The vicar, one Julius Ponsonby-Smythe was interrupted in his cogitations by the gardener tip toeing around the side of the church, 'Ah, vicar', he whispered, 'I'm glad I've caught you, I wanted to cut the grass but there's someone sleeping on a gravestone. All sprawled out, looks quite peaceful he does, I don't want to wake him, like.'

'Damnation man let's have a look at him. I don't want layabouts hanging around my church grounds. You'll never know what they'll be up to next. .... Oh, I see what you mean. He looks a bit of a ruffian to me. Probably out cold on drink or drugs, might even traffic them, you can't be sure. Filthy riff raff scum that they are. I'm thankful for your timely intervention and I am sure the police will confirm my suspicion. I shall call them immediately. Keep this our little secret; we don't want the dim-witted village rumour mongers making something out of it that it isn't.'

There was no secret to be kept though, not once the police tape went up and men in paper suits started to search the area. Tittle-tattle spread like sunrise on a clear day.. . . unstoppable. The vicar was beside himself with angst, that some waster of a tramp may have topped himself or been murdered in his very own church grounds. The embarrassment of it was almost too much to bear. The last thing he wanted was any adverse public interest in his beloved church.

Later that day-

'Ah, vicar, I'm Inspector Robert Arbiter, local constabulary. We've had a good look around, no foul play suspected. We've identified the deceased as a Mr Robert Loveless, 36, of no fixed abode. A sad young man who had been orphaned at a tender age and brought up by his grandmother, a local woman. We found a thermos and binoculars on top of the church tower, looks like he may have spent his last few days sleeping rough in the church.'

The vicar went red and snorted, 'filthy swine, no respect. No respect for the lord's place of sanctuary. Lucky that he didn't steal anything from my vestry. Almost a blessing he died before he could commit any more sacrilege . . .'

Inspector Arbiter held up an open hand to quiet the vicar's rant, 'I don't think that would have happened vicar, you see Mr Loveless was estranged from his wife. When he was made redundant a couple of months ago, he could no longer pay child maintenance, so his wife withdrew access to his two young children. They live in one of the houses, just over there beyond that wall, and it would seem likely that poor Mr Loveless was simply watching his children play in the garden. It's not possible to tell if he threw himself off the tower, the coroner would have to decide, perhaps he sought freedom from the pain that racked his tortured soul, or maybe it was merely an accidental fall. But fall he did and tragically the grave he landed on was that of the one person who loved him most in life, his grandmother, one Eliza Foster.

'We'll be out of your way soon vicar, then you can get back to normality. Who knows, you might be burying him here in a few weeks. Now, there's an irony for you. There but for the

grace of God and all that eh? Well, good day to you vicar, we'll be away now.'
Left to himself, the vicar mulled over the cost of padlocks. He couldn't tolerate further intrusion on his holy work by any more unwanted tramps abusing his church.

The only witnesses to his thoughts, a blood stain drying in the sunshine, children's laughter echoing from beyond the far wall and of course, God.

'Quick to judgement, quick to sorrow'

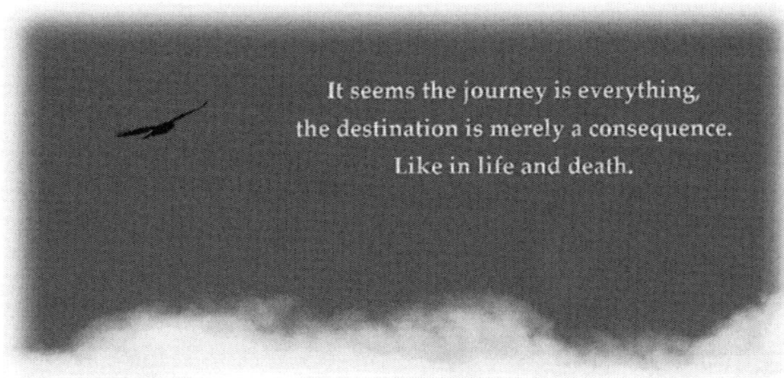
It seems the journey is everything,
the destination is merely a consequence.
Like in life and death.

For my boy. . . and his

You'll never see, what I have seen,
nor I, of what you will.
You'll never go, where I have been,
age keeps its secrets still.

Of all the things, that I have seen,
dread nightmares, fearsome bad,
I'm pleased it's somewhere, you've not been,
in truth, of that, I'm glad.

My soul can look upon a past,
where history books won't show,
all such things, not meant to last
and you weren't meant to know.

In later years, with half a care,
mem'ries, you may see,
but you will know, that you weren't there,
and that, they came from me.

Who is he?

Homeward, once again.

Autumn dead leaves scampered, as if alive, so, so quickly; quickly tumbling unfaltering across the sticky estuary mud; not stopping they, and all in a rush, seawards they were bent. Despite the ebbing tide, undaunted, little waves would come and lap the new-born shoreline. The wind was strong, as it ever can be, and it came from afar, from the North, the land of the white bear; it had travelled long to chill the bones of the watcher on the quay that day. The watcher saw it all, the leaves, the changing sky of grey, the retreating waves harried by the wind and he marvelled at it all. Then, seeing darkness on its way, he turned his thoughts and boots to homeward, once again.

'The dream world has immense power that often will not transfer to the waking world. In dreams, there appear amazing questions and answers of great intellect and intricacy, far beyond the wit of the woken mind that dreamed them. . . '

**

'What we deeply cling to imprisons us.'

I am a prisoner of the desire to be understood and valued. But I must accept, that the reasons I write,
are not the reasons you read.
One can only hope the two will conspire to meet sometime
on the great path of life.

Thank you.

The Wanderer, by Gibran

I met him at the crossroads, a man with but a cloak and a staff, and a veil of pain upon his face.

And we greeted one another, and I said to him, 'Come to my house and be my guest.' And he came.

My wife and my children met us at the threshold, and he smiled at them, and they loved his coming. Then we all sat together at the board and we were happy with the man for there was a silence and a mystery in him. And after supper we gathered to the fire and I asked him about his wanderings.

He told us many a tale that night and also the next day, but what I now record was born out of the bitterness of his days though he himself was kindly, and these tales are of the dust and patience of his road. And when he left us after three days, we did not feel that a guest had departed but rather that one of us was still out in the garden and had not yet come in.

**

My empathy with Gibran's wanderer is unbounded. Were I to beg for a desirous epitaph, I would ask for no other.

Richard J. Small

My writing has also been influenced by the lyrics of this 1960s song, something I heard on my journey.

'Could you tell a wise man
By the way he speaks or spells?
Is this more important
Than the stories that he tells?'
by M and B Hugg

A special gift story for you, dear reader.

Surviving the Blizzard

A sequel to 'Life, on the Moors', see page 24.

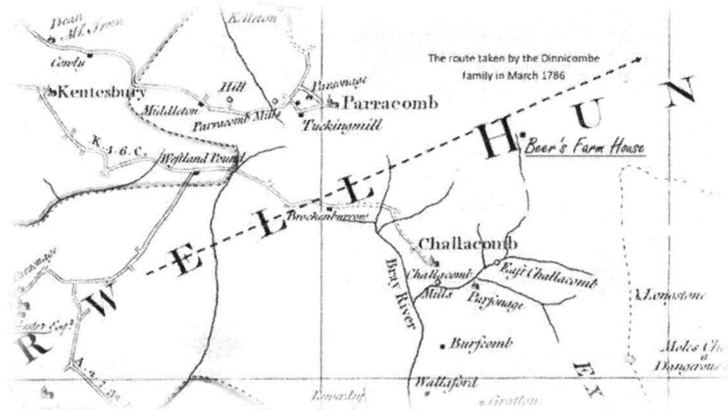

Some years later. . .

It is March of 1809, and on the continent, the Napoleonic wars ravage country after country, creating shortages of manpower and food in England. William, now at 34, is the same age as his father when he was lost in the great snowstorm on the moors back in '78 and the same fateful day when William himself was saved by his mother's final and enduring wish.

Before dawn broke, William had already sensed snow was approaching in the easterly wind and he had tirelessly, busied himself all day about the Beer's old farm, ensuring the livestock were safely sheltered, hay was in place, roots were dug, firewood collected, and fences checked.

As the first candle flame of the evening fluttered in a draught by the low casement window, William rested his tired body in his chair by the inglenook, the farm dog at his feet enjoying a treat by the fire. He began to reflect deeply on his dear wife Hannah and on their three children who were now growing up so fast. He wondered about finding a decent apprenticeship for the oldest boy Thomas, now 11 and named after both Hannah's father and his own brother. Thomas was the same age as William had been, when he had fought his way back through the great storm that spawned such tragedy, exactly twenty-three years ago to the day. He watched, fascinated, the falling snow filling the small panes in the window frame ... his eyes closed gently... he remembered it like it was only yesterday ....

Phoebe and her three children were trapped in a deadly snowstorm high up on the moors. Her husband, George, a confident and powerful man, had pressed on into the storm hoping to find a farm and help. Their old and ailing horse Molly had drawn both its last load and its last breath. The worm ridden sides of the cart and an old sheet of frail and tattered canvas their only shelter.

Phoebe carefully reconsidered Mr. Beer's earlier generous offer to care for her eldest boy, William. Perhaps six or seven miles back to the farm it was, but young William at eleven was a strong boy, well-nourished and big for his age, he had the determination of his father and the spirit of his mother. She had made her decision. Daylight would not last forever, maybe four or five hours left at best, if William started out now while he was still able, with the wind at his back and before the snow deepened, he could make a determined one-way trek to the farm before nightfall.

Phoebe gently lifted Sarah, who appeared to be sleeping quietly now, to one side, she took off her coat and made William put it on, she wrapped him up well and asked him, 'Tell me William, do you think you can find your way back to the farm?' William was subdued but nodded back in reply. 'Then off you go with my blessing, may God be with you and guide you all the way, safe to the Beer's farm,' she kissed his cold forehead, pulled his cap down tight and helped him off the cart. 'Don't you stop,' she said, 'if you are tired you do not stop, you keep going, say hello to them and that we send our love. Don't you stop William. . . whatever happens, you keep going!' she shouted after him.

William turned, nodded again, and was gone in an instant, he felt very grown up that his mother entrusted him with such a journey. . . he would not fail her.

Sheltered by two coats, with the snow blowing past him as if leading the way, his path was clearer, his body warmer and his intention steadfastly resolute.

Driven on, in part by fear, in part by the promise to his mother and in part the childish notion that the Beers would quickly organise a rescue and save his mother and siblings from the storm, William found the track relatively easy to follow, mostly it stayed with the contours of the hills. With the wind pushing him along, his progress was quick, though with no gloves his hands were painfully cold, his fingers had soon lost their ability to close, he pushed each hand into the opposite sleeve of his mother's coat and strode on. Once, he came across a huge snow drift that obstructed his way, he turned to look back, wondering if he should return, but the snow blinded his eyes and the east wind felt like a knife on his face. Now he knew for sure there was only one direction to take and became more determined than ever, not to let anything stop him, he bypassed the drift and plodded on with renewed vigour. It seemed he had been walking forever, and finding the Beer's farm seemed nigh on impossible, when suddenly he smelled wood smoke in the air. He had unknowingly passed by the slope down to the farm some quarter of a mile back. The smell of smoke on the east wind gave him renewed strength and it was with excitement, forgetting all else, that he ran the last few yards to the farm door. Despite his urgent quest, he was still respectful enough to knock. The door was soon opened, the Beers were thrilled to see him, they had fully expected the family to return not long after the snow had begun to fall. The old couple looked past William, peering into the storm, and fast falling dusk, eagerly looking for the rest of the family. Their expressions asked the question and William simply answered, 'I'm alone, mother sent me back.'

The old couple pulled William inside, closed the door to the world outside and gave him warm soup and a blanket. His hands fumbled to hold the spoon and his lips were numb with cold, and, as the burning pain in his hands slowly subsided, William realised that this dear old couple were in no state to carry out any rescue. It was not long after, that exhaustion and exposure took their toll and he succumbed to a deep and protective sleep.

Next day and for three days after, his body ached all over from his struggle to survive on the moor. Old William Beer, his wife standing behind him, her hands gently on his shoulders in support, called him over to sit at the table and spoke solemnly to young William. 'My boy, we must all of us face the facts, this is how life is and sometimes how it ends, we none of us can escape this. The snow is deeper now and the track impossible to follow. No one could survive out there, we must be grateful that you are here.' Old William could see the spirit ebbing out of young William as his loss fell heavily upon him. His voice calm but earnest, he continued, 'Young William, dearest boy, hear this and hear it well, your mother gave you life, in fact she handed you that most treasured of gifts twice. Now it is up to you to fulfil all she wanted for you. Now is your time to stand tall and honour her wish that you be chosen to live on and do well. Be strong, remember them as they were in happy times and live that life you were gifted to the full. Sarah and I will help you all we can. Time will be a great healer, you will see.'

Young William was shielded from the recovery of the family's bodies, carried out a week or so later by villagers and farmers near to the moor. Simple coffins were laid to rest in a small patch of sloping ground at the back of the farm where the graves of Beers also overlooked the track and gateway to the copse by the stream. The burial was a solemn and poignant occasion, followed by a hearty meal in the farmhouse for all those attending. Somehow, the warmth of good company and shared food made for a happy occasion. It was the beginning of a new era. William's father was never found, and it left a question that William might well take a lifetime to answer.

Old William and Sarah Beer were as good as their word, she loved him like the son she had always wanted, and he taught the boy all he knew about farming and life on the moors, he shared all the secret ways and wisdoms passed down through the ages. There was the planting of kale and potatoes, mangel beet for the livestock, leeks, onions, and other vegetables. Harvesting and thrashing the small barley crop, lambing and fleecing, watching the pig among the oak and beech trees at the right time of year. Storing the barley straw, picking fruit at harvest time, securing the ducks, geese, and chickens from the moorland fox, and so many other labour-intensive jobs. Young William, like his own father, worked hard, learned well, and had a respectful yet affable attitude to others. He grew from strength to strength and it seemed there was nothing he could not do. He was home where he was loved and valued.

**

The dog, stood, stretched, and lay down again by the fire, in doing so, brushed against William's feet and woke him from his dream, just long enough to hear Hannah tell George and Thomas to go to sleep, their six-year-old sister Sarah, already peacefully in her own land of dreams. Hearing Hannah's voice pleased William greatly and he settled himself comfortably in his chair and remembered their first meeting. Oh, they were good days back then, he was about sixteen, able to deal rationally with his past sorrows and had steadfastly gained old William Beer's respect. 'Find your coat young William and harness the horse to the small cart. I'm taking you to a horse fair.'

Though he was excited enough by that, it was nothing compared to what would happen later.

Old William Beer's experience proved invaluable as they made their way over almost trackless moor down the valley towards Challacomb.

'Stay by me boy, and best not speak unless I ask – we need to drive a good bargain, hill farming will never make us rich. My dear old horse has served me well but might only have another good year in her. We must find a fitting replacement today. Something suitable for a light plough and small cart would suit us fine.'

The village thronged with people from miles around, some to sell, some to buy, others for the spectacle and thrill. The horse fair was only held once a year. Now, old William had a good friend in Joseph Goulde, the village blacksmith and farrier, and it was to him they went first, to discover local news of any bargains to be had. Young William did as he was asked and stood quietly and close by the man he had come to treat as his father. The smells and the heat of the forge though, brought memories flooding back of happy days with his late family, but he had long accepted it was time to move on and he was now often referred to as young William Beer.

While peacefully walking the busy street, they were suddenly aware of a commotion in front. A pretty girl about William's age, with flowing auburn hair over her shoulders and carrying a basket full of eggs for sale, was being accosted by a much older man. A stooping man of slender build, wearing expensive clothes that had long since seen their best days. A silence fell swiftly over the watching crowd as the end of old William's stick jarred into the man's chest, stopping him instantly in his tracks. The girl showed her gratitude with a smile of recognition and the man showed his resentment and contempt with a sneer and a threat. A threat that came to nothing as the villain caught the look on young William's face, a look that spoke of untold strength and determination, a look reminiscent of someone else he once admired and feared. As young William moved shoulder to shoulder with old William, he did so with a new admiration for this old man's courage. Meanwhile, the evil villain of the piece, slunk away into the crowd, muttering. The young lady gave a little curtsey, thanked Mr Beer by name and with a swish of her russet dress and holding her basket in both hands, walked away. Young William's heart was in danger of being stolen by the young lady and even more so when after a few steps, she turned her head, tilted it to one side and smiled straight at him. A smile that lived forever within his soul.

Seeing that William was curious about events, old William explained, 'The man is an evil waster, well known for his drinking and gambling. He's been the utter ruin of many good folk round these parts. Luke Reid is his name – avoid him – he's always trouble.' Old William left a suitably lengthy and poignant pause, then with a knowing grin continued, 'Oh, the young lady is Hannah, Joe Richards' daughter, he runs a small farm not so distant from ours but not as high up the moor. We can call there on the way home, show him our new horse . . . once we've bought it of course. In fact, we can offer Hannah a lift home.' From that day on, there was only one other person on Earth for William – the lovely Hannah Richards

Old William Beer chuckled to himself, it was more than a horse he'd be taking home. His wife would be thrilled with the gossip.

The trip back to farm with the new three-year-old freshly shod horse, did not transpire quite as William had hoped. Yes, they gave Hannah a lift, and her older brother too. Hannah sat up front with old William Beer, chatting amicably about all manner of things, while the two young men shared the back of the cart. An occasional laugh from the merry pair at the front embarrassed the self-conscious young William that he might be part of the humour. They later spent about half an hour engaging with the Richards' family, though young William remained unusually quiet. Whenever he could, he watched Hannah, who, catching his glances, blushed and hid her face. The two young people hid their attraction for each other, except that it was amusingly obvious to everyone else. Old William Beer arranged some shared labour for harvest and shearing times, both he and Thomas Richards were getting older and it was time for the younger men to take over the heavier duties. They left the

Richards' farm for home in good spirits, though over the next few days, Sarah Beer good naturedly amused herself with young William's loss of appetite ... 'was he ill?' she enquired with a smile.

Over the months, William did manage to see Hannah a few times, though it was always a working visit, farming on the edge of the moors paid scant attention to the niceties of socialising for pleasure. What could have been intolerable was all made good by young William, now a fine young man with prospects, realising that Hannah felt just the same way about him. It was obvious to them both, when they saw each other the world was a better place, they felt whole.

Two years later, and when William looked forward to seeing Hannah at the horse fair, she wasn't there. He'd looked and looked but there was no sign of her. They met one of her brothers. . . Hannah? She's been sent away to stay with an ailing aunt, to look after her till she gets better. No idea how long, we don't need her at the farm anyway . . .

It was like a horse had kicked him in the chest, he felt sick and was poor company for old William as they made their way home. The farm work kept him busy and his previous losses had taught him that things can always get better. Though they were to appear to be worse in the months ahead. Another year had passed, and Sarah Beer fell ill, she took to her bed and showed no sign of recovery.

Life became difficult for the two men, more difficult than ever before. A farmer's wife was never idle, storing of fruit, making cider, butter, and cheese, collecting eggs, combing and spinning wool, pickling pork, smoking and salting meat, keeping house and feeding the men, and now this also fell upon the menfolk of the farm, and they were struggling badly. The doctor had been and thought it something akin to typhus, but unlikely, with no other cases. Sarah Beer deteriorated, young William felt the pain of not only his own loss but that of old William, a dear kind and devoted man if ever there was.

One early autumn morning, a cart drew into the yard, it was Mrs Richards come to help, and joy of joys, she had brought Hannah with her. There was little could be done for Sarah Beer except to comfort her until a peaceful end came. However, it had meant the men could return to essential prewinter farm labours and be fed properly as well. At the table with a fine warming soup, William looked lovingly across at Hannah as she stood by an embers fire in the inglenook, the glow of setting sunlight shining on her hair and face through the small farmhouse windows. Pretty as a picture she was, and my, how she looked like she belonged there. Young William could only dream.

Young William was twenty years of age when he stood once more by another burial in the farmyard plot. Old William Beer had been devastated by the loss of his lifetime partner, he only seemed to live on to complete his adopted son's education and to make arrangements for the farm. He died in his sleep, likely of a broken heart and yearning to be reunited with his dear Sarah. Mr William Beer had been a well-liked member of the community, his trials and his forbearance appreciated by the good people of the moor. Many that attended the farm for his burial and wake, knew of the infant deaths he and his wife had endured and how they had come to adopt and love an orphan off the moors. The Richards family were there in strength, Hannah and her mother brought potato and bacon pies and drink for the celebration of old William's life, to remember him with fondness and to console and cheer young William, now all alone in the world. He would need more than confidence and great strength to survive life on the moors, as his poor father had discovered to his cost.

Taking a quiet moment, William stood in silent thanks at the graveside for all he had received from the Beers, a decent life, the farm, a handful of sovereigns, the love of a family, nature's wisdom, the secrets of the moors. Someone came and stood respectfully close by. A kindly hand of strength touched his shoulder, it was Thomas Richards, 'sad day William, sad day. Now is your time to stand tall and honour their wish that you live on and do well. Be strong, remember them as they were in happy times. But you can't do this on your own, not on the moors you can't. What you need is a good wife. I'm not sure if you have ever noticed her, but ever thought of asking my daughter Hannah? She's strong, thoughtful, careful, loving, can read and write by God... and she's pretty too!'

In his slumber, William relived the warmth of joyful remembrance, turning ever hopefully to the smile, the hug and the knowing look on Thomas' delighted face. That afternoon he asked Hannah if she would consent to marry him. There was a short pause while she looked at the floor then threw herself deeply into his arms. It must be said, there was a fair amount of cheering and back slapping at the farm that day. The Beer's faith in their boy was vindicated, life on the moors would continue.

Though asleep in his chair, something in him sensed a presence from the past, something akin to his own spirit was nearby.
Outside, the ghost of William's father watched snow, falling upon the graves as it once had upon the living, he had at last found his family, now peace was his, his journey over, he need search no more.
Inside, William was reliving the enduring memory of last moments with his mother, he trembled as he felt the bitter cold of the east wind sleet, remembered the hands on his shoulder, the kiss on his forehead and her last words. Then suddenly he was awake, he felt the warmth of the fire's embers, kind hands on his shoulders and a gentle loving kiss on his forehead. He stood slowly, smiled, and embraced Hannah, forever the love of his life.
She smiled back at him, 'Time for bed William, it is late.'

**

The snow stopped falling and, where once the candle flame had given its life to the dark of evening, moonbeams brightly shone.

If you venture onto the moors one snowy night you might just see for yourself. If you search long enough.

**

Thank you for reading my stories.
Richard

'Not all those who wander, are lost' Tolkien
'but sometimes they are!' Me

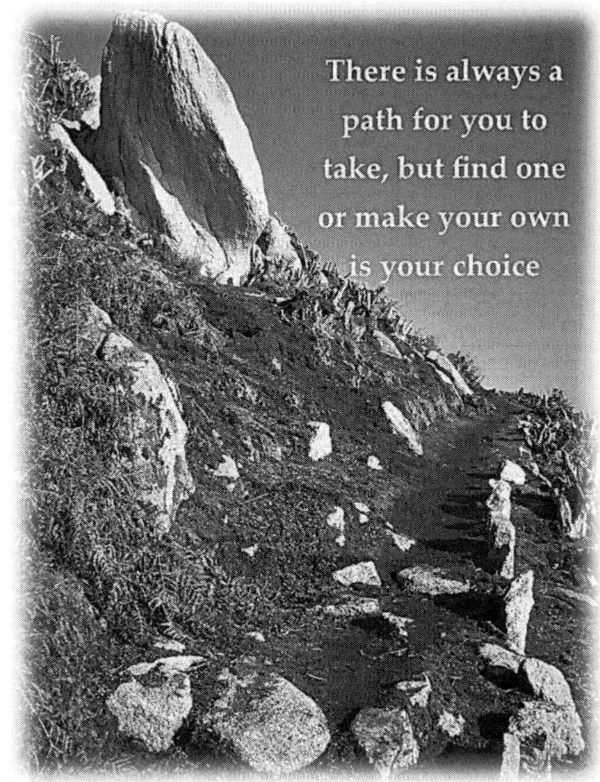
There is always a
path for you to
take, but find one
or make your own
is your choice

Printed in Great Britain
by Amazon